Remember Me and You

A Devil's Kettle Romance
Book Three

Susan Sey

OTHER TITLES BY SUSAN SEY

Author's Note:

Welcome back to Devil's Kettle, readers! You've waited a long time for this, and I can't tell you how much I appreciate your hanging in there. Georgie and Peter had a long way to go, and I made them earn every bit of their happily ever after. Which made it all the sweeter when they finally got there. I'm delighted you're here, and I hope you love Georgie and Peter's story as much as I do.

As always, I owe the thank yous:

To Claudia and Greta, who offer insightful solutions to imaginary problems on a nightly basis. If I didn't have these two at my dinner table, I'd never get to the HEA.

To Bryan, who takes my career seriously, even when it involves fictional sheep.

To Inara, who points out (with great compassion and bottomless love) when I've lost the thread.

To Wendy, Tammy, Joan and Alison, who round out The Squad. I'd never get these things plotted let alone written without you. So many thanks. ALL THE THANKS.

And to you, who trusted that Georgie had a heart and that Peter could be redeemed. She does, and he can. So read on, readers!

CHAPTER 1

Over the course of her 29 years, Georgie Davis had only ever prayed for three things. When she was 14, she'd prayed for her father not to be dead. When she was 25, she'd prayed for her brother Diego not to be dead either. She'd attended both funerals in flat black, her chin high, her eyes dry, just as her mother had taught her. (*They're here for the spectacle, Georgie. We won't give them one.*) So when she'd prayed at 28 for her scheming ex-fiancé to end up in a ditch somewhere, flat on his back in a cold, driving rain — preferably bankrupt — she didn't expect much. But there he was.

"Hallelujah," she muttered and pulled over. She wanted to verify this miracle with her own two eyes.

She parked her Range Rover on the edge of the narrow asphalt road that snaked along the basalt bluffs above Lake Superior and punched the hazards. She grabbed her umbrella from the passenger seat and stepped onto the pavement in a pair of schlumpy black rain boots that would've given her mother a heart attack.

A chilly November rain raced downhill in rivulets but Georgie was dry enough under her massive umbrella, and more importantly, her outfit was safe. Addy's bridal shower was three hours off yet, but she was the maid of honor and appearances were everything in this business. (*What business*? she heard her eight-year-old self ask. *Being a Davis, darling*, her mother replied.) She shivered inside her deep red trench coat and envied the sky-high heels she'd left toasting comfortably on the heated passenger seat. But Peter Zinc was right there across the street, lying in a ditch, blinking up into the rain while a black-and-white dog with intelligent eyes sat by his head.

Ah, hell. He couldn't be dead if he was blinking.

She crossed the pavement at lazy amble – her signature speed – and stopped in the clumpy grass lining the ditch to gaze down at him.

"Peter."

He flicked a glance her way, his eyes very black, the bones of his face as elegant as always despite the mud splattered across one sharp cheekbone. A sodden wool cap sat askew on the head he kept shaved bald. He closed his eyes.

"Peter, what are you doing?"

"Dying."

"Are you really?" Hope sprang eternal.

"I'd like to, yes."

"I'll just leave you to it, then, should I?"

"That would be lovely, thanks."

She peered down at him and waited. A minute ticked by. Then two. She'd have to get going soon but this was delicious.

"Any luck?"

He heaved a deep sigh. "Not yet."

"If you don't mind my asking…"

He kept his eyes closed. "Go ahead."

"I can't help but notice that you're, ah—" She paused. How to put it delicately? "—well, you're clutching your nuts."

"I'm waiting to die," he said reasonably. "A dying man is allowed his comforts."

"You've got your faithful dog by your side," Georgie

pointed out. "How much more comfort do you need?"

At Peter's shoulder, the dog grinned up at her, his pink tongue lolling companionably. She grinned back. Peter cracked a suspicious eye at her, then closed it again.

"You're laughing at me."

"Heavens no." Georgie let the smile spread across her face. "I'm enjoying your dog."

"That asshole?" Peter snorted and even flat on his back, soaking wet in the ditch, managed to pull off both derisive and gorgeous. Georgie suppressed a sigh. If there were any justice in the world, Peter would be as ugly as the betrayal he'd dealt her. Unfortunately, the world was stubbornly justice-free and Peter was still ridiculously handsome. It wasn't fair, really, all that male beauty lavished on such a terrible person. Those slashing cheekbones, those stark eyes, that super-hero jaw…

Careful, her mother whispered and Georgie started guiltily. *I hate him*, she reminded herself sternly. And she did. After what he'd done to her family, she hated him with a sincerity that involved every ounce of her soul and strength. That beauty was like some kind of superpower, though, transcending both her hate and his poverty, sneaking in under her radar and wrapping itself around her whenever she wasn't paying the strictest attention. It was like pheromones, invisibly working on her body with a primitive power she—

Her mother made a warning noise inside her head and Georgie realized her toe was in the quicksand. Again. God.

"He's no comfort," Peter said. "That dog is the reason I'm dying."

"Is he now?" Georgie jerked her attention with relief to the dog. Water ran down his silky coat and pooled on Peter's rain jacket. She stepped a little closer and leaned in, so the run-off from her umbrella dripped onto Peter as well. She reached out and gave the dog's sleek ear a gentle tug. "Good boy."

The dog's tail thumped the ground twice, a genteel acknowledgement of well-earned praise. Georgie fell a little bit in love, which was totally fine because this dog had evidently put Peter in the ditch and her enemy's enemy was a friend, right?

Peter sputtered, and Georgie realized her umbrella was now dripping onto his face rather than his coat.

"Sorry." She took her time rearranging the umbrella on her shoulder. "I thought you were dead."

Peter let go of his nuts to swipe the water from his face. He scowled up at her. "Not quite yet." He levered himself carefully to a sitting position and released a slow breath. "Looks like today's not my day to die."

"Are you sure?" Georgie asked wistfully. Her life would be so much easier if it were.

Peter addressed the dog. "But it might be yours, you bone-headed, miserable excuse for a sheep dog."

"What did he do?" Georgie asked. She really had to get going but the dog was still smiling at her, like it knew a wonderful secret. And if that secret had anything to do with what had put Peter in a ditch holding his boys, Georgie wanted to know it. Maids of honor were never late but Addy would understand.

He spoke to the dog instead of answering her question. "Take them to the barn."

The dog went nowhere. Peter pushed to his feet and stood there, up to his ankles in ditchwater, hunched against what Georgie surmised was a staggering pain. He hadn't been clutching his boys for comfort, she realized belatedly. He'd

4

suffered a nut shot. She suppressed a wince on his behalf. She had three brothers; she was aware that getting your junk racked was an event of some significance. It took Peter a moment, but he found his composure. He narrowed his eyes at the dog. "*Tag*," he snapped. "*Take them to the barn*."

The dog — was Tag his name, she wondered, or was that some kind of sheep dog command? — stood and gave a leisurely yawn.

"So help me, Tag," Peter muttered, and hauled himself out of the ditch. Tag — definitely his name — turned and slipped under the wire fence separating two dozen or so fat, woolly sheep from the road. They were milling about a small pasture, nosing at a giant circular something-or-other that was presumably filled with hay, but abandoned it when they saw Tag coming. They turned as if with one mind and trotted obediently through a gate at the far end of the pasture and headed for a picturesque barn.

"I hate that dog," Peter said from his side of the ditch.

"Why?" Georgie blinked through the rain at him, a little concerned for him despite herself. He had always been on the long, lean side, but he looked thin now. Thin and cold.

"He laughs at me."

She arranged her face into a parody of sympathy. "I noticed that."

"Of course you did," he muttered. He eyed the fence in front of him, took his nuts in one careful hand and stepped over it. He didn't release his manly bits until both legs were safely on the other side of the fence. Comprehension flashed bright and vengeful inside Georgie's mind.

"That fence is electric, isn't it?"

"Eight thousand volts," Peter said grimly.

"And you stepped over it less carefully the first time?"

"Significantly." Peter scowled at Tag, who was now sitting on top of the hay-feeder-thing, tongue lolling in a big doggie grin. "Tag decided to say hello to a hiker and his dog there on the road instead of putting the sheep in the barn like I asked. I was concerned that he was going to bite the guy, or maybe eat the other dog, so I didn't give the fence the respect it deserved when I tried to hurdle it."

"Like Tag would bite anybody," Georgie scoffed. He was far too smart for that sort of nonsense. She'd never had a dog in her life but she knew stupid when she looked it in the eye. She knew mean, too, and Tag was neither.

"He didn't," Peter conceded tightly. "He'd already sent the hiker and his terrified dog off at a sprint. He gave up the chase when I electrified my junk. I'm sure it was very entertaining."

"I'll bet," Georgie said cheerfully.

"Thanks for stopping. You didn't need to." He eyed her through the rain. "In fact, you had every reason not to."

"I know." Georgie held his gaze, and let him see that she was fully aware of what she owed him and what she didn't. "It was a pleasure, though." She produced a happy sigh. "Truly."

He nodded, accepting that as his due. Which it was. "Glad I could be of service, then." He pointed his chin at the sleek cocktail dress peeking out of her ruby trench. "Where's the party?"

"Davis Place. Addy and Jax's bridal shower is today."

"You're the maid of honor, aren't you?"

"I am."

"You'd better not be late."

She offered a languid shrug. "I'm not." Not yet, anyway. She gave him a spectacular smile. "Well. It was sure nice to see you, Peter." *In a ditch, clutching your electrocuted balls.*

He nodded curtly enough that she wondered if he'd somehow overheard her interior monologue. Would she even care if he had? She would not, she assured herself as he turned to stride across his pasture. Six months ago he'd been the king of Devil's Kettle. There wasn't a committee in town that didn't have his fingerprints all over it, or a business in which he wasn't a major investor if not the sole owner. He'd been about to marry into Devil's Kettle's oldest, richest family, too. Georgie's family, to be specific. Georgie herself had been the bride-to-be. Now Peter owned nothing but this farm, a couple dozen sheep and a dog who laughed at him. And he'd just zapped his nuts on his own electric fence. And Georgie, the fiancée he'd betrayed so vilely, whose family he'd used so badly, had been the one to find him.

If this kept up, Georgie might have to start praying more regularly.

Georgie really was later than she wanted to be. She was always a little late but there was fashionably late, and then there was falling-down-on-the-job late, and she was perilously close to the line between them. She wouldn't cross it, though. Addy was depending on her, and Addy was family. And Georgie didn't let family down. Not ever.

She skidded the Rover to a halt beside Davis Place with a speed and precision that would shock those who thought they knew her. A rambling, clifftop mansion that had been in her family since time immemorial, Davis Place overlooked not just a breathtaking expanse of Lake Superior and the town of Devil's Kettle, but also the geologic anomaly for which the town had been named. Just before the cliff's edge, the entire river tripped and fell improbably into a yawning black hole in an otherwise solid basalt slab. Half of it never reappeared, either. Nobody knew where it went or what it did; it was just gone. The other half, however, shot out of a crack in the cliff face some 100 yards below like a waterfall with power, reach and places to go.

In the summer, it was a sun-shattered rainbow of color and light. In the winter it was an abstract sculpture of ice and wind. Georgie's brother Diego — the man, the artist, the gone-too-soon legend — had painted himself famous trying to capture the view from Davis Place's front porch. Their father had done his share of art here, too, though not on the porch. As a potter, he'd worked in a basement studio. After he'd died in that very studio — also far too soon — Georgie's grandmother had locked the place up with her grief inside it and moved to town. And for 15 years, they had all just tried to forget it was even there.

It had taken Addison — the woman Diego had married, misused so badly, and widowed all before she was 25 — to see its potential. And with her bright ideas, her irresistible optimism, and her deep and abiding love, she'd transformed the place. She'd transformed their whole family. And now Addy was marrying another of Georgie's brothers — the right one this time — and Davis Place was about to be reborn as a high-end bed and breakfast for the art-minded crowd. Right after Georgie threw the bridal shower to end all bridal showers for the sister-in-law who'd become her best friend.

Georgie threw the Rover into park, shucked off the rain boots and wedged her feet into the punishing leopard-print heels she'd chosen for the festivities. That icy November rain continued to drive down in sharp needles but Georgie knew the value of an entrance. *Never let them see you undone*. Not even the people who'd undone you? *Especially not them*. What about family? *You love them best; give them your best self, always.*

Georgie sighed, her toes already going numb. She didn't disagree with her inner voice. She just sometimes wished it didn't sound so disturbingly like her mother.

Whom she loved. Adored. Bianca Davis was a force to be reckoned with, the kind of force Georgie hoped to be one day. She wondered uneasily if she would get to be her own force of nature, though, or if she would just turn into Bianca.

The back door of Davis Place flew open and Bianca herself appeared.

And love flooded Georgie's heart. Her mother was tall and elegant, all angles and edges and dramatic sweeps of color and emotion, with an enormous purple umbrella in her hand. She stepped to the edge of the porch and snapped it open, one imperious eyebrow raised in question.

In answer, Georgie cracked the car door, and popped open her own umbrella. She said a prayer for her ankles and strolled through the rain to her mother.

"Goodness," Bianca said, peering out at the rain. "I was beginning to worry about you."

Georgie wrestled her umbrella shut and leaned it against the pristine white clapboard. "I'm later than I wanted to be," she admitted. "I ran into a situation on the way up the hill."

"Oh?"

"I thought I saw Peter Zinc, dead in the ditch."

"How lovely." Bianca smiled, and Georgie recognized it from her own mirror. It was possible the transformation to her mother had already begun. "Was it a mirage, or did you really see it?"

"He was lying in the ditch, all right. But he wasn't dead."

Bianca made a disappointed noise and it warmed Georgie's heart. Bianca wasn't an easy person, or a traditional mother. She had impossible standards and made unreasonable demands but Georgie had never once doubted her loyalty.

Willa Zinc poked her head out the open porch door. "Who wasn't dead?"

Georgie gave her sort-of sister (and Peter's actual sister) an automatic once over. Willa had decent raw materials — even features, a curvy little figure, and truly spectacular eyes — but left to her own devices, the girl was a walking fashion tragedy. This had been great fun when Willa had been Georgie's favorite enemy. The fun had diminished somewhat when Willa became Georgie's prospective sister-in-law. It was downright burdensome now that Willa — even after the aborted engagement — was still family. (The relationship was complicated but sadly inarguable.) Georgie had still been digesting that bitter turn of events when Addy went and made the girl a bridesmaid.

And stuck Georgie with responsibility for ensuring that Willa didn't turn up to any wedding-related events in jeans and a dirty t-shirt.

Georgie nodded with grudging approval at the chocolate brown tuxedo pants Willa had tucked into soft leather riding boots of the same tone. She'd paired it with a creamy cowl-necked sweater with an asymmetric hem, the whole thing shot through with faint golden threads. She'd picked up the sparkle with a pair of chunky gold earrings, showcased by a neat French braid in which she'd confined the acres and acres of dark wavy hair she usually stuffed under a ball cap.

Maybe there was hope for Willa yet. Not that Georgie would ever admit such a thing out loud.

"Your brother," Georgie informed her. "Unfortunately, he wasn't as dead as he appeared."

"Not that we haven't all prayed for Peter's untimely demise, but why did you think he was dead?" Willa stepped back from the door. "And get inside. It's freezing out there."

Georgie stepped into the blessedly warm kitchen. The house centered on a massive brick chimney that Addy had lovingly restored. Twin hearths opened into both the kitchen on one side and the great room on the other. Addy had added a gorgeous granite surround in the great room but kept the original brick here in the kitchen. Georgie threaded through the caterers, busy in black and white, and stretched her hands toward the flames.

"He was lying in a ditch in the rain outside that sheep farm of his." She shrugged. "I had hopes."

Willa turned her butt to the flames and sighed happily. "He was alive though?"

"Sadly, yes," Georgie said while Bianca ran a proprietary hand over the smooth sheet of Georgie's stick-straight and unfortunately fine hair. All the product in the world would never give her a braid like Willa's. "He'd only stunned himself with the electric fence."

Willa chuckled. "I knew he was going to do that sooner or later. That thing runs at least 6,000 volts—"

"Try eight." She cut Willa a deliberately bland look. "He tried to step over it."

Willa yelped out a laugh. "He shocked himself in the crotch? Oh my God. I love it."

"I enjoyed it too," Georgie admitted.

Bianca smiled. "Just when you think nobody's in charge of the universe—"

"—somebody who deserves it gets struck by lightning, so

to speak," Georgie finished for her.

For a long, warm moment they all basked in the glory of divine justice applied directly to an offender's private parts, and Georgie slowly regained feeling in her fingers and toes. It was time to get to work.

"So, where's our bride-to-be?" She tugged Willa away from the fire by one soft sleeve. "Get away from there. You're going to set that sweater on fire, and I actually like it."

Willa shoved her hands into her pockets. "Upstairs with her parents."

Georgie slapped her wrist. "Stop that. You're ruining the line of your pants."

"I am not. I'm using my pockets." Willa scowled. "They wouldn't be here if I weren't supposed to use them."

Georgie turned to her mother. "She says stuff like that all the time."

Bianca studied Willa. "I think she really believes it, too."

"They're *pockets*," Willa said. Georgie sighed. So did Bianca, at the same moment, in the same tone. Willa's scowl deepened. "It's spooky when you two do that. You know that, right?"

Georgie did. She didn't know what to do about it, though.

Willa took her hands out of her pockets and held them out to the fire instead.

"Why are Addy's parents here already?" Georgie asked. "Jax is supposed to be picking them up right now."

"They got an earlier flight or something." Willa jerked a shrug. "According to Addy, her mom's got ultra elite premium status with so many airlines that they practically pay her to fly. She wants an earlier flight, she gets an earlier flight."

Bianca tipped her head. "And she wanted an earlier flight for some reason?"

"What reason?" Georgie asked, foreboding snaking into her gut.

"I don't know," Willa said grimly. "But they waved Jax off, rented a car at the airport, and showed up here about half an hour ago. Have you met either of them?"

"No, never." Georgie pursed her lips, thinking. "Diego and Addy eloped so there were no engagement parties or bridal showers where we might've. She's always said they were super career-focused, and they travel so much—"

Willa said, "Don't you think that's weird?"

"What, that we've not met Addy's people?" Bianca asked.

"Yeah."

"It is," Bianca conceded, a tiny line appearing between her brows, the only sign of maternal worry Georgie had ever been able to detect. "But I'm more concerned about why a pair of people who've never troubled themselves to visit their only child in the five years she's lived in Devil's Kettle would suddenly demand her undivided, private attention on the day of her bridal shower."

"Yeah," Willa muttered and, with flagrant disregard for the lines of her outfit, shoved her hands into her pockets again. "I'm worried about that, too."

"How long have they been up there?" Georgie asked.

"Twenty minutes?"

"Then they've had plenty of time to say whatever needed saying." Georgie flipped a length of shiny hair behind her shoulder with her haughtiest sigh. "I think I'll go introduce myself."

Bianca eyed her for a considering moment, then smiled

13

beatifically. "You should. As the maid of honor, it's your duty."

"Of course it is," Georgie sniffed and sailed toward the stairs.

"Entitlement Barbie to the rescue," Willa muttered, but she sounded relieved enough to give Georgie pause. Willa was never shaken, so she was never relieved. But she was relieved now, unmistakably.

What the hell was Georgie walking into?

CHAPTER 2

PETER WAS USED to shit. At this point in his life, he'd dealt with plenty of it. But if he was going to end every day smelling like sheep shit, he'd at least like to see his sacrifice reflected in his profit and loss statement.

His bottom line glowed stubbornly red from the sleek notebook computer in front of him.

He sighed and rose from the scarred kitchen table that served as his desk these days. He cracked his back and stalked toward the framed diplomas on his wall. He linked his fingers together on top of his smooth-shaven head and gazed at the school crests and the Latin words while a can of Campbell's tomato — dinner of champions — heated up on the stove. He stared at those achievements and accolades, and tried to remember why they'd once mattered so much.

Once upon a time, he seemed to recall, those diplomas had been proof. Proof that he was better than where he came from. Proof that he'd left this place behind. His childhood had put soap operas to shame, after all. Alcoholic parent? Check! Parental infidelity? Check! Domestic violence? Check! He'd taken the brains God had given him, though, and made more of himself than anybody could have expected. He'd gone to goddamn Yale and graduated with honors, hadn't he? Maybe he'd done it washing dishes and mowing lawns, maybe he'd driven a damn garbage truck and stunk like trash but he'd done it. And he had the diplomas to prove it, along with the real estate.

Not even six months ago, he'd owned half a dozen

vacation rentals and the only car dealership within 100 miles of Devil's Kettle, not to mention an entire block of goddamn Main Street. Half the town had called him landlord. The other half had called him boss. That was another life, though, and he didn't miss it. Most of the time, he barely remembered it.

An image of Georgie Davis floated into his mind, resplendent in a knock-your-eyes-out cocktail dress under a deep ruby trench coat and the ugliest pair of rain boots he'd ever seen. He'd been lying in a puddle trying not to puke from the sheer, miserable agony radiating up from his electrified balls, and even so his hands had twitched with the urge to touch the hair spilling shiny and endless over her shoulders. He smiled, bitterly amused. Had he really almost convinced himself he barely remembered that other life?

Sometimes he remembered it all too well.

Georgie Davis. The crown princess of Devil's Kettle. The most beautiful thing he'd ever seen, smelled, or touched, let alone been engaged to. He'd come back to Devil's Kettle for his old buddy Diego's funeral, intending to stay just long enough to show all the judgmental pricks in this town how wrong they'd been about him. He'd ended up trying to prove it instead. He couldn't be sure when he'd decided to stay. Maybe it was when he'd walked into the decrepit family bar his sister was mismanaging the crap out of and seen the centerpiece of an empire. Maybe it was when he'd rolled into town in a $3,000 suit and seen awed respect in the faces of people who'd only ever sneered at him before. Or maybe it was the moment Georgie Davis had stepped out of the smoked-glass SUV at the cemetery, the paparazzi's cameras strobing the whole thing into a damn dream sequence.

She'd been in black, of course, from her head to her

murderously high heels. Her hair had been pulled severely back, leaving the glorious bones of her face starkly revealed. She'd worn not a scrap of makeup, nor any visible sorrow. She'd been an oasis of grace and calm, a cool pool of water, utterly untouched by the madness of a funeral besieged by the national press.

She was exactly as he'd remembered her.

Before Diego had been an internationally renown painter, he'd been a friend of sorts. Not the kind of friend who'd ever invited Peter over for dinner — Peter was a Zinc, after all — but they'd been friendly enough in high school that Diego's kid sister had entered Peter's orbit a time or two. Even then she'd been like a distant moon — remote, beautiful and completely uninterested in her brother and his friends. She probably hadn't even known Peter's name, and he was dead sure they'd never spoken.

But as she'd stepped out of the SUV that day and taken her place in the front row of folding chairs set up at the edge of the hole that would receive her brother's body, she'd looked at him. Looked straight at him. Looked, and then *saw*. A shock had gone through him in that moment that rivaled his electric fence. Because she hadn't just seen him; she'd recognized him. And she'd smiled. Faintly, sadly, but truly. It was a smile that seemed to say *Diego would've loved this, wouldn't he*? And she'd given that smile to Peter, because she'd known — had she? *How* had she? — that he would understand. That he, too, had known Diego was an attention whore and a spoiled child and a goddamn genius, and that he really would've gotten a huge charge out of the media circus his ignominious shuffle off this mortal coil had triggered.

That smile had made Peter, for one brief, shining

moment, her equal. Georgie Davis, with her beauty, her money, her breeding, and the power that that holy trinity had invested in her, had raised him up. And it occurred to Peter for the first time that he could rule this place. This gorgeous little town that had given him the ugliest years of his life, the place he'd run so far and so fast from? He could *own* it. Which was different, he knew, than just buying it. He could buy every acre of property on the North Shore of Superior but he wouldn't *own* Devil's Kettle until its royal family accepted him as one of their own.

Next thing he knew, his five-year business plan had included buying most of the town and marrying Georgie Davis. It hadn't included the once-in-a-century recession and the ensuing economic collapse that had threatened to destroy everything he'd built, but hey, Georgie Davis was more than an impeccably bred quantum leap up the social ladder. She was also filthy rich. Their marriage would've given Peter access to her trust fund just in time to save his ass from financial ruin.

He should've known it was too good to be true. He should've known *she* was too good to be true. Because while she was undeniably well-connected, it turned out she was neither as rich as Peter had thought, nor as comfortably dim as she'd led him to believe. In fact, she was shrewd, smart, ruthless and broke. A sleazy accountant had beaten Peter to the punch and raided the Davis piggy bank months before Peter had maxed out his credit to pony up a diamond ring. Turned out Georgie had been making a golden parachute out of Peter at the same time he'd been making one out of her.

He should've called it right then. Should've just admitted he was broke, begged off the engagement and declared bankruptcy like a normal MBA.

But no. Peter was no quitter. There was still a path; he could see it. An unethical path, sure. A path littered with moral failings and casual cruelty but, hey, nothing in life was free, particularly not the social and financial miracle Peter was *this close* to pulling off. And it wasn't like he was committing murder, or asking anybody else to. Insurance fraud was white collar crime, country club stuff. And the pyromaniac he'd had his eye on was already burning stuff down for free, so…

So he'd sold his soul, then been forced to sell everything else he'd ever owned to mitigate the damage of that one, stupid, selfish decision. All he had left now was this stupid, ugly, stinky property that nobody in their right mind would buy, let alone occupy. Which was exactly what he probably deserved. Exile on a sheep farm. Shame roared in, familiar and heavy. It tightened his throat, roared in his ears like fire, filled his nose with the scent of…

Burned tomatoes?

"Shit." On the stove, a great wave of orange lava slopped over the edge of a sauce pan, suffocating the gas flame with a malevolent hiss. Peter seized up the pot, snapped off the burner and stood there, the dripping pot in his hand while half his dinner sizzled to a rock-hard crust on the stovetop. The scent of scorched soup mingled unpleasantly with the omnipresent smell of sheep.

"Great." He sighed and snatched a towel from the oven handle. He eyed the lava and said, "Screw it." He folded the towel in half, dropped it on the table and put the pot on it. Grabbed a spoon and settled in to eat whatever was left straight from the pot while he saw what could be done about the stubborn red line at the bottom of that profit/loss statement.

There was a knock at the door. Peter closed his eyes and set down his spoon. His stomach grumbled wearily. If the sheep had gotten out of the pasture again, he was going to have Tag made into boots. The damn dog was going to be the death of him, or vice versa. The world simply couldn't contain both of them. Surely some natural law forbade it. He pushed to his feet, shouldered open the kitchen door, and crossed the cavernous dining room to open the front door.

Georgie Davis stood there, ruby-red trench coat, ugly black boots, acres of moonlight hair and all.

He blinked at her, a little surprised but mostly just dazzled. He was out of practice looking directly into that face, up close and stunning. "Georgie?"

"Hello, Peter." She brushed by him and slinked into the foyer with the lazy entitlement of a house cat. "I have something for you."

"You do?" He stood there stupidly, holding the door open and gaping at her.

She pivoted like a model at the end of a runway, nailed him with those blue, blue eyes and a smile that edged toward mean. It sent off warning bells in his brain at the same time it sent sparks of interest zipping through his veins. It was the wretched stupidity of those sparks that slapped him back to the moment, directed his attention to the warning bells and forced him to focus. He'd thought of Georgie as comfortably dumb for so long that he had to constantly jump himself out of that well-worn track. Georgie wasn't dumb, not by any stretch of the imagination, and that laziness of hers was barely skin-deep.

And that was a dangerous smile. That was a switchblade of a smile. That smile meant he might be seeing his own guts up close and personal any minute now.

"I do." She looked beyond him to the still-open door. "Come on in, Mike."

Peter's head swiveled back to the door and he saw what he'd missed the first time: A guy standing on the front step with a wheeled suitcase. Peter put him in his late fifties, early sixties, with good shoes, an excellent suitcase, and a build that said he'd be murder on the soccer field but would actually *get* murdered should he attempt football. He was a little short for basketball — even in her rain boots, Georgie had him by an inch or four — but something about those eyes had point-guard potential.

The man stepped into the house and aimed a weary smile at Peter.

"You're Addy's," Peter heard himself say. He sighed. He spent so much time alone these days, his mouth sort of operated on auto-pilot, the thoughts making words of themselves just to keep Peter company. He barely made sense to other humans anymore. "I mean, you must be Addy's father."

"Guilty," Mike said with a grimness under the surface bonhomie that made Peter wonder if he meant that literally. "What gave it away? The hair or the face?"

"The smile," Peter said, closing the door behind him. "But now that you mention it, the hair's a dead ringer, too."

"Yeah." Mike reached up to touch an abundance of nutmeg-and-pepper curls. "Poor kid."

"Looks good on her," Peter offered. "Addy's a peach."

"She absolutely is," Georgie said, that switchblade smile still in place. "She's our peach, which is why Mike and I are here."

"Okay." Peter waited for it but Georgie only rubbed her hands up and down her arms and frowned around the formal dining room, empty and chilly.

"Why is it so cold in here?"

"This place is 4000 square feet and I'm one guy. I heat the part I use."

"Which is?"

He pointed toward the kitchen.

"We're having this conversation there, then." She galumphed across the room in her rain boots — actually *galumphed*. The boots made that noise precisely, and Georgie Davis made walking in them look easy. Slinky, even. Jesus Christ. Would the punishment never end? She disappeared through the swinging door Peter had hung to keep whatever heat he could in the kitchen.

He looked to the man at his side. "Do you have any idea what's going on?"

"Some," Mike said. "Mostly I just know that I'm more afraid of that girl in there than I am angry at my wife, and I'm pretty angry at my wife."

"It's the face." Peter rubbed his chin and considered the kitchen. "Georgie's like the sun — you can't look directly at her without going blind."

Mike gave that a dubious beat. "I think it's more that she's eight moves ahead of me and I don't even know what the game is or when I agreed to play it."

"There's that, too." Peter slipped his hands into his pockets and tipped his head toward the kitchen. "After you."

"Hell, no. You go first. It's your house."

"It is, isn't it?" Peter sighed and steeled himself to face the staggering one-two punch of Georgie's brains and beauty, along with the bitter regret of losing something he hadn't even known he had. "Let's go."

CHAPTER 3

THE KITCHEN WAS cozily cluttered but warm, which made it a nice change of pace from Peter's mausoleum of a dining room. It smelled like lemons and burnt tomatoes, and Georgie remembered suddenly that Peter's house — *houses*, really, as he'd never had a place of his own but moved around from rental to rental as he rehabbed them and waited for them to lease — had always smelled lemony. She'd assumed at the time that he must use the same cleaning service for all his properties, but it occurred to her now that he must just have a favorite soap or detergent. Because Peter could no longer afford a cleaning service. She'd made sure of it.

There was a laptop on a kitchen table, a handful of framed diplomas on the wall and a cot with a sleeping bag on it against the wall. She lifted a brow. He hadn't been kidding about only heating the part of the house he used. Things must be dire indeed if he was using the kitchen as an efficiency apartment. She tried to decide how she felt about that. A warning twinge danced through her stomach and she thought of Matty. Thought of her beloved baby brother at his most vulnerable, of the way Peter had used him, the damage he might've done. Rage surged inside her, rolling through and over the pain, obliterating it. Peter was being punished, she reminded herself. He'd *earned* this punishment, and she wasn't going to think about it beyond that.

She helped herself to a seat at the table. It was a farm-house style table, probably built with the house because

23

there was no way this table would fit through any door she'd seen so far. It was a big old chunk of rectangular wood with chairs at the head and foot, big, solid things that Georgie would have to use some muscle to pull out. There were benches on either side, though, and she'd chosen the one in front of the laptop to plop down on. She was just considering tapping a key or two — wouldn't it be interesting to wake up that dark screen and peek at what Peter entertained himself with while eating his sad little can of soup right out of the pot? — when Peter pushed through the swinging door, Mike on his heels.

Georgie smiled. "Have you two been getting acquainted?"

"Sure," Peter said. "We've both agreed that you're up to something, and it's probably not a good something for either of us."

She beamed at him. "Smart boys."

"Smart." He huffed out a little laugh. "I used to think so, too. I know better now."

"Do you? How nice." She shrugged. "I've brought you company."

"So I see."

"Peter, this is Mike Tate, Addy's father. Mike, this is Peter Zinc. He's…" She trailed off delicately. "Well, he's family of sorts." She lifted a lazy shoulder. "It's complicated."

"Okay." Mike offered a hand and the men shook. She gestured Mike toward the bench opposite hers. He sat cooperatively.

She turned to Peter, who'd leaned back against the counter beside the stove, arms folded, his dark eyes pinned to her. She said, "Mike's decided to stay in Devil's Kettle until the wedding."

"Has he?"

"Indeed. As he's separating from Addy's mother, he's a bit at loose ends and thought he'd like to spend some time getting to know his only daughter before she gets married again."

Peter's eyes shifted to Mike briefly, then came back to Georgie. "Is that so."

"The timing isn't good, I know," Mike offered apologetically. "But you have to understand about my wife. She's just so—"

"Stubborn?" Georgie asked. "Bone-headed? Impossible? Selfish?"

"And a liar," Mike said bitterly. "Because we had a deal. We prioritized work above everything — even, I'm ashamed to say, raising our child — so we could retire at sixty and enjoy our damn lives. Maybe even enjoy each other, if we remembered how. I've been retired for nine months now. Jennifer, on the other hand, is still putting in forty hours weeks, and thinking it counts as retirement because she used to put in eighty. And I'm sick of trying to—"

"I'm sure we understand." Georgie waved a dismissive hand. "Bottom line?" She met Peter's eyes. "Mike and Jennifer ambushed Addy two hours before her wedding shower with the news of their separation, then proceeded to wage a custody battle in her bedroom."

"A custody battle?"

"Over Addy."

Peter blinked. "Addy's, what, twenty-five? Twenty-six? Doesn't she get custody of herself?"

"One would think. But Jennifer's not about to cede the field if Mike's hanging around. She decided to stay in town, too."

Mike gave a derisive snort. "I'll believe it when I see it. Work's an addiction with Jennifer. She won't stay. She won't be able to."

Georgie ignored that. If the guy knew his wife that well, he wouldn't be pulling stunts like this. He wouldn't have to.

"And of course," she told Peter, "they both wanted to stay at Davis Place."

"At Addy's bed and breakfast? Isn't this week her grand opening?" Peter tilted his head and considered that. "How is she fixed for reservations? Does she need the guests?"

"I have no idea, nor is that remotely the point." Something he'd understand if he were remotely human. *Which is why*, her brain pointed out with her mother's voice, *it isn't safe to forget we hate him*. "The point is, I'm her maid of honor."

He digested that in cautious silence. Georgie sighed and spelled it out.

"Which means that until I hand both Addison and my brother into one another's keeping, I have one job and one job only: keeping the bride happy." She slid a pointed glance Mike's way. "But happy is a tall order when *your divorcing parents move in with you*."

Mike had the grace to drop his gaze to the table. Peter pursed his lips thoughtfully. "Fair enough. What does that have to do with me, though?"

Georgie smiled. She'd been hoping he'd ask. "Well, Mike obviously can't stay at Davis Place."

"Obviously."

"But he's family so we can hardly send him to a hotel."

"All right."

"So we're sending him to you."

He stared. She met his incredulous gaze wide-eyed, unblinking. Daring him to argue.

Eventually he lifted a hand to his face, dragged it wearily down a jaw that hadn't seen a razor in a good couple of days if Georgie was any judge. She could hear the rasp of stubble against his palm across the room, and an entirely inappropriate shiver danced into her blood. Knee-jerk, she told herself. She'd slept with this man once a week for the better part of two years, and the body had a memory, just like the brain.

And the heart? her mother's voice asked.

Don't be ridiculous, Georgie told it. She'd trusted Peter, which was bad enough. She hadn't been stupid enough to love him.

A cramp seized her stomach, the pain intense and dazzling. She closed her eyes against it, but only briefly. The psychologists — all of them — had agreed with the medical doctors — all of them — in that there was nothing physically wrong with her. She was evidently hard-wired to transform mental discomfort into physical pain, that was all. It was sort of like being in a bad dream, they'd told her. No matter how real it feels, it isn't. You just have to tell yourself it isn't really there.

Which worked about as well as you'd think. But she'd rather her stomach hurt than anything more vital, so she just breathed and waited for Peter to speak.

"Let me get this straight," he said finally. "A hotel's not good enough for family but a barely operational sheep farm is okay?"

Georgie cast her eyes modestly down. "Well, you're family, too."

Peter went still. "You keep saying that."

"Because it's true."

"No, it isn't," Peter said. "I don't have family."

"Of course you do." Georgie rolled her eyes lavishly and turned to Mike. "Addy's other bridesmaid, Willa? That's Peter's sister. You probably met his dad Brett at the shower, too."

"Tall guy? Blue sweater? Big hands?"

"That's him."

"Sure. Nice guy."

"I left them behind years ago," Peter told Mike, his eyes still on Georgie. "I had no use for family when I was rich. I have no use for family now that I'm poor. And they have no use for me."

Georgie snorted. Like family was about use? "We also share a brother."

Which was, she realized suddenly, the very crux of her problem with Peter. If he'd just been Willa's brother, Brett's son, or her own ex-fiancé, she'd have been able to cut him dead. Toss him into exile exactly as he deserved. But he wasn't just related to her through friends and disastrous personal history. He was also her brother Matty's half-brother.

Which was what happened when your horndog older brother fathered a bastard at sixteen with the hot neighbor lady (who also happened to be Peter's sociopathic mother) and your own mother adopted the baby, making your nephew your brother.

It was, as she'd told Mike, complicated. Very.

Bottom line, though? It didn't matter that she and Peter shared not a scrap of DNA; he was her brother's half-brother. He was family.

Which didn't release her from her responsibility to hate

him.

The pain roared back in like the tide, sickening and inevitable.

"Matty doesn't claim me any more than I claim him," Peter pointed out with exaggerated patience. "Nor does the rest of your family." He cut his eyes toward Mike, who was silently absorbing what must be a largely incomprehensible conversation. "For good reason," Peter told him. "I once used the kid as a torch-for-hire to commit insurance fraud."

Mike blinked owlishly.

"Yeah." Peter nodded. "I blackmailed him into blowing up a Dumpster, burning down a resort and then starting a fire at Davis Place that could've killed both your daughter and her fiancé, who happens to be Georgie's oldest brother."

Mike took a long pause, then cleared his throat. "Why?"

"Because I owned all three properties, either outright or with partners, and I needed the money."

There had been more to it than that, Georgie knew. Yes, Peter's financial problems had been entirely self-made, and sure, he'd been trying to marry his way out of them, but Georgie had been pulling much the same scam, hadn't she? (Hindsight was brutal, and Georgie had spent a few sleepless nights, breathing through her pain and thinking this one through.) Her hands weren't entirely clean when it came to their spectacularly broken engagement, a little fact Peter was well aware of but had never made public. Georgie peered at him, leaning there against his sturdy cabinets, painting his admittedly shitty decisions in the worst possible light. She wondered why he wasn't painting hers with the same brush.

"I see," Mike murmured, and Georgie wondered if he did. If so, she envied him.

"It worked out about as well as those schemes usually

do," Peter said with a wry smile. He untucked one of his folded arms and waved it magnanimously around the kitchen. "What you see now is all that's left of my once-legendary empire. One sheep farm that some hipster convinced me to invest in, then abandoned at the first sign of a North Shore winter."

"Ah," Mike said. He'd likely run out of agreeable words and was now just making soothing noises. Which made sense. If Georgie remembered correctly, he'd spent most of his career as a flight nurse on med-evac choppers. It seemed like the kind of work that would reward the ability to be reassuring without making any promises.

"I sold everything," Peter said to Georgie. "Paid the debts money could settle but the rest of them? The ones money can't touch? Those are why I have no family, and never will." He held her eyes with his — dark, straightforward, and so impossibly naked it was hard to meet his gaze. "I don't want it."

Georgie forced her lips into an amused curve. The pain was fading but she was still sweating. "Oh Peter," she said. "You're adorable. Family isn't something you get to want or not want. Family is just something you have, and you have us, like it or not. Or, more to the point, we have you." She let the smile fade. "Because as you said, there are some debts money can't settle. You still owe us."

Peter went perfectly still, and simply watched her for the space of three slow heartbeats with those brutally honest eyes. Georgie wondered uneasily when he'd stopped even trying to put up a good front. She wondered also if she was shiny with sweat. "For Matty," he said finally.

"For Matty."

He nodded abruptly. "Fine." He glanced toward Mike.

"There are four bedrooms upstairs but this is the only heated space right now. I don't even know if the furnace works. Until last week it was warm enough that I didn't need to know. Even if it does, I can't afford to turn it on."

"Right," Mike said. "Okay."

Peter shifted his eyes back to Georgie. "Where did you send the mother?"

"Home with *my* mother."

"Ooof." Something flickered at the corner of his mouth, the stirrings of a smile. He lifted a hand to scrub at that jaw again, hiding that maybe-smile from view. And his jaw, Georgie couldn't help but notice, was still as firm and heroic as it had been when she'd first decided Peter would do, and do nicely for her. How wrong she'd been. It didn't seem fair that he got to keep the heroic jaw but hadn't had to keep the promises. He sent Mike a serious look. "You dodged a bullet, my friend."

"I kind of got that impression," Mike murmured, and rose. "I'll find a room to stash my bag."

"Bianca's no bullet," Georgie said to Peter. "That would imply the existence of a gun, and somebody else pulling the trigger." She smiled. "My mother is the whole terrifying package."

"Truth." Peter held up both hands. "I respect Bianca only slightly less than I fear her." Once again, Georgie had the strong impression that this was the bald, unvarnished truth. "Which is to say tremendously." He leaned to one side to call after Mike. "I hope your wife is made of stern stuff."

"You have no idea," Mike said grimly and disappeared.

Georgie rose with a lazy smile. "Well, that was fun."

"Glad you enjoyed yourself."

"You've been extremely entertaining all day, Peter." She

crossed the kitchen to him, laid a hand on those tightly folded arms. She rose to her toes and pressed her lips to that stubbly cheek. "Thanks." Those low-grade shivers multiplied and cascaded down her back all the way to her rain boots and she dropped back to her heels to smile into his face. "I'm sure I'll see you around. Now that you're family."

He said nothing, just gazed at her with those bleak eyes, so she turned and strolled out of the kitchen. She didn't look back, and she didn't pause. It wasn't until she was safely in her Range Rover again, lights on, heater blasting, that she allowed herself to press a hand to her poor abused stomach in wonder. It still hurt — it always hurt — but publicly claiming Peter as family had unwound something inside her that had been painfully clenched. Forcing him to do something to pay back the debt he owed her — owed Matty — had been a good decision, then.

Kissing him goodbye, though?

She shook her head at the sparks and shivers still multiplying and dancing around her libido.

Bad decision. Very bad.

She wondered if she'd do it again.

She just might.

CHAPTER 4

THE NORTH SHORE of Lake Superior was a funny place. Peter hadn't thought of it often when he'd been a business mogul, not beyond the way tourists seemed to love the view. That vast inland sea, all rugged and fierce, juxtaposed against the colorful optimism of Main Street, with a picturesque harbor sandwiched between them and a forbidding basalt cliff shearing straight up behind? It was something to behold, and he'd bought every acre of it he could afford. A few acres more than he could afford, actually, which was how he'd ended up in his present circumstances.

That and some lamentably amoral decision-making.

Now that he was a shepherd (a *shepherd,* for Christ's sake), he spent all day with the outdoors underfoot and in his face instead of politely outside his window. This had given him many soggy, sweaty hours to become exquisitely familiar with each and every one of the 50 acres that comprised what was left of his empire. Redemption Farm (the name should've been his first clue that he'd gotten into bed with an unreliable farmer) was situated about halfway between Devil's Kettle's two most photographed properties, if you didn't count Buck's Bait and Tackle down on Main Street, with its enormous papier mache fish. The Davis family owned them both, of course.

Hill Top House, the current family seat, was parked a couple miles below the farm in a gorgeous meadow at the cliff's edge. All gleaming glass and cutting edges, it boasted a wall of windows and a post-card ready view of Lake Superior sparkling all the way to the horizon. A few miles above the farm was Davis Place, and its view was the stuff of legend. The Davises weren't rich for nothing; artistic talent and business acumen ran like twin threads through their DNA. So when some enterprising ancestor had stumbled across a disappearing damn river, he'd snapped up the overlooking property and built himself a massive house with front row seats. The Department of Natural Resources (when it eventually came into existence) had had to settle for building their state park around Davis Place, and tourists gawked at the Kettle from the second best vantage point.

The road connecting the two properties meandered toward and away from the cliff's edge for half a dozen miles, curling back on itself when the going got steep, stretching out when it hit a meadow. Peter's property lay in an elbow of that road several hundred yards inland from the cliff's edge, 50 or so acres of lumpy grass punctuated by the occasional copse of quaking aspen.

The entire North Shore of Lake Superior had been pushed into place by the glaciers eons ago, which was the only reason an anomaly like Peter's farm even existed. The glaciers had acted like some giant hand scraping thousands of miles of the earth's crust one direction then making only a half-assed attempt to put things back where they belonged on the way home. Stuff had gotten left behind, jumbled up. Devil's Kettle itself was the most famous example of this scatter-shot take on geology, born as it had been of a strange patch of soft rock that had gotten stuck somehow in the middle of an otherwise erosion-proof basalt cliff. Peter's farm was another example. There shouldn't be 50 acres of protected, grassy pastureland on top of a rocky cliff, of course, but the glacier had scraped out a shallow depression in the clifftop on its way south, then on its retreat north, had filled it in with a bunch of rich black soil.

At least this was how the hipster farmer had explained it all to Peter when pitching the investment.

The guy had been wrong about so many things, but not geography. Peter was, indeed, standing on a cliff, and yet somehow also in a low spot. He could tell by the way the water was pooling around his ankles, and the way his wet toes ached with the cold. He was wearing a pair of waterproof boots that came nearly to his knees, but today's rain was of the misty variety that didn't fall so much as sneak. And so far it had snuck into Peter's boots, his collar and his goddamn underwear.

"Tag!" he shouted. "Come on by!"

According to everything he'd read, this command would tell a well-trained sheepdog to hang a left around the sheep, and begin gathering the flock into a single unit, ready to be moved. Tag veered obediently left. When he was behind the flock of damp sheep placidly munching late-season grass, he loped to the top of a lumpy rise and sat, waiting patiently for his next command.

Hope sparked to life inside Peter. Maybe Tag was going to cooperate for once. Maybe they'd get these sheep out of the middle pasture and into the near pasture where fresh grass awaited so Peter could go inside to mainline coffee until his toes either warmed up or fell off. He'd be equally satisfied with either outcome at this point.

"Tag, to me!"

Tag rose to his feet, circled once, then sat again. Peter, standing maybe 50 yards away in the open gate between the middle and near pastures, could see the smug bastard cocking a defiant brow. Peter had never before realized that dogs had eyebrows but Tag did, and he used them eloquently. *Yeah,* those eyebrows said, *I don't think so.*

"Tag!" Peter shouted again. "*To me!*"

Tag yawned and glanced over his shoulder, beyond which lay the far pasture. A moderately electric fence subdivided Peter's pasture into three sections — far, middle and near — with gates between them that Peter could open or close at will. A more emphatically electric fence enclosed the whole thing, running from the barn all the way to the road. Tag sat on a rise of earth that hid most of the far pasture from Peter's view, along with the road and the this-means-business fence on which Peter had likely lost his ability to father children. At Peter's shout, the dog got to his feet once more, circled in place, then sat again, tail wrapped neatly around his feet. The sheep didn't even lift their heads. They just chewed.

"Damn it, Tag!" Peter stomped around the flock himself. When he was on the rise beside Tag, he put his fists on his hips and glared down at the dog. "I said, bring them to me!"

Tag's eyebrows said, *exactly how much closer do you want them?*

"I hate you," Peter said.

Tag rose and trotted down the back of the rise toward the far pasture. He dropped his haunches and scooted under the moderately electric fence with a grace and ease Peter envied reluctantly.

"What," Peter called after him, "do you have a lunch date or something? Anybody I know?"

Tag kept trotting until he reached the far fence, the one Peter still couldn't look at without wincing. Then he dropped his haunches once again and slid easily beneath it. He disappeared briefly into the ditch where Georgie had found Peter cradling his smoking nuts nearly a week before, and came up on the other side. He planted his rear on the asphalt shoulder and faced Peter with a deliberate air of expectation that had Peter frowning.

"What, are we going to play Lassie now?" he muttered. "What is it, boy? Did Timmy fall down the well? Was it Colonel Mustard with the lead pipe in the conservatory? What?"

Tag did the eyebrow thing again.

"Fuck's sake." But he trudged down the rise.

He stopped short when he saw the ewe lying on her side in the shallow ditch. Tag sat above her, eyes patient, tongue lolling out.

"What the hell?" Peter stepped carefully over the fence and jogged to the sheep's side. There was no blood, nothing was obviously broken, but she was panting, and the one eye he could see was wide and full of suffering. Peter dropped to his knees and ran his hands over her legs anyway. Her joints seemed intact, and she didn't respond to any particular pressure anywhere. Her ear tag said 14, and Peter wracked his memory for anything in the somewhat haphazard medical records he'd inherited from Hipster Farmer that might explain this.

Fourteen gave a bawl of sheer, pitiful misery. Then she lifted her tail and farted out a bloody spurt of something Peter could've happily lived his entire life without seeing or smelling. "Oh dear God," he murmured, staring. "Jesus, Mary and Joseph."

Because Peter had made two very large mistakes, one of which a guy should never make about a female of any species.

First, what he'd taken for the ewe's anus was actually her vagina. Men should know those two orifices apart, Peter believed firmly, and never confuse them without a lady's express permission.

Second, what he'd taken for some kind of vile diarrhea was actually some kind of vile liquid associated with the birth process. Because Fourteen now had a pair of tiny hooves protruding from her backside. Which was, as far as Peter's records were concerned, a total impossibility.

"No," Peter told the ewe firmly. "We are not doing this. This is not happening right now."

Fourteen keened sadly. Peter didn't blame her.

"I read about this," he told her. "The records were crystal clear on this point. The wether—" That would be a male sheep of which Peter had only one. "—was castrated." Which was why he was a wether, not a ram. "The only working penis on this farm is mine." He hoped. He sent the fence a reproachful glance. "Hipster's journal made this very plain. You are not pregnant."

The ewe clenched her jaw and another steaming jet of fluid squirted from around the tiny hooves. Which were, Peter saw with a sense of encroaching horror, now attached to a pair of knees. He gripped his own knees helplessly and looked at Tag.

"What now?" he asked the dog. "What in the bleeding hell am I supposed to do now? Do I pull it out? Leave it there? I skipped this chapter. I'm not supposed to need it yet!"

Tag maintained a skeptical silence. He wasn't getting involved in this, not with an amateur like Peter. Peter didn't blame him.

"Mike!" he bawled. There was absolutely no chance

Mike would hear him back at the house. Even less, he realized bitterly, since Mike wasn't even at the house. He was picking up the chickens. Chickens, for sweet lord's sake. Peter was attending a virgin birth, and the only other sentient human adult who might've helped was in the next county picking up experimental chickens.

Fourteen's eye narrowed with determination and Peter said, "Oh God, please don't—"

There was no liquid this time, just another inexorable couple inches of spindly lamb legs.

"Please don't do that again," Peter said when she'd subsided, her pink tongue hanging out as she panted. He buried his fists in her wool, which was somehow both wet and warm at the same time. Her sides heaved with effort, and sympathy twisted Peter's dancing guts. "I'm sorry, I know you have to but I really have no idea what the hell I'm doing here and if you could just wait while I call the vet—"

Tires sounded on the road behind Tag and relief jetted up inside him. Mike was back with the chickens, thanks be to a merciful God. He shot to his feet and waved both arms in the air. The chickens could wait to be unloaded for a few minutes. Mike needed to pull over the farm truck and take charge of this situation *now*. He was a nurse, for crying out loud. Surely he'd done this before. Probably not on a sheep but how different could it be, species to species?

Except that wasn't Peter's beat-up farm truck rounding the bend in the road.

That was Georgie's sleek black Range Rover.

Peter didn't even care. Georgie wasn't a nurse but she was a woman. She had a vagina. He knew this for certain, having once been on a first-name basis with it. (Those were the days.) This fact alone made her far more qualified to attend an unauthorized birth than Peter.

He saw her behind the wheel, her eyes huge and amazed at the sight of him in his ditch yet again. He saw the flash of her smile, too, and he realized that she was wondering if he'd also shocked his crotch again. Was *enjoying* wondering if he'd shocked his crotch again.

He didn't care about that either. He was too happy to see her pulling over.

"Peter," she said, her voice cool and amused as she stepped out of the Rover. "We've got to stop meeting like this. People are going to talk."

He ignored that, dropped to his knees again beside Fourteen. "Let them." The sheep lowed softly and Peter dug his hands back into her woolly side, found his way to the hard drum of her belly. It was alive under his hands, and in spite of his roaring panic, a spark of wonder surfaced. There was a lamb in here, *inside* his sheep, fighting to be born. A life, tiny and stubborn and impossible. "We're having a baby here."

He heard her galumphing across the street — must be in those rain boots again — and then she was splashing into the ditch beside him. "Holy hell," she breathed, her blue eyes huge and fixed on the skinny legs protruding from Fourteen's bottom. "We are."

"We are not supposed to be having a baby," he informed her. He spoke to the sheep. "You are *not* supposed to be doing this."

"I don't think you should argue with the lady," Georgie said. "She seems...determined."

"Tell me about it." The belly writhed under his hands and Fourteen's single visible eye wheeled. "Okay, now, take it easy," he murmured to the sheep and smoothed his palms over the war being waged inside that tight belly. "Easy there, shhhh." He spoke to Georgie without taking his eyes off Fourteen. "My phone is in my right jacket pocket. The vet is in the favorites menu. Will you please—"

Fourteen lifted her head and bawled, and Peter felt her gathering for a mighty push.

"No time for the vet," Georgie said grimly and dropped to her knees in the muck behind the ewe. "This is happening right now."

CHAPTER 5

PETER GLANCED IN surprise at Georgie, and winced. "That was a nice outfit."

"Thanks," she returned, utterly unconcerned about the trim black pants currently soaking up ditch water and the fluffy sweater that lived somewhere between gray and purple but was in grave danger of ending up more placenta-colored. Whatever color placentas were.

Oh God.

Georgie, bless her, seemed unworried about any of this. She laid a comforting hand on Fourteen's rump and gathered the little lamb knees in her other hand. "Okay, sweetheart," she said to the sheep. "Let's do this thing."

A wave of gratitude nearly swamped him but guilt followed immediately after. Georgie was the last person who should be helping him at all, let alone sacrificing what was surely couture for him.

"Georgie, listen, you don't have to do this," he forced himself to say. "Seriously, just get my phone and look up—" Fourteen thrashed suddenly, stabbed determinedly at the earth with sharp hooves. "Jesus Christ," he breathed, horror and shock mingling unpleasantly inside him. "I think she's trying to get *up*."

"Well, don't let her," Georgie snapped.

"I thought we weren't arguing with the lady."

"Peter, I have lamb knees in my hand. Keep her *down*."

"Right." Peter threw himself across the sheep's neck, pinned her like a wrestler. "Sorry, Fourteen." Moisture trickled from his collar down his back, and it was actually sort of nice, given that he'd broken out in a flop sweat 15 minutes ago. Fourteen fought for a moment, then subsided with a wounded, whinnying *baaaaaaaaah.*

"Oh, love, I know," Georgie crooned to the sheep. "It hurts, and you want to get away from it."

"You and me both," Peter informed the sheep.

"And that mean man won't let you."

Mean man? "You're the one who said—"

"But there's nowhere to go." Georgie spoke calmly over him. "Not for you, not for me, not for him." She nodded toward Peter, as if Fourteen saw him or cared about his whereabouts, beyond the fact that she'd prefer to give birth on the hoof and he was pinning her to the ground. "The only way to the other side is through. You have to go through it, darling, but not alone. We'll be with you the whole time."

"God help us all," Peter murmured.

Fourteen shifted restlessly beneath him, not trying to get up again but definitely trying to squirm away from the contraction Peter could feel starting to grip her belly.

"Oh crap," he said to Georgie. "Here we go again."

"All right, love, all right," she said to the sheep. "Don't fight it, okay? Just roll with it. Get on top of it and use it. Push, baby. Give us a good one, hmmm?"

Peter found Fourteen's soft ear with his free hand and gave it a caress. "Do it, Fourteen," he told her grimly.

"Fourteen?" Georgie asked.

"It's her name, I guess."

"You named a sheep Fourteen?"

"They don't have names, per se. Just numbers. The other nineteen — including Nineteen — are over there, along with Twenty-one, the boy sheep responsible for this mess. I'm

43

naming him Bastard. I just decided." He jerked his head toward the middle pasture, and caught sight of Tag still sitting near the road, tongue out, eyes watchful. "Tag, go to the flock."

This wasn't an official sheep-dog command but for once, Tag didn't balk. He leapt to his feet, jumped the ditch, slipped under the fence and planted himself on the rise at the edge of the middle pasture, his back to them. Watching over the sheep, Peter thought, but from a vantage point where he could continue to supervise Peter as well. Damn dog didn't trust him.

Fourteen strained and heaved under Peter's weight and bawled pitifully, but Georgie said, "Oh, good girl! Oh my good, *good* girl! Look!"

Peter turned his head and found Georgie cradling a ball of bloody wool the size of a football to that pretty smoke-colored sweater, damp hair plastered to her cheeks, eyes shining. And Peter lost his breath. Georgie had smiled at him before. She'd smiled at him all the time when they'd been engaged, and she'd continued to smile at him afterwards. Some of her smiles were designed to flatter, and he'd gotten plenty of those in the good old days. Some of them were designed to slice a man to the bone, and he'd been on the wrong end of a few of those in recent months. He thought he'd seen every one she had to offer but he'd never seen this.

"Peter, look!" She hefted the squirming, bleating ball of slime higher up on her chest and simply *beamed* at him. Her eyes, shockingly blue against the gray sky, were filled with a simple, uncomplicated joy and her perfect face was suffused with wonder. "Holy smokes, we made a baby sheep!"

Peter stared, too overwhelmed by the blunt instrument of her beauty to form words.

44

"I *know,* right?" She'd evidently mistaken his speechlessness for a wonder that matched her own. She shook her head and turned that smile on the squirming, bloody mess in her arms. "Can you believe it? We have a sheep here! An actual, real-live sheep, size extra adorable."

He found himself grinning at her. Grinning! Fourteen had called into question everything he understood about the farm he'd somehow found himself running, and he still had the wherewithal to grin at Georgie Davis, filthy and falling in love with the ugliest, stinkiest thing said farm had yet produced. "And all it cost you was a very nice sweater."

"Aw, listen to Mr. Grumpy Pants," she crooned to the disgusting ball of mucus in her arms. "Talking about laundry at a time like this! Who cares about sweaters? You'll just grow me a new one, won't you?" She lifted the lamb in both hands, *Lion King*-style. "She's going to be the queen of wool, and her sweaters will put all other sweaters to shame!" Four stick-like legs unfolded from the lamb's wet body and pawed uncertainly at the air. Given this context clue, Peter was able to locate a tiny pink nose somewhere near the top, and a hungry little mouth just below it. That mouth opened and a distinct *baaaaaaaah* emerged, affronted and hungry.

"Aw, you want your mommy, I'll bet."

Georgie patted Fourteen's rump approvingly and leaned forward to snuggle the little ball of grossness under its mother's chin. Fourteen should've started licking it clean but instead stirred uncomfortably under Peter's weight. He eased cautiously to his hands and knees.

"Can I let her up yet?"

Georgie wiped her hands on her pants and frowned up at him. "How the hell do I know? You're the farmer in this scenario."

"No, I just play one on TV. In reality, I have no idea what the hell I'm doing. Fourteen here isn't even pregnant as far as I know."

"Well, she isn't *now*."

Fourteen stirred again, more alarmingly this time. Peter lay back down on her. "She's acting like she might be. Does she have to deliver the, I don't know, the afterbirth or something? Because she's supposed to be licking little Twenty-two there—"

"You are not naming the precious little lambkin I just delivered Twenty-two."

"I'm not naming her anything," Peter said. "That's her number. She's a farm animal. She's a commodity. That's all she gets."

"Fine," Georgie said serenely. "I'll name her. She's growing me a new sweater. It's the least I can do."

He didn't have the heart to tell her his flock was bred for meat. Fourteen bawled and hunched again and Peter said, "How about after you deliver the placenta?"

Georgie wiggled herself back into the hot zone and punched one bloody fist into her other palm with a wet slap that Peter would never unhear. "Okay, Fourteen. Let 'er rip."

Fourteen obligingly heaved through another series of brutal contractions. Peter caressed that soft ear again and mentally apologized on behalf of males everywhere.

"Well?" he asked. "Did she do it?"

Silence.

He turned to look at Georgie, found her round-eyed and open-mouthed, staring at Fourteen's bottom. Unease gripped him. Sometimes sheep pushed so hard, they delivered their own uteri. He'd read about it. Well, skimmed, really. He'd only skimmed the chapters on birth because he wasn't going

46

to need them. A castrated ram couldn't get sheep pregnant, and he'd needed to focus. But a little fact like that — the ability to accidentally expel a vital body part — had jumped out and stuck with him.

"Georgie? What is it?"

She blinked at Fourteen's bottom and bit her lip. Scrubbed her filthy hands down her pants and finally looked up at him, her eyes filled again with astonished wonder and a purity of joy that knocked him predictably stupid even as suspicion filled him.

"It's hooves," she breathed, and a smile dawned across that perfect face that severed him from his rational thought process entirely. "It's another set of hooves. We're having twins, Daddy."

Several hours — and one very thorough shower — later, Georgie breezed into Davis Place with a contraband pie.

There were no guests in the great room though a fire crackled merrily in that enormous hearth, but something smelled delicious so she followed her nose.

A swinging door to the left of the hearth separated the kitchen from the great room and Georgie nudged it open. "Hello?"

Addison sat at the generous island counter anchoring her industrial-yet-cheerful kitchen, her elbows propped on the granite, the heels of her scuffed Keds hooked on the rung of her stool. She had her fingers knotted around the stem of an otherwise untouched glass of wine.

"Hey," Addy said and sent Georgie a weary smile over her shoulder. Oh, hell. Georgie didn't like that smile. Addy loved to work. She *thrived* on work. She got a little squirrelly when she didn't have enough work to do, in fact,

47

and had been looking forward to her first week of business as an honest-to-goodness innkeeper with an almost religious fervor. Georgie would bet her recently (if only partially) restored trust fund it wasn't the work that had drained Addison's bottomless stores of energy. This left Jax (the groom-to-be) or Addy's parents as the most likely source of trouble. And Georgie knew for a fact that her brother adored Addison and doted on her to a degree she personally found nauseating, so smart money said this was a parental issue.

Of course it was.

Willa stood on the far side of the island counter, an apron tied on over her usual uniform of jeans and a t-shirt while she tended a bubbling pot on the built-in range. Georgie glanced a question her way but Willa only gave a tiny shrug. So Georgie sauntered up to the counter and slid the pie box onto it. She put her cheek next to Addy's and gave her a lazy squeeze. "Hey, Addison." She straightened and paused deliberately. "Willa."

"Well, well." Willa bared her teeth in a wide smile. "Look who finally decided to show up."

"Oh, am I late?" Georgie rounded her eyes innocently, though she *was* late and to a bridesmaids dinner, too. Ouch. In her defense, she'd been trying to save her poor sweater. "And you waited dinner." She gave a disdainful sniff, as if there were something vaguely obscene about the scent of excellent chili. "You shouldn't have."

"That's what I said," Willa returned gamely but Addy didn't even frown. Normally nothing got her fired up like a little spat between her bridesmaids but she wasn't biting tonight. Georgie's gut tightened ominously and Willa soldiered on. "That's what I've been saying for months now. *Let's just go ahead without her*. Addy wasn't having it,

48

though." Willa tipped her head to the side and studied Georgie like she was a weird bug or an animal Willa had never seen before, which would be very odd indeed, as Willa made her living handling, trapping and evicting every kind of wild animal the North Shore had to offer. "She seems attached to you for reasons that remain mysterious to me."

Georgie sent her a close-lipped smile in return. "Same."

Addy finally looked up from her knotted fingers. "I knew you'd get here," she said, and sent Georgie a crooked smile that had relief sloshing through her tense stomach. "Sooner or later."

"It's always later with her, though, isn't it?" Willa muttered and hid her own relief by fetching bowls from the cupboard behind her. "Much, much later."

"Yes, well." Georgie flipped a length of meticulously blow-dried hair over her shoulder. "Some of us take the time to shower and change before having dinner at a friend's house. Just as, you know, a common courtesy."

Willa snorted and marched back to the counter with a trio of sturdy bowls. She used some kind of prong-covered spoon to dump an enormous scoop of noodles into each one, then pointed the spoon at Georgie. "You sit on your bony butt in an art gallery all day being the spokesmodel of Devil's Kettle. How dirty could you possible get?" She dropped the spoon into the colander and pulled a ladle from the pot rack overhead. Georgie watched with mild fascination as she topped Mt. Pasta with half a gallon or so of chili.

"We're having spaghetti *and* chili?" Georgie asked, blinking. Her stomach spasmed in pre-revolt. "Together?"

"It's just chili," Willa said and tossed at least a cup of shredded cheddar into each bowl. "Cincinnati-style." She finished it off with a fat blob of sour cream and pushed a bowl Georgie's way with a sharky smile that reminded her of Peter. She'd never seen the resemblance before, but there it was.

Georgie gazed down at the bowl. "How is everybody in Cincinnati not dead?"

"Of happiness?" Willa shrugged and dealt out the silverware. "Hell if I know. They created a goddamn miracle." She lifted the bottle of red wine in front of Addison, poured Georgie a generous glass and said, "Dig in."

"I'll do my best," Georgie murmured, poking at the sour cream with her fork. The scent rising from the bowl was incredible — hot, greasy, spicy. This couldn't be ground turkey. Willa cooked with real ground beef, she was almost certain of it. And she was no slouch in the spice department, either. If her nose didn't deceive her, that was smoked paprika doing the tango with a generous helping of cumin, a pinch of cinnamon and possibly some cocoa powder. And Willa hadn't settled for plain old kidney beans, either. Those were garbanzo beans and…Georgie shifted aside that generous scoop of sour cream…hominy? Oh, mercy. If Georgie could live on smell alone, she'd be set. But there was no way she could put this in her stomach. Not without serious consequences. "Unfortunately, I left all the starving orphans in the car. Should I go get them?"

Willa was already chewing with apparent bliss and waved a *whatever* with one hand.

Addy picked up her fork and began twirling up a more modest bite of her own. Georgie got up, found a clean bowl — a much smaller one — and helped herself to a more manageable serving of plain pasta. She drizzled it with olive oil, ground some sea salt over it and took it back to her stool.

"I really wish you'd eat more," Addy said. She frowned and reached over to tap the bony knob of Georgie's wrist. "You've always been thin but ever since the break up, you've gotten downright skinny."

"You think she's pining for Peter?" Willa asked and lifted the beer she'd opted for.

"No, of course not." Addy tipped her head and studied Georgie. "Are you?"

She thought about Peter's stubbly jaw and suffered another wave of inappropriate shivers.

"Of course not. And I eat. See?" Georgie took a deliberate bite of pasta. "Mmmm." Willa snorted again while Georgie chewed and swallowed. "As Willa pointed out, however, I lead a relatively sedentary life. I don't need to eat like a lumberjack."

"Plus, she has an entire size zero wardrobe," Willa added. "Which is inherently incompatible with the caloric intake normally required to sustain a six-foot-tall human."

Addy only frowned thoughtfully at Georgie's collarbones which, she could admit, were a bit more prominent than she liked. The sweater she'd pitched in the trash an hour ago had camouflaged that fact nicely. The one she was wearing now evidently did not.

"Speaking of wardrobes." Georgie consulted her stomach and decided that the pasta was settling better than usual. "Your brother owes me a sweater, Willa."

"Does he now?" Willa's eyebrows shot up and she leaned against the counter.

"How on earth?" Addy leaned forward, too, eyes sparkling with an interest the bickering bridesmaids routine had utterly failed to produce. Peter wasn't exactly Georgie's favorite topic but she was the maid of honor, damn it. She knew her duty.

"Turns out, Peter sucks at birth control."

Addy's eyes went huge in her pointed little face. "Excuse me?"

Even Willa froze. "Tell me you're not somehow pregnant with my niece or nephew."

"What?" Georgie blinked, then released a burbling laugh. "Good heavens, no! Like any woman with a functioning brain stem would leave the birth control up to a man? Please." She waved that off. "Peter became a daddy today, but I'm not the mommy. That would be Fourteen."

CHAPTER 6

"Fourteen what?" Addy asked blankly.

"Oh God." Willa set down her bowl with a thump. "Fourteen delivered a baby today?"

"Fourteen *what*?" Addy asked again.

"Fourteen isn't a what," Georgie told her, grinning. "It's a who."

"What?"

"Technically, it's a sheep," Willa said. "Farm animals don't get names. They get numbers. Peter's sheep are all ear-tagged with their number."

"So sheep number fourteen had a baby today?" Addy asked cautiously.

Georgie held up two fingers.

Addy's eyes went round. "Fourteen had *two* babies today?"

"Evidently, sheep do that," Georgie said. "According to Google, their first births are more likely to be singletons, but after that twins are common, sometimes even triplets."

"But Peter's sheep aren't pregnant," Willa said. "I checked the records myself. Twenty-one is his only ram—"

"That would be a boy sheep," Georgie informed Addy loftily.

"—and it's a wether, which means it's been castrated."

Georgie and Addy winced.

Willa said, "Hipster's plan was evidently to—"

"Hipster?" Addy shoveled in another bite of chili, eyes avid and sparkling. Georgie didn't look at Willa but could feel the other woman's relief matching her own. Addy was coming around.

"That's what Peter calls the farmer he invested with who bailed out and stuck him with a sheep farm," Willa informed her. "Fucking Hipster Farmer is his full name, as far as I'm aware, though at this point, Peter mostly just calls him the Hipster." She paused. "Or sometimes That Fucker."

"It was definitely That Fucker this afternoon," Georgie said.

"I'll bet." Willa shook her head. "At any rate, Hipster's records were quite clear. I looked them over myself. He purchased the flock in the spring and it included one ram which was mostly Columbia so he immediately castrated it."

"Is Columbia bad?" Addy asked.

"Not at all. They're ideal for Minnesota, actually. Super hardy. He decided to cross breed for better wool, that's all."

"I beg your pardon." Georgie set down her pasta bowl with an indignant thump. "Rag and Bone have top quality wool. I nuzzled it myself."

"Rag and Bone?" Willa blinked at her. "You named the lambs Rag and Bone?"

"Oh no," Addy breathed. "You were wearing your Rag and Bone sweater for the delivery?" She pressed her fingers to her mouth in horror, but her green eyes laughed. "You got that at Barneys last time we were in New York. You loved that sweater."

"I did." Georgie grimaced. "Placenta stains are the worst."

Addy rolled her lips inward, bit down hard. Georgie felt a laugh bubbling up herself but somehow maintained an air of mournful disgruntlement.

Willa snagged Georgie's empty bowl with one finger and

drew it across the counter. "Am I to understand," she asked, and dumped another scoop of plain pasta into the bowl, "that Rag and Bone is a brand name?"

"A fashion house. One of Georgie's favorites," Addy said and drew the refilled bowl her way. She drizzled on the olive oil with a more generous hand than Georgie would've used and nudged the bowl and the salt grinder Georgie's way. Georgie consulted her stomach, found it amenable and gave a mental shrug. She ground on some salt and picked up her fork again.

"So, yes, I was wearing my favorite Rag and Bone sweater today when I happened across Peter in his ditch again."

"Ah." Willa drained her beer, and pointed the empty bottle at Georgie with a grin. "You were hoping he'd shocked his nuts again."

"I was." Georgie admitted this serenely. "I really was. But he was only kneeling in the grass trying to talk Fourteen out of having a baby."

Addy scraped up the last of her chili. "Why do people do that? Try to talk a woman in active labor out of giving birth?"

"In this case? Pure panic, I think." Georgie twirled up another bite of pasta. "With maybe a touch of denial built in."

"Right," Willa said, and eyed the pie box Georgie had arrived with. "Because how the hell did Fourteen get pregnant if good old Twenty-one is shooting blanks?"

"That's the question of the day, isn't it?" Georgie set her bowl down, her stomach pleasantly full for once, and free of pain. "You should look into it, Willa."

"Me? Why me? I'm not exactly Peter's favorite person,

you know."

Georgie wasn't so sure of that. The news of Willa's probable death by wildfire back in August had given them all a bad hour or two. Up until that moment, however, Georgie had been firmly convinced that Peter was a heartless bastard. But she'd been standing beside him when he'd learned his only sibling was supposedly dead, and she'd watched that nonexistent heart silently break into a thousand pieces. He hadn't said a word or moved a muscle, but Georgie knew when a soul was shattering in front of her eyes.

"You might be surprised," she said finally.

Willa snorted. "I might not be."

She shrugged. "Hey, he's not exactly my favorite person either, but I have to hand it to the guy. He's trying. He got on our bad side in a big way—"

"—which is why he used to be the king of Devil's Kettle but is now broke and farming sheep for a living in a place desperately inhospitable to farming," Willa finished for her.

"And that's delicious," Georgie said with a deeply satisfied sigh, "no question. But he's been broke for six months, and reduced to farming for three, and he continues to take his punishment like a man. It might be time to move out of the punishment phase and into rehabilitation."

"What are you saying, Georgie?" Addy asked slowly. "Do we not hate Peter anymore?"

"Like I'd waste my effort hating an ex-boyfriend? Please. That's what my family is for." She gave Addy's knee a fond pat. "And you've done it beautifully. Thank you."

"Our pleasure, truly." Addy lifted her wineglass, found it empty. She refilled and toasted without taking her large green eyes off Georgie. "But?"

"But Peter is family, too." She pressed a tentative hand to her stomach, waiting for the warning spasm, but nothing hurt. She released a tiny sigh and accepted the inevitable. If her stomach was at peace, then bringing Peter out of exile must be the right move. Damn it anyway. "He's Matty's brother as much as Willa is."

"He gave up any right to call Matty brother when he blackmailed the kid into burning down his money pits," Willa said flatly.

"It's problematic," Georgie admitted. "But family is complicated. Believe me, I know what it is to have a difficult brother. To love him anyway."

There was a silence, and it was filled with Diego. Each one of them had had their own tangled relationship with Georgie's dead brother. With the famous artist, the incurable addict, the charismatic genius, and the selfish bastard. He had been all of those things and more, and each of the women in this room had once loved him anyway. Some of them — well, maybe only Georgie — loved him still. But nobody hated him anymore. It was a waste, and life was too short. On that, they all agreed.

"But we all saw how well it worked out when Mom tried to deny Matty his blood," Georgie told Willa. "And Peter is Matty's blood, same as Matty is my blood and your blood."

"And my mother's blood," Willa pointed out grimly and Georgie only shrugged. Most of Devil's Kettle thought Willa was Matty's birth mother, a little lie Georgie's stomach had no problem with. Matty's biological mother — who was also Willa and Peter's mother — was a real piece of work, and nobody wanted Matty exposed to her. Which was easy enough for the moment, as Shay Zinc had been missing for Matty's entire fourteen years on earth. But that might change if she thought she could squeeze either fame or money out of claiming the boy. And if Matty's shocking resemblance to Diego went any deeper than his face, it was a distinct possibility. Bianca looked at Matty's work and saw burgeoning genius. And Georgie, who made her living deciding what was art and what wasn't, couldn't disagree. She just didn't agree out loud. Not with Matty's crazy birth mom out there somewhere, hungry to profit off an innocent kid.

Addy sighed. "He's not my blood."

"He's your heart," Georgie said promptly, and it was nothing less than the truth. Addy loved Matty like he was her own child, and nobody had ever doubted the strength or legitimacy of their attachment. "It counts."

Addy reached over, and Georgie took her hand for a fond squeeze.

"So as much as I'm enjoying seeing Peter punished for his many and sordid crimes," Georgie said, "I think it might be time to bring him back into the fold."

Willa narrowed her eyes. "Why?"

"He could be useful. In fact, he already has been."

"How so?"

"He took in Addy's dad, didn't he? How do you think I managed that little miracle?"

Addy's eyes went round. "Whoa. You played the family card?"

"And he *bought* it?" Willa asked, incredulous.

"He did," Georgie said.

"I'll bet he did, actually." Willa nodded thoughtfully. "Even when we were filthy little urchins, Peter hated being us. He wanted to be you."

"Me?" Georgie echoed blankly.

"Sure. What little boy doesn't want to grow up to be an anorexic clothes hanger?" Willa rolled her eyes. "No, not *you*, Georgie. He wanted to be a Davis. He's always had a thing for that *lah di dah* you do so well."

Georgie only arched a derisive eyebrow.

Willa scowled. "You know what I mean. It's hard to describe, but you know it when you see it." She met Georgie's eyes frankly. "Or when somebody who has it rubs your nose in the fact that you don't."

Georgie shifted uncomfortably. She'd rubbed Willa's nose in her poverty without mercy when they were younger. She wasn't proud of it but she'd been operating on limited information and out of a deep love for the baby brother she'd believed Willa had wronged. Her stomach gave a warning spasm so she blurted, "I'm sorry, Willa. I was such a bitch to you."

Addy sat up like she'd been shocked by Peter's fence, but Willa waved an impatient hand. "Of course you were. And I just called you an anorexic clothes hanger. We have a thing here, Georgie. It works. Don't get sincere on me now."

Georgie's stomach settled and a smile curved her lips. "Right."

"All I'm trying to say is that Peter used to care about all that appearance-and-status shit, whereas I did not." Willa held out her arms, inviting Georgie and Addy to inspect her outfit. "Do not."

"Obviously," Georgie murmured, and normalcy was restored. She wondered if there was any more pasta then decided not to press her luck. She lifted her wineglass instead.

"It appears that a return to poverty, plus a new career in animal husbandry, has been good for our Peter," Willa concluded. "Given enough time, he might just grow himself a soul and rejoin the human race." She cracked a fresh beer. "So I have to ask: why would we risk stalling his progress by just handing over the big prize?"

"The big prize being what?" Addy asked. "The Davises acknowledging him as family?"

"That's how he'd see it, yeah." Willa grimaced at Georgie. "Beauty really is in the eye of the beholder."

"No, beauty exists in the space between wanting and having," Georgie said.

Willa's beer paused halfway to her mouth. "What?"

"Never mind." There were limits, Georgie decided, to aligning her private and public selves. Now probably wasn't the time to get into her theories on beauty. "But I'll agree that it wouldn't be beneficial to anybody to just up and forgive Peter."

"Then what are you proposing?" Addy asked.

"Just that. *Proposing* forgiveness." She smiled. "Floating the possibility of it. Of family unity. Of eventual reconciliation. It's time to make Peter aware that it's a possibility. That redemption could be his."

Willa took a contemplative sip of beer. "Could be?"

Georgie smiled and polished off her wine. "If he's a good boy."

Addy grinned. "Georgie. I love your devious, vengeful mind."

"I'll take devious but I'm over vengeful. Now I'm on to practical." Was she? Or was she just flirting with the edge of that hypnotic quicksand again? "Peter's already proven himself a useful resource. The next few weeks leading up to the wedding are going to be busy and potentially dangerous for the family." Far more dangerous than Peter was to her, she reminded herself firmly. Which was why she was risking this. Risking *him*.

"I know." Addy's smile faded. "You know that Jax and I would be more than fine just doing a courthouse wedding."

Willa and Georgie shared an eye roll. "We've covered this ground," Willa said and pitched her empty bottle into the recycling. "You and Jax are the real deal. So you're getting a real wedding. Big white dress, doughnut trees on every table—"

"Which you know I'd love," Addy said, "and I love you guys for wanting that for me. But Diego's Angel marrying Diego's brother? The press is going to go nuts."

"Screw the press," Willa said succinctly.

"What about Julia Gates, though?" Addy asked, her generous mouth flattening into a grim line.

"That face-lifted reporter Diego banged when he was too stoned to know better?" Georgie's lip curled. "What about her?"

"Well, she's hardly rational when it comes to Diego. You heard that she called Peter after the fire, right? That she was pumping him for info on Willa maybe being Matty's birth mom? She's got the bit between her teeth on that story, you guys. Just because we haven't heard from her in a while doesn't mean she isn't dangerous. It feels like a mistake to give her any excuse to come up here again."

"You deserve a wedding," Willa said.

"And she'll have one." Georgie nudged aside her empty wine glass and slid the pie box she'd brought into the center of the island. "Which is why we're putting our arsenal in order."

"That's a Wooden Spoon pie," Addy said, her eyes hopeful on the white pastry box. "I thought we were boycotting the Wooden Spoon after Gerte's behavior this summer."

"We were. But her mouth's a weapon, and it's probably better to have it on our side," Georgie said, and her stomach — damn her stomach anyway — was as happy as a sailor on shore leave with a hooker on each knee and a wad of cash in his pocket.

"Thanks be to a merciful deity," Addy breathed and drew the pie box closer. "Gerte is a bitter old pill but her pie crust makes angels sing."

Georgie smiled. "I got the North Shore triple berry."

Addy was silent. "I may cry."

"I thought Gerte might shed a few grateful tears herself when I stepped up to the pie counter after a three month hiatus, especially when I mentioned I was buying it for a bridesmaids dinner." Georgie grinned. "I think she's missed you."

"I've missed her, too," Addy breathed, and lifted a gorgeous concoction of whipped cream, deep purple berries and the aforementioned miraculous crust from the box. "I missed this, anyway." She set it reverently on the counter, grabbed a knife and whacked the pie into massive wedges that made Georgie's unusually cooperative stomach balk preemptively. She rested a reassuring hand over it. She knew when not to press her luck.

She said, "I figured if we're going to have ourselves a high-profile wedding here—"

"And we are," Willa said, dealing out forks.

"—then we'll need all the help we can get managing the press."

"Which is why we love Gerte again?" Addy asked, forking up a generous bite of pie.

"Exactly," Georgie said while Addy whimpered with ecstasy over the pie in her mouth. "If anybody can shut down a nosy reporter, it's Gerte."

"No kidding. She lives to tell other people what to do and where to get off," Willa said around an obscenely huge mouthful of pie. "What do you have in mind for Peter, then? What's his job in our arsenal?"

"I'm not sure yet," Georgie said. "He owes our family some favors, though. Big ones. I say we put him on notice that we plan to call them in."

"And if he does his duty like a good boy—" Willa began.

"*When* he does his duty like a *man*," Georgie corrected, "he may get his fondest wish after all."

"To be your husband?" Addy asked, a sly grin on that pixie face.

"To be family," Georgie said mildly, though her stomach slid alarmingly. Peter very nearly had been her husband.

"Once upon a time, being family would have included access to your trust fund and your bed," Willa pointed out, scooping up another dripping mouthful of berry goodness. "Is any or all of that still on the table?"

Addy gaped across the counter at Willa. Then, at Georgie's considering silence, shifted the gape to her. "Well?" she demanded. "Is it?"

Georgie recalled the scrape of Peter's three-day beard against her lips the other day, the purity of those bones, the grim duty in the way he held down his laboring sheep, the tenderness with which he'd stroked poor Fourteen's silky ear when he thought Georgie couldn't see.

"Of course not," she said lightly. "I just got that trust fund back."

"What about your bed?" Addy asked.

"My bed's always been my own. And as he sleeps on a cot in his kitchen these days, I doubt I'll be tempted to share his." She smiled complacently. "A girl has to have her standards."

"Good for you." Addy toasted her with the last forkful of her pie.

"But I do want Willa to swing by the farm later to find out why Peter's sheep are having babies."

"Yeah, I will."

"And when you do, he'll owe us yet another favor." Georgie sighed happily. "Now then, let's get down to business." She leaned forward. "How was your first week in business, Addison, and what have your parents been doing to make you insane?"

Addy sighed. "Where do I even start?"

"At the beginning?" Willa asked, and slid a second slice of pie onto Addy's plate.

"I'm not even sure where the beginning is. But the middle involves my mom relentlessly critiquing my business plan and my dad buying me chickens," Addy said and picked up her fork. "I'm not sure where it ends."

"Not murder, hopefully?"

She took an enormous bite. "We'll see."

CHAPTER 7

THE CHICKENS WERE noisy and stupid but the sheep didn't seem to mind them, so Peter decided he didn't either. For his part, Tag mostly ignored them. Mike, however, adored them. He stood next to Peter in the thin, cold sunlight outside the barn, beaming Addy's brilliant smile at a bizarre contraption he'd spent the morning building.

"Okay," Peter said finally. "I'll bite. What is it?"

"It's a chicken tractor." Mike sighed happily.

Peter cocked a skeptical brow and blew on his frozen hands. "I'm no expert, but isn't a tractor something you ride on and plow fields with?"

"That's the primary definition, sure. But it's also defined as a two-wheeled apparatus designed to be pushed by an operator."

Peter squinted at the thing Mike had constructed. Maybe ten yards long by one yard high by one yard wide, it was essentially a tunnel of chicken wire wrapped around a PVC pipe frame, the bottom open to the grass. At the far end was a pair of training wheels from a toddler bike, the kind that could be raised or lowered depending on how steady the kid was feeling. At the near end was a couple of handles, sticking out of the sides of the frame like a pair of ears. This end was butted up against Peter's barn, covering a chicken-sized trap door Mike had cut into the wall.

"You're going to put the chickens in that thing?" Peter asked doubtfully. "And push it around?"

"Yep." Mike wiggled with delight and he looked so much

like his daughter that Peter had to smile. "I've always wanted chickens."

"Why didn't you have any?"

His delight faded. "Not home enough. Jennifer built her company from scratch and at the beginning we had to move every few years. Even after she got established, her travel schedule was brutal."

"Yours can't have been much better, not as a flight nurse."

"No, it wasn't." He slid a screw driver into his back pocket and frowned at his chicken tractor. "I married an ambitious woman, and I was stupid enough to think it made me less of a man if I didn't keep up. So I did." He cut a sideways look at Peter, a look that concealed nothing. "Which left Addison to more or less raise herself, of course."

"You have regrets," Peter said carefully. Talking with Mike was a mildly disorienting experience. Before the farm, Peter's primary goal for all social engagement had been to elicit information he could use to maximize profits during later negotiations. But Peter didn't have negotiations now that he didn't have a business. Now he just had *conversations*, and he didn't know what to do when people just handed over the goods so guilelessly.

He wondered briefly how Mike had survived for so many years in what he knew to be a tough, competitive business. For that matter, how had he survived in what sounded like a tough, competitive marriage? The guy had zero aptitude for self-preservation.

"Of course I have regrets," Mike said easily. "Any life well-lived comes with a hefty serving of those." He shrugged and wiped his dirty hands down his still-stiff Carhartts. He'd bought the iconic indestructible work pants at the farm supply store down in Hornby Harbor his first full day on the farm. "The life lesson here is it's never too late." He aimed a finger Peter's way. "If you're still breathing, you're still in the game, son. Don't drop the ball."

Insight dawned with a satisfying flash.

"You haven't always wanted chickens," he said. "Addy did."

Mike's dimples flashed ruefully. "I'm pathetic, aren't I?" he said cheerfully. "Getting chickens because my twenty-five-year-old daughter wanted them when she was twelve."

"Not pathetic," Peter said, though he wasn't sure that was the truth. It might very well be pathetic for a parent to do such a nakedly vulnerable thing for an adult child. How would he know? His parents wouldn't have even known he'd *wanted* chickens as a child, let alone remembered it a dozen-odd years later. He couldn't even conceive of one of them deciding to satisfy that desire now. "Maybe just…"

A car horn cut him off and Peter turned to see Willa's truck pulling into his yard. Thank Christ. He had no idea what adjective he'd have replaced *pathetic* with. Peter lifted a hand and Willa parked her ancient pickup next to the even older pickup Peter had acquired along with the farm.

"Is that your sister?" Mike asked.

"Yep." Peter tucked his fingers into his pockets. The cold leached through his jeans into his hips but it was better than letting his fingers freeze off. "Georgie told her about Fourteen."

"Mary." Mike grinned. He'd started calling the sheep Mary in honor of her virgin birth.

"Fourteen," Peter said. "You can't go around giving names to future food."

"Fair enough," Mike said, though Peter noticed this

wasn't actually an agreement. Mike was sneakier than he first appeared. That must've been where Addy had gotten it.

Willa arrived at Peter's side. She eyed the chicken tractor.

"It's a chicken tractor," Mike said helpfully.

"I know." Willa tilted her head, squinted. "Have you tried it out yet?"

"Nope. We were just about to embark on the maiden voyage." Mike was all but dancing. "You have time?"

"To see a chicken tractor's maiden voyage?" Willa grinned. "I'll make time."

"Yes!" Mike bounded off to the barn door. "I'll just fetch the feeder."

Peter and Willa stood shoulder to shoulder and watched him disappear into the dark maw of the barn.

"I don't think Georgie intended for Mike to enjoy his stay on the farm quite so much," Willa observed, still grinning.

"He's always wanted chickens," Peter offered.

Willa slid her fingers into her pockets. "No, Addy's always wanted chickens."

"That was my call, too."

She glanced at him. "You're not even invited to the wedding. You didn't need to get the bride a gift."

He shrugged. "I wouldn't have let him do it if the numbers hadn't lined up. The chickens will earn their keep."

"I'd have liked you better if you hadn't run the numbers first."

"Better than what?"

"Better than I did."

That she liked him at all was news to Peter. He'd assumed her sporadic visits to the farm were inspired by a commitment to animal welfare at best, a morbid curiosity at worst. He hadn't even considered that she might feel some kind of personal interest in his own welfare. Not that Peter blamed her. Their family had been a sinking ship and he'd abandoned it as soon as humanly possible, without a backward glance for his little sister stuck on the deck. It was a choice he could've revisited any time over the intervening years — when their mother had gone missing, when their dad had gone to jail, when Peter had moved home, when he'd gotten engaged, when their dad had been released from jail — but he hadn't. He'd left his old life behind him for good, and Willa along with it. He could hardly change his mind now just because his shiny new life hadn't turned out the way he'd hoped. Or because he'd discovered that family wasn't something you actually could just walk away from. Turned out blood went deeper than anything you could cut through. But he'd discovered that too damn late, hadn't he? He was on his own now, dragging his mangled family relationships behind him like a botched amputation, and that was that.

"Sorry," he said with patent insincerity. Insincere was better than pathetic. "I'm a farmer now. I'm doing business on a cash-only basis these days."

"Which is why I like you a little better than I used to," she said. "You're not such an asshole when your pockets are empty."

Mike emerged from the barn again with a round metal chicken feeder wantonly leaking seed. "Okay, let's get this thing set up!"

He trotted to the wheeled end of the tractor, opened a nifty door in the top and hung the feeder inside from a hook built into the ceiling. He closed it up, then trotted back to the barn wall the handled end of the tractor was butted up against.

"Ready?" His eyes shone wildly and Peter found himself suppressing a smile. Willa didn't bother.

"Ready!" she called back, grinning openly.

Mike unwound a rope from a cleat he'd screwed to the side of the barn. The rope had been threaded through a pulley bolted to the wall directly above the tractor, and when Mike pulled, a little door slid open at the base of the wall. A dozen chickens streamed through the door and raced down the length of the tractor to attack the feeder suspended at the wheeled end.

Mike cackled delightedly. "Holy crap, it worked!" He turned to beam at Peter and Willa. "It actually worked!"

"Yeah, yeah." Willa waved a dismissive hand. "That was the easy part. Now I want to see you move it."

Even Tag showed up at this point, seating himself on the ground next to Peter's boots. Peter glanced down at the dog, at those skeptical eyebrows. "I know, right?" he murmured.

"What?" Willa asked.

"Nothing." Peter cleared his throat. He'd gotten into the habit of talking to the dog. Out loud. Like he was a person or a peer. Or (God help them all) a friend. That probably wasn't good, was it?

"You're on!" Mike said, and raced back to fuss with the training wheels. In a matter of moments, he'd gotten them lowered and locked, then headed back to the end with the handles. He shimmied the thing a foot or two forward and wedged himself into the space between the tractor and the wall. Then he gripped the handles, lifted and slowly began walking. It was like the longest, most awkward wheelbarrow Peter had ever seen but it moved. And the chickens stayed glued to the feeder.

Mike drove the thing around the yard for a while, laughing like a lunatic, then finally settled it in the near pasture. He closed a flap of chicken wire over the handled end that had been open to the barn, retracted the wheels, then opened the top and retrieved the feeder.

"They'll eat whatever they find in the grass now," he informed them. "Eating up bugs and invasive plants, pooping out fertilizer, and essentially improving your pasture one tractor-sized patch at a time."

"And making eggs we can sell for twice the standard commodity price because they're cage-free." Peter touched the brim of his stocking cap in salute. "Well done, sir."

"Now we just need a rooster," Mike said, his eyes going dreamy.

"We do not need a rooster," Peter said immediately. "I'm already making unauthorized sheep. I don't have the bandwidth for baby chickens."

Willa laughed. "Yeah, speaking of your unauthorized baby sheep—"

"Hail Mary, full of grace," Mike intoned, and headed for the barn with the metal feeder, "the lord is with thee..."

"Fourteen," Peter called after him. "Her name is *Fourteen*!"

The show over, Tag hopped to his feet and trotted off to check on the sheep in the far pasture, delivering a shoulder check to Peter's calf on the way by. Peter scowled after him. "That dog does not respect me."

"Nobody does," Willa said idly, head cocked, still studying the chicken tractor. "You're an asshole."

"But the dog doesn't know that," Peter said, still frowning after Tag. "He's a dog."

"Dogs are smarter than people," Willa said. "And Tag is

smarter than most dogs. If he had thumbs, he'd be running this place."

"If he had thumbs, I'd let him."

"That's why you're an asshole." Willa met his eyes, unsmiling. "Now let's have a look at your supposedly castrated ram, shall we?"

"Well, there's your problem right there," Willa said. She muscled Twenty-one's tail into the vertical position and gripped the filthy wool just south of its anus with a clinical detachment that had Peter wincing on the ram's behalf. "Feel that?"

Peter gingerly poked a couple fingers into the questionable wool and said, "Uh, no?"

"Use your whole hand," Willa said impatiently. "Feeling up a boy sheep won't make you gay."

"Gay isn't contagious," Peter told her primly. "Shame on you. Plus, this animal is clearly heterosexual. Just ask Fourteen."

"Mary's busy with Rag and Bone."

He let the Mary thing go but... "Rag and Bone?"

"The lambs you'd know as Twenty-two and Twenty-three, I imagine." Willa met his eyes over the ram's tail, and they were full of unholy amusement. "Georgie named them after the sweater she ruined delivering them. She says you owe her a new one."

"Hell." Like he had five hundred dollars lying around to replace one of Georgie's designer sweaters. "I'll just give her the lambs and call it even."

"Good luck with that." Willa nodded at the ram's butt again. "Now come on. Get your fingers in there. What do you feel?"

Peter gave up and just shoved his hand into the ram's crotch. "Nothing," he said. "This guy's a eunuch as far as I can tell. No nut sack, no nuts."

"Exactly." Willa let go of the ram's tail and he began placidly munching hay as if he hadn't just been violated by a pseudo-farmer and his sister. "That's the problem with the whole Cryptorchid thing."

"Cryptic Orchid? What the hell is that?"

"No, *cryptorchid*," Willa said patiently. "It's a method of castration, not an Asian spy. It's where you amputate the nut sack but not the nuts."

Peter winced involuntarily. "What?"

"You push the testicles up into the body cavity rather than removing them along with the scrotum. The theory is that the body heat kills the sperm so the ram's infertile, but you haven't actually removed the testicles so the ram — now technically a wether due to said infertility — grows faster and better than either an intact male or a true wether. Plus you can pasture him with the ladies since he's shooting blanks. It makes a certain amount of sense."

"Except when it doesn't work," Peter muttered.

"Except when it doesn't work," she agreed.

"Which is how often?"

"It's not a particularly reliable method of birth control."

Peter took off his cap and scrubbed a hand over his head. "Which means that any number of my ewes could start dropping lambs any minute."

"It could mean that," Willa admitted. "Speaking of, where are you keeping Mary and the babies?"

"Over there." Peter hooked a thumb over his shoulder. "I'm giving her a week's maternity leave, then they're all going back into the pasture."

Willa strode deeper into the barn and arrived at the pen that he and Mike had hammered together based on some plans they'd found on the internet. It was a four foot by four foot enclosure with a heat lamp hung over it.

"Sweet set up," Willa said, and leaned her elbows on the railing.

"It's called a jug. It's supposed to encourage bonding and nursing." Peter joined her at the railing. "And if you know the babies are coming, you can put the ewe in here so she doesn't have to deliver in a ditch." In the rain, with the help of only a panicked not-farmer and his ex-fiancée. And her atrociously expensive sweater.

"Okay." Willa held out a hand and one of the lambs bounced over to touch her nose to it. "Aw. Is that one Rag or Bone?"

"How the hell do I know?" Peter consulted the ear tag. "It's Twenty-two."

"First borns are always more social," Willa said, grinning down at the fluffy little thing with its pink nose, bright eyes and impossibly skinny legs. "Hey, Rag."

Peter swore the thing smiled at her. "Don't get attached. It's growing up to be meat."

"Are you trying to convince me or yourself?"

"I'm not the one calling it by name and making girlie noises over it." Bone — damn it, *Twenty-three* — bounced over to the railing this time and blinked up at Peter. He touched the little pink nose before he could stop himself. Willa laughed.

"And yet you'll boop it on its little lamby nose."

"Boop?" He squinted at her. "Is that a technical term?"

"You tell me." She pushed away from the railing and grinned, and Peter realized he actually liked his sister. Had things been different — had *he* been different — she might've liked him, too. Wasn't that just a kick in the teeth?

"Now, let's go look at your ladies," Willa said. "I'd like to see how many of them are in line to use this jug."

Terror replaced his regret.

"Right. Okay. Let's do this."

They were still inside the barn when a blue sedan glided into the yard and parked beside Willa's truck.

She stopped and squinted into the comparatively bright outdoor light. "You expecting company?"

"Just you." Peter squinted too. There were two people in the car, women, he'd guess from their silhouettes, but they didn't seem to be in any hurry to get out. "I don't suppose there's like a child protective services for farm animals?" he asked hopefully. "Like somebody coming to take custody of the lambs on grounds of gross incompetence?"

Willa snorted. "You wish."

"I do," Peter said fervently. "I really do."

The driver's door opened and a woman stepped out. Peter put her in her forties somewhere with an angular haircut, sharp bones, stylish glasses and a brightly painted mouth.

"Oh fuck," Willa said. "That's Julia Gates."

"You know her?"

"Of her." Willa pressed her lips into a hostile line. "That's the reporter Diego used to sleep with, the one who thinks I'm Matty's mother and wants to break the story."

"Stay inside," Peter murmured. "I'll get rid of her."

Willa spun on one boot heel and headed back to the jug. Peter put on his let's-do-business face — he hadn't worn it in so long, he'd forgotten what it felt like — and sauntered out of the barn toward the car. When he was within hailing distance, he said, "Can I help you?"

"Well, now, I don't know." The woman smiled warmly, still standing in the vee of her open car door. "I'm looking for Peter Zinc."

"You've found him." He slid his fingers into his pockets and waited.

"I have something for you."

"Do you now?" He smiled, his as genuine as hers.

"Well, some*one* anyway." She leaned down and spoke into the car. The passenger door opened and a woman stepped out. She blinked into the watery sunlight and sent him a tentative smile. "Peter?"

He stared, stunned. "Mom?"

CHAPTER 8

"YOU'RE SUPPOSED TO be dead," Peter said. The air was cold inside his nose, and his whole head went hollow. The rest of him was curiously numb. He wondered what the correct emotion was to feel in this situation, because he felt nothing. His mother had just returned from the dead, and there was nothing inside him but a weird emptiness. Did that make him a sociopath? Probably. He wondered why it had taken so long for him to arrive at this conclusion. Clearly, something was broken inside him, something that made normal people, well, normal.

Shay Zinc gripped the top of her car door as if it were a shield. As if Peter were the threat. "I'm very much alive," she said, her lips curving in a tremulous smile. "Um, surprise?" It came out more like an actual question than a jaunty punchline and Peter only continued to stare at her. Her smile flickered and disappeared. The car door came practically to her chin and her hands were small and vulnerable on the door frame. She was tiny, he realized dully. He'd forgotten how small his mother was. She was maybe Willa's height but gave off an air of exquisite vulnerability that was the exact opposite of Willa's blazing self-sufficiency. But those were Willa's giant silvery eyes blinking moistly at him in his mother's face. That was Willa's princess hair spilling down Shay's back, albeit in blond rather than black. And that was Willa's curvy little body, packed into a wasp-waisted trench coat and shoes that screamed *it doesn't snow where I'm from.*

"You've been dead for fifteen years," he told her, as if the math had slipped her mind.

"Fourteen," she said softly. "Almost exactly."

"Everybody thought Dad killed you." Peter studied his mother helplessly. "You let them think that."

"He was going to," Shay murmured, those eyes going shinier. "I believed he was going to."

"Did you?" Peter had avoided the house — along with his parents and their drama — as much as possible when they'd been kids but Willa had been different, and she'd been younger. She'd been around, and she'd seen things Peter hadn't seen. Things like Shay provoking their father into bitter arguments. Things like Shay taking the first swing, always. Things like Shay leaning into Brett's drunken flailing when anybody who didn't truly want a shiner would've leaned out.

"Of course I did. Your father was dangerous. You saw how he was. You must have—" Shay's eyes filled, and she dropped her gaze to the dirt in front of Peter's boots. "I shouldn't have come," she murmured brokenly. "I'm sorry. I—" She turned a stricken face to Julia Gates who smoothly took over.

"We'll find a room in town," Julia said soothingly, "and we can have this conversation another time." She turned that professional smile on Peter. "Maybe when everybody's over the shock, and can discuss the situation calmly."

Peter ignored that and watched his mother visibly tremble. Maybe he wasn't a sociopath after all, because it was starting to tug on him, her naked vulnerability. He believed Willa without reservation but Shay looked...older. Fine lines fanned out from her eyes and her lips were thinner than he remembered. That small hand wasn't as smooth as it once had been, either.

"Have you seen Dad yet?"

Shay's hand went to her throat. "No."

"Willa?"

She shook her head. "I wanted to see you first." She tried another smile, more tremulous than the first. "We were close once, you and I. You were my sweet boy. I thought you might be—" Her voice caught and she stopped. "It doesn't matter what I thought. This was a bad idea."

"No, it's a very good idea," Julia said firmly. She pressed a hand to the roof of the car between them, and leaned toward the other woman. "I know it's hard but, Shay, you need to work through this. If you don't put the past behind you, you'll never be free. So don't lose courage now. We've come this far, haven't we?"

Shay nodded reluctantly.

"Damn right we have." Julia slapped the car's roof and grinned. "Now let's go find a cup of coffee and see if there are any open rooms in town. Because we came here for closure, and we're not leaving until we get it."

"Is that right?" Peter asked softly. Shay's gaze fluttered his direction but she got obediently into the car without responding.

"Absolutely," Julia said. "The truth will out, Mr. Zinc. It always does."

"I'm sure you're right," he said equably. "The Wooden Spoon serves pretty good coffee, and there's free wifi."

"That's the diner on Main Street?"

"Yep. Make sure Mom says hi to Gerte. They go way back."

"I will. Your mother's been through a lot. She could use a friendly face."

"Gerte will love seeing her." Or she would once she got past the shock of seeing the woman she'd repeatedly and publicly accused Brett Zinc of murdering, alive and well and sipping coffee in her diner. Peter would pay good money to see that, actually. Gerte had strong opinions, aired them frequently and didn't enjoy being wrong. Seeing Shay alive might chap her ass but she'd dearly love being the first to hear the news. She'd love spreading the news even more.

"Well, maybe we'll stop by." Julia smiled at him before sliding into the driver's seat. If he were still swimming in the bloody waters of high finance, he'd have enjoyed seeing that sharp smile. It would mean the gloves were off, and it was time to do business. If he'd still been a shark himself, he'd have known exactly what that business was, too, and what he wanted from it. What he'd get from it.

In this case, he didn't know shit. He wondered if Julia did. Did the reporter have any idea who she was playing with, or did she really think Shay was nothing but a pawn in whatever game she was playing with the Davis family?

Peter had no idea. He was going to find out, though. And he knew who to ask.

CHAPTER 9

GEORGIE'S ENTIRE FAMILY had already assembled in Addy's great room by the time Peter showed up at Davis Place. He strode across the gleaming hardwood floors like a male model playing a farmer for an ad campaign, his jaw dark with stubble, his cheekbones starkly perfect under a damp woolen cap, his boots authentically battered. Georgie thought about closing her eyes. It was so much easier to maintain focus when her image-oriented brain wasn't overloaded by the sheer visual impact of him. She snuggled deeper into one of Addy's giant leather chairs by the fire and watched him anyway. He sat on the hearth near Matty, propped his elbows on his knees, and grimaced down at his boots.

"Sorry," he said to Addison who sat on a generously stuffed couch opposite the fire, "I should've asked. Should I take my boots off?"

She gave him a smile, warmer than usual though still a bit reserved. "I'm not running a shoes-off kind of establishment, Peter. You're fine."

"Yeah, tracking a little mud across the great room is actually a step up for you," Georgie observed acidly. *Because the last time you were here, you burned this place to the ground.* She left that bit unspoken but felt confident that everybody heard it anyway.

"That's true," Peter said, and met her eyes directly. She sucked in a startled breath. When was she going to get used to the raw openness in that dark gaze of his? She'd seen

Peter's naked body dozens of times but had never seen him truly naked until after he'd moved to the farm. It was as if losing his money had stripped away some essential artifice, or given him permission to drop some pretense she hadn't been aware of. It had left his eyes black and almost too honest to meet anymore. She glanced away. It was almost rude, really, the way he looked at her. Manners dictated a *little* polite artifice, didn't they?

"Mud is small potatoes compared to the damage I did up here," he told her. "And I don't mean just financially. I'm sorry for what I did to Matty. To your whole family. I know words aren't enough but until there's something I can do, they're all I can offer you."

She met those eyes again but found nothing hidden there. No challenge, no malice, no layers of meaning. It was a simple acknowledgement of his actions. And she had to remind herself that the eyes weren't a decoy. He didn't just look honest; he *was* honest these days.

He looked to Addy. "You did a fantastic job on the place, Addison. How much of the old structure were you able to save?"

"After the fire? Not much," Addy said while everybody else in the room just stared, breathless, waiting to see if Georgie would allow the subject change. "We kept the central chimney and the basement, but otherwise started fresh from the ground up. We had the original plans, though, so managed to recreate everything we wanted."

"Only with updated electricals and modern plumbing," Jax put in with a wry smile from beside his fiancée on the couch. He hadn't gotten the Davis looks, was neither tall nor lean nor beautiful, but he was solid, he was strong and his roots in Devil's Kettle went all the way to the center of the earth. And he was Addy's all the way to the center of himself. It had been months since Georgie had discovered her brother and her best friend had fallen in love, and it still caught at her heart to see them so *together*. Was she happy for them, or envious? She wasn't totally sure. She didn't see why she had to choose, honestly. That kind of happy ending wasn't in Georgie's cards, but that didn't mean she couldn't want it anyway. Or admire it when she saw it.

"An unexpected silver lining," Addy conceded with a gracious tip of her curly head.

"I'm glad to hear there was one," Peter said. He knitted his fingers together between his knees and turned his eyes to Georgie's mother, sitting in the chair opposite Georgie's like a queen. Bianca had a knack for turning every chair she used into a throne, Georgie noted, amused. She hoped she herself would grow into that particular gift one day. "I don't know if we'll be so lucky this time," he said. "If there was a silver lining to today's little surprise, I don't know what it is."

"Yes, well." Bianca rested her clasped hands on one knee and gave him a regal smile. "We'll have to see about that, won't we? Why don't you start at the beginning and we'll see where we land?"

"Yeah, okay."

He spoke for a few minutes, tersely summarizing the conversation he'd had with his mother and Julia Gates. It had been short, she gathered, if fraught with double meanings and veiled threats.

"She didn't say what she was doing here?" Addy asked.

"Who?" Peter said. "The reporter or my mother?"

"It sounded like Mom was after *closure*," Willa said from a leather footstool she'd stolen from Georgie. She gave the word the derisive emphasis it deserved.

"Mom didn't actually say that," Peter pointed out slowly. "Julia did."

"That's true," Bianca said thoughtfully. "Julia was the one pressing Shay to stay, to put her past to rest or some psychobabble to that effect?"

Peter nodded.

"Well then." Bianca steepled her fingers and gazed into the fire. "This begs a few questions, doesn't it?"

"Such as?" Jax lifted a dark brow at their mother.

"Such as where Shay's been these past fifteen years, for starters—"

"Fourteen years," Willa said bitterly, and her fiancé Eli who sat on the arm of the couch beside her put a quiet hand on her shoulder. "Almost exactly." She touched the back of Eli's hand even as she met Matty's eyes across the room. "She took off when you were barely three months old."

Georgie sent a sharp look Matty's way. Her baby brother wasn't really a baby anymore, was he? He sat on the hearth to her immediate left, elbows on his knees and one hand clasped around the other skinny wrist. But even with Peter on the far side of the hearth in essentially the same posture, the kid looked like nobody so much as Diego. The older Matty got, the more pronounced the resemblance became, from his rangy height to those angular bones to the way he held his pencil and the magic that came out of it. His eyes were the only deviation, and even those weren't his own. He shared them with Willa, didn't he? And with Shay.

"Okay," Matty said, not looking away from his knuckles. "So why's she back now?"

"That's the question, isn't it?" Brett said softly, and Georgie frowned at Willa and Peter's father. He sat silently on the footstool that matched Willa's, though he hadn't had to steal it. Bianca had offered. "I haven't laid eyes on the woman in fourteen years, mind, but the Shay I knew thought closure was for butthurt losers, if you'll pardon the expression. And Shay was a winner. Not because she was beautiful but because she was smart. Smart enough to use her looks as a weapon and make the world cough up whatever she wanted, whenever she wanted it."

Georgie studied the man who'd given Peter that tall, rangy build, the big, capable hands and those dark, dark eyes that no longer hid a damn thing. That didn't even try, damn it.

"What could she possibly want here after so long?" she asked, just as softly.

"Hell if I know. I still don't understand why she disappeared that way. Seems like divorce would've been a whole lot less complicated."

"You don't go to jail for divorce," Willa said flatly.

"You think it was that intentional?" Peter asked slowly. "That Mom actively *hoped* Dad would go to jail for her murder?"

Willa met his gaze impassively. "You think she didn't?"

He lifted those wide shoulders. "I wasn't here," he said simply. "You were."

"And Brett wasn't convicted of Shay's murder," Bianca pointed out. "He was never even charged as far as I'm aware."

"It was discussed every few years," Willa said tightly. "And I have the legal bills to prove it. But absent a body, there was never enough evidence to charge him, let alone convict him."

"Of a murder that didn't even happen," Eli said, and rubbed Willa's shoulder comfortingly. A little spasm of pain darted through Georgie's stomach and she identified it reluctantly. Envy again. She was jealous of Willa? Shit. It was one thing to be envious of Addy whom she loved. But why was she jealous of Willa whom she barely liked? Because she had a nice boyfriend — well, fiancé — who was at least an inch shorter than Georgie herself?

But her stomach had eased the instant she'd given the pain its true name — jealousy. She suppressed a weary sigh. Okay, fine. Maybe she wasn't personally attracted to Eli, though there was something to be said for a truly beautiful pair of sky-blue eyes. But any fool could see that there was something real and precious in the way he touched Willa, in the comfort it offered her and the way she accepted it without an instant's hesitation. Willa trusted him, she realized with a pulse of wonder. Willa, who trusted nobody, who liked animals better than people, trusted Eli Walker implicitly.

It was, she had to admit, enviable. She glanced involuntarily at Peter, and found him gazing at his sister with that same perplexed wonder that filled Georgie. He met her eyes and for just a moment, they shared that wonder, marveled together at its very existence.

Georgie forced herself to hold that gaze until he looked away but damn it, her heart was knocking against her ribs by the time he did. She *had* to stop letting him get under her skin like that. While any little bit of him still fascinated her, even if it was just that stupid, stubbly jawline of his, Peter was dangerous to her. She had to remember that.

"No, they never put me in jail for Shay's murder," Brett said ruefully. "I managed to get there all by myself." He curled one of those big hands into a fist, looked balefully at it and released it. "Don't drink and fight, kid," he said to

Matty. "It never ends well."

Matty absorbed that in silence, which was probably the only wise way to receive advice from a guy who'd accidentally turned a fellow drunk into a vegetable during a friendly-disagreement-turned-violent-brawl.

"Your jail sentence was obviously enough to keep Shay satisfied for a time," Bianca mused. "I wonder if she heard you'd been released?"

"I wonder if Julia told her," Willa said darkly.

"How would Julia even find her?" Georgie countered.

"Why would Julia even think to look for her?" Jax asked.

"Because of me," Matty said.

There was a moment of taut silence and Georgie's stomach tensed for the inevitable cramp so she did the only thing she could do. She told the truth. "That's what I've been thinking, too."

CHAPTER 10

BIANCA'S EYES SHARPENED on Georgie. "You think this has to do with Matty's…history?"

Georgie stared right back. "You think it doesn't?"

Bianca released a slow breath. "You're right. Perhaps this isn't entirely about Matty, but the idea that it's not at all about him simply doesn't wash."

Matty's shoulders, sharp and skinny, rose up nearly to his ears. "Do you think she knows?" He spoke to his shoes. "Julia, I mean. Do you think she knows Shay is my birth mother? Is she going to write a story about it?"

"I don't know," Addy said slowly. "The last time she was here, she was focused on going public with her and Diego's affair."

"Because of the naked pictures Diego had painted of her?" Matty asked. "She thought you were going to show them."

"She knew your mom would have a hard time *not* showing them," Addy corrected, with a wry smile for Bianca.

"I still say it would've been a tremendous show," Bianca muttered.

"No question," Jax said. "Tremendously inappropriate."

"There is nothing inappropriate about art," his mother shot back. "Especially art that challenges conventional—"

"There's challenging convention, and then there's cruelty," Jax cut in. "And you never seem to know where the line between them—"

"Okay." Addy put a hand on his forearm. "Let's all take a breath here and remember that I let Julia's naked pictures burn to ashes along with this entire building."

"Let them?" Jax turned his scoff on Addy this time. "You kicked open the door of a burning kitchen and threw them inside!"

Along with the wedding ring Diego had put on her finger when she hadn't even been old enough to indulge in the champagne toast. The ring she'd kept wearing nearly three years after he'd widowed her just as abruptly as he'd married her. Tossing it into a roaring fire had left her finger open for the very pretty, if significantly smaller, diamond Jax had given her a few months back. A diamond Georgie could almost guarantee Addy would never feel compelled to heave into a house fire.

"Did I? It's all a bit hazy." Addy lifted innocent shoulders. "My point is, Julia is ambitious, vindictive, and revenge-oriented."

"And possibly just a little unbalanced." Georgie held up her thumb and forefinger, an inch apart.

"Agreed," Addy said. "But Diego could have that effect on people."

"No kidding," Willa muttered. Addy patted her knee with honest sympathy, demonstrating for the millionth time that she was a far better person than Georgie would ever be.

"She wanted Diego to love her, but he loved me," Addy went on serenely. "And then when he didn't love me anymore, she wanted him to humiliate me. And when he refused, she tried to do it herself by coming forward as the subject of those naked paintings. And when I didn't show those paintings, when I let them burn—"

"And refused to be humiliated by Diego's own

89

shortcomings and mistakes," Georgie murmured.

"—she took off to regroup." Addy sighed. "The moral of the story here? Julia Gates is no quitter. I think it's safe to say she hasn't given up on her ultimate goal."

"Which is?" Peter asked.

"Hurting me," Addy said lightly while Jax scowled beside her. "Plan A was to show the world that she was Diego's true angel, of course, and to prove it with those naked paintings he did of her."

"The ones you burned," Peter said.

Addy shrugged. "Just one more reason for her to hate my guts. She all but promised me last time she was here that she'd be back and I'd be sorry to see her. But dragging Shay into it?" Her brows drew together uncertainly and she glanced at Matty. "Julia's been at war with me for years but Matty's just a kid. Surely she wouldn't—"

"Of course she would," Georgie said, her stomach gripping tight. She followed Addy's eyes to Matty. He sat silently on the hearth, his eyes fixed on the rug between his big boots. The conversation had flowed around him all this time while he sat there, stoic and resigned, splitting the current like a rock. "You know she would."

"But she's an adult!" Addy shot to her feet to pace, hands twisted together. "What kind of adult would exploit an adopted kid's birth story in service of some years-old cold war nobody even cares about anymore?"

Georgie sent a significant glance Peter's way. What kind of adult indeed? He met her eyes, acknowledged the silent question, raised no defense. Her stomach fluttered uncertainly and she looked away.

"Julia cares about it." Bianca leaned forward. "She cares a great deal. She's devoted her adult life to it, in fact.

Meanwhile Addison — the only other armed combatant — has moved on so completely she probably doesn't even remember the petty disagreement that started it."

Georgie thought *petty* might be understating it a bit, given that Julia had slept with Addy's husband, posed nude for him multiple times, and encouraged the drug habit that eventually killed him. Regardless, she couldn't argue the larger point, as Addy really had moved on.

"Look at you with your new fiancé, your new job, your new life. Everything's coming up roses for Diego's Angel, just like always." Bianca smiled thinly. "It has to be killing her."

"Truth," Willa said. "But what's she going to do about it?" She paused. "More importantly, what are *we* going to do about *her*?"

Nobody spoke, and Georgie finally turned to Matty. "Well?"

Beside Peter, the kid's head jerked up. His eyes were wide and startled when they met his sister's. "You're asking me?"

Georgie, curled in her armchair like a lazy cat, lifted a shoulder. "Why not?"

"I never get a vote."

She arched a perfect brow. "Did you want one?"

"Since it's my life story she's planning to publish world-wide? Yeah, I do. And thanks so much for asking."

Teenage sarcasm, Peter noted, applied with a big, fat brush.

"Aw," Georgie crooned. "Was our sweet boy waiting for somebody to ask for his precious opinion?" She snuggled deeper into her chair and let those eyes drift shut. "What are

91

you, adopted?"

Peter suppressed a wince. That was harsh, even for Georgie, but Matty just laughed.

"Yeah, that must be why nobody in this family ever listens to me."

"Either that or you're boring." Georgie cracked one eye. "Falling asleep here, champ. Either dazzle me with your opinion, or be quiet."

Matty's grin faded and he dropped his gaze to his linked fingers. "If my birth mom wants to go public with the truth, I say we let her."

Peter blinked at that, and he shot a look at Georgie. She wasn't looking back, of course. She was still cuddled up in the corner of that big chair looking snoozy. "And if Shay's not planning to go that route?"

"If it's just the reporter behind all this?" His face hardened and Peter saw Diego, his old friend's terrible beauty and merciless rage. "How bad can we hurt her?"

On Peter's other side, Bianca smiled. "My son," she murmured. Was she talking about Matty, Peter wondered, or did she, too, suddenly see Diego all over the boy?

Jax tipped his head and considered the question. Considered the boy who'd asked it. "I'm going to assume you mean financially, legally and professionally," he said finally.

Matty scowled. "As opposed to what, taking a hit out on her?" He jerked a bony shoulder. "Not that I'm opposed. She's been a stone-cold bitch to Addy for years."

"Language," Bianca said mildly while Georgie murmured, "Amen."

Jax frowned at his sister. "You're not helping."

"Did you expect me to?" Georgie poked Matty with one

bare, elegant foot and said, "Hey, maybe *Jax* was adopted." The twin smiles they turned on Jax dripped with the smug pity enjoyed only by two siblings double-teaming a third.

"I wish," Jax muttered, but he was clearly suppressing a grin of his own. Peter found himself doing the same, though he wasn't in the least amused. He was…relieved.

Of all Peter's sins, the worst by far was making Matty question his status as a Davis. He hadn't known at the time how irregular the kid's birth story really was but he'd known exactly what it was to grow up in a house full of people you didn't trust. Peter had deliberately poisoned Matty's faith in his family, and that was an atrocity that had haunted Peter for months now.

But watching Matty engage in this kind of effortless bickering with his siblings around the family hearth laid that fear to rest. Matty was giving and receiving goodnatured shit, just like any kid in any family. It was maybe a bit sharper and more stylish than your ordinary family shit, but these were the Davises. Stylishness was their stock-in-trade, along with wealth and talent. And you couldn't fake this kind of give-and-take. It was rooted in the unshakeable faith that no matter what anybody said to your face, they would always have your back.

Matty was just fine, and the relief of that was staggering.

"If this is just the reporter," Matty said, "I want her to go away and never come back. And without the story she came for. I want her to *lose*. After everything she's done to Addy? She deserves to lose."

"And I love you for wanting that," Addy said, beaming the full-on dimples at the kid. "But I don't know, Matty. She's not quite rational. Engaging her at all might just be gas on the fire."

"But not engaging her hasn't made her go away," Willa pointed out. "If anything, it's brought her back."

Addy grimaced. "True."

"I'm not generally a fan of the nuclear option, but in this case it might be our only one." Willa drew in a deep breath, let it out slowly. "I'm with Matty. Let's finish her."

The quiet held for a long moment. Then Bianca said, "We'll need more information, then. A great deal more."

"Agreed," Jax said. "But how are we going to get it?"

"Never ask any questions," Peter heard himself say.

"What?" Bianca swung that laser focus his way and Peter fought not to squirm. Damn, had he really ever thought having this woman as his mother-in-law would be a good thing?

"That you don't already have the answers to, I mean," he said quickly and cleared his throat. "By the time you enter negotiations, you should never ask a question you don't already know the answer to. Opposition research is everything. My lawyer was expensive but she was worth every penny."

"You had your lawyer research us?" Bianca's eyes were matte black, and colder than the ninth circle of Dante's hell. "Before you offered that ring to Georgie?"

"I could've saved us all a lot of trauma if I had," he said evenly. "But no. I was bleeding red ink, and I made a desperate move without my usual due diligence." He met those eyes and refused to flinch. "Everything that came after only proves my point." He lifted two empty palms. "From financial raider to sheep farmer with one rash decision."

"It was significantly more than one," Bianca said tartly.

"No, he's right," Georgie said. "Our engagement *was* his only rash decision. The rest of them were fully thought out and terrifically selfish." She shook back her hair and gave him a dazzlingly cold smile. "Rash isn't really your problem, Peter. It's more the soulless and evil thing."

He inclined his head. He'd had the same thought himself, more and more often lately. Tag wasn't a great conversationalist, but his eyebrows were eloquent.

"But take heart," she said. "You're about to redeem yourself."

He blinked. "I am?"

Addy went still and Willa sighed "You're really doing this, then?"

"I think she is," Bianca murmured, her eyes still uncomfortably intent on Peter.

"Doing what?" he asked uneasily. He hadn't even realized he and Georgie were *in* negotiations, let alone done any opposition research on what they might be negotiating for. And here he thought *he'd* called this meeting.

"I am," Georgie said, her eyes never leaving Peter's face.

"If you want a pet, fine," Bianca said and dismissed him with one elegant hand. "I recommend a very short leash, though."

A *pet*? What the hell?

"I know, Mom. I've got this." She was studying him like he was a potential outfit, or a piece for the gallery she hadn't figured out yet how to show.

"Sorry, what are we doing here?" Peter asked. Was he sweating? He thought he might be sweating.

Georgie didn't smile. "We're negotiating."

"I get that." He resisted the urge to wipe his palms down his filthy jeans. "What are we negotiating, though?"

She did smile now, and it chilled the sweat on his skin. "Your return to the family, Peter."

CHAPTER 11

PETER STARED AT her, astounded. "I don't have a family." Why did he have to keep telling her that?

"Nice," Willa muttered. "We're sitting right here, you asshole. Remember us? Your sister and your dad?"

Like he ever forgot. "I don't think that's what she's talking about."

"Oh but I am." Georgie uncurled one long leg, rolled her ankle languidly and tucked it back under her derriere. "Willa and Brett are your family, of course, but so are we. Because of Matty."

Peter closed his eyes. Not this again.

She said, "Matty's my brother, of course, but he's also Willa's brother. Your brother. And Brett's your dad. Matty connects each and every person in this room."

Peter opened his mouth but Georgie held up a stop-sign hand.

"Don't," she said. "It's boring."

He closed his mouth.

"Long story short? What you see gathered together under the very expensive new roof you bought Addison with the proceeds from your late and unlamented empire is a family. It's *your* family."

Bianca made a soft noise, somewhere between a snort and a sigh. Peter didn't blame her.

Georgie went on. "But your behavior in recent months—"

"Years," Willa said crisply.

"—has called into question your commitment to family."

"I have no commitment to family," Peter reminded her.

"As you've made clear." Georgie propped an elbow on the arm of her chair, rested the point of her chin on her palm and studied him with sleepy blue eyes that missed nothing. "But I believe I've been clear as well. Family isn't something you choose. It's something that is. Whether you honor or abuse it is up to you, and you've made the wrong choice again and again. I'm giving you the chance to make the right one for a change."

"Julia is giving me that chance, you mean." Peter wasn't totally sure what was going on here but he hadn't been a sheep farmer *that* long. Surrender simply wasn't in him. After the Davis Place fire, he'd put it on like a scarlet letter but he hadn't *lost*. He'd simply acknowledged the immoral nature of the war he'd waged on them and ceded the field. But this was different. He might be just a humble sheep farmer these days but he was nobody's pet, and he wore no man's leash.

No woman's, either.

He leaned back on the hearth, folded his arms and stretched his boots out in front of him. "All right," he said. "I'm interested."

"I'm so glad." She gave him a smile that might've disemboweled the unsuspecting but that wasn't Peter. Not anymore. He was wide awake for the first time in months. "Then you'll be—"

"Why don't we discuss this over a drink?"

She blinked slowly, the only sign of surprise on her perfect face. "Excuse me?"

He smiled at her, and he could feel the shark swimming in it. God, it felt good. "A drink, Georgie. It's about the oldest way to do business there is."

"I don't want to have a drink with you, Peter."

"You'd rather golf?" He lifted doubtful shoulders. "Okay by me but it'll be chilly."

"I don't want to golf, either."

"You want my lawyer to call your lawyer?"

"You can still afford a lawyer?" She blinked again, even slower this time. He suppressed a delighted grin. Damn, this girl was fun now that he knew who he was dealing with.

"There are times when you can't *not* afford a lawyer," he returned. "I'm hoping this isn't one of those times. I'm hoping this is just one of those hash-it-out-over-a-friendly-drink times." He studied her. "We're family, after all."

Jax laughed. "Damn, Peter. I remember now why I liked you."

Liked. Past tense. Peter knew he deserved nothing less but he'd always liked Jax, too. He'd lost a lot while trying to be the king of Devil's Kettle.

"Heaven's sake, Georgie," Addy said. "Let the man buy you a drink. And get all these people out of my house while you're at it. I have an inn full of art students and they like to catch the early light. I need to get the dough on for tomorrow morning's cinnamon rolls."

"And I'm due back by tomorrow noon to critique whatever they produce while catching the early light." Bianca rose and held out a hand. "Come on, Matty. Let's go see what Jennifer's making us for dinner."

Addy goggled. "My mother is making you dinner?"

"Of course," Bianca said, all innocence.

"My mother *cooks*?" Addy asked.

"Every night."

"How on earth are you surviving?"

"That bad?" Jax asked his fiancée, amused.

"All but inedible," Addy assured him. "My mom's one of those first-generation feminists who thought she was proving a point by refusing to learn even the basics of any traditionally girlie skill."

"How is feeding yourself a girlie skill?" Willa asked.

"Why cook when there's take-out?" Georgie countered blandly.

"Listen to Trust Fund Barbie," Willa sneered, and Georgie lifted a lazy middle finger her way.

Willa grinned. "You'd have to buy me a drink first."

Georgie sighed lavishly. "Apparently I'm booked this evening."

"Yeah, way to take one for the team." Willa rolled her eyes just as lavishly.

"Girls, please," Bianca said mildly, and Peter realized with a pulse of amazement that Georgie and Willa were behaving like…sisters. Good God, was Georgie right? Was this oddball conglomeration of people really some kind of Frankenstein family?

"Jennifer and I understand each other," Bianca said to Addison. "I'm giving her a place to stay while she sorts through the mess she's made of things with your father. In return, she cooks for us." She shrugged. "It gives her something to do."

"Not enough to do," Addy muttered. "She's still up here every day."

Bianca leaned down to kiss Addy's cheek. "She's your mother and she's trying."

"Trying to drive me crazy. I wish she'd just go talk to Dad." She turned beseeching eyes on Peter. "Hey, now that you're family again—"

"Still in negotiations, sorry. You could always try talking to your dad yourself, you know." He paused thoughtfully. "Did you know we have chickens now?"

She sighed. "Yeah, sorry. I always wanted chickens when I was a kid. I guess Dad remembered."

"Humor the guy. Swing by sometime."

"I'll think about it."

In moments, the room was empty except for Peter and Georgie.

"So," he said, anticipation bubbling in his veins. "You up for that drink?"

She rose slowly, patted all that shiny hair smooth. "Can you afford to buy me one?"

"One," he returned equably. "And since you've never had a second drink in your very thin life, I think my budget will be okay."

"You can drive," she said.

It was nearly sunset by the time Peter pulled into his barren and depressing farm yard. Georgie sat serenely in the passenger seat of his farm truck like a flower growing on a trash heap. She turned curious eyes on him.

"I thought you were taking me out for a drink?"

"You thought I meant in town?"

"I did."

Peter shoved open his door. Had to put some muscle into it. The truck's engine was a champion but the body had a few issues, one of them being extreme old age. He got out, then leaned back into the cab to smile at her. "You thought you could spring your little plot on me—" Whatever it was. "—and I'd just cede home court advantage?" He shook his head. "What are you, adopted?"

He slammed the truck door on her reply. Probably for the best. He rounded the hood and yanked open the passenger door for her.

"Such a gentleman." Her tone was pure battery acid.

"Nah. Just didn't think you could get out otherwise." He waited for her to step into the barnyard, then swung the door back and forth a few times. It howled unhappily. "This one's sticky."

She studied it with pursed lips. "So I hear."

He glanced down at her feet and found a pair of buttery soft knee-high riding boots that had never seen a barnyard in their Italian lives. He offered her his elbow. To his surprise, she took it. She pressed his biceps between her warm hand and her side. Perilously close, he realized, his blood jumping violently, to her breast.

Oh, she was good. She was very good.

He patted her hand. "This is going to be fun."

"You're delusional," she said fondly.

And they strolled off through the chilly almost-sunset to the farm house.

Fun wasn't the word Georgie would've chosen, but she couldn't deny that Peter was keeping her attention. He opened the big farmhouse door with a courtly flourish and she paused in the empty foyer, sent him a questioning glance.

"To the kitchen, I assume?"

"That's where we keep the heat," he said. "It's also where we keep the booze."

"Then by all means, to the kitchen," she said and threaded her arm through his again. She took her time studying the empty living room and an equally empty dining room as they passed through. The farm house was brutally cold and painfully barren but the bones of the place were astonishing. Low ceilings, exposed beams, rough wood, ancient floors. The overall effect was uncompromising and austere, like it had been built by Norwegian farmers who knew that heat was precious and luxury was for fools. But there was beauty in the tense space between what was necessary and what pleased the eye, and whoever had built this place had lived in that space. And if anybody ever opened a door or window and let the light in? A tingle brewed in her blood, the kind she usually only experienced when a new artist's work caught her eye. Fascinating.

They reached the kitchen and again, Peter pushed open the door and allowed her to precede him. Just like on her previous visit, it was warm and relatively clean. This time, however, two coffee cups rested in the sink rather than one, and nobody had burned the soup. "Where's Mike tonight?"

"If I had to guess? Crooning to his chickens."

She considered that. "Why?"

"It's complicated."

"Okay." She unbuttoned her navy peacoat, shrugged out of it. She kept her cashmere scarf — warm was a relative term in Peter's farmhouse — but held the coat out to him. He hung it on a row of pegs behind the door where a stack of firewood stood ready to feed the potbellied stove near Peter's cot.

"Don't tell me Mike sleeps with the chickens, too."

Peter grinned at her. "It's not *that* complicated a relationship."

"Why only one cot then?" She blinked innocently. "Unless the two of you—"

"—have the complicated relationship?" He gestured her

toward the big kitchen table while he opened a small door on the front of the stove. A blessed wave of heat reached out and touched Georgie's knees and she sank onto the wooden bench tucked beside the table, as close to the stove as possible. "No. He's camping out in one of the upstairs bedrooms. He bought a space heater."

"Ah."

Peter grabbed a few logs from the woodpile, fed them to the little black stove and wiped his hands down the thighs of his jeans. It was a habitual gesture, judging from the state of his jeans, and sawdust looked to be the least offensive thing he'd encountered all day. The same thought must've occurred to him because he went to the sink and gave his hands a quick scrub. Then Georgie realized he wasn't washing his hands; he was washing the coffee cups.

"We're drinking out of coffee mugs?" she asked.

"Unless you want to go at it straight from the bottle?" He sent her a look over his shoulder. "Wouldn't be the first time I've done business that way but I don't recommend it." He wiped the mugs dry and brought them to the table. "Not for you, anyway. If you have five percent body fat, I'd be amazed."

She crossed her legs, slowly. Enjoyed the way he followed along with his eyes. Men were so easy sometimes. "Feel free to be amazed," she purred. "But yes, I'll admit that drinking like a sailor isn't a strong suit." She picked up one of the mugs. It had a chipped handle and sported the logo for the Devil's Tap Room, the Zincs's family bar. "But you did promise me at least one."

"While we talk," he said mildly.

"Of course," she said.

"All right, then. Let's get down to business." He headed

to the cupboard and opened it wide. "Pick your poison," he said grandly. "Beer's in the fridge."

She rose to inspect her options. "You stole all this when you sold the Tap Room, didn't you?"

"Stole is such a harsh word. Besides, I still own twenty percent of the place. I don't think you can steal from a place you own."

"Sure you can. It's called embezzlement." She nudged aside a middling bottle of pinot grigio. "And I thought you sold your share of the bar to Eli." She sent him a look. "Stealing from your own future brother-in-law? For shame, Peter."

"Yeah, I only sold him forty percent."

"Why forty?" Lord, apple brandy? She'd never really known Peter at all, had she?

"Because it was all he'd take. Willa and I had a sixty-forty split, her forty to my sixty, and Eli didn't want to own a single share more than his bride." Peter sighed. "He was very stubborn about it."

"So you're stuck with both the bar and the family." She turned around a dusty bottle in the back of the cupboard to get a better look at the label. "Is this a Laphroaig? It is! The twenty-five-year-old stuff, too. Well, angels sang. You've been holding out on me." She sent him a chiding look. "*Beer's in the fridge*, indeed."

He shrugged cheerfully. "It works on Mike."

"Mike sleeps with chickens."

"Beg pardon?" A new voice entered the conversation and Georgie turned to find Addy's father poking his curly head in the kitchen door.

"Hi, Mike." Georgie sent him a slow smile. "How are your chickens?"

"Adorable," he said. "And you're just as terrifying as ever."

"Aren't you the sweetest thing?"

Mike turned to Peter. "Are you okay in here?"

Peter frowned at him. "Why wouldn't I be?"

"Because the last time I saw you, a reporter who evidently bears her family—" He jerked that curly head toward Georgie. "—some serious ill will had just ambushed you in your own front yard with your mom who's been dead for fifteen years. Then you take off up the hill like your hair's on fire, and the next thing I know your truly frightening ex-fiancée, whom I understand to be either responsible for or at the very least delighted by your financial troubles—" He glanced at Georgie. "No offense."

"None taken," she said and nudged aside an inferior vodka so she could liberate that 25 year-old scotch.

"—is making herself at home in the sin cupboard."

Georgie grinned. "That's what you call the liquor cabinet?"

"I was raised by teetotalers."

"I'm sorry," Georgie said sincerely.

"Me, too." His dimples flickered though Georgie wouldn't have called it an actual smile. She really did like this guy. He turned his attention back to Peter. "So I ask again, are you all right in here?"

"I'm fine."

"You're going to meet your fate like a man, then."

"I've read *Oedipus Rex*," Peter said solemnly. "I know better than to run."

"Better you than me."

"But we've got scotch." Georgie held up the bottle and wiggled it. Mike's eyes widened.

"Is that a Laphroaig?"

"It is, and a quarter century old, too."

"We have that?"

"You do." From the corner of her eye, she saw Peter sigh sadly. "Well, you do for now. Peter promised me a drink while we do business so we'll see how things go. I'll try to save you some but I'm not promising anything." She tipped her head, as if struck. "I can offer you dinner, though, if you head down to Hill Top House. Jennifer's cooking."

Mike stared. "Jennifer Tate? My wife?"

"Your soon-to-be-ex-wife, you mean?" Georgie did a slow blink. "Yes. She cooks every night."

"I don't believe you."

"I said she cooks. I didn't say we ate."

His brows shot up. "Damn. She *is* cooking."

Georgie sighed. "It's a sight to see. One you really ought to go see for yourself because, Mike?"

"Yeah?"

"I don't think she's coming to you." She set the scotch on the counter. "I'm sorry but I don't think she is."

His mouth tightened, and incongruously it flashed his dimples just like that almost-smile had. Sympathy ached in her throat. Why did pain and pleasure have to live so close together? "Yeah, I was just coming to that conclusion myself."

"Addy says Jennifer spends a lot of time at Davis Place."

"I know."

"I think she's hoping to see you there."

"She knows where I am."

Georgie glanced at Peter. Those naked eyes of his met hers and she passed the baton with a barely-there nudge of her chin.

"Mike, come on," Peter said. "This is your wife. You know her. She's an entrepreneur. An alpha. She doesn't know how to do anything but win."

"So I have to lose?"

"No, but you could find a way to win that doesn't require her to lose."

"What the hell does that even mean?"

"He means it's not a zero-sum game," Georgie said gently. "You can both win if you find a way."

"But why do I always have to find the way? Why is it always me who has to bend?"

Pain fluttered through Georgie's stomach but it wasn't hers. It was Mike's. He hurt. God, he hurt so much it leaked into the air around him. Georgie was getting a stomachache on his behalf.

"I'm tired of finding a way." He leaned wearily into the doorjamb. "I'm so damn tired of always finding the way."

"Then go win." She didn't want to foment unrest in an already troubled marriage but something needed to knock these two out of their stalemate. Mike's abandoning the marriage bed hadn't done the trick. Maybe this would.

"How?"

"Have dinner at Hill Top House."

"What, go to her? Reward her for refusing to bend?"

Peter waved him quiet. "Just listen, Mike." His eyes were dark and interested on Georgie. "She's onto something."

Warmth gathered under her heart at the vote of confidence and she leaned into her subject. "For goodness' sake, Mike, think! Jennifer knows you're not coming to her. You've all but served her papers. And maybe you don't love her anymore but she knows you'll always love Addy so she's counting on running across you at Davis Place. That's the scenario she's planned for. She probably has her speech all ready, her moves rehearsed. The last thing she expects is for you to show up for dinner at Hill Top House. She's not prepared for that, plus she'll be flustered because dinner didn't turn out." Georgie put a hand to her stomach. "It never does."

Mike studied her. "Jennifer's a terrible cook."

"The worst. But Peter's right. She's an alpha. She doesn't do failure."

"But she fails at dinner?"

"Every night. If nothing else, you deserve to witness the spectacle." Inspiration struck and Georgie smiled. Mike blanched and she wondered if she was wearing Bianca's smile again. "You know, my mother's single."

Mike drew back, horrified. "I'm not interested in—"

Peter laughed. "She's not suggesting you date Bianca."

"Definitely not." Georgie laughed, too. Bianca would eat Addy's sweet, chicken-loving dad alive. "But if Jennifer thought you were looking that way, and that maybe my mom was looking back…"

"You are truly, truly frightening." Mike crossed the room, took her by the upper arms and pressed smacking kisses to both her cheeks. "But you're a genius."

Georgie hadn't been kissed in that particularly fatherly way for nearly 15 years, and her heart squeezed in painful wonder. Mike snatched up the bottle of scotch, twisted off the cap and took a belt straight from the bottle.

"Jesus Christ." He shook like a wet dog.

Peter said, "Easy, champ. You're driving."

"No, I know. I just needed the one."

Georgie patted his shoulder. "Come home with your shield or on it, Spartan."

"Pray for me." He snatched the farm truck keys off the counter and bolted.

CHAPTER 12

GEORGIE GRINNED AT the swinging door then turned to find Peter grinning at her.

"What?"

He shook his head. "You."

"What about me?"

"You're in love with that guy."

"No, I'm in love with my stomach lining, and his wife's cooking qualifies as a biohazard." She picked up the scotch and brought it to the table. She sank to the bench while Peter did the honors, splashing a generous measure into each mug. She lifted hers, swirled it under her nose. "Sometimes she saves me a plate but if Mike eats my share…"

He ignored that. "It's the dimples," he said sympathetically. "I could tell you Addy's are worse but you'd only point out the flock of chickens I now own that I don't actually want." He arched a brow at her mug. "Rocks?"

"Please."

He retrieved a few ice cubes from the freezer with his bare hands and plunked them into her mug. Something jumped in her stomach at the intimacy of it. It wasn't pain exactly, but it wasn't pleasure either. It was whatever lived at that fascinating balancing point between the two. She shivered and he lowered himself to the bench beside her, his knees only inches from hers.

"You're cold." He took the end of her scarf and draped it more securely around her throat. This close he smelled like dish soap and sheep and healthy man. That strange, compelling tension coiled tighter inside her. Intrigued, she breathed in deeply, pulled the scent of him into her lungs and held it there. "Better?"

She wasn't sure. She was definitely awake, though.

She lifted her mug to him. "Let's do business, shall we?"

He touched his mug to hers. "Let's."

She brought the scotch to her lips and sipped. Lord, it was gorgeous. She closed her eyes and held it in her mouth a moment, unwilling to rush the experience. Rich soil and oak barrels filled her sinuses and curled through her mind, then slid away like smoke when she finally allowed herself to swallow. She opened her eyes, found Peter gazing at her.

Heat that had nothing to do with the alcohol climbed into her cheeks, and she was gripped with a self-consciousness she hadn't allowed herself to feel since she'd decided as a six-foot-tall eighth grader with Viking cheekbones and near-white hair to get over being stared at.

"Peter."

"Hmm?"

"You're staring."

He smiled. "Am I?"

"You are. Why?"

"Because you liked that." He nodded at her mug. "The Laphroaig."

She sipped again. It really was wonderfully smooth, with a sooty finish that reminded her of campfires on rocky beaches. "What's not to like?"

"No, I mean you genuinely, physically enjoyed the taste of it. The act of putting it in your mouth and swallowing it. You *savored* it."

"How clumsy of me." Mortification soured the lovely

aftertaste. She was used to being stared at. She *wasn't* used to being seen. "A lady mustn't have appetites."

"I'm all for a lady with appetites," Peter returned. "I just didn't think you had any."

"Really? How...honest." She smiled politely. "That does explain a few things, however." She gave his knee a brisk pat. "Well, let's leave past disappointments in the past, shall we?"

"Wait." His eyes narrowed. "Are we talking about my disappointments or yours?"

"If we're talking about appetites gone undetected or unsatisfied, is there a difference?"

"Hell, yes."

"There shouldn't be," she returned promptly. "Maybe that's the biggest disappointment of all. Now, can we get down to business?"

"Not yet. Not with this business still unfinished."

"Which business is that?"

"Your appetites."

Something deep inside her drew up, interested, and she had to reach for her customary languor. "Peter, please."

"No, seriously, let's explore this for a minute." He tapped a finger to his lips and considered her. "You're different."

She gave him her profile, let him look. "Am I?" She sounded bored. Good. For God's sake, he'd thought she didn't have any *appetites*? She'd slept with this man for close to two years!

He lifted his mug for a sip, studied her over the rim. "Or maybe I'm different."

"Of course you are. You're poor now. Then again, you were poor before, and I just didn't know it, so maybe you're not that different after all." She sipped, too, purposefully left a drop of scotch on her upper lip. She flicked out her tongue to catch it, and his eyes followed along with an intensity she'd never seen before.

Oh, he'd been a capable lover. Very. But their relationship had been built more on mutual interests than any grand passion, and that had been fine with Georgie. More than fine. She wasn't in the market for passion and never had been. How could she be with her mother's voice in her head at all hours of the day and night, murmuring about the dangers of unguarded behavior? (*People are watching, Georgie. Always. Don't ever forget that you're a Davis.*)

So she didn't. She never forgot she was a Davis, not even when she was naked. Which meant she'd never allowed herself a lover who might *make* her forget. And Peter never had. Oh, he *could* have. She saw that now with unsettling clarity. But during their engagement, he'd been nothing but respectful, polite and undemanding. He'd been perfect.

How wrong she'd been.

"You're saying we might be the same people we've always been," Peter mused, and she could feel those dark eyes *touching* her, wandering over her skin, her lips, her hair with frank interest. A fizzle ignited inside her everywhere that gaze landed, like champagne bubbles climbing up the inside of the glass. "And I'm only now noticing?"

She tried one of her laziest smiles. "Noticing what?"

He leaned an elbow on the table between them. "Your true nature."

"Ah." She sipped her scotch and reminded herself to be careful. It was the kind of smooth that went down so easily you didn't really know you were in trouble until you stood up. And while she definitely had more than five percent body fat, she probably shouldn't belt back straight scotch and expect to keep her head on straight. "And what is my true nature?"

"You're smart."

She gave that her signature slow blink, and to her surprise he laughed.

"Christ, you do that so well. We dated for how long? Two years?"

"Over."

"And not once did I look past the lash extensions."

She drew back, offended. "I beg your pardon. I don't use extensions."

"Oh, are those real?" He peered at her. "Huh."

"See for yourself." She lowered her lids to half-mast and leaned in. "What you see is what you get, Peter. I'm not putting on a show for you, or anybody."

His palm came up to cup her cheek and he brushed a thumb across the very ends of her lashes. "Wow, they *are* yours." That interesting fizzle under her skin edged toward an actual simmer. She fought the urge to recross her legs against the strange restlessness gathering low in her belly. "Who knew?" He took his hand back. An involuntary mew of disappointment rose in her throat and she swallowed it down with a pulse of horror. Good lord, what was wrong with her? "My point, Georgie, is that you're beautiful. Dazzling, really."

"Aren't you sweet," she murmured, and the simmer in her blood faded abruptly. She understood why people always wanted to discuss her face but she'd lost interest in the subject years ago.

"Hardly. Because back in the day? Back in our day? I never once thought there might be anything more to you. You were so beautiful that it was all I expected you to be."

He moved those shoulders again and just like that, the fizzle was back.

"But now that you're...noticing," she said carefully, because between the fizzle and the scotch, she was close to being dazzled herself, "you think there's more?"

"I know there is." He reached over, slid a warm hand along the line of her jaw, under her hair. She shivered and her stomach leapt back onto that dangerous balance point between pleasure and pain. He freed a lock of hair from her scarf and smoothed it into the rest. "I just don't know what that *more* is, exactly." He caught himself and drew back, that hand lifted in apology. "Sorry, force of habit." He gave her a rueful smile. "Your hair was stuck inside your scarf but I wasn't invited."

"Invited?" She sat back, too, a little dizzy. She should definitely ease up on the scotch. She glanced in her mug. Still mostly full. Huh.

"To touch," he clarified. "I took liberties with your person that a boyfriend or a fiancé is allowed. Liberties that are his privilege and his honor, if he's doing it right. Liberties that I don't enjoy anymore."

She frowned at him. "Don't lie to me, Peter."

"Lie to you?"

"Those liberties, as you so charmingly call them, were yours, and you were proud of them. But you never enjoyed them."

"No," he said slowly, "maybe I didn't." He paused. "Why didn't you ever talk to me this way when we were together?"

"Why didn't you enjoy touching me when I was yours to touch?" She lifted her shoulders, her stomach confused, that odd fizzle racing madly in her veins. "Life's a mystery and people are strange. Now can we get this discussion back on track?"

"I wouldn't say I didn't enjoy touching you." He propped an elbow on the table again and leaned his temple against his fist. He studied her openly, his mug cupped loosely in the other hand on his knee. "I'd say more that back then being allowed to touch you was the goal, and I've always been a goal-oriented guy." He pursed his lips, and Georgie fought the urge to drop her eyes to them, to study each curve and dip, all utterly familiar and yet startlingly new. "Achieving the goal was everything. Enjoying what I'd achieved? Not so much."

"And now?" she heard herself ask. She hadn't meant to ask.

"Now I live in the moment. I have no goals."

She smiled at that. "Liar." She propped her elbow on the table, too, leaned her head against her curled fist. "I wouldn't be here drinking your best scotch if you didn't have a goal."

"No, you wouldn't be here drinking my best scotch if *you* didn't have a goal."

"Touché." She toasted him and sipped her drink. Pretended to, anyway. She'd had enough alcohol, and this verbal fencing match required all her wits. "But you're counterpunching for all you're worth and you don't even know what I want yet."

"I haven't ever known what you wanted, though, have I? How could I, when I didn't think you knew how to want?"

"Why, Peter." She smiled brilliantly, suddenly delighted with him. "Are you having a crisis of manly confidence?"

"A what?" He scowled. "No, I'm not having a crisis of manly confidence."

"You are!" She reached over to pat his arm. She could feel the animal heat of his biceps even through the thick wool of his sweater. "That's adorable!"

"I'm not, and it isn't." He lifted his scotch for a healthy swallow. "Jesus Christ." He put a fist to his chest. "That is *not* for gulping."

"Aren't you sweet!" She gave his arm a friendly squeeze. "All those years you thought I didn't enjoy sex, or maybe that I'd starved myself beyond the point where I was in touch with appetites of any kind." She deepened her voice. "*If you have five percent body fat, I'd be amazed!*"

"First of all, I do *not* sound like that—"

"But now that you're all awake, you're suddenly wondering if the appetites were there all along and you just missed them." She bit down on a chuckle. "If you failed to do your manly duty by me."

"I did my manly duty just fine."

"Well of course you did." She realized her hand was still on his arm and gave it an encouraging rub. "You were a fine lover. Lovely. You were quite dear, actually."

He narrowed his eyes. "Okay, now you're *trying* to be mean."

She sighed. "You're going to obsess about this, aren't you?"

"About what? You rewriting history?"

"Men are such fragile creatures." She set her mug on the table with a plunk and swung one leg over to straddle the bench so she could face him fully. "If your lot had to give birth, we'd have died out as a species eons ago."

"Amen," he said promptly, Rag and Bone's unannounced arrival clearly tripping through his mind. "But as to the fulfillment of my manly duties—"

"Are we still talking about that?" Georgie scooted a few inches closer, tucked her knees companionably against the long line of Peter's thigh.

"Only because you brought it up." He pointed his drink at her. "Because you said I was *dear.*"

"You were."

He closed his eyes, pained. "Dear is for finger paintings by kindergartners. Dear is for macaroni necklaces and valentines made out of doilies. Dear is *not* for orgasms.*"

She shook her head sadly. "I can see that we're not going to get anything done until we deal with this."

"This?" he asked, suddenly wary. The simmer in her veins flirted with a boil and she arranged her face in lines of perfect sympathy. "What this?"

"Your manly confidence." She scooped her hair out of her scarf and tossed it all behind her shoulders where it wouldn't get in the way. "Okay, I'm ready."

"For what?"

She took the mug from his unresisting fingers and set it beside her own on the table.

"Kiss me, Peter."

CHAPTER 13

PETER STARED AT Georgie, his pulse pounding in uncomfortable places, his thoughts scattered like his stupid sheep. She sat in front of him, her knees on either side of the bench, her perfect face turned up to his, her mouth soft and ready, those impossible lashes resting on those camera-ready cheekbones.

"You want me to kiss you?"

She opened her eyes. "I asked you to, didn't I?"

"Well, yes. But why?"

"Because you're having—"

"—a crisis of manly confidence, yeah, so you said." His lip curled; he felt it. "I'm not, but—"

"So just kiss me and prove it."

"Prove what? That I can kiss you? We already know I can. I can't even count how many times I've kissed you."

"But you've obviously never done it to your satisfaction, or you wouldn't be in such a snit."

"A snit?" He stared. That was worse than dear. "Men don't have snits. Plus we're not talking about my satisfaction, we're talking about yours."

"Then there's no need to discuss this any further." She smiled brightly and scooted back. "I already told you you were fine in bed. Lovely." She paused. "Sweet."

Dismay trickled into his stomach. "Sweet?"

She put one cool, slender hand on his knee. "Sweet," she told him, her eyes large and earnest. "I have no complaints about our sex life, Peter. Truly."

"No complaints?" The trickle grew into a flood. "No *complaints?*"

"None," she assured him.

"All right, then," he said. "Let's do this thing."

"Excellent." She swung her leg back over the bench and crossed it over the other knee. "So Julia Gates and your mother are obviously our primary—"

"No, I meant the kissing."

Her brows shot up. "Oh?"

"Yeah. I mean, I never really thought about it before but now that you bring it up—"

"Actually you brought it up."

"—you have a point. I'm not satisfied as to your satisfaction. And I really don't think I can concentrate on the business at hand until I am."

"Satisfied?"

"That you're satisfied, yes."

"And how do you propose to measure such a thing?"

He smiled, slow and warm. "A gentleman knows."

"A gentleman actually doesn't, or we wouldn't be in this situation."

"Ah, but I'm awake now." He threw a leg over the bench this time, scooted toward her. "Aware of those appetites I missed the first time around."

She gave that a moment's thought, and Peter waited her out, his blood pooling hot and interested in all his most interesting places. Because Georgie was right — they had been fine in bed, but hadn't exactly rocked each others' worlds. He'd been okay with that because he'd thought it was all that was possible between them. The old Georgie was somewhat limited, mentally and emotionally, and Peter hadn't exactly been interested in depth himself. But this

Georgie was something else entirely. This woman wasn't just beautiful; she was fascinating. She was complex. She was inaccessible. And she'd offered to let him kiss her.

Peter wasn't the king of Devil's Kettle anymore, but neither was he anybody's fool. When opportunity knocked, you kissed the hell out of it and apologized later if you needed to.

"Fine." She blew out a breath and straddled the bench again. She scooted closer until her knees touched the insides of his spread thighs and he could smell expensive shampoo and fresh snow. Winter air. That invigorating, head-clearing first breath of frigid sunshine. Georgie smelled like that. How had he never noticed it before? She put her hands on his knees — his pulse jumped to attention — and leaned in. Closed her eyes and offered her mouth. "Whenever you're ready, Peter."

"I'm ready," he said. "You might want to brace yourself."

"I think I can take it."

"If you're sure."

Her eyes drifted lazily open. "I'm sure."

"Close your eyes."

She complied with a tiny sigh.

"Good girl."

"This is a limited time offer, Peter, and you're on very thin ice."

"Fine, okay. Here we go."

"Finally."

He didn't kiss her. He lifted both hands, laid his index fingers at her hairline, right at her perfect center part.

"This isn't kissing," she murmured.

"Shh." He traced the fine curtain of her hair all the way to her jaw and slid his fingers into the silky warmth behind her

121

ears. Cupped the sharp edges of those jaw bones in his palms. He closed his own eyes and followed that same path with the very tip of his nose, pulling the wintery scent of her deep into his lungs. It shimmered there, sparkled like new snow. When he got to her ear, he paused, exquisitely aware of the delicate muscles of her neck against his fingers, of the tension growing there. He drew his nose along the arc of one cheekbone, brushed past those long, long lashes and followed the curve of one skeptical eyebrow.

A minuscule shiver seized the back of her neck and he smiled. "Cold?"

"A little. Are you planning to kiss me anytime soon?"

"I am kissing you."

She sighed and he felt it against his throat. Desire rose like the tide to meet it and he pushed it back. If this was the only chance he ever got to kiss the new Georgie, he wanted to do it right.

She said, "Most people use their lips, in case you were wondering."

"Really?" She wanted his lips, then. She wanted, period. Satisfaction twined with the desire flowing through his veins. "Okay, have it your way."

He pressed his mouth to the outside corner of her eye, and she pulled in a slow breath. Held it while he moved on to her hairline. Let it go as he drifted kisses over to her ear and traced that vulnerable shell with the point of his nose. He took the naked lobe between his lips. Her breath caught at that, then released on a tiny sigh, and the desire in his blood leapt into lust. It raced, savage and hungry, through his veins, and Peter had to take a moment to breathe through the pain. He hadn't wanted — hadn't allowed himself to want — anything for so long. The piece of him that knew how to want had frozen over, but that tiny hitch in Georgie's breathing had wrenched it back to life, far faster than was probably wise. It ached like frostbitten fingers being warmed too quickly, because Georgie wasn't cold. Georgie was subtle. You had to pay attention, really *listen*, but it was all there. She was giving him a road map and all he had to do was follow it.

That and keep his own lust under control while he fed hers. Because hunger was clawing and howling inside him now, urging him to take, to snatch, to satisfy.

"Peter." Under her customary laziness, her voice was a little thin, perhaps even a trifle unsteady.

"Hmm?" He nudged her chin up with one gentle finger and pressed his lips to the vulnerable hollow of her throat.

"Is this going to go on much longer? I'm getting bored."

"Are you?" Liar. He could feel her pulse jittering against his lips. He smiled and dragged his teeth delicately up the column of her neck to press a kiss to the secret darkness behind her ear.

"A little." But her hands weren't bored on his thighs. They were in tight fists on top of his dirty jeans. That hunger roared inside him, made his own hands needful and greedy. Demanding. They wanted everything but he forced himself to touch only her hair. He speared his fingers deeper into that silky spill, and combed them through the glorious length of it all the way to the indent of her waist. "Can we get on with it, please? The actual kissing?"

"Your wish," he murmured. "My command."

He kissed her.

Georgie froze, her palms flat on Peter's thighs, her fingers splayed in the air, stiff and shocked. Her mind spun uselessly, trying to sort through the crash of sensory input, and the corresponding images it tore from her memory. The scent of him filled her mouth and nose, and sent her lungs begging. Oxygen was replaced by the clean citrusy fact of him, mingled with darker notes of something essentially male, and she couldn't breathe. She couldn't think. Her brain spun sideways, flickered through a crazy kaleidoscope of scenes, then settled on the night she'd opened her eyes.

She normally kept her eyes closed during sex. During kissing. During any of it. She kept the lights off, too. It wasn't that she was a prude. It was more that she suspected her partners kept *their* eyes open, and she didn't want to see them seeing her. Didn't want to be reminded that what they saw when they had sex with her was so much more important to them than what they felt. Than what *she* felt. Then again, did she really want to feel much? Who knew what her face did at orgasm? She'd never allowed herself to have one in front of anybody for precisely that reason.

But she'd opened her eyes this particular night, and Peter hadn't had his eyes open. He'd been frowning, in fact. He'd hung above her, propped on his elbows, his face a mask of concentration as he moved inside her. A wave of tenderness had filled her. He was probably naming all the states of the union in his head, or listing the presidents in alphabetical order in order to maintain coitus long enough to give a girl a chance. Georgie had appreciated that gentlemanly attention to detail, so she'd always let him pump away for at least three or four minutes before faking the lady-like orgasm that would give him the all-clear to have his own.

But her heart had swelled inside her with an unexpected tenderness that night and she'd had to turn away from his face. From the endearing effort he was expending on her behalf. She didn't want to feel tenderness toward Peter. Affection and respect was enough. Anything more would be extraneous, not to mention dangerous. So she'd turned away.

And found him anyway in the mirror above his dresser. It was angled so that Georgie could see Peter but not herself beneath him and she'd stared. She'd suddenly understood the appeal of keeping your eyes open because, dear God, he was beautiful. He was a symphony of muscle and bone limned in moonlight, all of it striving toward the most ancient satisfaction. The silvery light had worshipped the hard cut of his deltoids as he'd held himself above her, had slid over the clench and release of his buttocks as he'd pushed his body into hers, had thrown a spotlight on the primal rhythm of that thrust and withdrawal that she could both see in the mirror and feel in her body. Something had fluttered inside her, something strange and light and desperately dangerous. It rose and reached low in her belly, and she'd wanted to follow it. Wanted to lift her knees, grip Peter's flanks with them like a jockey and ride this *feeling* anywhere it wanted to go. She was suddenly liquid and hot between her legs, her inner muscles swelling and clutching around him. She'd shifted helplessly, trying automatically to find her way either into or out of that discomfort, and Peter's breathing had hitched.

"Oh, Christ," he'd said, and his face had twisted in what she now recognized as neither pleasure nor pain but that glorious place exactly in between. "*Georgie*."

He'd surged hard and held there, straining against her. And she'd realized that he'd mistaken her finally entering the race for her crossing the finish line. She didn't know whether to laugh or cry.

Then he'd released that breath and lowered himself to

her, warm and heavy and satisfied. "Georgie," he'd murmured again and patted her fondly. And Georgie had patted him back, disappointment mingling with wonder, relief and a little fear. What on earth had that been, anyway? Was that what other women felt during sex? Was that what *men* felt? No wonder they were such idiots about it. Georgie had been grateful in that moment to have been spared such idiocy.

But here she was months later, fully clothed, being spared nothing.

She froze under the chaotic onslaught of sensation, though why something as familiar as Peter's kiss should overwhelm her she had no idea. She knew what Peter smelled like. Knew what he felt like. Knew the size of his hands, and the way they fit into the dips and hollows of her body. She knew the taste of his mouth, even when layered with the peat smoke and the ancient patience of good scotch.

But it wasn't just the scotch that was patient tonight. It was Peter.

He'd always been patient, though. He'd always been polite. He'd always approached their sex life like it was a test and he was going to ace it.

But this was different. Her body insisted on it, even if her brain couldn't pinpoint just why.

His mouth lingered on hers, neither asking nor taking, simply experiencing. Exploring. Those hands at her hips were warm and firm but demanded nothing. They simply held her. He wasn't just kissing her, she realized on a pulse of anxiety. He was *tasting* her. He was savoring her the way she'd savored the scotch. He was breathing her in, lapping up the scent of her mouth, and *enjoying* it. Enjoying *her*.

And that lightness floated up again, the same one she'd

felt when she'd spied on Peter in the mirror. It lifted and reached low in her belly and the urge to participate seized her once again. She wanted to squirm. To *move*. To rub against the bench between her legs until she either was consumed by the lightness and floated away with it, or ground it into nothing.

Never let them see you undone.

It was her mother's voice in her head — or was it her own at this point? — but it did the trick. It crushed that strange yearning, clipped it off like a rose destined for a vase. What on earth must her face be doing right now, and in front of Peter? The man she'd promised to keep on a tight leash, who had every reason to use against her any weapon she was stupid enough to hand him?

She forced her fingers to relax. They fell lazily to Peter's dirty jeans and she concentrated on making a blank white canvas of her mind while Peter lazily learned her mouth.

An endless moment later, he drew back.

She gave him a slow blink. "You didn't want to use your tongue?"

"I didn't need to. I got what I was after."

This time her blink was real. "You did?"

"Not every kiss leads to sex, Georgie." She lifted a skeptical brow and he laughed. "It's every guy's much-cherished goal, sure, but horny teenagers eventually grow into men who understand what a kiss can be."

It occurred to her — far, far too late — that asking him to kiss her might've been a tactical error. "And what was this one?"

He smiled guilelessly. "Delicious."

"It was excellent scotch."

"I wasn't talking about the taste. I know what you taste

like, Georgie." His hands slid from her waist, followed the long line of each thigh and curled into the hollows behind her bent knees. He held her there, her knees tight in the vee of his own thighs, then leaned forward and spoke into the warm, intimate space between them, the space shared only by lovers or people who've just kissed one another stupid. "I was talking about you."

"Me?" She gazed at him, mystified. How was she not what she tasted like?

"You. I was right about you." He met her eyes directly. "You've never really been satisfied."

He didn't make a question out of it, and Georgie wasn't foolish enough to answer what hadn't been asked.

"The question is, do you want to be?"

God, yes.

"Oh dear," she murmured instead. "I've given you ideas. Peter, please, let's not make this awkward."

"Awkward is the only way to go, unfortunately."

"Excuse me?"

"We've been naked together hundreds of times, Georgie. But it occurred to me as I was kissing you just now that we hadn't ever gotten naked enough to do it right."

She narrowed her eyes, fighting to focus. Her well-kissed mouth still sang from what he'd done to it, and the memory of his body, all moonlit skin and leashed need, floated up in her mind's eye again. That ominous lightness rekindled in her belly. Oh lord. "I'm not taking my clothes off, Peter."

"Did I ask you to? All I asked is if you wanted to be truly satisfied."

"Are you offering?"

He considered that. So did she. If he said yes, would she? She honestly didn't know. But the lift in her belly morphed into a buzz, a fine vibration that ran through her blood, danced along her bones, sang against her nerves. And she was tempted. If his version of satisfaction took her farther into that feeling, she was definitely tempted.

"No," he said finally. "That would be missing the point."

"What point?"

"There's something really interesting between us, Georgie. Something that only happens when we're completely honest with each other. We were there for a minute just now."

He didn't ask her to acknowledge it, only dipped his chin and met her eyes. She didn't flinch, though she wanted to, and she didn't deny it. Something *had* happened between them just now. She'd been trying to get the upper hand, knock him off balance before she extorted what she wanted from him, but everything had gone sideways when he'd kissed her and meant it.

"You meant it," she heard herself say, and heat climbed into her cheeks. Oh, Christ, she was blushing. But she didn't take the words back. She wanted to know. "When you were kissing me. You meant it."

He squeezed the backs of her knees, delighted with her. "You felt it, too."

"It was…different."

"It was honest. Now I've been a liar my whole life, up until a couple months ago, anyway. Shitty upbringing, fatally flawed moral structure, greed and vanity my besetting sins." He shrugged. "I don't know what your excuses are but you're as big a liar as I ever was."

"I beg your pardon?"

"Please. I had sex with you once a week for nearly two years and I never kissed the real Georgie Davis until just now. And the old Georgie, whoever you were pretending to be, whoever you think you need to be? I could go the rest of my life without kissing her again. But the woman I kissed today? Just now?" He let out a whistling breath. "I'm going to dream about her at night. And Georgie?"

"Hmm?" It was about all she could manage.

"I don't even dream anymore." He gave her knees one last fond squeeze. "Just think about it." He let her go and swung his leg over the bench, picked up his mug and said, "Okay, let's get down to business."

CHAPTER 14

"So my mom's back in town," Peter said, and forced himself to taste the words with the same exquisite attention he'd just given Georgie's mouth. He wondered if she'd been even half as taken aback by that kiss as he had been. It was hard to tell. He was feeling his way in the dark with this new Georgie. He was going to have to feel his way through this bizarre development with his mom, too.

"She is." Georgie crossed her legs and turned to lean her back against the table. Sent him a sideways look under those impossible lashes. "I take it that was a genuine surprise to you."

"It was." He turned his back to the table as well, stretched his boots out in front of him and frowned at the sin cabinet across the room. "All these years, I just assumed the gossip had it right. I thought Brett had finally gone too far."

"You thought your father murdered your mother? Really?"

"Everybody thought my father murdered my mother, Georgie." He sent her the sideways look this time. "Even you."

"Yeah but it was just scurrilous home-town gossip for me. For you, it was family."

"Scurrilous." Improbably, a smile threatened. "Did you always have such an interesting vocabulary or was I really just not paying attention?"

"A little of both. Now answer the question."

"I don't do family the way you do, okay? I left home a

long time ago." At her expectant silence, he lifted his shoulders. "My parents fought. A lot. Physically. By the time I left, I didn't care what they did to each other anymore." Or he'd told himself as much until he'd believed it. "Murder made as much sense as anything. Way more sense than any elaborate plot where Mom disappeared herself then rose from the dead fifteen years later."

"Fourteen."

"Okay." But, damn, had it really been that many years since he'd lit out of this place, on fire to change the world? To change himself? "What do you suppose would bring her back after all that time?"

"Ah." Georgie sipped her scotch contemplatively. "That's the question, isn't it?"

"She can't imagine Brett would be happy to see her, not after the way she deliberately set him up for prosecution." And he had no reason to doubt Willa's take on the situation. She'd been there; Peter hadn't. Story of his life. "Given what she put Willa through, she has to know she's not welcome there either." He tick-tocked his boots lazily from side to side, and tried to find that dark, sketchy mindset his mother had taught him to think from. "So what could she possibly want here? And how can Julia Gates help her get it?"

"Excellent question." Georgie tapped a thoughtful finger against her mug. "But it's just as likely, if not more likely, that Julia's driving this train and Shay is just along for the ride."

"It would take one hell of a carrot or a stick to get Shay to agree to that ride."

She lifted her shoulders agreeably.

"What are you thinking, Georgie?"

"I have a few ideas."

He waited. He could almost hear her mental gears engaging.

"I'm worried about Matty," she said finally.

"Well, sure. He's at the heart of all of this. There's no way what goes down next doesn't touch him." He took in the pugnacious set of that perfect jaw. "And you don't want him touched."

"I refuse it." Her voice was flat, almost frightening. At the same time, though, it woke up a bittersweet yearning inside him. What would it have been like to be Georgie's family for real? To live under the umbrella of that fierce protectiveness? To have somebody — anybody — prepared to go to war for you at any time, simply because you were theirs?

"How do you plan to prevent it?" And what was he supposed to contribute? Because she wouldn't be sitting here, drinking his scotch, kissing him into an alternate reality if she didn't need him for something.

"Jax is a firefighter." She switched brothers without so much as a turn signal. "He's been pounding fire safety into our heads for years. We pretend not to listen because we don't want him getting a big head but I've learned a few things. Fighting fire with fire, for example. It's effective but expensive. It's always safer — not to mention cheaper and easier — to smother it if you can."

"You think you can smother what's coming before it touches Matty?"

"I sure as hell don't want to feed it." A faint line appeared between her brows that made her look heart-stoppingly like her mother. Peter didn't know if he was intrigued or appalled.

"What do you need from me, Georgie?"

133

"I want you to take Matty."

"Take Matty?" Peter frowned. "Take him where?"

Georgie smiled. "Here."

"You want him to visit the farm?"

"I want him to move to the farm."

Peter stared, disbelief a big, ringing emptiness inside his head. "You do recall that I'm the bastard who blackmailed him into insurance fraud?"

"Emotional blackmail, and show me a single family that doesn't use it daily." She waved a lazy hand. "And since neither you nor Addy filed the claim on Davis Place, and since you withdrew your claims on your other properties before you got paid, no insurance fraud actually happened."

"Which doesn't make what I did any less evil."

"Of course it doesn't."

"So how the hell can you want the kid in my custody?"

"I want him safe."

He arched a brow. "I believe my point stands."

She sighed. "You've got your issues, no question, and our personal history is messy—"

"At best."

"—but bear in mind that Julia Gates is ambitious, ruthless and addicted."

"Addicted? To what?"

"To Diego." She rolled her eyes. "Jesus, Peter, keep up. She wanted to be Diego's Angel and Addy stole that from her. Addy won. But now there's Matty, and he's young, he's beautiful, and he's blazingly talented, all of which would make her want his story. But guess what? He's also Diego's son."

"The son that should've been hers," he murmured, finally

connecting the dots. He felt ill. "The son who loves Addy like a mother."

"Exactly," Georgie said grimly. "Why do you think Julia wants to give him his real mommy so bad? It's sure as hell not because she's a fan of the truth. She wants to hurt Addy, and what would hurt her more than damaging her relationship with Matty?" She shook her head. "Julia's more dangerous to Matty than you'll ever be and, given our history, she'll never think to look for him here. Just keep him busy and don't let Julia Gates across the property lines. Have her arrested for trespass if you need to."

"Okay. What about Shay, though?"

"I wouldn't invite her over but it would be weird if you refused to see her at all, don't you think? There's a reason they came to you first. You're the most likely to be sympathetic to Shay's story." She rested the mug thoughtfully against her chin. "She wants a conversation? Give her one. What are you doing here, what happened all those years ago, why did you leave, where did you go, et cetera, et cetera." She glanced his way, her eyes alive with curiosity. "We've allowed Willa to become Matty's de facto birth mother by never denying the rumor. I wonder what Shay thinks about that."

"You want me to find out."

"She'll tell you what she wants you to know."

"Or what Julia wants *you* to know."

A sleek smile spread across her face. "Now you're thinking."

"And of course I'll let slip whatever you want her to know."

"You'd have made an excellent Davis."

"I thought I was one. Isn't that what this exercise is all

about?"

Her lashes came down coyly. "You're auditioning."

"So I can turn down the part if I get it?"

"It's a family, not a choice." The contradiction didn't seem to bother her.

"Right."

"Meanwhile, I'll let Julia reach out to me. She's not interested in me, per se, but once it becomes clear that she's not getting anybody else, she'll come around. Plus I'm just dim enough that maybe I'll let something worthwhile slip accidentally." She blinked slowly and a reluctant chuckle lodged in Peter's throat. If you didn't know her, you'd swear she'd just dropped 50 IQ points. Suddenly, those lashes swept his way and Peter found himself staring straight into a pair of razor-sharp blue eyes, snapping with intelligence and demand. "We need to know what exactly they want, and what they're prepared to do to get it. Until we do, we're not safe. None of us."

He'd have told the old Georgie not to worry her pretty head.

With the new Georgie, he couldn't disagree.

Trouble was coming, and they were going to have to negotiate eventually. It was their job, evidently, to make sure there were no unanswered questions when eventually became now.

CHAPTER 15

NEARLY A WEEK later, Georgie's stomach was in open revolt. She wasn't surprised. Her digestive system was a delicate snowflake that demanded perfect alignment between her public and private selves. Unfortunately, Georgie didn't have the luxury of living her most authentic life just now. She was on a stake out.

Maybe she wasn't hunkered down in a cop car with binoculars and a camera but she was on a stake out nonetheless. She was both bait and trap, her beautiful dim-bulb exterior the come-on Julia Gates would eventually be unable to resist. The trick was keeping that exterior firmly in place while her nerves were wound up to DefCon 5 twenty-four hours a day. She'd been waiting a week now while Julia played coy, poking around in the shops, haunting the local library, turning up at the Wooden Spoon every day with Shay to share a slice of pie and sip coffee. They'd been everywhere, it seemed, except the gallery. At this point, Georgie's stomach was accepting nothing but applesauce and chicken broth. And coffee, because while her stomach was her unrelenting conscience, it also seemed to grasp the vital role caffeine played in a stake out.

Speaking of which. She rose from the gleaming white table that sat in the center of the Davis Gallery and went to the back room to refill her mug. It was part of a set her father had thrown when Georgie had been maybe 12. He'd formed this very mug from a shapeless lump of clay before her astonished eyes, then handed her a lump of clay of her own.

The resulting disaster had killed once and for all her mother's notion that every Davis child must surely have *some* kind of artistic ability. (Georgie decidedly did not.) But she'd been entranced by the sight of her dad's long, skilled fingers, coaxing dirt and water to transcend themselves and serve his vision. That tension, that quivering space between the humble and the exalted, the visceral and the cerebral, was what Georgie still looked for in the work she chose for the gallery.

She carried her full mug back to the front desk. The gallery was a ghost town so she fished her cell from her purse. She needed to check on the wedding dresses. Addy had insisted on off-the-rack dresses for bride and bridesmaids alike — no high fashion wedding for her! — and Georgie hadn't argued. She'd simply ordered the dresses online and had them shipped straight to a Latvian woman whose work with silk embroidery had caught Georgie's eye a few months ago. Georgie knew better than to rush an artist but those dresses needed to be in hand by Thanksgiving if the local seamstress was going to have time to do a proper fitting. Georgie would have preferred to do the fittings first and the embroidery second but the bride had a pie habit and parental issues. Better to take measurements as close to the actual wedding as possible.

The phone call took all of five minutes, leaving Georgie reassured that her dresses were on track, but without much to fill the hours before closing. She gazed out the gallery window at Lake Superior churning away under a leaden November sky. The days were brutally short this time of year but without the summer's tourist traffic — and without any move on Julia's part — they felt endless enough to Georgie.

She sighed and flipped open her laptop. She hadn't found an artist who'd really made her sit up and take notice for a year or more. She called up the homepage for a North Shore artists' cooperative she took seriously. Maybe she'd find somebody—

Her cell phone rang and she snatched at it. Addy's picture flashed onto the screen.

"Hey," she said while her stomach weathered the useless surge of adrenaline. Like Julia was just going to call and schedule an appointment? "What's up?"

"Your sheep," Addy said.

"Excuse me?"

"I said your sheep. What are you calling them, Rag and Bone?"

"The babies?" She rose, pressed a comforting hand to her stomach and wandered to the gallery's central wall where *Diego's Angel* hung. It was hard to even recognize the woman on the wall as her sister-in-law sometimes. She knew Addy so much better than Diego ever had. "What about them?"

"They're on a field trip."

"Where?"

"My front yard."

"Are you kidding me?"

"Unless I'm having an irritation-induced hallucination — which is entirely possible given that Mom and Dad are *still* not talking to each other but won't *stop* talking to me — I have two tiny sheep in my front yard, hopping back and forth over each other, falling down, and being generally adorable."

"Rag and Bone are in your yard?" She was having trouble internalizing it. "What on earth are they doing there?" And how did they get away from Tag? Peter wasn't much of a farmer but Georgie had the impression that Tag knew what he was about.

"Like I know how sheep brains work?"

"Have you called Peter?"

"He's not answering, and Mom won't let me call Dad while she's here in case he thinks it's secretly her who wants him to visit. That's why I'm calling you."

"What do you want me to do?"

"Take them back to the farm, Bo Peep. They're cute and my artists are in love, but none of us can catch them and I'm afraid they're going to gambol their way right over the rock wall."

Fear snaked into Georgie's abused stomach, icy and thin. That rock wall was all that separated Addy's yard from a cliff that plunged straight down into Lake Superior, and Rag and Bone were just babies. They didn't understand walls or cliffs, and Tag wasn't there to protect them. "What if I can't catch them?"

"You're their mommy. You were there when they hatched. Of course you can catch them. But you need to get up here soon."

"Right." She glanced at the computer, winced at the hours left before closing time. "I'm at the gallery right now, but maybe—"

Behind her the door jingled and a chilly blast of sullen air bit through Georgie's light sweater. Out of habit, she waited a beat before turning, giving her audience a moment to orient themselves to the scene she was about to present. *Eagerness is the opposite of confidence, dear,* Bianca said inside her head. She curved her lips into a cool smile and turned.

Julia Gates and Shay Zinc bustled into the gallery in a

mishmash of colorful scarves and pretty shopping bags. Georgie gave them a slow blink even as her stomach seized up in protest. She tipped her head toward the displays in a welcoming gesture and went back to her phone call, her hands numb and slippery.

"Maybe?" Addy prompted.

"Maybe I can make it up there in a bit." She set herself off on a deliberate stroll around the perimeter of the room, her high heels clicking slowly on the gleaming pine floor. "What does your evening look like?"

"My evening?" Addy's frown came through the phone as clearly as if she was standing in front of Georgie. "The lambs are here now, Georgie. You need to come take care of this."

"I will," she said airily, every cell of her body tuned to the pair of women who'd planted themselves in front of *Diego's Angel*. These weren't just any women, though, were they? They were both the artist's ex-lovers, both seriously messed-up women. The kind of messed up that slept with teenagers on one hand, and the kind of messed up that devoured talent and destroyed marriages on the other. "Of course I will."

"Good. How about right now?"

"I have customers." She made it sound like a mild inconvenience. "Why don't I get back to you in a bit?"

"Customers?" Addy said blankly. "Wait, do you mean customers like tourists, or customers like Julia and Shay?"

She sighed lavishly. "Okay, chat soon. Bye."

She hung up on Addy's sputtering. She strolled back to the desk, slid her phone face-down onto the shiny surface beside her laptop, and bent to tap a few keys. Not because she was interested in what was on the screen, of course, but because she couldn't seem interested in the women circling the central display. They were in front of *Broken* now. If *Diego's Angel* was a chick flick, *Broken* was *cinema verite*. It was Addy's broken heart and shattered innocence, smeared across the canvas with unflinching honesty and piercing regret.

A fierce cramp seized her stomach and Georgie closed her eyes. Inside her mind, the pain was a hot red light but she didn't shrink from it. No, she'd learned better. She sank gracefully — always gracefully — into the chair and leaned into the pain. And discovered that it *wasn't* pain, not precisely. She sifted through it, let it slide through her fingers like sand, let it sit on her tongue and dissolve. It was more like...hunger?

Yes. She was starved, her mind as hungry as her malnourished body. It was both a physical and emotional imperative for her to see Julia and Shay's faces while they absorbed Diego's last testament to his marriage. While they came face to face with the proof not only that Addy had been the only woman Diego had ever truly loved, but that he'd known it. That he'd known just as certainly that he'd destroyed her, or come viciously close, and in the process had finally destroyed himself.

He'd died not two weeks after finishing *Broken*, and Georgie didn't imagine that was any accident. She didn't think it was suicide either, not exactly, but Diego had been the perfect storm of impulse and arrogance. It would have been just like him to punish his body with an impossible quantity of illegal drugs and simply expect he'd be fine.

But he hadn't been fine. His body had finally failed him, as he'd failed his soul. As he'd failed his wife.

To be fair, Addison hadn't been fine either. Not for a

long, long time. But she'd had the courage to hang around. To risk her precious heart again. If she'd gotten the happy ever after Diego hadn't, it was because she'd *earned* it.

Rage rose up, burned the light in her head bloody and fresh. She was still so angry at Diego sometimes. He'd left so much shit behind, such a goddamn mess. A mess that included the two women now quietly circling the gallery like sharks, exchanging soft whispers and covert glances. Georgie's eyes were still shut but she could feel those glances bouncing off her sleek exterior. It was armor, she told her wonky stomach. The lies protected her, kept her whole and strong and unreadable while she did the work Diego had shirked. While she got his final mess cleaned up and put away where it would never again touch anybody she loved.

The cramp released and Georgie sighed with gratitude.

"Georgie?" A soft voice spoke a few feet in front of her. Georgie gave it the usual extra beat, then lifted her lashes slowly. "Georgie Davis?"

She kept her face professionally blank though she recognized Shay Zinc easily. She really did look like her daughter, though Georgie knew better than to say as much to Willa. Besides, when she broke it down, there really wasn't *that* much resemblance aside from those startling gray eyes and a couple acres of cartoon-princess hair. Throw in a general air of small-and-curvy, though, and nobody was going to mistake them for strangers. "Yes?"

She gave a nervous chuckle. "Oh, lord, you probably don't remember me. I'm Shay Zinc. You might've gone to school with my Willa?"

Georgie gave that a slow blink. "I knew Peter better."

"Of course." Shay kept her hands twisted together in

front of her coat. "I'd heard you were even engaged for a while?"

"I'd heard you were dead."

She blanched and those pale eyes darted past Georgie. To Julia, she assumed. "I guess you would've."

"You aren't, though," Georgie observed.

"No." Those hands wouldn't settle down. They plucked at her coat front, pulled at the buttons. "I'm not."

Georgie let that rest between them. A normal gallery clerk would've leapt to her feet by now with a flurry of *what can I do for you*s. Georgie just let the woman fidget. She considered closing her eyes. She could feel Julia lurking behind her, ostensibly taking in the Angel and *Broken*, moving just enough to keep the oxygen moving over her gills. Sharks couldn't stop swimming, right? That was a thing? Would she just keep pacing back there endlessly or would she eventually step up and help Shay spit it out, whatever it might be?

"I was wondering," Shay began, and Georgie wanted to slap her hands away from her coat. That button was loose and she was going to twist it right off. Instead, Georgie pulled in a slow breath, let an even slower one out. Shay chewed the inside corner of her mouth and color climbed into her cheeks. "I was wondering where the rest of Diego's work is."

"The rest?"

"Yes." Now that she'd said it, her lips firmed up and her shoulders straightened. Her eyes still flickered past Georgie's shoulder, though. "I'd heard you were showing new works. Old works, I mean." She shook her head. "Drawings from when Diego was young."

Georgie let her lips curve without humor. "He was

twenty-eight when he died, Mrs. Zinc. All his work is considered young."

"Of course. My goodness, I'm so sorry. How insensitive of me. You must miss him terribly."

Georgie let her smile drift toward polite boredom.

"I only meant—" Another glance, a fortifying breath. "I was referring to drawings Diego had done when he was a teenager. Pencil sketches? You showed them for Devil Days? I heard about it all the way out in California and I remembered that he used to draw right there at my kitchen table sometimes when he'd come home from school with Peter. And even decades later, I remembered what it felt like to be in the room when he drew. I could still *feel* it, Georgie. Right here." She put a fist to her heart. "Your brother was an astonishing talent. I'm so sorry for your loss."

"Thank you," Georgie murmured.

"I thought maybe I could see them while I was here. The sketches." Shay blinked those large clear eyes. "But I can't seem to find them."

"That's because we don't show them." She glanced at her laptop, tapped a few random keys, flicked through a few artists' portfolios without really seeing them. "*Diego After Dark* was a limited-run exhibit. We put those works back in storage. They're not scheduled for another showing until next summer."

"Oh." Shay's brow crumpled. "Oh, dear. That's disappointing. I'm in the gallery business myself these days. I'd really hoped—" A rustle behind Georgie's shoulder, the shark approaching. "Well, timing is everything. Maybe I'll have to come again next summer."

"Mmm," Georgie said, and let her eyes wander to her laptop screen. A fiber artist she'd never seen before smiled back at her.

"Anybody interesting?" Julia spoke from behind Georgie's shoulder. Satisfaction flowed thick and delicious into Georgie's tender stomach. Finally. The shark had come to her.

Georgie turned to the reporter. "Excuse me?"

"I couldn't help but notice." Julia nodded at Georgie's screen. "You do the gallery's acquisitions?"

"I do," Georgie allowed. She followed Julia's eyes to the laptop. "Are you in the business, too?"

"Goodness, no." Julia laughed lightly and Georgie had to admit the woman was aging nicely. Good bones, and she obviously moisturized religiously. "I'm an art lover, but I'm no professional. I'm terminally curious, though."

A common failing among the journalistic set, Georgie imagined.

"You must see hopeful artists every day," she went on, "dying to get their work hung next to Diego's. How do you decide?" She edged closer and pointed her chin at Georgie's screen. "Her, for example." She leaned in to read the bio. "Isla Wickersham. A fiber artist? I don't know what that even means."

Georgie doubted that. Julia was a senior reporter for the *New York Art Report.* She knew exactly what a fiber artist was.

"I don't really have set criteria," Georgie said idly. "I just know what I like."

"And you like this Wickersham woman's work?" Julia leaned closer yet to the screen. Georgie wondered what she thought she'd see. Her email program wasn't open, her phone was face-down on the desk and there weren't even any other open tabs. "What are those, placemats?"

"Oh I don't know." She nudged the laptop lid closed with one finger and crossed her legs. "I'm just poking around." She sat back, partly so she could study both Julia and Shay at once and partly because Julia had a heavy hand with the perfume. Her stomach was too tender for that nonsense. "And how about the two of you? Just poking around today as well, or are you looking for something in particular?" She gave Shay a close-lipped smile. "Apart from the pencil sketches you were interested in, I mean."

"Oh, did they not have them on display?" Julia asked Shay. "That's too bad. I know you wanted to see them." She flashed a bright smile Georgie's way. "Shay came all the way from California, you know."

"So she said." Georgie held that gaze and offered nothing.

"Surely you could be persuaded to make an exception, considering her…connection to your family."

"Connection?" Her stomach tensed, as if suddenly aware that it was surrounded by a thread-thin net of pain. That net was relaxed now but if it were suddenly drawn taut, Georgie would be awash in agony. For now there was only potential, and it was a risk Georgie was willing to take. She lifted a brow in silent question.

Julia's smile didn't falter. "I understand the Davis and the Zinc families share some rather delicate history."

"Then you misunderstand." She smoothed a lock of hair. "Peter Zinc and I were engaged for a time, yes. We decided we didn't suit before anything permanent or complicated could come of it. It was unfortunate but mutual, Ms.—" She stopped, blinked. "I'm sorry, we haven't been introduced."

Which was true enough. She *hadn't* ever been formally introduced to Julia Gates.

"Well, where are my manners?" Julia gave a light laugh and offered her hand. "I'm Julia Gates. I was very close to Diego back in the day, and both your mother and Addison are acquaintances of mine."

"Julia Gates," Georgie said slowly, as if tasting the words, placing the face. "You're a reporter."

"For the *New York Art Report*, yes." Julia beamed and Georgie finally took the offered hand for a brief shake. "I was in town last summer for the *Diego After Dark* showing, and was even able to meet your Mattisse. How strange that you and I wouldn't have met!"

"So strange." Georgie didn't smile back. People rarely expected her to. "So you've seen the sketches Mrs. Zinc is interested in?"

"Of course." Her blue eyes sharpened. "I found them extremely provoking."

"Diego was a provoking man."

"And a provoking boy, evidently." Julia lowered a hip onto the edge of Georgie's desk and perched there. "Always pushing limits and boundaries." She shook her head. "Not to mention social and ethical standards."

"If you know my mother then surely you know what she always says." Georgie gave Julia's butt planted presumptuously on her desk a pointed glance, then slid her gaze lazily back up to meet those avid eyes. "If it doesn't challenge the viewer, it's not art."

"And what of the subject?"

"What *of* the subject?"

"Must art challenge the subject, too?"

"I don't know what you mean."

"What if the subject is unwilling to be challenged, Georgie? What if the subject's been coerced into participating?" She leaned in, still smiling pleasantly, though those eyes were arctic blue. "That would make the art itself a kind of crime, wouldn't it?"

"I'm sorry, I'm not following you." She let her forehead wrinkle prettily while that finely-woven net cinched her stomach in a breath-taking grip of pain. "Are you suggesting there was something illegal about my brother's teenaged sketches?"

Julia patted Georgie's hand where it rested on her laptop case. "We're not suggesting anything." She rose. "Not yet. But I do hope you'll reconsider showing us those sketches."

"Why?" Georgie imagined her spine was melted butter, that her high-heeled ankle boot was a wave kissing a white-sand beach.

Julia circled the desk and linked her arm cozily through Shay's. "Just tell your mother what I said, dear. Word for word, if you can manage it." She gave Shay's arm a little squeeze. "Do you have the umbrella? It's going to get nasty out."

Georgie glanced doubtfully into the leaden sky. "It's been like this all day. Damp but no rain."

"It's always best to be prepared, though, isn't it?" Julia said brightly. "I'm sure your mother agrees with me." She produced a card out of nowhere and slid it onto the desk with one polished nail. "Just in case she ritually burned my last one."

"Excuse me?" Her tone was semi-bored bafflement but it cost her. Her stomach lunged fiercely and her sweater stuck sickly to her clammy spine.

"Come on, Shay." Julia nestled her shoulder companionably into the other woman's. "I hear a slice of Gerte's pie calling our name." Shay offered a weak smile and allowed Julia to lead her to the glass door. She stepped obediently onto the sidewalk while Julia turned and sent that blade-bright smile Georgie's way one last time. "Oh, and Georgie, do tell Addy I said hello."

CHAPTER 16

THIRTY MINUTES LATER, Georgie pulled her Rover into Addy's jam-packed side lot. She slipped off the velvet-and-suede Alexander McQueen ankle boots she'd paired with a black pencil skirt that morning, tossed them on the passenger seat and dug her trusty rain boots out of the footwell. She jogged through the lot and into the front yard.

A tearing wind greeted her with a solid slap to the face. It smelled like cold dirt and wet rocks, and she shivered inside her heavy wool peacoat. Julia hadn't been wrong. This wind was about to serve up some precipitation. It wasn't quite cold enough to snow just yet but it was close. They were well within the danger zone for a good shot of freezing rain. She had a hand-span of skin showing between the hem of her skirt and the top of her boots, and it was already numb.

She swiped at her streaming eyes and squinted into the wind.

She had to smile. Addy had formed a human fence of her aspiring artists, seating them at intervals along the rock wall separating the yard from the drop. They all had sketch pads on well-bundled knees while the sun sank toward the matte-pewter lake at their backs. One lamb — Bone, Georgie thought for no reason she could articulate — bounced in cheerful circles in the grass. The other lamb — Rag, obviously, by process of elimination — lay on the front porch, chewing contentedly on a leather glove. One of the artists, a man in his early seventies with a full head of white hair, lifted a hand to her. The other hand, Georgie couldn't help but notice, had a leather glove on it. She waved back.

"Sorry," she called over the rushing wind. "I think my sheep is eating your glove."

"No worries," he called back, grinning, and wiggled a sketch pad. "I'm getting some great stuff here."

"I'm so glad."

She jogged back to the Rover, reversed it to the edge of the yard and opened the rear hatch. She strode back into the yard and stomped up the front porch steps. Rag paused mid-chew and blinked up at her with big, innocent eyes. Georgie reached down and heartlessly snatched away the leather glove. Rag leapt to her tiny hooves with a forlorn *baaaaaaaaah*.

"Oh, cry me a river." Georgie shook the glove at Rag's adorable pink nose. "You're a thief. You're a thief and a truant and you can be as cute as you want. I'm still mad at you."

Rag lowered her woolly head and said, "Bah."

"Thank you." Georgie sniffed. "Now get in the truck." She marched down the steps to the open tailgate and threw the glove inside. Rag tumbled down the steps after her and boinged into the Rover. Georgie propped the flat of one hand to her forehead and shouted over the wind to the gloveless sketcher, "I'll bring your glove back if she doesn't digest it!"

The man waved her off, his pencil flying madly across the page.

Georgie turned her attention to Bone next. This was her second-born, and it was immediately clear that Bone was no people-pleaser. The little lamb stood facing Georgie with her front hooves splayed, her woolly bottom in the air, her tail twitching. Her entire tiny body vibrated with suppressed joy, and Georgie had the impression that if she made even the slightest move, Bone would shoot into the air like an overexcited poodle.

A smile tugged at her mouth but Georgie was no amateur. If she hadn't broken when Julia had gotten all snide and quasi-threatening at the gallery, she wasn't going to break now.

She deliberately turned her back on the lamb and slammed the tailgate of the Rover. Inside the truck, Rag immediately bounded to the back window and squashed her nose against it. A muffled *baaaaaaaaaaah?* emerged from the interior of the car. Georgie couldn't resist. She tapped a finger against the warm little nose through the glass. Rag sneezed and Georgie sighed. She had lamb mucus on her back window. Love was a miserable thing.

Behind her, Davis Place's front door opened. "What?" Addy said. "You're only taking the one?"

"Don't blow my cool." Georgie leaned against the back bumper like she had all day and her knees weren't numb. Like freezing rain wasn't going to come needling down out of the sky any moment. Like she didn't have lamb snot on her back window and another lamb with a suspicious mind still to corral. "Bone's not sure if she's being left out, or if her sister's being kidnapped."

"Ah." Addy wiped her hands on a dishtowel and slung it over her shoulder, amused. "While we wait for her to make up her mind, do you want to tell me what the heck was going on at the gallery when I called earlier?"

Georgie ignored Bone, who stood up straight, ears wary, nose twitching. The lamb took a tentative step toward the Rover and said, "Bah?"

"I do want to tell you, actually," Georgie said. "I really, really do. Unfortunately, it's complicated and I think it's

153

about to rain on me."

"Yeah." Addy sniffed at the cold, swirling air. "I have to agree." She lifted her voice to the artists. "Who needs a refill?"

Four or five hands went up along the rock wall and Addy leaned back into the house. "Mom! Can you bring the carafe out here?"

Georgie arched a brow and avoided eye contact with the lamb now nosing around the grass at her feet. "Your mom's here?"

"She was just about to head back to your place." Addy's smile was pure innocence. "It's about time to start dinner, isn't it?"

Jennifer Tate appeared in a pale blue sweater set and trim charcoal pants under a sensible wool coat, a coffee pot in her hand. "Hello, Georgie."

"Hey, Jennifer." Georgie nudged Bone away from her skirt hem with a gentle boot. "Making yourself handy, I see."

"I don't do well with time on my hands," she said briskly and marched off to do the refills. Georgie tried to remember what Addy had said her mother's company did. Something about implementing hospital-wide software programs? That would fit with the no-nonsense practicality sparking off that neat figure of hers. It was Addy's figure, actually, thirty-ish years down the road. There might be a little something of Addy around the cheekbones, too, but that was where the resemblance ended. Nobody with Addy's wide-open heart could ever end up with such tightly pursed lips, nor the brackets of dissatisfaction habit had carved on either side of them.

Georgie lifted a brow Addy's way.

Save me, Addy mouthed, her eyes comically wide. Bone

lifted her front hooves to Georgie's bumper and bleated a question toward the rear window. Inside the truck, Rag bleated back happily, slobbering her delight all over Georgie's interior. Georgie relented enough to glance down at the little lamb.

"You want in?"

Bone bounced back onto all fours, then sproinged into the air for a full 360.

"Impressive," Georgie allowed and opened the tailgate. Bone bounded in and Georgie slammed it shut again.

"Very impressive," Addy said. "Are you going to be able to drive with those two in there? They're adorable but not particularly well behaved. No offense, Mommy."

"None taken." She smiled. "You're right, though. It wouldn't be safe for me to drive with a truck full of unrestrained sheep."

"Good luck getting them into seat belts," Addy said, dimples winking. Jennifer mounted the porch steps and Addy took the coffee pot. "Thanks, Mom."

"You're welcome, darling." Jennifer didn't seem to know what to do with her hands now that the coffee pot was missing. Her eyes glanced off Addy's hair, her shoulders, her cheek, like these were all potential targets for landing a bit of motherly affection. In the end, she simply squared those shoulders and clasped her hands at her waist. "I'm glad I could be helpful."

No wonder she and Mike were at an impasse in their marriage.

Addy's dimples dimmed. "You don't need to be helpful, Mom."

Jennifer's shoulders didn't wilt. "Of course I do."

"No, really. You don't. All you need to do is be you. It's

enough."

Jennifer's mouth tightened. "Now you sound like your father."

"He's right."

"He's a child. Being me didn't provide health insurance or mortgage payments or private school tuition. Being useful did."

"I might not've needed—"

"You know what I need?" Georgie cut in brightly. Because she knew the next words out of Addy's mouth would've been *boarding school*, followed closely by *if you'd been less useful and more present.* And Georgie wasn't sure this was quite the time for that level of honesty. "A co-pilot!"

Addy and Jennifer turned to her with identical frowns.

"Because Addy's right. It's not safe to drive with a couple of demented lambs in my backseat. I need somebody who can keep them in line while I'm driving, and I'm sorry, Addy, but you're too nice. I need her." She pointed at Jennifer. "I need somebody who can do what must be done and won't be swayed by their adorable lamby noses."

Jennifer turned back to Addy. "I should be going anyway."

Addy sighed and wrapped her free hand around her mother's shoulders, drew her in for one of her signature hugs, the kind that smelled like sunshine and felt like home. "Thanks, Mom. I'll see you tomorrow."

Jennifer didn't speak, just closed her eyes and absorbed her daughter's love. Georgie looked away, her eyes suddenly stinging and damp.

"This wind," she muttered and inside her truck one of the lambs bleated knowingly. "Quiet, you. What do you know?

You're two weeks old. Plus it's raining."

And it was. Thin needles of icy rain had begun slicing down out of the sky. The artists jumped up, squawking like chickens. They pelted for the house.

"Okay," Georgie called above the clatter. "Time to go!"

Jennifer frowned. "You'll bring me back up here afterwards for my car?"

Georgie eyed the lowering sky, the thin slick of ice already sparkling from each individual blade of grass in Addy's yard. "Sure," she lied while her stomach gave its customary protest. "No problem."

Peter blamed the rooster.

"Fucking rooster," he muttered and kept his hand — his *hand*, for sweet lord's sake — inside Number Three.

Matty lay across the bellowing ewe's shoulders. Number Three was understandably put out by the situation but wasn't allowed to get up just yet. Not while she was still trying to deliver her own damn uterus. Matty jerked his hood up with one hand. Peter just let the rain (or ice or hail or what-the-fuck-ever) pelt down onto his bare head. He couldn't feel his ears anymore anyway and didn't imagine a hood was going to help much.

"I don't know much about farming," Matty panted, "but I'm pretty sure a rooster didn't get this sheep pregnant."

"Just keep the baby under your coat and see if you can get it to nurse."

Matty obligingly shifted to better shelter the tiny lamb snuggled up against Number Three's woolly belly. "It isn't moving much," he reported.

"Well find a nipple and get its mouth on there."

"Life on the farm is so much more interesting than I

thought it would be." Matty swiped a filthy hand down his equally filthy jeans and started patting around Number Three's belly. "It's all *nipple* this, *vagina* that—"

Number Three decided it was time to try getting up again, and Peter threw his own weight more securely over her hindquarters. "If you don't help me keep this ewe down, we're going to get up close and personal with her uterus, too."

"Right." Matty planted himself more securely across the sheep's shoulders. "I have a nipple."

"Great." Number Three's internal muscles clamped down around Peter's hand with crushing force and he spoke through his teeth. "Milk it a little, see if you can get some colostrum on your fingers."

Matty hesitated. "It feels a little personal."

"You don't have to tell me about personal. I have my hand in her *vagina* holding in her lady parts, for Christ's sake."

"Okay, okay." There was some furtive rustling, then Matty said, "Why do I feel like I'm jerking off a sheep?"

"Because you're a fourteen-year-old boy. All roads lead to jerking off eventually."

He huffed out a laugh. "Truth."

"You've got the skills. Work your magic and get this lamb something to eat."

"Right. Okay." The rustling grew more purposeful. "Ew. Climax achieved."

"You've got the milk flowing?"

"I've got something flowing." He shifted the baby around, and there was a weary bleating from Number Three. "God, it's so tiny. How do I get its mouth open?"

"Stick your thumb into the hinge of its jaw. It shouldn't

take much."

"Got it. Okay, I stuck the nipple in there. Take it away, little dude."

Peter could feel the kid's frown. "What?"

"It's not sucking."

"Then keep milking."

"God. Okay." The rustling resumed. "I should tell you, this is the weirdest thing I've ever done. And I once burned down a house for you."

"And a resort and a Dumpster, I know. I was there. Sorry about that, by the way. Desperate times and all that."

"Normally I would say fuck you—" He had said it, actually. At least once. Peter hadn't objected to either the content or the language. "—but I suddenly have a new insight into desperate times. Do you do this every day?"

"Only one other time so far." Number Three's internal muscles released and Peter sighed with relief. "Last time, your sister was the lucky Davis who wandered by and got dirty."

"Right. The twins. Thank God this is a singleton, huh?"

"Small mercies," Peter muttered. "But fuck you, rooster."

"This isn't the rooster's fault," Matty reminded him. "I'm pretty sure we can pin this on Number Twenty-one and his magical nut sack."

"But if Mike weren't off picking up a goddamn rooster, he'd be here right now, wouldn't he? He could call the vet to come stitch Number Three's vagina closed so she can't expel a vital internal organ, and you and I could go inside, take showers and never speak of this again. Oh, Jesus, here she goes again."

"Come on, Three," Matty crooned. He curled his body more securely around the baby lamb without allowing the ewe to struggle to her feet. "Knock it off with the contractions. You're done here. There are no more babies."

Number Three didn't care. She pushed for all she was worth, her wounded bleat ringing in the air. Peter's hand was summarily crushed, and he found himself breathing through the pain like he was the one in labor.

Matty's head jerked up. "Hey, is that Mike?"

"Thank you, Jesus," Peter said as Three's contraction dialed down. He lifted his head as well, and heard the glorious sound of an engine pulling into the barn yard. "Tag!" he bellowed. "Get Mike!"

He had no idea if normal sheepdogs were capable of following such instructions but Tag was no ordinary sheepdog. He was Tag, and he could probably drive the stick-shift into town, pick Mike out of a crowd and fetch him home before Peter could dial his cell phone number. Not that he could dial anybody at the moment, as his phone was dead as a doornail. Whatever the fuck a doornail was.

Also, Mike had the truck and Tag couldn't drive what wasn't on the farm.

Tag disappeared in a flurry of imperative barks and Peter finally let himself relax. Help was here. "Okay." He lowered his forehead to Three's woolly rump. "Okay."

Then he heard it — the distinctive *galumph* of Georgie's ugly rain boots pounding across his rain-slicked pasture.

"Peter? Matty? What the hell?" She skidded to a halt and dropped to her knees at Three's back. Peter winced. Shit, that skirt looked as expensive as the sweater she'd lost birthing Rag and Bone. (*Twenty-two and Twenty-three*, he reminded himself sternly. You didn't name food.) She gave Matty a lightning-speed pat down, then gave Peter the same treatment. Her hands were warm and competent and he could suddenly feel his ears.

"Christ's sake, Peter." She snatched his hood up to cover his head. "You're going to freeze to death. Where are the babies?"

"There was just the one this time." Matty lifted his coat to show Georgie the tiny ball of wool curled up to Three's heaving belly. "Hey, look! He figured out the nipple!"

"Aw." Georgie leaned in for a look and she smelled like snow and money. Or, fuck, maybe he was smelling actual snow. He blinked and his eyelashes crunched. Or ice. It was a goddamn ice storm. Great. "Peter, what are you doing back there?"

"He's holding the sheep's uterus in," Matty said cheerfully. "She won't stop pushing."

"God."

"I know, right? His phone's dead and I don't have the vet's number or internet this far from the house."

"Dr. Beauregard," Peter told her. "Hornby Harbor."

"Got it." Georgie leapt to her feet and jogged off toward the farm house, presumably to get internet access. She was about twenty yards away when she gave a shriek and gulumphed into a depression in the middle pasture.

"What?" Peter shouted, his heart thudding, his ears and fingers roaring back to painful life. "Georgie, what? Are you all right?" He turned to look but without getting off Three, all he could see were Matty's huge silver eyes. His mother's eyes, he couldn't help thinking every time he saw them. *Their* mother's eyes.

"She never yells," Matty whispered, shocked. "Georgie never yells, and she never runs. Can you hold Three? I want to go see if—"

She came galumphing back over the rise at a sprint, her

hair streaming behind her like a glorious flag. "It wasn't just the one this time!" She had her arms lashed around something small and lumpy, pressing it frantically to her chest, and dread pooled in Peter's stomach. "There was another one! I found another baby!"

CHAPTER 17

THE LAMB WAS so cold. God only knew how long it had been lying there in the freezing rain, too weak to follow its mother while labor drove her to her feet and across the pasture to deliver the twin. Georgie raced into the kitchen. She yanked open the potbellied wood stove in the corner and dragged a heavy chair around to face the heat. Behind her Jennifer said, "What should I do? What should I *do*?"

"Get me a towel." Georgie jerked her chin toward a dishtowel of questionable provenance hanging crookedly over the lip of the sink. Jennifer snatched it up and ran it over. Georgie lifted the lamb — it wasn't even shivering — while Jennifer spread the towel over what used to be Georgie's favorite skirt. Lamb snot was the least of her worries now. She laid the lamb on the towel, folded the edges over it and began rubbing, mindful of its tiny bones.

"God," she said. "It's like a fleece sack filled with sticks."

"Newborns are like that." Jennifer sidled from foot to foot, those hands worrying each other. "You can't imagine how fragile they are. And they just send you home with them!" Georgie glanced up and Jennifer's eyes were round with remembered indignation and terror. "Twenty-four hours after you have a baby, they just put her in your arms and send you home. Like you're supposed to automatically know how to keep her alive! Can you imagine?"

"I hadn't ever really thought about it, honestly," Georgie said. "But now that you mention it, no. It seems ridiculous."

"It is." Jennifer stalked over to the wood stacked behind the door, grabbed a few logs and fed them to the fire.

The kitchen door flapped open and Mike stepped in.

"Close the door, close the door!" Jennifer flew at her husband, yanked him out of the doorway and shoved the door shut. "You're letting the cold air in!"

"I saw Peter in the pasture," he said and came to crouch next to Georgie's knee. "Is it still alive?"

"Barely." Georgie's throat cinched down tight and she shook her head hard. She wasn't crying. Not now. There wasn't time. Her stomach sent a warning shot over the bow. *I'm busy*, she told it. *Fuck you.* One more sullen twinge, then nothing. She sighed and burrowed the flat of her hand between the lamb's spindly front legs, pressed it against the tiny sternum. "I can feel the heartbeat."

"Good," Mike said. "That's good." He rose. "The vet's on her way. I'm going to go unload the rooster. I'll let Peter know you guys are okay in here."

"Okay?" Jennifer's eyes narrowed. "We are *not* okay in here! We're doing deathwatch on a sheep that's barely an hour old! How are we supposed to be okay?"

Mike put a hand on her shoulder and squeezed. "Come with me."

"I don't need a walk, Michael."

"No, but that lamb needs some nutrition, and it needs to get warmed up from the inside out. Walk with me to the pasture and Peter will tell you how to make the milk substitute."

Jennifer's shoulders melted with relief. "There's a milk substitute?"

"Of course. The recipe is in one of these manuals." He nodded toward a shelf over Peter's cot. Georgie hadn't noticed it on her last visit but saw now that it held a row of neatly filed books. "Hell if I know which one, though. Lucky for us, Peter has a brain like you wouldn't believe. I'm pretty sure his memory is photographic. He'll be able to tell you exactly where to look. More likely, he'll just tell you the recipe."

"Thank God." Jennifer snatched up her coat and shoved her arms into the sleeves. "Let's go."

Then Georgie was alone with the tiny lamb, and even its nose was cold. Her throat ached miserably and a high-pitched whine filled her ears. It was, she recognized dully, her internal gears grinding. The pain and horror on the inside clawing to make themselves seen and felt on the outside.

"Oh, please," she whispered to that frail, flickering life cradled between her shaking hands. "Please hang in there. Please don't die on my lap." Tears filled her eyes and dropped onto the filthy towel. Instinct had her blinking them away (*Never let them see you cry,* her mother murmured), but nobody was around. Nobody was going to see her cry but this poor, doomed creature on her lap and it would be dead before it could tell anybody. Her hands went blurry again but this time she let them. She concentrated instead on massaging the little belly, rubbing the little back, dipping her fingers into the curls of two paper-thin ears. "Please don't leave. Not yet. There's so much to do! You haven't seen this place yet when it's sunny and warm, and I'm telling you, it's gorgeous. There's no place on earth like it. Just ask my brothers. Any of them, really, but mostly you should talk to Diego. Nobody loved Devil's Kettle like he did. Nobody saw it with his eyes, though God knows he tried to show us."

Her voice wobbled but the words wanted to be born and she was helpless to stop them. They spilled out of her,

165

tumbling headlong over one another like Rag and Bone on their illicit holiday.

"But you, you're a lamb, so paintings aren't your jam, I get it. You'd be interested in the grass, I imagine. Well if you hang in there, you can eat green grass all day with the sun warm on your wool, and Tag will keep you safe while you play with the other lambs." She gave a mighty sniff, trying to stem the flow but her mouth crumpled and she kept talking. Kept crying. "You have a sister, you know. Maybe a brother, I guess, but I'm calling sister. You haven't even met her yet but sisters are the best. They love you like nobody's business, and they kick your ass when you come off the rails. All you need to do is listen to your sister, and you'll be fine. I'm a sister myself, so I know what yours would tell you if she were here. She'd tell you to stay. She'd tell you to *stay*, goddamn it, because family doesn't give up. Family doesn't bail out. I know life gets hard, and I know it hurts. God, sometimes it hurts so much. Sometimes you only know you're alive because you can see yourself bleeding, but alive's better than dead any day. Because dead means you're done, even when you're not done. Even when you've got a daughter who needs you, or a sister who loves you, or a wife who'd forgive you. When you give up, you're just *done*, and nobody gets to be okay ever again. So I'm asking you to *please*—"

"Georgie."

She jerked but didn't look up, instinctively shielding her tear-ravaged face from view. Peter's hand came to her shoulder, cold but firm. Comforting, somehow. She opened the towel on her lap, showed him the lamb.

"It's still alive," she managed, her voice a phlegmy mess.

"Good." He nudged her chair a little closer to the fire.

"Let's get something warm into that belly."

Relief washed through her. "Do you think it'll eat?"

"Only one way to find out." He pulled a pot from a cupboard and put it on the stove, then bent to rummage around under the sink. "Keep it warm over there and I'll have dinner ready in five minutes."

"What's dinner?"

"A truly disgusting combination of this—" He held up a can that Georgie assumed was some form of baby formula for lambs. "—plus corn syrup, cod liver oil and eggs." He reached into his coat pocket and retrieved two. Sent her a wry smile. "Score one for Mike's chickens."

She tried to smile back. "Speaking of scoring, I hear Mike brought them a rooster?"

He shook his head. "Don't even ask how he talked me into it because I don't know." He measured out his ingredients, cracked in the eggs and whisked. "But, yes, I understand my chickens will be having sex shortly." He tested the temperature of his concoction on his wrist. "They may be having sex right now." He sent her a look over his shoulder. "You're welcome, while we're on the subject."

She lifted her head, too surprised to hide her puffy eyes. "Of sex?"

"Yep. Matty's been on the farm for less than a week, but after today, any gaps in his sex education have been completely and definitively filled in. He can also use the words *vagina, nipple* and *uterus* correctly, and in coherent sentences. When pressed, he can also milk a sheep."

She laughed, something she'd have said wasn't possible five minutes ago. "Well, thanks, then. Have you scarred him for life, do you think?"

"Not sure. If he does ever gather his courage to try his

hand at sex, though, at least we know he won't pass out during the birth of his first child." He sent her a look she had trouble deciphering. Pride? Admiration? "He was solid out there, Georgie. That situation was unpleasant, to say the least, but Matty didn't choke. He hung in there, and did what needed to be done. If you've ever worried about him—"

"He's fourteen," she said. "We worry about him all the time."

"But if you've worried because he looks so much like Diego," Peter said. "If you see that face, that talent, and you wonder if maybe Diego's on the inside, too? If maybe whatever was in Diego that made him so selfish and weak when it mattered most is in Matty, too?" He held her eyes steadily. "It isn't."

Her throat closed and tears flooded her eyes again, even as relief and gratitude flooded her heart. Because she *had* been worried about it. More than she'd obviously known, if a simple reassurance from a man who wasn't precisely trustworthy was all it took to open the floodgates. She dropped her head, let her hair hang forward and stared at the lamb in her lap until the world steadied around her. Peter, bless him, allowed it. He stayed at the stove, stirring silently.

"Okay," he said finally. "It's ready."

Georgie dragged the ragged edges of her composure together while Peter filled a baby bottle with the truly vile-smelling mixture, sealed it up and handed it over.

"What do I do?" she whispered. Peter eyed the lamb on Georgie's lap without a lot of hope. It was as limp as the dishrag she'd wrapped it in. He crouched beside her knee and slipped one hand under its head, the other between its front legs. Its fleece was dry, if a bit crunchy, but its eyes were shut and it appeared to be barely breathing. Only the flutter of its fragile heart against his palm assured him it was still with them.

"I'll open its mouth and you slide in the nipple. Let's see if it'll feed on its own."

"And if it doesn't?"

"Let's just see if it does."

He wiggled his thumb into the corner of the lamb's mouth and eased open its unresisting jaw. Georgie slipped the rubber nipple into the lamb's mouth. Peter massaged the miniature throat, encouraging it to swallow, but nothing happened. Georgie gathered the lamb to her chest, adjusted the bottle and crooned softly, rocking it like a fretful infant. Her hair shone pale gold in the flickering light of the open wood stove, and he could see the silvery tracks of her tears still staining that porcelain skin. Her eyes were puffy and her nose was running, and he'd never seen anything so beautiful in his life.

Something shifted inside his chest, something alarming and vital that shouldn't be moving. Something that, heretofore, had always remained so firmly anchored within his own soul that he hadn't been aware it *could* move. But it shifted today. The sight of Georgie grieving so desperately sent it on a long, dizzying sideways swoop. It lurched aside and made room for her. For this new Georgie who not only would cry over a farm animal, but *could*. The Georgie Peter had almost married wouldn't have known how. But this Georgie...this Georgie was extraordinary. Blazingly strong and terribly fragile, and so very exposed.

He lifted a fist to his chest, pressed it against the unfamiliar new arrangement there, and made himself step back. Because what he wanted was exactly the opposite. He wanted to wrap himself around those hunched shoulders. He wanted to press himself against that slender back, hook his chin into the snow-scented hollow under her jaw and comfort her. Offer her the heat and the yes she wasn't getting from the poor creature in her arms. To put himself between her and anything that hurt her.

And that, he recognized, was crazy. Not to want it — Peter was an old hand at wanting more than he deserved — but to offer it. He was the last person on the face of the planet Georgie would accept comfort from.

He glanced at her, murmuring soundlessly to the lamb in her arms who *still* wasn't feeding, damn it, and her grief was so thick in the air, he couldn't breathe. His heart staggered under the weight of it, and he turned back to the sink, shoved his hands deep into the sudsy water.

And wondered who would comfort him when this was all over and Georgie went back where she belonged.

Which was not, he knew, Redemption Farm with him.

CHAPTER 18

"Peter."

"Hmm?" He didn't turn. He didn't need to. The sight of her was burned on his brain. He saw her in his sleep.

"It's not swallowing." Her voice was thick, but steadier.

"I know."

"What's the next thing? You said there was a next thing."

"I'm getting it ready."

The kitchen door opened a crack and Mike, Jennifer and Matty slid in, careful not to let out the heat.

Mike went to his knees beside the patient. "How's it going in here?"

"Not so good," Georgie said. "It won't eat."

Matty dropped to his haunches on her other side. He stroked a knuckle down the sheep's back. "Poor little dude."

Jennifer marched over to Peter at the sink like she was reporting for duty. "The vet repositioned the uterus and stitched Number Three's vaginal opening shut," she announced. "Number Twenty-four is nursing. The vet gave her — it's a her, by the way — the vaccinations and popped in the ear tag."

"I put them both in the jug," Matty told him, still petting the lamb who would be Twenty-five if it lived. "I turned on the heating lamp over them and gave Three a bunch of hay. Twenty-four's a feeding machine, and Mama needs fuel, right?"

"Right," Peter said. "How's the rooster settling in?"

Jennifer's lips tightened. "You mean the rapist?"

"Excuse me?"

Mike rose. "His seduction technique could use a little work." He dusted his hands on his jeans. "I had planned to call him Romeo but he might be more of a Mr. Darcy — makes a rotten first impression but has leading man potential in there somewhere?"

Jennifer snorted. "He went after the flock like the Romans sacking Jerusalem. It was all feathers and screaming and destruction."

Mike's dimples flickered with his grimace. "It wasn't pretty," he admitted. "It's possible he was coming off a long dry spell, though. Maybe once he realizes it's a 24/7 all-you-can-eat buffet, he'll calm down."

"For your hens' sake, I hope that's true." She sniffed and shook back her wet hair. Shivered inside her coat which, while it looked warm, clearly wasn't waterproof. "It's miserable out there. I should get back up the hill before the roads get too bad." She glanced at her husband. "My car's still at Addy's, and Georgie was supposed to drive me back up to fetch it after we'd delivered Rag and Bone. She's obviously otherwise occupied. Do you mind—"

"You're not going anywhere," Mike told her sharply. "It's raining ice outside, and you heard the vet. She barely got up here in her four-by-four, and that was half an hour ago."

"I'm sure if I'm careful and go slowly—"

"—you'll end up planting your rental carefully and slowly in a ditch, if you don't just crash through a guard rail and *Thelma and Louise* yourself straight into Lake Superior."

She lifted her chin. "We're divorced. What do you care?"

"We're not divorced yet, and I care plenty. I was slipping

and sliding all the way here from town. You're not going anywhere tonight."

"I beg your pardon," she said coldly. "We're separated. So your opinion, while appreciated, hardly matters. Now if you'll excuse me, I'm going home."

"Christ's sake, Jennifer!" Georgie snapped, her voice thin and dangerously fragile. "Your husband just admitted he still cares about you! Yes, he hurt you. And yes, he scared you. But you can either keep punishing him for that, or you can save your marriage. But you can't do both, so pick a lane." She glared at the older woman over the lamb in her arms. "And do it now, because we have bigger problems than your poor hurt feelings."

Jennifer's customary self-assurance cut out like a blown circuit, and she fell awkwardly silent. Peter almost felt sorry for her. She'd likely never before encountered a problem that could withstand her signature blend of efficiency, logic and a stiff upper lip, but Mike wasn't going down so easily. No, Mike was going to have either proof of love — a terrifying demand for such a tightly controlled woman — or a divorce. How interesting that a person as bright as Jennifer didn't understand that, while Georgie, whose mental deficiencies were the stuff of local legend, could put her finger on the crux of the problem so precisely, even while hard in the grip of her own crisis. Tenderness bloomed bloody and dangerous inside Peter's chest. This new Georgie was a goddamn wonder.

"Do what you want," Mike said woodenly to his wife, then turned and walked out the kitchen door.

"Okay," Peter said into the ringing silence Mike had left in his wake, "everybody out. Including you, Jennifer. Mike's room is warm enough and, unlike everything else in this house, the water heater is a champ. Go take showers, get warm and dry, then report back here for dinner. Georgie and I have this."

Matty exited the kitchen without argument, and Jennifer drifted after him, a thoughtful frown replacing her usual pinched dissatisfaction. Georgie lifted troubled eyes to Peter's. "It's still not eating. The lamb."

"I know."

"What now?"

Peter held up a feeding tube and a funnel with a resigned sigh. "This."

Georgie studied them warily. "Where are we putting that?"

"Into its stomach, via its throat. I don't think it'll fight us."

"I don't think it can."

"Which is why we have to do this."

"I know." But she edged away from him, the lamb clutched protectively to her chest.

"You have to give it to me, Georgie."

Her arms tightened around the ragged bundle. "You know how to do this?"

"Sure." It was a dirty lie. He'd read about it. He knew in theory what to do but there was a very real possibility that, instead of threading the tubing into the lamb's stomach, he'd miss and end up in the lungs. A mistake like that would mean the difference between feeding the poor thing and drowning it. "Farmers do it all the time, Georgie. It's not rocket science. Hand him over."

Her eyes darted to the door. "Maybe we should get Mike."

Excellent idea. Peter had had it himself. "Mike's upstairs,

face to face with his wife for the first time in weeks."

"So?"

"So maybe they're talking, maybe they aren't, but do you really want to head off a potentially marriage-saving conversation so Mike can intubate a lamb?"

Her eyes narrowed. "I hate you for negotiating at a time like this."

His naked heart bled a little at that. Which was stupid, as her hatred of him was longstanding, well-deserved, and not limited to today's shitstorm. "I'm not negotiating."

"Yes, you are! Because of *course* I want Mike to do this. He's a flight nurse. Intubating people is his job! But now if I say yes, I look like a terrible person because I'm willing to sacrifice Addy's parents' marriage for a farm animal." She glared at him. "But it isn't that black and white. There's a life at stake here and I won't let you treat it like—"

"—like money?" he cut in, his tone deliberately even. "Like it's destined for the slaughter house in eight to twelve months, depending on how well it grows?"

She drew back as if he'd slapped her, and he supposed he had. Before tonight, he'd had no idea she was still grieving so actively for her father or her brother, not until he'd stepped into his own kitchen and heard her pleading with this damn lamb to live. To stay. To fight. She hadn't actually said *for me* but Peter had heard it loud and clear. Her father's death had been ruled accidental but there had been whispers. Diego's death, too, had carried that same unpleasant whiff of *maybe* underneath the official *accidental*. Which meant it was possible that either or both of the most painful events of her life had been deliberately inflicted on her by people who didn't care enough about her to fucking hang in there. It would've been devastating for anybody, but how much more so for a woman so intensely private about her feelings that most people assumed she didn't have any, let alone any that ran this impossibly deep?

It took everything he had not to throw himself at her feet and promise her that the lamb would live. That he would cheerfully beggar himself for its survival. But he had no idea if that lamb would live, just like he had no idea if her father or her brother had committed suicide. There was no way to know, and no use pretending otherwise. Giving your heart away was a fucking gamble, and when you didn't win, you paid up. End of story.

"This is a farm, Georgie." He said it as gently as possible. "Be reasonable."

"You think I'm being a diva." Hurt ghosted across her face, barely there before disappearing behind one slow blink. Before *she* disappeared behind that slow blink. Her withdrawal opened a bloody gash on something soft and defenseless deep inside but he gritted his teeth and soldiered on.

"I don't. But that lamb has, at best, a five percent chance of surviving the night, even with Mike's expert medical care. It'll be less on my watch, yeah. But I have a decade of business experience that says when you're operating in the under-five-percent range, the deal is generally done."

"So you're just giving up on it."

"I'm not. But Mike and Jennifer could be upstairs saving their marriage right now. I'm giving them their chance." He held up the feeding tube. "The lamb's chance is right here. Give him to me, Georgie."

In the end, Peter turned on the furnace. He could hear his bank balance whimpering but Mike's space heater had its limits and there was no way everybody was going to sleep in the kitchen. Fortunately, the boiler had fired up without protest, and ancient steam radiators were now cheerfully glugging and burbling throughout the house. Unfortunately, all that glugging and burbling wasn't exactly conducive to a good night's sleep. Neither was doing deathwatch on the silent lamb in a nest of blankets on the floor beside his cot.

He flopped onto his back and dropped one hand down to check on the lamb. By some miracle, they'd managed to avoid the lungs with the feeding tube, and by the time Mike had ventured back down the stairs, Twenty-five's belly had been warm and full. Mike and his stethoscope had pronounced the lungs clear and offered Peter a job. Peter had offered Mike a farm. But when Mike only smiled and gripped Georgie's shoulder with quiet sympathy, Peter had understood that Mike didn't have any more hope for the lamb than he did.

Peter patted around the nest of blankets on the floor, just as he already had three dozen times since midnight. Only this time, he knew. The lamb was still warm, still nestled snugly in those blankets, but the fragile flicker of its life was gone.

"Ah, hell." He sat up, the floor warm under his bare feet for once, and dragged a hand down his face. "Just…hell."

He scooped up the bundle, placed it on his lap and went through the motions with the stethoscope Mike had left him but it was a formality. The lamb was dead. Georgie was going to…

What? What would Georgie do? He was used to thinking of her as fragile, but she wasn't. Not at all. But he'd caught a glimpse of her heart earlier today, and finally understood why she'd guarded it so well. When she loved, she loved ferociously. Her loyalty was a force of nature.

Shame crawled up his esophagus like heartburn. She'd invited him into her family when she'd accepted his proposal all those months ago. Maybe it hadn't been a love match but he understood now that Georgie believed in family the way other people believed in God. She might never have loved him with romantic passion but if they'd gotten all the way through to *I do*, she'd have honored him and fought for him and protected him with everything she had for the rest of their life together. She'd have been his and he'd have been hers in ways the old Peter could never have imagined, let alone properly valued. The new Peter could imagine them very well but would never have them. Didn't deserve them.

He knew one thing, though. He couldn't deal with this lamb's body without letting her say goodbye. Not when so many of the people she'd loved had left her without word or warning. He stood, settled the little bundle on his sleeping bag and carefully covered its face with the blanket. Then he went to find Georgie.

CHAPTER 19

MATTY SAID, "GEORGIE."

Georgie continued to fake sleep. It was a skill she'd mastered so well that she now fake-napped in broad daylight and people bought it.

Matty's pointy elbow found her ribs. "Georgie."

"Ow." She kept her eyes closed. "What?"

"I know you aren't asleep."

"How could I be? You just punctured my lung with your elbow. But before that I was definitely asleep."

"Liar." He flopped over to face her on the creaky queen-sized bed they were sharing in one of Peter's spare rooms. He slapped the quilt flat between them. A blast of musty air and teenaged boy hit Georgie in the face. "Plus you're creeping me out over there."

She cracked an eye. "I beg your pardon?"

"Seriously. Like if you got body-snatched by aliens who didn't know how humans slept, they'd lie there just like you. Flat on your back, hands together on your stomach, all that Sleeping Beauty hair spread across your perfect pillow. You look like you should be in a coffin." He paused. "Now that I think about it, that's one weird-ass fairy tale, isn't it? Sleeping Beauty? I mean, she's totally lying there like a corpse. What kind of guy sees a dead girl and is like *I have got to get me some of that*?"

Georgie gave up and opened both eyes. Gazed at the sturdy beamed ceiling above her, pale and geometric in the moonlight. "Is there something you want to talk about,

Matty?"

"There are a lot of things I want to talk about."

"And I'm not going to sleep until we talk about them?"

He grinned. "And people say you're slow."

"People say what I want them to say."

"I know. I just enjoy the joke sometimes."

"It's a good one," she conceded. It was now, anyway. It had grown on her over the years, as the sting faded and the utility made itself more apparent. "Now what's so almighty important that it's getting between me and my eight nightly hours of corpse impersonation?"

"I've been stuck on this farm for a week now, Georgie."

"I know. I'm sorry."

"Don't be. I'm actually having a good time."

"Now who's the liar? It's miserable and cold, the sheep are dropping lambs all over the place, and when I showed up this afternoon, you were pinning a ewe to the ground in the middle of an ice storm so she wouldn't get up and deliver an internal organ." She wrinkled her nose. "And then there's Peter."

"And then there's Peter," Matty said cheerfully.

"You're awfully nonchalant about moving in with him. You do recall that ugly little incident in the spring when he turned you into an arsonist?"

"Sure. But do you recall that ugly little incident this afternoon when he stopped a sheep from delivering its own uterus with his bare hands?"

"I remember." She cut him a sideways glance. "You seem very comfortable with the word uterus."

"Life on the farm has been very educational."

"So I hear," she murmured. "You've been having a good time, have you?"

"Yeah, I have. It's beautiful here, Georgie." He stopped, shook his head impatiently. "No, not beautiful. That's such a stupid word. It doesn't even mean anything."

"Amen."

"This place is brutal." He said it with reverence, though. With a light in those silver eyes that reminded her of Diego when an idea had caught his subconscious and was smoldering there, trying to figure out what to be. "You should've seen the rooster go after those hens today. It was…disturbing. But afterwards, the hens just shook out their feathers and wandered off to the feeder like nothing even happened. Sex is just another bodily function here, like eating or peeing. So is birth. Some sheep are good at it, at delivering healthy babies, and taking care of them afterwards. But some sheep can't figure out how to stop pushing, and they squirt their insides out."

"Ew."

"Other sheep drop a lamb in the ditch like they're taking a dump and walk off. They just leave it there, and it's either strong enough to get up and follow along or it dies." He moved his shoulders, clearly not satisfied that he was articulating what was inside him. On the quilt between them his fingers curled around an invisible pencil and Georgie's stomach gave a bittersweet pang. Words were failing him. He wanted his sketch pad.

"Have you been drawing?" she asked quietly.

"Yeah," he returned just as quietly. "Don't tell Mom, though, okay? She'd only want to see and I'm not ready for a critique yet."

"What kind of sister do you take me for?"

He released his imaginary pencil and grinned at her in the moonlight. "The kind who loves me for my own precious

181

self and not what I can do for the family fortunes?"

"Thank you." She gave a haughty sniff. "Plus, the family fortunes have been restored." Partially, anyway, mostly due to Bianca's ability to calmly and relentlessly browbeat law enforcement into pursuing their feckless financial advisor all the way to Bimini. "Pressure's off."

"For now," he said and Georgie couldn't disagree. He couldn't hide this kind of talent from their mother forever. Probably not even for another month. "Peter doesn't know shit about farming, you know."

"I gathered."

"No, I mean he really doesn't know what the hell he's doing. Imagine you have an MBA from Yale. Imagine your closet is full of fancy suits. Imagine you own half of a town, and do enough business to support a whole staff of lawyers. Now imagine that you're suddenly broke and living in a drafty house all by yourself. Imagine that you're responsible for twenty-plus sheep that may or may not be pregnant and a dog that laughs at you."

"I do imagine it," she told him. "Whenever I'm having a crappy day, whenever I think fate is out to get me, I remember Peter living up here on this farm and it renews my faith in the universe."

"He doesn't have to be here, Georgie."

"Of course he does." She frowned. "Where else is he going to go?"

"He could abandon this place like Three abandoned her lamb today. He could just drop it in a ditch and let it be somebody else's problem. That's what bankruptcy laws are for, you know. Clean slate, fresh start. If anybody needs one, it's Peter. He should've declared bankruptcy three months ago and gotten the hell out of here but instead, he's downstairs, sleeping next to an orphaned lamb that probably won't live till morning. He didn't even check the book earlier, did he?"

"What book?"

"The book with the recipe for substitute lamb's milk. I'll bet he came in from the barn and just made the stuff from memory, didn't he? Because guess what he does every night?"

"What?"

"He reads those books on the shelf over his cot. He reads them and he memorizes them, so that when a farm he didn't even want goes haywire, he knows how to fix it. Mike and I never panic when things fall apart because Peter knows what to do." He paused, wonder in his voice. "He stopped Three from delivering her own uterus today with his *hand*, Georgie. He knew what to do."

"And you think that makes it all okay?" she asked slowly. She wasn't arguing against it, she just wanted to know how he was doing the math. Peter had tried to use Georgie, Matty and their family for his own desperate ends. He'd done no permanent damage but she didn't know if she could get past the way he'd held her most precious people so cheaply. The way he'd held *her* so cheaply.

"It doesn't work that way," Matty said.

"What doesn't?"

"Forgiveness."

"You think we should *forgive* him?"

"I thought we were working on it. He's family, remember?"

"He's on probation." But something scrambled inside her, something nervous and shaky. She'd toyed with the *idea* of bringing Peter back into the fold. She wasn't prepared for the reality of actually and sincerely forgiving him. What would that even look like, to have this new Peter in her life? In her family?

"I had a thought today." Matty rolled onto his back now, folded his hands across his stomach and spoke to the ceiling. "Shay Zinc is like Three."

"How so?"

"She's the kind of mother who can squeeze out a kid and not care. She delivered me and walked off without a second thought, didn't she? She sold me like I was a farm animal."

Georgie's heart ached. "Matty—"

"I got lucky."

"What?"

"Three's out in the barn right now stuffed into a four-by-four jug with a lamb she doesn't care about. And that lamb's getting fed and staying warm but it doesn't have a mother. Not really. But I did. Because of Mom. Because of you and Jax and Addy."

"Oh." Tears squeezed her throat.

"You guys found me, just like you found that lamb in the ditch today, Georgie. You found me and brought me inside. You kept me warm and filled my belly. But more importantly, you gave me a family. That lamb out in the barn is full and warm, but it doesn't have a family because Three doesn't care. Maybe she can't. Who knows? All I know is that I'd rather be the lamb down in the kitchen right now than the one in the jug, because the lamb in the kitchen has people who care about it. Even if it dies — which, honestly, Georgie, it probably will — I'd rather be that lamb than the one in the barn whose mother doesn't want it."

Her throat closed completely. She didn't have words, let alone breath to speak them. Her heart was too full of love for him.

"I got lucky, but Peter didn't. He got a shitty break."

"What do you mean?"

"He got stuck with a Three. Shay Zinc probably tolerated him but she never wanted him. Never loved him. No wonder he's so messed up."

"By that logic, Willa ought to be at least that messed up, if not more. But she never tried to marry my money or burn down Addy's house."

"Willa had the woods. What did Peter have?"

Something creaked in the hallway while Georgie was still trying to decide what to say to that. How to feel about it. It wasn't a particularly welcome paradigm shift. Peter was the villain in her story, and she was comfortable with that. She wasn't comfortable recasting him as a lost lamb of a boy, doomed to love a broken mother.

Matty flopped immediately onto his belly and feigned sleep. "You're asleep, Georgie," he hissed. "When farmers start poking around at two in the morning to see who's awake, trust me, you don't want to raise your hand."

The creaking drew closer, became footsteps. Matty did a very credible imitation of an unconscious teenager, she realized with a twinge of pride. She wondered how many times he'd pulled this one over on Peter in the last week. Then Peter himself was in the doorway, his smooth head shining softly in the moonlight, his bones sharp and clean.

"Georgie," he whispered. "I need you."

Peter peered into the darkness of Georgie's room. Matty lay in the bed beside her like a long, skinny log, and Georgie tossed off the blankets. Moonlight limned her shoulders and Peter withdrew hastily into the hallway before he saw any more. She joined him moments later in a tank top and a slightly-too-short pair of sweats she must've borrowed from Matty and drew the door shut behind her. It left them in total darkness.

"It's the lamb, isn't it?" she asked.

"Yeah. I'm sorry, Georgie. It died."

She released a long, slow breath. He reached for her without thinking and, despite the utter blackness of an interior hallway after midnight, his hands knew exactly where to find her. Her skin was chilly against his palms, and he drew her into his chest. She allowed it, her shoulders curling inward, her arms folded between them like fragile wings, her cheek coming to rest on his shoulder. She didn't cry but he felt her sorrow anyway.

"I'm so damn sorry, Georgie."

"It's all right." She lifted her head and stepped away. "What do you need me for?"

"I just wanted to tell you before I dealt with the body. In case you wanted to, I don't know, say goodbye."

She said nothing, and it suddenly occurred to Peter that he'd pulled a woman from her warm bed to see a dead farm animal.

"Have you slept?" she asked.

"What?"

"Have you slept?"

He scrubbed a hand over his scalp and dragged it down his face. "Do you mean tonight, or in general?"

She took his hand. "Show it to me."

"Yeah, okay."

CHAPTER 20

PETER LED GEORGIE into the kitchen. The air was stiflingly hot with both the wood stove and the boiler going, and it smelled of wool and the grilled cheeses Mike had made everybody for dinner.

"Where is it?" she asked.

"There." Peter nodded to the lamb he'd left bundled on his cot. "You don't have to look at it if you don't want to."

"Why am I here, then?"

He shrugged. "You found it, you fed it." You loved it. You cried over it. "You deserve a goodbye."

"All right."

She drifted across the room and sank onto his sleeping bag with that curious boneless grace of hers. She drew back the edge of the towel and gazed down at the dead lamb. Peter came to stand next to her. It wasn't pretty. The lamb's eyes were closed to slits, and its tongue protruded darkly from between slack lips.

"Poor thing," she murmured but Peter frowned down at her. She'd wept over this lamb with a keening grief only a few hours earlier. She'd wanted this lamb to live more than she'd wanted Addy's parents to work their shit out, and she loved Addy ferociously. And now that the lamb had lost its fight — if it had ever even waged one — all she had to say was *poor thing*?

He studied her uneasily. She was perched on the edge of his cot, leaning on one hand to look down at the lamb, her head tipped lazily to one side. The firelight from the open stove door painted roses onto her perfect cheekbones, and he realized it wasn't an accident. The image she presented, the gorgeous picture she made? It was calculated. Pre-fab. His kitchen was a stage, and Georgie had hit her mark like a pro.

"Don't do that," he said.

She blinked up at him. "Do what?"

"That." He waved a hand at her. "You. Her."

"Her?" Her eyebrows rose.

"You're not even just sitting on my bed." A spark of anger flared inside him. "You're *posing*. The cameras are off, though, Georgie. It's just you and me here, and that poor dead creature you cried over earlier today, so you can knock it off. I don't need the Georgie Davis show."

"I beg your pardon?" She widened innocent eyes, and he *hated* it. She'd taken herself from him, and though she wasn't his to have, he howled at the loss of her.

"Can you just be yourself right now? Can you be real?"

She held out her arms, studied them as if verifying the fact of her reality. Lifted those eyes back to his, and smiled with skeptical indulgence. "You really haven't slept, have you?"

Peter suddenly understood what women the world over felt when men dismissed their rage as hormonally-induced instability. But all he said was, "No. I haven't. I haven't slept much since I took this place over, and I haven't slept at all tonight. So maybe you're right. Maybe I'm not making sense." He folded his arms and glared down at her. "Or maybe I'm just too tired to play this stupid game anymore."

"I'm sitting next to a dead lamb, Peter. If this is your idea of a game—"

"It's not my idea. It's yours."

"My only idea is getting back to bed." She rose from the

cot and strolled toward the door with her usual lazy aplomb. Given her borrowed sweatpants and her bare toes, it was an impressive feat. "Thanks for letting me know about the lamb, though. And Peter?" She paused to toss him a sympathetic glance. "Get some sleep, okay?"

Rage smoked inside him because he knew she wasn't this cold. Beneath that brittle, beautiful mask, she was hiding a grief deep enough swim in, to drown in. Grief she hadn't wanted him to see, but he had. He'd seen it and he'd seen *her*. The real her. The true her. It was possible he'd even kissed that woman, right here in this kitchen, barely a week ago. After that, this lazy, shallow Georgie felt like junk food, and he was a starving man. It wouldn't be enough. Not tonight, maybe not ever.

"Do you want to know what comes next?" he asked.

She froze. "What do you mean?"

"Don't you want to know what I have to do next? With the body?"

"I don't—" She smoothed a hand down hair that was already as shiny as the ice-slicked windows. "I don't know. Bury it?"

"This is Minnesota, Georgie. The ground is frozen solid half the year. Plus we're sitting right on top of the Canadian Shield, geologically speaking. It takes a backhoe and a jackhammer to dig a grave up here, even in the summer. But this is a farm. Things die."

Her throat worked in the flickering light, the first small fracture in that god-awful composure. She didn't speak, but she didn't turn away either.

He pressed on mercilessly. "Incineration facilities are outrageously expensive, and the closest one's down in Duluth anyway. A five-hour round trip isn't practical for the busy farmer."

"Practical." She blinked those large empty eyes. "You have to be practical."

"Poor people do."

"Rich people do, too," she told him. "But about different things."

"Is that so." He hadn't considered that before, certainly hadn't thought of it when he'd been young and poor and badly dressed and so ashamed of his parents' high-volume dysfunction he could barely breathe. Back then, he couldn't conceive of any problem money couldn't solve, especially for a golden girl like Georgie Davis. *Pregnant at fourteen? Mommy will just take you on a trip to Europe when you start to show. She'll pretend the baby is hers, and you can start ninth grade like nothing ever happened.*

Except it hadn't exactly happened that way, had it? Instead, it had been Peter's mother who'd delivered the baby she'd then sold to Bianca to raise. Georgie had come home with a new baby brother and a barely suppressed scandal revolving around her virtue, or lack thereof. And she'd stared it all down with the same cool serenity she was now using to stare Peter down. The same cool serenity she'd shown the paparazzi at Diego's funeral.

But Georgie was more familiar with grief than anybody in this damn town knew, aside from Peter. And Bianca, who'd handed her fourteen-year-old daughter a burden that required more strength of will than most adults could claim, and trusted her to carry it.

And Georgie had. To protect her brother, she'd carried it. And Peter, for reasons he didn't quite understand, wanted her to put it down.

Her lips curved without humor. "Being practical is what I

do best."

"You and me both," he assured her. "Take a walk with me."

"To dispose of a body? How romantic."

"We're practical people. We'll multitask."

She glanced at the glazed window. "It's raining ice out there."

"It's nearly done. Besides, the lamb doesn't care about the cold. It doesn't care about anything, if it ever did. It's gone." He lifted heartless shoulders. "Cold—" Pain. Agony. *Grief.* "—is only a problem for the living."

Which she knew better than most. It occurred to him suddenly that he was asking a lot of her. Maybe too much.

"Yeah, thanks," she said. "I think I'll pass."

He studied her closely. She was right. He had no right to ask her for a walk. He certainly had no right to howl with missing her when she dropped the curtain and retreated into that empty beauty she wore so well. He might ache with wanting this brave, wounded woman, but that didn't mean he could have her.

"Okay. I'm sorry I woke you. Go back to bed. I'll take care of it." He went to the pegs behind the door and retrieved his oiled canvas jacket.

"How?"

He shot his arms into the sleeves and ran up the zipper. "How what?"

"How will you take care of it?"

"The lamb?" He pulled a wool cap from his pocket and snugged it onto his bald head. The stubble caught like velcro and he made a mental note to shave it in the morning when he showered.

"Yes. What does that mean, take care of it?"

"This is a farm, Georgie. Do you really want to know?"

"No." She scowled and marched over to the pegs herself, snatched up Mike's heavy raincoat and shoved her arms into it. It was about twice as wide as necessary but the sleeves weren't bad. She was a tall drink of water, his Georgie, and impossibly strong. A ridiculous pride glowed inside him, and he reached over and ran her zipper up himself. Flipped the collar up to protect that long, vulnerable neck. She found Mike's fleece beanie in a pocket and yanked it down over her ears. She glared up at him. It put dissatisfied brackets on either side of her mouth, and a line between her brows that matched her mother's. "But I'll be damned if I'll let you throw my lamb into the Kettle. Now where are my boots?"

It never had gotten cold enough to snow. The world crunched under Georgie's boots, though, and tree limbs that had been dull and naked just hours ago danced delightedly inside their sparkling new coats of ice. Peter walked ahead of her on a single-file path through the woods. They'd crossed into the state forest adjoining the farm without comment some minutes ago. Peter's breath hung in crystalline puffs in the air, and the moonlight painted his sturdy canvas jacket a silvery gray. She couldn't see the lamb bundled in his arms but the set of his shoulders said he'd hunched over it. The rain had stopped but he was protecting it from whatever was still sliding off the branches overhead.

"I thought you said the lamb didn't care about the weather," she said.

"It doesn't." He kept walking, that long measured stride of his eating up the yards.

"So why are you hunched over it like you're worried it's going to get wet?" She picked up the pace, squished herself onto the path beside him, though it really wasn't wide enough. This felt like an important question; she wanted to see his face when he answered. "It's *dead*, Peter." Her stomach seized up mercilessly at that off-hand acknowledgement of such a terrible truth but she barreled on. "We're about to pitch it into the Kettle. Keeping it warm and dry on the way there seems a little pointless."

"First of all, we're not pitching it into the Kettle."

"Then why are we walking there?" Georgie had grown up in these woods. She knew the Devil's Kettle Trail like her own living room.

"We're multitasking, remember? As for the lamb, I already told you. Rain and cold are only problems for the living."

"I know. So do my toes. But that lamb is dead." Her stomach sent a vicious wave of pain slopping over the edges of her ability to contain it. God. She'd wanted so desperately for that lamb to live. To *want* to live. But it hadn't. Or maybe it had simply packed a lifetime of suffering into its brief few hours on earth and letting its light flicker out had been a mercy. Georgie's heart didn't know, and it didn't care. It just hurt, but she didn't allow that hurt to swim up to her face. She let it migrate to her stomach instead, which magnified the pain but at least Peter couldn't see it there. She'd shown him enough of herself already, too much probably. And now that Matty had forced this new version of Peter into her head, showing him any more would leave her all but naked. And she didn't want to be naked with Peter.

Her stomach found another level of pain and lunged for it.

Okay, so maybe she *did* want to be naked with Peter. *Fine*. Naked with Peter — this new Peter — sounded kind of amazing, actually. A wicked heat pulsed up from her lower belly, rolled slowly out from her center in slo-mo shockwaves, bringing welcome relief to her frozen toes and a disconcerting tingle to her bra-less nipples.

Peter said, "Ah, but we aren't, are we?"

She folded her arms more tightly across her chest and wrenched her focus back to the conversation at hand. "We aren't what?"

"Dead." He smoothed a hand over the bundle in his arms, and her stomach gave another vicious twist. "This little guy is but we aren't. I'm not. Keeping him warm and dry is for me, not him. Showing respect isn't the same thing as showing weakness, Georgie. Same as breaking shit doesn't show your strength. I learned that one the hard way, and at your expense." He caught her gaze, and his eyes held an acknowledgement of everything that had gone before. Of his betrayal, his disregard, and the harm it had done her and her family. It also held a universe of regret, silent and vast. It was the most powerful apology Georgie had ever received, and he'd packed it into a wordless, unguarded glance. It knocked the breath from her lungs. Those eyes of his were so goddamn naked. They shamed her. She'd been so worried about him seeing her cry, but here was Peter's world of sorrow, revealed without a flinch. He looked back to the path at their feet. "So, yeah, maybe the lamb doesn't care about the wet but my obligation isn't just to him. It's to my own soul, too. And I've done enough damage there, don't you think?"

They walked in silence under the moonlight, the minutes stretching and twisting in the peculiar way that post-midnight minutes sometimes did. The path climbed and twisted as well, and Georgie let it hypnotize her. There was nothing now but the rhythm of her boots and the burn of her muscles and the cold air moving through her lungs. Finally they came to a crest where the trees thinned out and water murmured below.

"Look," he said and she did. They were standing at the edge of a ravine. The earth dropped sharply away a few yards ahead of their boots, angled steeply down to the Devil River. It was a silver ribbon in the moonlight, lying crumpled among the rocks and fallen trees at the bottom of the ravine. It meandered south, all the way to the cliff at the lake's edge and the gaping black mouth of the Kettle, waiting to swallow the river whole. It was a sight she'd grown up with. Davis Place — which had been nothing but Granny Nan's place back then — had front row seats to the spectacle, including the part where the river blasted triumphantly out of the cliff face sheering down to Lake Superior.

"Addy's artists are going to be thrilled," she said. "Tourists love it when the waterfall freezes."

"No," Peter said, and aimed Georgie's face to the north with a single warm finger under her chin. "Look that way."

Charred wasteland. Georgie's throat seized up. "The forest fire," she murmured. "This is where it turned?"

"Yeah," Peter said. "This is where Willa and Eli got burned over, actually."

She frowned up at him. "You came to see it?"

He shrugged. "Willa's the only family I have."

She didn't point out that both of his parents were still alive. The truth didn't always line up so neatly with the facts, and she was hardly one to point fingers on that score. Matty was technically her nephew, after all, but she'd be damned if she'd ever call him anything but brother.

195

She studied the ranks of blackened trees stretching away into the distance like a skeleton army in retreat. It had been August when a lightning strike had sent fire roaring down from the northeast. It had leapt the Devil River and climbed partway up the ravine upon which they were currently standing. Then something had happened. The wind had changed, the universe had intervened, who knew? But the fire had been slapped abruptly north, leaving Georgie's side of the river — along with Davis Place, Hill Top House, Peter's farm and the town itself — untouched.

"They deployed their fire shelter right there." He pointed to an elbow in the river below where some silty muck had collected to form a sort of sandbar. "See those rocks?"

A collection of large crescent-shaped rocks lay maybe five or ten yards uphill from the river bend, pale in the moonlight. "The ones that look like a bunch of giant orange sections?"

"Yeah. Eli said it was one big boulder when they deployed their fire shelter. After the burn over, it looked like that."

"Damn."

"I know, right? Fire hot enough to break rocks." He shook his head. "But look there." He pointed to the far side of the ravine this time, to the naked lip of ground spiked with blackened tree trunks.

"What?"

"Grass."

She squinted. Sure enough, random tufts of grass sprouted up here and there, like the forest had gotten hair plugs in the off season. But Peter gazed at it like it was a miracle.

He said, "When Eli brought me here in August, this place

was nothing but ash and bedrock and death. But look at that grass, Georgie. Look at that goddamn grass growing."

"Why did you bring me here?" she asked, her lungs tight, her stomach light and wary.

"I wanted you to see the grass." He adjusted the lamb in his arms. "There's always death but there's always life, too. Before we put this little one to bed, I needed you to know that. To see that."

She slipped her cold hand into the crook of his elbow, tipped her head onto his shoulder and stared across the ravine at the lumpy grass sprouting up between blackened boulders and the dead trees. She kept his arm as Peter turned and led her back down the path and onto his property once again. She stood silently by when he placed the lamb still wrapped in dishtowels into a half-buried metal container that evidently served as a graveyard for rocky farms this far north. He closed the lid and latched it, and Georgie was glad. Nothing would bother it here. No scavengers would prey on it. Nothing would make a meal of its fragile bones or a nest from its newborn wool. It would be a dust-to-dust deal, without any messy food chain business in between, and Georgie's stomach could handle that.

"Do you want to say anything?" Peter asked, his eyes serious and dark.

"Like a prayer, you mean?"

"Anything."

He meant it. Those eyes of his were fearlessly naked, and in that moment she knew she could pray out loud in front of him, should she have any desire to. Any ability to. Any faith that such a prayer would even be heard, let alone answered.

"No," she said. He'd said everything that needed saying while they'd stood over the Devil River and marveled at the

November grass slowly erasing the ashes.

He laid a hand on the lid of the vessel, as if in benediction, then turned to her.

"Let's go home."

He held out his hand and she took it.

CHAPTER 21

THE NEXT MORNING, Peter slid — quite literally — down the hill into town for groceries. There had never been any fruits or vegetables in the house (they were men, after all) but last night's grilled cheese fest had put a nail in it as far as breakfast was concerned. Peter would have been perfectly happy feeding everybody nothing but scrambled eggs (they were men, after all, and owned chickens) but then he'd discovered they were also out of coffee.

No human should start the day without coffee.

So he'd fired up the farm truck shortly after dawn and trundled carefully into town, grinning the whole stupid way.

Because Georgie Davis had held his hand last night.

He'd reached for her hand before he could think better of it. But she'd taken it without hesitation, and Peter was no fool. He'd twined his fingers through hers, tucked their hands together into his jacket pocket and walked the girl home. And for the first time since he'd come back to Devil's Kettle — maybe for the first time in his life — he'd felt like he was actually walking *home*.

They hadn't spoken, not even after they'd gone inside. They'd hung up their coats and she'd reached for him, slid one hand around the back of his upper arm. He'd been immediately paralyzed with breathless anticipation but she'd only leaned in and kissed his cheek, then disappeared like a dream. He didn't know how long he'd stood there, pressing that kiss to his skin with dazed fingers, but eventually he'd climbed into bed and slept for the first time in days. Weeks.

Maybe months. He'd woken up with the dawn, filled with something effervescent and compelling and so foreign that he was still trying to put a word on it as he negotiated the slippery road into town.

Was he...happy?

No, not happy. Happy was too small, too simple.

Hopeful?

Mmm, too much, but closer.

Optimistic?

Yeah, maybe that one.

That stupid grin widened, threatening to split his face in two. Because for the first time in recent memory, Peter was optimistic about the future. Oh, he didn't imagine Georgie was going to hop into his bed any minute. Or at all. (Well, he probably *would* imagine that, and enjoy it. He just wasn't going to make a goal of it.) No, it was more that he could finally see a path forward. He could finally see how he might get past what had gone before. His sins would always be there, but this morning, a narrow gleam of possibility shone where yesterday there had been nothing but darkness and endless regret. This morning he could see forgiveness glimmering on the horizon, and the sweet relief of it made him realize how very lonely banishment had been.

This was as surprising as the possibility of forgiveness, honestly. Peter had never been a people person. He'd been good at the social stuff, of course. When you had nothing but big dreams and empty pockets you learned to sling the charm, but it always drained him. Recharging meant some time alone with his beloved spreadsheets, making the numbers line up and dance to his tune.

So when he'd found himself with nothing but a sheep farm and the cash reserves (barely) to run it, he hadn't flinched. Had he known about Twenty-one's iffy vasectomy, he might've hesitated but he'd been blissfully unaware of that looming disaster. He'd moved to the farm embarrassed about his diminished prospects but not worried about being alone. He *liked* being alone. Or so he'd thought.

But alone was one thing when you'd chosen it. It was something else entirely when you'd been such a dick that nobody wanted your company. And when you knew they were right to hate you, and topped it with the dawning awareness each day of what exactly you'd thrown away? He'd been living in hell, even if it had taken him months to realize it.

But this morning, this glorious, frozen morning, there was a breath of hope. Peter wouldn't ever be the king of Devil's Kettle but that was an old dream, and he didn't want it anymore. Today he had a new dream. The details were blurry yet, but he had the broad strokes. Mostly, he wouldn't be at war with Georgie anymore. He wouldn't be at war with anybody. He could retrieve his lambs from Davis Place next time they wandered off and Addy would probably smile at him. Smile for real, instead of the polite shit she'd been handing him since his and Georgie's engagement had blown up. He could swing into town for a slice of pie at the Wooden Spoon, and Gerte wouldn't even bother trying to rope him into her eternal feud with Bianca Davis because he'd be solid with the Davises and everybody would know it.

And at the end of the day, if it was pretty, he could ask Georgie if she'd like to take a walk, and she might say yes. She might hold his hand. It wouldn't have been enough for the guy he'd been a few months ago, but that guy hadn't known how to value anything but money. Georgie's friendship would be more than enough for the man he was now. It would be a gift. It would be the key that unlocked the rest of his life. If she forgave him, he'd be able to breathe again. Asking for anything more would be criminally greedy, and Peter wouldn't dare. He would want her for the rest of his life but that was his cross to bear and it could be a hell of a lot worse.

He suddenly realized he'd been sitting in the grocery store parking lot for at least ten minutes, grinning foolishly at the darkened windows and the CLOSED sign hanging on the door.

He checked his phone. It wasn't even eight a.m. yet. He laughed at himself. Damn, he really was becoming a farmer, wasn't he? He'd fed the chickens and let the sheep into the pasture before he'd taken off, too.

Plan B, then.

He pulled back onto Main Street. Nothing was open at this hour but the Sugar Rush and the Wooden Spoon. Had it been just men back at the farm, he'd have snagged a dozen doughnuts and a gallon of coffee from the Sugar Rush and called it a day. But he had women on hand this morning, and experience told him they'd be more apt to accept sugar for breakfast in muffin format.

He stepped into the Wooden Spoon. The scent of warm butter and blessed coffee hit him full in the face and he inhaled greedily. It was a good crowd for this early, but nobody paid him any mind as he stepped up to the retro-chrome bakery counter and bent to inspect the offerings. He would never understand how *muffin top* had become an insult, not with these beauties nestled together like a lushly curved harem. Fat blueberries made purple halos in dough so tangily yellow it had to be lemon. His mouth watered in anticipation and he mentally ordered half a dozen of those.

202

The morning glory muffins all but winked a come-on at him, their sugar-spangled tops ribboned with carrot strips and chunky with walnuts. He'd get the other six of those, he decided, because vegetables. Women liked vegetables, right? And he could clearly see carrots in those muffins, so they were obviously healthy.

"Peter Zinc! I haven't seen you in an age. What can I do for you?"

He straightened and found Gerte's daughter Lainey smiling over the counter at him. Her straight blond hair was pulled back from a fine-boned face and pale blue eyes that warmed genuinely with the smile. Proof, he thought giddily, that the universe had gotten the memo. His banishment was all but over. He smiled back at her, delighted with her, with the day, with life.

"Hey, Lainey. I need a dozen muffins and about a gallon of coffee."

"Decaf or regular?"

"Is that a trick question?"

She laughed. "Regular it is. Hang on a minute and I'll brew you a fresh pot. Jax's guys are drinking us dry."

He took a second glance at the crowd. Mostly male, distinctly sooty, a bit sweaty. "Was there a fire last night?"

"A cabin south of town. I guess the ice storm dropped a tree on the roof and brought a power line along for the ride. Thankfully the owner wasn't there — he's from the Cities — but I'll bet he's not a happy camper this morning."

"I'll bet his insurance company isn't best pleased either." They got touchy when well-insured stuff burned down, a little fact Peter knew from personal experience.

"Truer words." Lainey rolled her eyes. "What'll it be on the muffins?"

"Half of those blueberry beauties, half the carroty ones."

She laughed. "A balanced diet." She snapped open a bakery box and loaded it up. Turned and set a new carafe on the burner and punched the brew button. She leaned back against the counter and gave him that friendly smile again. "So. Haven't seen you much since your engagement broke up. Sorry about that, by the way."

"It's fine," he said. And it was. It was better than fine that he and Georgie had put that sham behind them. "I don't get to town much anymore now that Eli's running the tap room."

"I heard you moved onto the sheep farm up the hill after that idiot farmer-kid bolted. What're you doing up there?"

"Farming." He was surprised at how easily it came out. At how proud he was to say it.

Her brows shot up. "You didn't sell the sheep? How many do you have up there, anyway?"

"There were twenty-one when I got there, but they've been multiplying." With or without his permission. "And then there are the chickens."

Her brows arched. "There was a guy in here just yesterday talking about a rooster he was picking up."

"Yeah, that would be Mr. Darcy."

"The guy's name was Mr. Darcy?"

Peter laughed. "No, the rooster's name is Mr. Darcy. The guy's name is Mike. Addy's dad. You've met him?"

She frowned blankly, then laughed. "Well of *course* he's Addy's dad. Now that you say it, I can't imagine how I missed it." She tipped her head, perplexed. "Why was Addy's dad picking up your rooster?"

"Long story. Let's just say he's helping out on the farm."

"Is Addy's mom helping out, too?"

She had last night. He gave a non-committal shrug.

"They came for the shower, decided to stay until the wedding. Prerogative of the retired, I guess."

"It'll be the event of the season." She leaned a hip on the counter between them and sent him a glance under her lashes. "You going?"

"What, to the wedding?"

"Yeah." She gave him an oddly tentative smile. "Because I was thinking, if you're going and I'm going, maybe we could—"

"Hey, Lainey!" At a table across the room, Mason Kennebec lifted an empty coffee cup and a pair of hopeful eyebrows. He sat with Frank Wilson, both of them looking cheerfully grimy. "You got any decaf yet?"

Color rose in her cheeks and she lowered her eyes. "It just finished brewing. Hang on." She turned to grab the orange-handled pot but shot a finger at Peter. "Don't you go away."

"You still have my coffee. I'm not going anywhere."

"Good." She went to refill Mason's cup.

Somebody behind him leaned forward and murmured, "You realize she's asking you out?"

Peter turned and found his sister's fiancé Eli Walker standing there. Beside him was Georgie's brother Jax, whose wedding Lainey was so excited about. They were as cheerfully grimy as Mason and Frank, but the receipts and to-go cups in their hands said they were waiting to cash out. "What?"

"Lainey," Eli said. "She totally just asked you out."

Peter stared. "She did not."

Jax grinned. "She was getting there."

He took a second. Well, damn. They were right. "What the hell am I supposed to do now?"

Jax and Eli exchanged a look. "I think you're supposed to answer her."

"And say what?"

"What do you want to say?" Jax asked.

"No." It was automatic. "I like Lainey just fine but I don't want to go out with her."

"Why not?"

"She's just not—" Georgie. He suppressed a scowl. Goddamn it, she wasn't Georgie. "—my type." He glanced at Lainey, weaving her way through the dirty crowd with her coffee pot, topping off cups right and left. "Were all these guys at the fire last night?"

"Yeah. It was a good one." Jax grinned and clapped Eli on the shoulder. "Gave my newest recruit his first taste of structural fire fighting."

"Ah." Peter had forgotten that Eli, a former wild land firefighter, was one of Jax's volunteers now. "Have fun?"

"Good times." Eli waved that off and refocused on Peter. "So Lainey's not your type, huh? Why not?"

Peter shrugged helplessly. He didn't do subterfuge anymore but he didn't think the truth was quite appropriate either. "She just isn't." He watched Lainey bee-lining her way back to the counter. To him. He lowered his voice. "How am I supposed to say so in front of all these people, though?"

"Hell if I know," Eli said cheerfully. "She asked me out once, too. I declined as politely as possible but Gerte's still half-convinced I burned down her Dumpster." He shook his head. "The other half of the time, she thinks it was Matty." His gaze shifted over Peter's shoulder and he smiled, big and bright. "Speak of the devil!"

Peter turned and found that Gerte had taken over the

register. Lainey must've gotten that sweet smile of hers from her father, God rest the guy's soul.

"And the devil will appear?" Gerte asked, and gave Eli a sour up-and-down. She'd never forgiven him for costing her cousin Paul his forest service job back in August. Never mind that Paul had allowed a wildfire to nearly devour the entire town. Eli was on Gerte's shit list in permanent ink.

Eli laughed. "Am I the devil in this scenario?"

"Given the way things seem to burn down around you," she returned, "it's not out of the question."

"Here we go again." Eli handed over his ticket and a ten dollar bill. "For the last time, Gerte, I'm not the reason your cousin lost his job. He was crap at forest management. If he'd been any good at it, he'd have been prescribing controlled burns for decades before I came along."

"I'm not making any accusations," Gerte said airily. She punched a few keys on the register and passed over his change. "It's just interesting, that's all."

Eli dropped the change in the tip jar. "What is?"

"The way fire seems to follow you."

Jax handed over his ticket next. "Fire doesn't follow fire fighters, Gerte," he said. "You know that, right? We follow the fire."

"After somebody calls it in, sure. But with Eli, things just seem to spontaneously combust, don't they?" She punched some more register keys and caught the drawer as it popped open. "First there was that terrible business with the hotshots out west, then ten minutes after Eli sets foot in town things start burning down everywhere!" She tucked away Jax's twenty, leisurely counted out the change. "There was your mother's garage, then the Dumpster out back." She shifted those pale eyes to Peter. "Even that ugly old resort you used

207

to own!" A triumphant little smile curved her lips. "And then Davis Place on top of it?"

Lainey arrived at the counter. She stopped as if the tension were a wall and she'd run into it. "Davis Place on top of what?"

"That happened after Eli left town," Peter pointed out, guilt sliding into his nascent optimism like a snake slipping into a lake. It happened every time somebody mentioned the fires. He'd paid for his sins, of course, but never taken public credit for them which had created a vacuum custom-made for conspiracy theorists. Or for vindictive gossips like Gerte. "There's no way he could've—"

Gerte plowed right over him. "And the minute he comes back, lookie loo! Suddenly the forest is on fire, and right after he'd finished harassing poor Paul about how he should've set it on fire years ago!"

"Oh my God, Mom, stop." Lainey shoved the decaf onto its burner. "You can't just say things like that. You know they aren't true."

Gerte widened wounded eyes. "Goodness sakes, Lainey! I'm not saying Eli started that fire—"

"Oh good." Jax didn't smile. "Because it was starting to sound like you were."

"It's just that we've known and trusted Paul O'Malley his entire life. And all we know about Eli is that trouble seems to follow him." Her mouth soured. "And so does fire."

"Okay, Mom, that's enough." Lainey put herself firmly at the register. "You needed some coffee, Peter?"

Peter ignored her and spoke to Gerte. "But we also know that Willa, who doesn't like anybody, likes Eli. Loves him, in fact."

"Willa," Gerte sniffed dismissively and Eli stiffened. His

smile stayed fixed but everything else about him tensed. "The girl is half-feral, and always has been. Paul is family, though. He deserves better than our doubt, and he certainly deserves better than to be fired after thirty years of dedicated service on a stranger's say-so. Goodness' sake, he's one of us!"

"And Willa's not," Peter said slowly. "Willa's not *one of us*. Why not just say it out loud?" The room was, he noticed suddenly, very quiet. "Who exactly is this *us* we're so proud of, though, Gerte? It can't be just the business owners of Devil's Kettle, because Willa definitely qualifies. It can't be just native-borns, because Willa was born right here. So what is it about her that you can't stomach? Is it that she grew up poor and trashy?"

"Peter, don't," Lainey said desperately. "Just ignore her. She'll stop."

He knew she was right. He knew he should stop. He just couldn't seem to. "No, that couldn't be it," he mused. "I grew up poor and trashy and you were delighted when I took over the Chamber of Commerce last year."

Gerte's smile could've drawn blood. "You didn't give birth to Diego's bastard in eighth grade, though, did you?"

Peter was dimly aware of Eli taking a step forward and Jax hooking a hand in the guy's elbow. Eli subsided but Peter sympathized. Gerte desperately needed a good punching but she was an old lady. What the fuck was a guy supposed to do?

He did the only thing he could do. He bypassed Gerte's little smoke bomb and zeroed in on another truth she didn't like to say right out loud.

And he said it.

CHAPTER 22

"THAT'S NOT WHAT bugs you so much about Willa," Peter said. "It's more that she doesn't give a fuck what you think of her."

"Language!" Gerte snapped.

"She's always been like that, if it makes you feel any better. It drove me crazy when we were kids. I hated her for not caring, for being so absolutely unconcerned about you all. Because I was so damn concerned all the time. Concerned enough for both of us. It ate me up, knowing what people saw when they looked at us. What they said about us when we weren't around to hear it. *Oh, the Zinc kids. Products of the most fucked up gene pool in town. Trashy as hell, and going nowhere in a tearing hurry.*" The silence was a palpable presence in the room and he patted his hands on the tense air. "No, no, calm down. I get it. I totally do. It makes you feel better, doesn't it?" He took in the entire room, including Jax and Eli now standing silently by the door, Jax's face stoic, Eli's wary.

"Knowing somebody else is more messed up than you?" Peter went on. "That's priceless. Because no matter what stupid shit is going down behind your closed doors, at least you know it's a whole lot better than the shit going on at the Zinc cabin out in the woods."

"Be that as it may," Gerte returned acidly. "At least you've never tried your hand at arson."

"Really? That's your bright line for us versus them?" Peter stared at her, and the truth lurched up his throat like vomit. He'd always thought it was shame keeping it down but now he knew better. It was fear. Fear of finally, irrevocably crossing the line from *us* to *them*. He'd worked so damn hard to get into that rarified *us*, it made sense that he'd be loath to get kicked out. But if Gerte was *us*, and Willa was *them*, he knew without question which side of the line he wanted to be on.

"You really want to know who burned all those buildings down, Gerte?"

"Oh, I already know." Her eyes skated over his shoulder to Eli.

"It was me," Peter said flatly. "The Dumpster, the resort, Davis Place? It was all me."

Behind him, he heard somebody — Jax? Eli? — give a long, slow exhale. He also heard the door jingle open, shockingly loud in the brittle silence. He didn't even care. The faster the word spread, the happier he'd be. This was the last lie, the last bit of flotsam still lingering from the shipwreck of his life, and he'd been clinging to it for far too long.

"You?" Gerte's eyes were wide, stunned. Lainey gave a small moan. They weren't alone in their shock. It was slack jaws and popped eyes all over the place, along with a general air of startled dismay. Even so, a dizzy lightness bubbled up inside him. Because there were no more secrets after this. Nothing to hide, nothing to regret. Maybe he'd never be part of Gerte's precious *us* again, but what did that matter when he had a farm to get back to? When he might, judging by the grins spreading across Jax's and Eli's faces, have a family, too?

"Yeah, me," he said. "You may have heard rumors of my financial troubles. They're all too real. Real enough that I felt compelled to attempt a little insurance fraud." He shrugged. "My empire might've been crumbling, but it was very well insured."

"You owned all of them," Gerte murmured, struck. "The Dumpster was yours, the resort was yours. You even owned a chunk of Davis Place, didn't you?"

"It almost worked out, too. But I got sloppy, Matty caught on and next thing you know I'm in a family meeting I'll never forget." He rubbed his jaw, as if remembering a blow. "Suffice it to say that you should *not* mess with Bianca Davis, or anybody she loves."

"Any idiot could've told you that," Gerte said.

"Some people only learn the hard way," Jax murmured.

"I'm one of them, I guess." He lifted his shoulders. "So you can put your mind at ease, Gerte. Eli isn't your fire bug. Neither is Matty. I am."

She shook her head slowly. "I never would've believed it."

"Of course not. That was the beauty of it. But you don't mess with the baby Davis unless you're prepared to deal with the wrath of the clan, and when people started looking Matty's way, when the whispers started—"

"He *did* burn down the carriage house," Gerte pointed out.

"Accidentally," Jax put in.

Peter hooked a thumb Jax's way, an unspoken *what he said*. "Matty's little mishap was convenient timing for me, I'll admit. Unless you count the irreversible damage I did my own soul and an innocent kid, of course."

"Why are you telling us this?" Lainey asked, her voice shocked and hollow. "Why now?"

"Who the hell knows?" He shrugged and it felt light,

easy. "But if your mom's going to keep talking shit about those fires, at least she can aim her shit the right direction. Eli can handle himself but Matty's just a kid."

Gerte snorted. "He's a Davis."

"Who's worked like hell on the farm all week and deserves a hot chocolate with extra whipped cream. Put one on my order, will you, Lainey?"

Gerte's eyebrows shot upward. "Matty's working at the farm?"

Peter ignored her and smiled at Lainey. "The rest of us worked hard yesterday, too, so I'll take four large coffees as well."

She shook her head and started ringing up his order. "If anybody deserves a coffee for each hand, I guess it's you."

"Each hand?"

"Unless you've got somebody besides Matty and Addy's parents stashed away with the sheep, you've got one extra coffee by my count." She caught the register drawer as it slid open and met his gaze with curious blue eyes. "That'll be twenty-eight thirty-three, unless you want to take off the fourth coffee."

"Hell, no," he said automatically. "Georgie would murder me, then take my coffee."

"Oh," Lainey said softly. "Georgie's at your place, too?"

And Peter remembered belatedly that she'd been trying to ask him out before her mom had hijacked the conversation. "Oh," he said awkwardly. "Um, yeah. She is."

"Well, well, well." Gerte's brows lifted slowly. "I guess we don't need to wonder anymore why Peter's suddenly defending the baby Davis."

"Because he's an innocent kid?" he said, suppressing a wince on Lainey's behalf. She'd spent her entire life coming in second to Georgie. She'd probably only asked Peter out because she'd figured she wouldn't have to compete with Georgie for him. She couldn't have gotten it more spectacularly wrong.

Gerte went on as if he hadn't spoken. "Or why he doesn't need a wedding date." She put a comforting hand on her daughter's arm. "If at first you don't succeed, after all..."

Peter dragged his wallet out of his pocket. He needed to pay and get the hell out of here before he said something truly regrettable. Or got arrested for assaulting a mean old lady. Or prolonged Lainey's agony by a single second. He opened his wallet which contained a twenty dollar bill, his driver's license and nothing else, his daily reminder that if something cost more than twenty bucks he probably couldn't afford it. Fancy coffee and muffins for five, unfortunately, fell squarely inside that category.

"Looks like I only have a twenty on me," he said, an old shame creeping up the back of his neck. "I'll have to pass on the muffins today."

"We take credit cards," Gerte said sweetly. "I'm sure you don't want to go all the way back up the hill empty-handed. Your guests must be hungry."

"No, it's fine." Peter didn't have any credit cards. He barely had credit anymore, thanks to his previous abuse of the bank's trust. And there was no room for baked goods and coffee-shop treats in his budget, not if he was going to feed both the sheep and himself until the spring when the farm was scheduled to make its first profit. But the urge was there regardless, riding the greasy crest of that shame. What kind of man couldn't buy a woman a goddamn muffin, for pity's sake? He held out the twenty to Lainey, the sweaty panic of being poor in public snuggling up to him like an old lover.

"Just the coffees and the cocoa."

She took it silently and re-rang his order. Gerte lifted the white bakery box off the counter and made an unnecessary bustle out of reshelving the muffins. Lainey gave him his pitiful change with a wan smile, and nudged a cardboard cup carrier across the counter. He dropped a buck or two he couldn't afford to spare in the tip jar and returned the smile as best he could. Fuck, coffee was expensive by the cup. He should've just waited for the grocery store to open. He could've had a whole bag of coffee beans, a gallon of milk, a can of cocoa mix and a loaf of bread for his twenty without the side dish of public humiliation.

He stepped over the shreds of his earlier optimism and headed for the door. Jax and Eli moved aside — without comment, thank Christ — to make room for him. And revealed his mother and Julia Gates, standing just inside the door staring at him. Julia's eyes were bright and avid; reporters liked nothing better than conflict first thing in the morning. But his mother's eyes were full of something else. Something familiar and bitter. Something he recognized all too easily.

Disappointment.

And it wasn't because he'd grown up to be a lying, amoral arsonist-turned-farmer.

It was because he was poor.

His dad had never been able to buy nice shit for her, either.

CHAPTER 23

GEORGIE ALWAYS HAD a camera in the car. She'd once harbored delusions of talent but she'd shrugged those off years ago. These days, she used her camera not to make art (or attempt to make art) but to document any art that caught her eye, and the artist that went with it. If she took enough pictures, the right pictures, it didn't matter how many artists she'd seen on a scouting trip. The photos told her the story, and she remembered not only what she'd seen but what it had made her feel, and that was what mattered when it came to art.

She wasn't sure whose story she was telling herself this morning, but good God, it was glorious. The entire world sparkled and melted and swam around her, the temperature hovering in that magical in-between place where water didn't know what to do with itself. Was it rain? Snow? Fog? Ice? Some incandescent melange of everything? It all depended on where the sun was, she decided, and held the camera to her eye. She found one of Addy's artists sitting cross-legged on the glistening grass near that big circular hay-feeder-thing in the middle pasture, raptly sketching Tag, who sat on top of it keeping an eye on his charges. She clicked, capturing the woman in the hoarfrost squinting thoughtfully up at the sheep dog, her pencil arrested over the sketch pad on her knee.

Most of the sheep surrounded the feeder, placidly pulling out mouthfuls of hay. The babies, though, *her* babies bounded around the meadow playing some game known only to the two of them. Their little bleats hung in visible puffs in the chilly air, and joy radiated off them in near-palpable waves. Bone raced up to Rag and tried to hurdle her. Rag was having none of it, though, and bucked just as her sister hit the crest of her leap. Bone tumbled to the ground, all hooves and ears and flappy tail, then boinged away smugly like she'd pulled off a sweet trick. Chuckles drifted up from the artists scattered throughout the pasture and pencils flew over sketch pads. Bone bounced over to her and Georgie couldn't resist. She knelt, zoomed in through the fence on that naughty nose and snapped.

"Bah!" Bone said, delighted.

"Bah," Georgie said and tapped that nose. "Now go play. People want to draw you."

Addy joined her in the near pasture and handed her an insulated mug of coffee. "This was a fantastic idea, Georgie. You're a genius."

"I woke up this morning and the whole farm was an art project." Georgie let the camera dangle from the neck strap. "And you have a house full of artists, so it only made sense to invite them over." She wrapped her cold hands around the coffee. "God, I needed this." She sipped, closed her eyes and gave thanks to a benevolent creator.

Addy grinned. "Hence the other reason you called."

"Peter was completely out of coffee and nowhere to be found." She shook her head in wonder. "How does that even happen?"

"Got me." Addy sipped from her own thermal mug, and the tag of her tea bag twirled on the wind. Georgie zoomed in and snapped.

"You still have dough on your hands." She lowered the camera. "Your engagement ring is a mess."

Addy smiled fondly at it. "It's perfect. Plus there's a tray of fresh cinnamon rolls waiting for you in the kitchen. You'd better get in there if you want to eat."

Georgie consulted her stomach, and found that she wasn't at all averse to the idea of eating a little something. "I take it back. Your ring is perfect. You should always have dough stuck to your diamond."

"I probably always will."

"You sound happy about that."

"I am." Addy sighed wistfully. "I just wish I were as happy about everything else."

Georgie's brows shot up. "Jax?"

"Lord, no." Her smile was smug. "He's perfect, too."

Georgie rolled her eyes. Her eldest brother was far from perfect but love did things to a woman's brain. "I think your folks are on the right track," she offered.

"I hope so." Addy sipped. "Dad took Mom back up to Davis Place to fetch her car. If nothing else, at least they're talking again."

"They're doing more than that."

"What?"

Georgie grinned. "I saw Jennifer tiptoeing out of your dad's room last night around three a.m., looking extremely disheveled and a lot satisfied."

Addy stared. "Really?"

"Really."

She closed her eyes and released a sigh from the very depths of a weary soul. "Thank you, Jesus, for this miracle you have bestowed upon us." She opened her eyes. "Did you have anything to do with this?"

Georgie shook her head. "I don't think so. Though I had yelled at them earlier, if it counts for anything."

"I've been yelling at them for weeks without discernible effect." Addy frowned. "For future reference, what magical words did you yell?"

"I don't remember precisely. Something along the lines of *either grow up and get over your damage, or get divorced because we're all sick of your shit.*"

"Sage advice." She lifted her mug for a sip and arched a brow at Georgie through the steam. "And did you take it as well as give it?"

"Excuse me?"

"Make up sex can be contagious." She grinned. "What exactly were *you* doing wandering the halls at three a.m. in Peter's farmhouse?"

"Not having make up sex."

"Too bad. Why not?"

Georgie gaped at her. When Addy only blinked at her in expectant silence, she groped for reasons that had seemed very clear just a few days ago. "He only wanted to marry me because he was broke, remember? And when he found out *I* was broke, he tried to blackmail my brother into arson so he could commit insurance fraud. That hardly seems like the kind of thing you get past with a little make up sex."

"True," Addy conceded and sipped her tea. "But it's also true that he didn't dump you when he found out you were broke."

"No, I know." The coffee went sour in her mouth. "That's when he took aim at Matty."

"To save you both."

"I beg your pardon?"

Addy met her gaze steadily. "I was curious so I ran the numbers."

"Of course you did." Addy had never met a spreadsheet

she didn't like. "And what did they tell you?"

"As a substantial investor, Peter knew exactly how deep our family was in with Davis Place, financially speaking. An accidental house fire — not unheard of during a rehab of that scope — would've sent insurance money to each and every one of us. We could've tabled the rebuild and used the cash to float us until either you and your mom got jobs or the cops dragged your financial advisor back from Bimini with your money. As far as he was concerned, it was win/win. Nobody would have to declare bankruptcy, nobody would get publicly shamed, and he would still get the girl of his dreams."

"And all it costs us is Matty's mental health?"

"I talked to Matty this morning," Addy returned. "His mental health is just fine, and so is his appetite." She shook her head fondly. "Kid put away half a pan of cinnamon rolls while assuring me that life on the farm isn't all that bad." She glanced up at Georgie. "He's drawing again."

"I know." Georgie blew out a breath. "He told me last night."

"Something about this place speaks to him. He likes it here."

"He doesn't just like it here," she said slowly. "I think he likes who *he* is here." The rumble of an engine floated to her across the sparkling air and she saw Peter's truck pull into the farm yard. "He likes the work."

"Peter's putting him to work?"

Georgie smiled despite herself. "I heard him say *vagina*, *uterus* and *nipple* yesterday without blush or hesitation. He was pinning a laboring sheep to the ground when he said them, but still."

"Wow. Peter's putting him to *work*."

"He is. And Matty likes it." Her stomach gave a warning twinge and she lifted her shoulders, defeated. "Matty likes him, too."

"He said as much?"

"Last night." She sent Addy a disgruntled glance. "He gave me pretty much the same speech you just did, minus the math."

"Which boils down to *grow up and get over your damage*, essentially. At least the damage you've been holding against Peter." Addy grinned at her. "It's good advice, Georgie. You might consider it."

Across the pasture, Peter wrenched open the sticky door of the truck and stepped out, carrying a cardboard holder of what looked like coffees. Her heart — stupid, sentimental thing — gave an alarmingly tender squeeze.

"He brought me coffee," she murmured.

"Is that what it takes?"

Nerves rushed up inside her, tangled with a bright streak of hope and a whiff of joy. Her stomach twitched but her face wanted to smile so she let it. "Maybe it is," she said and went to meet him.

Peter squinted into the glare of his ice-coated farm and found Georgie galumphing across the near pasture toward him in those ugly boots of hers. The sheep were in the middle pasture where he'd left them under Tag's expert surveillance, but they'd been joined by half a dozen strangers with sketch pads and cameras.

"You're back!" Georgie smiled at him, the kind of genuine, open smile he'd have given his left nut to see on her face even half an hour ago. "And you brought coffee!"

He glanced at the thermal mug in her hands and the tide

of shame rose inside him. He'd spent everything he had for something she didn't even need. "A little too late, looks like." He nodded at the strangers in his pasture. "Who are all these people?"

"Addy's artists." She slipped a hand through his elbow and drew him toward the near pasture. "It was so pretty this morning, with everything all coated in ice and the sheep breathing in frosty little clouds. The artists had enjoyed drawing Rag and Bone so much yesterday. I figured they'd go nuts for the whole farm and I was right." She gave his arm a companionable squeeze and bounced on her boots a little. "Plus you were out of coffee, and Addy's is fantastic."

They'd reached the fence dividing the pastures and Addy lifted her own mug to him in greeting. "Hey, Peter. Thanks so much for letting my students overrun your farm."

"No problem." He smiled tightly and jiggled his unnecessary coffees. "I should get these inside before they get cold, though."

"There's a pan of cinnamon rolls on the counter," Addy said, her smile not tight at all. "My version of a thank you note."

Georgie eyed the Wooden Spoon logo on the coffee cups. "Did you eat in town? I'd have been hard pressed to resist one of those morning glory muffins Gerte does."

He held onto his smile through sheer force of will. "I managed."

"Well, I'm starving," Georgie said, "and if you didn't bring me one of those muffins?"

"Nope. Just the coffee," he said for the second time that morning. It didn't feel any better with repetition.

"Then I'm having a cinnamon roll. Come inside with me." She turned him toward the house, her hand still hooked companionably through his elbow. "I want to talk to you about something."

Addy said, "I'll stay here and supervise the artists." She lifted a brow. "You'll tell Peter what we talked about?"

"Of course."

"*All* of what we talked about?"

Georgie gave her a bland stare and Addy grinned serenely back.

"Well." Addy buried that grin in her mug and turned back to the artists. "Have fun, you two."

Georgie tugged on his elbow and Peter let her lead him toward the house. He couldn't imagine what she and Addy had discussed that might involve him. Wasn't sure he wanted to know. Every time those two put their heads together about him, he ended up with another roommate.

As they passed the barn, one of Addy's artists stalked out, a small, round woman with a pencil in one hand, sketch pad in the other. Matty jogged behind her, but she ignored him. She marched straight to Georgie and glared, her face framed with steel-gray curls squashed onto her cheeks by her earflap hat. "Do you own this place? Are you in charge here?"

Georgie stopped, surprised. It had evidently never occurred to her that she might look like a farmer to anybody, even wearing knee-high muck boots. "No, I'm just visiting. Peter's the farmer."

The woman shifted her attention to Peter, and he nearly stepped back from the anger in her face. "Your rooster is a monster. He's raped at least five chickens in the last half hour. You need to get him out of the coop. Now."

"I tried to explain—" Matty started but the woman shot up a hand and he subsided.

Peter stared at the woman all but vibrating with righteous

fury in front of him, and felt nothing but tired. He dredged up a smile from his dwindling reserves and said, "Mr. Darcy's new at the whole roostering business. We're monitoring the situation but we're giving him a day or two to get the hang of it before we—"

"He's not getting the hang of anything," the woman snapped. "He's a serial rapist."

"Animals can't even *be* rapists," Matty said behind her.

"If you don't get verbal consent before sex, you're a rapist," the woman informed him. She turned to give him a critical up and down. "You're old enough to know that, young man."

Matty goggled at her. "What, now *I'm* a rapist because I don't think chickens are able to give verbal consent before sex?" He turned beseeching eyes to Peter and spread his hands. "Seriously?"

"Listen," Peter said to the woman, "I agree with you." Behind her, Matty rolled his eyes toward the heavens. Peter sympathized. He was digging deep into an ancient well of people skills on this one. "Verbal consent is crucial to a healthy, legal sex life."

"For people," Matty muttered.

"But given a chicken's cognitive abilities and communication skills, I think verbal consent is a pretty high bar—"

"Bottom line." The woman planted her fists on her hips and leaned in to fire that glare at him from close range. "Either you get that rooster out of that coop right now, or I will. And then I'll report you to Animal Control, because—"

She was interrupted by a flurry of barking, and not Tag's bark, either. Peter recognized Tag's bark in his sleep. This was a new bark, a stranger's bark, and it held an edgy excitement that verged on hysteria. Oh, Jesus. He glanced over and saw Tag come to his feet on top of the feeder to give a sharp warning bark of his own. He circled in place, caught Peter's eye and barked at him, too. And Peter had no trouble deciphering the meaning. That bark meant *get your ass over here, pronto.*

Shit.

He shoved the tray of coffee at Matty. "Hold that."

"What? Why?" He paused. "Hey, is that hot chocolate?"

"Yeah, enjoy." He spun and started for the pasture Tag was barking at.

"Peter?" Georgie asked, bewildered.

"Do *not* walk away from me!" the artist snapped.

But Peter was already doing just that. He was running.

CHAPTER 24

Jesus, Jesus, Jesus. He didn't know if he was swearing or praying as he charged across the slippery grass. He didn't even bother to unlatch the gates, he just leapt over the fences. Which was the kind of behavior that could put a guy in the ditch clutching his smoking nuts but he ignored that. He'd read about barking like this. He knew what it could mean.

Tag launched himself off the feeder and streaked past him, but Peter shouted, "Tag, no! Take them to the barn! For God's sake, Tag, *take them to the barn*!"

For the first time in Peter's memory, Tag didn't balk. He simply put his rear down like a barrel-racing horse, pivoted on the spot and streaked back to the middle pasture where he'd left the flock. He could hear Georgie galumphing along some yards back but he couldn't pay attention to that. He was too busy saving her babies.

His babies, damn it.

Oh Christ, they were in the street. How the hell had they gotten into the street? Rag and Bone shot back and forth like pinballs on the blacktop between a pair of beagle/terrier mixes sporting matching collars. The dogs raced around and through them, nipping at their tails, their ears, sending them clattering in desperate circles, looking for shelter. The lambs' bewildered bleats rang in the air, mixed with the dogs' frenzied barking. One of the lambs spotted a break in their coverage and bolted toward the safety of the pasture. The dogs barked furiously and one streaked after her. It was on her in moments, its white teeth flashing at her ears, at her flanks.

"Bone!" Georgie wailed behind him. The little lamb squealed back desperately and Peter realized it hadn't been bolting for the pasture at all. It had seen Georgie. Its sides heaved and it bounded for her with everything it had but it was a baby, and the dog was bigger, stronger, and lost to an ancient blood-lust buried deep in its DNA.

The dog drove its flank against the lamb's, and Bone stumbled to her knobby knees. The dog gave a triumphant yelp and skidded to a halt, its paws splayed on either side of the downed lamb, its lips peeled back from the teeth that were seconds from tearing out Bone's throat and smearing it all over the pavement.

Peter was three long strides from the dog, and he didn't slow down. He ran through the dog like the football player he'd once been, putting a boot solidly in the dog's hindquarters on his way by. The dog yipped and became an airborne jumble of fur and legs. Bone lifted her head a cautious inch and satisfaction flowed hot and feral in Peter's veins.

He left her to Georgie and sprinted into the street where Rag still veered in increasingly erratic circles while the other dog relentlessly nipped and feinted. She bleated wearily, stumbling like a drunk. Rage roared into Peter's mind, filled it like a swarm of bees. He was still ten yards off when Rag gave up. She folded to her knees with one last weary bleat and lay down. The dog was on her in seconds, but so was Peter.

A new voice shouted, "Barnum! Barnum, come!" but Peter barely registered the words. He didn't look away from those bared white teeth aiming for his lamb. Lungs burning, chest heaving, he closed the final yard. He reached out and snatched a handful of the dog's scruff. He yanked the dog up, and its teeth snapped harmlessly closed on the air.

"No, goddamn you!" He gave the dog a ferocious shake, then bent and pitched it like a bowling ball toward the far shoulder of the road. "No!"

"Oh my God, *Barnum*!" A woman in hiking boots and an earflap hat raced past him, a leash in her hand, panic in her voice. "Barnum!"

She skidded on the gravel on the far shoulder, dropped to her knees and threw her arms around the dog which had already come to its feet and given itself a vigorous shake. It panted over its owner's shoulder at Peter, its tongue lolling out in a big doggie smile. It had clearly had the time of its life. Peter's boot twitched. Before he'd become a farmer, he would never have considered kicking a dog. He wouldn't have thought much of anybody who did. Then again, he wouldn't have guessed that any pampered family pet with the right DNA could become a lamb killer in the blink of an eye. He knew better now.

"What the hell is the matter with you?" The hiker cuddled her dog and glared at Peter with reddened eyes. "I saw what you did! You *threw* him! I'm calling the cops!"

"Go ahead, lady." He stooped and carefully lifted Rag into his arms. She bleated weakly and snuggled in. "Save me the trouble. Your stupid dogs nearly killed my lambs."

"Where's Bailey?" She scanned the ditch frantically. "What have you done to Bailey?"

Peter jerked his head toward the grass behind him. "He's back there." With one of Georgie's ugly boots on its fucking neck, hopefully. "He almost killed my other lamb."

"She would never." The woman stalked past him toward

the pasture fence. "Bailey's the gentlest creature on earth. So is Barnum." She nuzzled the dog, who had indeed transformed into a sweet-looking lapdog, its head tucked trustingly under its owner's chin. Bailey chose that moment to trot out of the ditch, tail high, eyes sparkling.

"Bailey!" The woman dropped to her knees and scooped up the second dog. And burst into tears. The dogs squirmed all over her like toddlers, lapping at her tears and stepping on each other's heads. "Barnum, Bailey, you naughty, naughty dogs! When I say come, you're supposed to *come*."

Peter walked around her and stepped carefully over the electric fence. Georgie stood there with Bone in her arms, fury sparkling in her eyes. "Is Rag okay?"

"All worn out but not hurt."

"Bone's ear is bleeding."

Peter glanced at the lamb in her arms. "It's not bad. I have some antiseptic in the barn."

"Okay." She shifted the lamb. "Hold Bone, will you? I want to go punch that lady."

"Oh thank Christ. Hand her over."

She didn't pass him the lamb. "You'd let me punch her?"

"Somebody has to, and I'd probably go to jail. You'd do it right, too."

"I would?"

"Hell, yes. You might look strictly ornamental but I know better. You'd cut a bitch. Go make me proud."

"I might be in love with you," she said, still frowning darkly at the woman weeping in his ditch.

His heart stuttered inside his chest and he pressed poor Rag to it. "Less talking, more punching."

"Right. Hold my sheep."

Before she could hand Bone over, a strident voice rang

out behind them. "How dare you run away? I'm not done with you!"

Peter closed his eyes. "Fuck me. The chicken lady."

She reached Peter's side, her anger a palpable presence. "Fair warning, sir! If you don't have that rooster removed from the coop within the next fifteen minutes, I'm calling Animal Control."

Matty appeared next, the tray of coffees still in his hand. "What happened?"

"The circus came to town," Georgie said.

"What?"

Peter pointed his chin toward the lady in the ditch. "Couple of off-leash dogs nearly took Rag and Bone down."

Matty studied the fawning lapdogs on the other side of the fence. "Seriously?"

"I'm telling you," the woman in the ditch snapped, "Barnum and Bailey are the gentlest dogs alive! They would never—"

"I watched them," Peter interrupted grimly. "They did."

The chicken lady lifted a skeptical brow at the pair of dogs scrambling over one another to cover their owner with lavish kisses. "Those dogs couldn't hurt a fly. Plus these are electric fences. How did they get in?"

"They didn't," the dog owner replied tearfully. "The lambs were in the street."

"They wandered up to the resort I'm staying at yesterday, too." She turned back to Peter with cold dislike. "It appears you have a number of problems on your farm. Problems I'm sure Animal Control would be very interested in."

"Go ahead and call them," Peter said flatly. "You and your new best friend can bail Barnum and Bailey there out of dog jail for being off-leash and out of control. That's a misdemeanor right there."

"You threw my dog!"

The chicken lady's eyes narrowed dangerously. "You threw a dog?"

"I bowled it. But I was within my rights to kill it."

"Excuse me?" She drew back, horrified.

"Minnesota Statute says that any dog found chasing, worrying or injuring livestock can be killed by the owner of said livestock."

"Your sheep don't look worried," the dog owner said bitterly, eyeing the lambs snuggled peacefully in his and Georgie's arms.

"No?" Georgie turned to show off Bone's bloody ear. "I suppose this was a love bite?"

The dog owner blinked, startled.

The chicken lady didn't budge. "That could've happened while it was getting out of your faulty fence."

Peter opened his mouth but Georgie put a hand on his arm and turned into her mother. It was uncanny. The emotion drained from her face, leaving nothing behind but the blunt instrument of her beauty. She drew privilege and wealth around her like a cloak, and was suddenly every inch of her six feet.

"Matty?" Her voice clinked like ice cubes in an expensive glass.

"Yes?"

"Take our guest to the barn, please, and put the rooster into accommodations that meet her approval. Then let Addy know that today's visiting hours are over."

"Got it. One rooster in solitary confinement, coming up." He pried the hot chocolate out of the cardboard carrier and took a fortifying slug. "God, that's good. I want to hate

Gerte but I'd miss the hot chocolate too much."

"Welcome to adult life," Peter told him. "It's a series of compromises."

"You're telling me." Matty eyed the chicken lady who put her nose in the air and stalked toward the barn.

"As for you." Georgie shifted that glacial gaze to the woman still cuddling her dogs on the side of the road. "Your dogs were clearly off-leash and out of your control. I suggest you keep them leashed for the rest of your hike. If we see them anywhere near our sheep again, we won't hesitate to exercise our rights to the full extent of the law."

The woman rose shakily to her feet. "Believe me, I won't be coming back here." She clipped the leash onto her dogs and marched down the street. There was a small parking lot down there, Peter remembered belatedly, for a spur trail leading to the Kettle. He'd have to remember that come tourist season, or he'd have off-leash dogs crawling all over the place.

"That's a tourist we won't be seeing again," Georgie murmured, watching her go.

"Lucky for me, I'm not in the tourist business anymore."

"Maybe you should be. The chicken lady notwithstanding, Addy's artists are in love with this place. This probably isn't the best time to bring up the idea of regular visits—"

Peter wanted to palm his face but his arms were full of lamb. "No, it's not."

"—but we're going to talk about it anyway."

"Of course we are." Because poor people had to be practical in ways rich people didn't. "Give me a minute to see about Bone's ear." And to get his damn coffee from Matty. And drink all of it. "I'll meet you inside."

Georgie watched Peter stalk to the barn with a pair of exhausted, frightened lambs. Violence still shimmered in the air around him, his tight shoulders and hard jaw plainly telegraphing a sincere desire to punch whomever happened across his path next. But those big hands on her lambs were exquisitely gentle. Fiercely protective. She lifted the camera still dangling from its neck strap to her eye, focused and shot before she was even conscious of moving. She recognized art when she saw it.

"Lord have mercy," Addy murmured beside her. Georgie hadn't heard her arrive. She'd been too busy staring. "Farmer enraged."

Georgie lowered the camera and blinked her friend into focus. It was like surfacing from a long, deep dive. Her head felt dangerously light, her lungs clean and pure and empty. "Sorry?"

"The portrait you just shot of Peter," Addy said. "You should call it *Farmer Enraged*."

"I don't shoot portraits," she said automatically but she frowned toward the barn Peter had disappeared inside, her fingers itching on her camera. Whatever she'd just done, she wanted to do more of it. "I'm not a real photographer."

"Okay," Addy said easily, and sipped her tea. "But you should call it *Farmer Enraged*." She shook her head in wonder. "I have never in all my days seen anything like that."

"What?"

"Peter defending his lambs. If you'd asked me ten minutes ago to come up with a scenario where it was okay to kick a dog that wasn't actually eating a toddler, I'm not sure I could've done it. But then there was Farmer Enraged."

233

"I know." Georgie pressed a hand to her stomach. For once it didn't hurt but it was jumping all the same. Because she was thinking about doing something she, too, couldn't have imagined doing even ten minutes ago. "He's changed."

"He has." Addy pressed her mug thoughtfully to her chin. "The old Peter would never have risked tourist dollars over future meat." Georgie glared at her but Addy only lifted sympathetic shoulders. "I'm sorry, Georgie. It's true, though. Rag and Bone aren't pets."

She sighed. "I know. I hate it but I know. And you're right. He would never have spoken to a tourist that way, not even if her dogs were Cujo-style murderers. Her money would've meant more to him than any pre-lamb-chop possibly could have." She paused, that strange purpose bubbling up inside her, turning her stomach into a wonderland of pain-free anticipation. "He apologized last night."

Addy arched a brow. "Was this before or after your three a.m. sexcursion through the halls?"

"It wasn't a sexcursion." But her mouth wanted to smile. "Heaven's sake, Addison."

She made a disappointed noise. "He apologized though?"

"He did."

"He's done that before, though, hasn't he?"

"Loads of times. But he meant it this time."

Addy studied her. "How could you tell?"

"I just could. We'd gone out to bury the dead lamb—"

"What?"

"Long, awful story." She waved a hand to fill in the blanks. "Suffice it to say that I'd already bawled all over the poor thing and begged it to live—"

"In front of Peter?"

"Yeah, a few hours earlier." She grimaced. "Which is why, when he woke me up at like two in the morning to let me know it had died, I was trying to play it cool. Damage control, you know?"

"You were feeling vulnerable," Addy said softly. "He'd caught you crying, and you don't even cry at funerals." She didn't say *you're not allowed to*. She didn't have to.

"Exactly." Her stomach relaxed into the precious luxury of Addy's immediate understanding. "So anyway, there we were, trudging through the last of the ice storm, me in these very attractive Wellies, Peter with a bundle of poor dead lamb in his arms. I'm doing my best impression of detached irony of course—"

"Damage control," Addy murmured sympathetically.

"—so I give him a little poke. I ask him why he was being so damn careful to keep the dead lamb dry. The lamb's beyond caring, obviously, so why all the theater?"

Addy winced. "You didn't."

"Of course I did." She shook back her hair haughtily. "I'm Georgie Davis."

"Oh, honey." Addy gave her arm a little rub.

"Yeah, that's about what he said." Wonder dawned inside her as the scene replayed itself inside her mind. *Showing respect isn't the same thing as showing weakness, Georgie. Same as breaking shit doesn't show your strength.* "Then he looked at me."

"Looked at you how?"

"It's hard to describe. He has a way of looking at me these days and it's almost unbearable. He's not hiding anything anymore. He looked at me like that last night, with this ridiculous honesty, and I just knew he was sorry. Deeply, truly, sincerely. And it made me ashamed."

"Honey. Why?"

"Because he was being exactly who he is now." She swallowed, forced the truth out. "And I was still hiding like a coward."

"It's different for you," Addy said gently. "Women who look like you have to protect themselves. I didn't always get that but I do now. The world would eat you alive if you let it."

Georgie shook her head. "Peter's not the world, though, is he? He's just Peter." Her stomach lifted and bloomed, joy unfolding inside her petal by petal. "He's a guy who knows exactly how important public opinion is. It used to control him but it doesn't anymore. That's how he's different." And the relief of putting her finger on it was exquisite. "He's doing what's right, and not just for him, but in general. It's probably the most courageous thing I've ever seen another person do. He's *real* now."

"He wasn't real before?" Addy asked carefully.

"He was a Ken doll before, and I was his perfect Barbie." She frowned. "And if you ever tell Willa I said that, I'll shave your eyebrows off before the wedding."

"Like I would." But she smoothed a protective finger over one brow.

"A Barbie was all the old Peter wanted," Georgie said, almost to herself. "It was all I wanted to be to him."

"But you want to be something more to him now?" Addy said.

"I'm not sure." The joy blossoming inside Georgie climbed up, curled across her face and announced itself to the world. "But I want to see if I can be. If I even have that much honesty in me."

Addy's answering smile was brilliant and warmed

Georgie like the sun. "I'm getting my artists off your land, then, and taking Matty with me. And if Mom and Dad try to come back here or even try to get away from each other before dinner at the very earliest, they'll face my wrath."

"Your wrath is a fierce and terrible thing," Georgie said solemnly.

"Truth." She seized Georgie up in one of those signature hugs of hers, all strong arms and sunny affection. "Now go get your man."

CHAPTER 25

GEORGIE SAILED INTO Peter's kitchen and, out of habit, sank with a boneless grace she didn't feel onto one of his sturdy wooden benches. Her stomach fired a warning shot over the bow and she popped back to her feet. Right. The room was empty. No point keeping up expensive appearances. Her stomach suggested she might try pacing instead of pretending she wasn't close to hyperventilating. She shrugged. She'd never paced in her life but she'd seen it done.

She marched to the far end of the room, spun on one rubber boot and stalked back. The plop and slap of her boots rang satisfyingly in the empty space, and soothed her stomach surprisingly well. It made sense, she supposed. Pacing obviously took the chaos in her head and channeled it into some kind of organized physical effort. Which was good because that chaos had been threatening to morph into cowardice, and if Peter took much longer in the barn, she'd bail on this ridiculous plan.

Because it was a ridiculous plan, wasn't it? What was she thinking? She wasn't an aggressive person, not in her career, not in her love life. Things came to her — men, friends, jobs — not the other way around. So why was she standing in Peter's kitchen, ready to throw herself at a man she'd had to *ask* to kiss her a few weeks ago? A man who'd held her hand all the way home last night, then let her go back to bed without even *trying* to kiss her again?

It was, she had to acknowledge, an ominous sign. Men

were competitive by nature. Nothing proved a guy's
superiority to his buddies like bagging the prettiest, richest
girl in the room. As a result, parties had been a straight-up
misery for Georgie since puberty, and she'd been fielding
invitations to the Devil's Kettle high school prom clear
through college. Which might've been flattering had she
been even remotely acquainted with any of those hopeful
young men bombarding her with emails and text messages
every spring. But as she'd exchanged less than a dozen
words in total with the lot of them combined, it was quite
clear that she wasn't a person to them so much as a status
symbol. A stretch goal. When men wanted something, even
something they weren't entitled to, they went after it.

Peter, she couldn't help but notice, hadn't come after her.
At all.

She squirmed at the memory of how she'd blatantly
maneuvered him into kissing her the other night. Of how,
when he'd finally given in and done it, he'd *sniffed* her
longer than he'd actually kissed her. (Never mind that her
blood ran hot even now as she remembered the way he'd
soaked her up with every sense available.) And maybe he'd
woken her up when the lamb had died last night but surely it
was because he'd caught her weeping over it like a baby and
didn't want to be the guy who'd denied a hysterical woman
her goodbye scene. And yes, that goodbye scene had
included a beautiful stroll through an icy wonderland but
instead of putting the moves on her he'd spent the time
gently but unmistakably scolding her for being such a fake
hairdo. What the hell was she *doing* thinking of jumping
him?

Never risk what you can't bear to lose, darling.

Oh great. Now her mother (or the piece of her own brain

that spoke with her mother's voice) was wading into the battle. The scales inside her head were already see-sawing wildly and now she had Bianca bouncing away on the *hell, no* side. But Bianca was one of the most fearless negotiators she knew. You ignored her advice at your peril, and Georgie wasn't one for unnecessary peril.

She sighed. Her mom (or her brain-mom or whatever) was right. She was just getting to know this new, improved Peter. She shouldn't risk whatever might bud between them on such an impulsive move. Her stomach tightened in warning but Georgie pressed a shaky fist to it. Maybe she should get out of here before Peter showed up and the recklessness uncurling inside her took the wheel for real. Maybe she should—

The phone in her pocket rang and she jumped violently. She dragged it out and frowned down at her brother's photo. "Jax? What's up?"

"Are you at Peter's place still?"

Her heart collided uncomfortably with her sternum. "How did you know I'm at Peter's?"

"Everybody knows you're at Peter's. He announced it to the breakfast crowd at the Wooden Spoon this morning."

"Did he?"

He laughed. "He announced a lot of stuff actually."

"Color me interested." Her voice was light and lazy, but her stomach twisted mercilessly inside her. It didn't like this sudden return to dissembling. "What else did he have to say?"

"Plenty. Bottom line, though? Your boy came clean."

Her boy? Since when was Peter her boy again? Did she even want him to be?

Yes, her stomach said. *Maybe just for an hour or two.*

No, her mother/brain said. *But even if you do, for God's sake don't tell Peter that.*

All she said out loud was, "Did he? About what?"

"All of it." Another laugh, this one a strange mix of incredulous and admiring. "He told Gerte straight to her face that Willa was a quality individual he was proud to be related to, and that neither Eli nor Matty was an arsonist of any kind. The only person burning shit down in Devil's Kettle last summer was Peter."

"What?" Georgie's face — and her stomach, thank the lord — went numb.

"Yeah, that's pretty much what Gerte said. Nobody else had the presence of mind to say anything. They just let Peter make his grand exit with as much dignity as a guy can muster when he's trying not to let the whipped cream blow off his girlie hot chocolate."

"It was for Matty." Her heart knocked audibly against her ribs. Or maybe that was the blood beating against her eardrums.

"I know. It's getting embarrassing. That kid's old enough to drink black coffee like the rest of us."

"He'd earned a treat. He helped birth a couple of lambs yesterday."

"Shit. Are Peter's sheep still dropping impromptu babies?"

"Just twice so far. I don't know if anybody else is pregnant."

"Make Willa find out. I'm no fan of Peter Zinc's, but the guy's starting to look downright haggard. I mean, he did the right thing this morning, no question, but I wonder whether he really meant to, or if he was just so damn tired it slipped."

"It was on purpose," Georgie said. Her stomach knew it

241

and so did she. She rubbed a comforting fist over it anyway.

"You sound awfully certain of that."

The kitchen door opened behind her, the cool air kissing her hair, her ears. Her blood jumped hotly and she turned to find Peter there in the door jamb studying her with those brutally honest eyes. "I am."

Jax said, "Did he tell you he was planning to come clean like that?"

"No. But it doesn't surprise me." A man who looked at her like that, who *could* look at her like that, wouldn't have been able to stand somebody else bearing the burden of his sins. She should've known a public confession was coming.

Jax said, "You know, now that I think about it? I'm not super surprised either."

She met Peter's bleakly open gaze, and tenderness for him welled up inside her. He owned a truly suicidal brand of courage these days, didn't he? "I've got to go."

"Georgie, wait," Jax said, "there's something else—"

"Tell me later." She hung up on him and slipped her phone into her pocket. Folded her arms and leaned back against the counter. "Well look who finally came in from the cold."

He didn't smile at her. "I'm an arsonist, Georgie, not a spy."

"So I hear. So everybody heard, I gather."

He pointed his chin at the phone she'd tucked away. "Jax or Eli?"

"Jax."

"What else did he tell you?"

"There's more?" She arched a skeptical brow. "What, did Gerte slap your face off?"

"No, it didn't get physical."

"Lucky you. I hear Gerte has a swing on her. Now get in here, Farmer Zinc. You're letting the cold in."

"Sorry." He stepped into the room, let the door swing shut behind him. It was just the two of them now, and the scent of him filled the room, filled her lungs. She swallowed down a ridiculous surge of breathlessness.

"You smell like sheep and wind," she blurted.

"Sorry," he said again. He took off his coat, hung it on its peg behind the door and crossed to the sink beside her.

"Don't be. You're a farmer." God, she was bad at this. How on earth did men do it? How did they just *ask* for what they wanted from a completely disinterested person?

"Yeah," he said, his voice strangely flat. "I know." He began washing his hands. She watched, fascinated by the flow of water over those banged-up knuckles, those dirt-rimmed fingernails. He dried them on a dishtowel and sent her a sideways look. "You wanted to talk to me?"

She cleared her throat and focused. "About a couple things, yeah."

He leaned a hip against the counter and ran a weary hand over his smooth scalp. "All right," he said. "Let's hear it."

She frowned. What was the word Jax had used? Haggard? It fit. She'd noticed it lately herself. Peter wasn't just lean these days; he was skinny.

"Have you eaten this morning?"

A smile twisted his mouth, bitterly unamused. "I had plans to but—" He lifted his shoulders.

"You're eating now then." She opened the cupboard and brought a plate and a fork to the table where Addy's cinnamon rolls sat. What was left of them, anyway. Matty was a one-man eating machine. She picked up the gooey knife sitting in the pan and aimed it at the bench. "Sit."

He hesitated and she thought he might argue but he didn't. He straddled the bench obediently while she carved off a massive hunk of frosting-covered sweet bread and plunked it on a plate. She slid it his way and lowered herself to the bench as well. Propped an elbow on the table and studied him. He didn't eat.

"You look like shit, Peter." She nodded at the cinnamon roll. "For God's sake, eat something."

"You're not looking so healthy yourself, if you'll pardon my saying so."

"My stomach hurts," she said, surprising herself. She didn't talk about her digestion issues to anybody but her gastroenterologist and her therapist. "It always hurts."

He lifted a slow brow. "Always?"

"Not always." She tipped her head, considered him. Considered the stark honesty that seemed to be his only gear these days. "Only when I lie."

He reached over, braceleted her wrist with his fingers. Frowned at how easily his thumb and fingers overlapped. "How often do you lie, Georgie?"

"Pretty much all the time." She had no idea why it was such a relief to admit that. He *knew* she was a chronic liar. He'd said as much to her face a few weeks back when he'd kissed her at this very table.

He had the good grace not to mention it, though. He said simply, "About what?"

"Everything."

He released her wrist and sat back. "Everything?" He kept his eyes on hers even as he reached for the fork and used the edge to cut off a generous bite of cinnamon roll.

"Well, that might be a bit broad." She watched as he speared that gooey hunk of sweet bread and dragged it through a puddle of cinnamon filling. "Let's just say you were right last night."

"About?"

"The Georgie Davis show." She gave him that slow blink she'd used so effectively for so many years then looked away while an unfamiliar shame lapped at her belly. No pain, just shame. "It's easier to give people what they expect than to force them to see what's really there."

"Safer, too, I'll bet."

She studied him carefully. "A lot." *Don't risk what you can't bear to lose.* "People can't exploit what they don't know exists, and I'm kind of a high profile target." She lifted a vague shoulder that somehow encompassed her face, her fortune and her family name. "People see me and they want things. They'll do what it takes to get them, too." Use whatever weapons she gave them. "I learned early on to keep a fair bit of daylight between my internal and external selves."

"Ah." He didn't lift the cinnamon roll to his mouth. He just kept dragging it lazily through that glistening pool of liquid sugar. And watching her. Her stomach sat up, interested. So did a few other portions of her anatomy that hadn't been fed in a while.

"But the more daylight I manufacture," she murmured, mildly fascinated by the appetite unspooling inside her like the thinnest thread, "the worse my stomach hurts."

"I see." He lifted the fork finally, held it over the plate to let it drip. Cinnamon filling plopped onto the dish, and Georgie's stomach clenched on a shocking spasm of pure want. But did she want the food, or the man holding it? She couldn't tell. Need filled her so completely, emptied her so thoroughly. It left her with nothing but an urgent desire to taste. Heat mingled with shock, pooled low in the cradle of her hips. "And does your stomach hurt now?"

"No." She pulled her focus back to the conversation, pressed a hand to her stomach in wonder and delight. "No, it doesn't."

"Good." He didn't smile. He lifted the fork to her. "Eat."

She was powerless to disobey. She closed her lips over the fork, then froze while a spicy-sweet bombshell of buttery sin laid waste to her senses. Sugar and cinnamon melted on her tongue, and she closed her eyes while Peter dragged the fork slowly from between her teeth. She didn't even chew at first. She couldn't. Her brain was too devastated by the nuclear-grade punch of scent and texture and flavor to coordinate that kind of effort. She simply breathed and let it melt.

"Damn it, Georgie." Peter's voice was rough but the fingers he brushed over her cheek were exquisitely gentle. "It's a cinnamon roll, not crack."

She managed to chew and swallow, then opened her eyes and found him there, right where she'd left him. But his jaw was hard, his eyes snapping with fury. She wanted to taste him next. Wanted to put her lips against that prickly jaw, use her tongue to lap up the salty man taste of his throat. Her stomach did that unnerving float-and-reach thing only Peter had ever inspired, and she finally recognized it for the hunger it was. She wanted her teeth on this man.

"You're angry," she heard herself say. She hadn't meant to say any such thing but now that it was out there, she found she genuinely wanted to discuss it. "Why are you so angry?"

"Why are you so damn hungry?" He speared another generous hunk of cinnamon roll, swirled it through a puddle of frosting and held it up to her. "How the *hell* did this happen?"

She opened her mouth to answer but he stuffed the cinnamon roll in. And then she was too overwhelmed again to do anything but experience it. She hadn't enjoyed food in so long. She'd forgotten what it was like to savor a perfect sweetbread — the way the dough could be both elastic and tender between your teeth, the way the cinnamon filling could cling to your tongue like pudding, the way real cream cheese frosting sent a subtle tang up your nose. Dizzy delight swept through her, and she reached out to steady herself. She wrapped her fingers around his wrist, the one still holding the fork to her lips, which didn't help at all. His skin was warm against her palm, and a little rough with the dark hair she knew he wore everywhere but the head he shaved clean. Even as her stomach sighed in satisfaction, that other appetite rumbled through her. It gripped her belly, kindled in her womb. A prickly heat stiffened her nipples, tangled her thoughts, and shone a merciless spotlight on a needy emptiness growing inside her. An emptiness food wasn't going to fill.

She swallowed the cinnamon roll with a tiny, involuntary moan of appreciation and opened her eyes once again to find him glaring at her.

"You kissed me right here on this bench," she said baldly. "The real me, for maybe the first time. You said that."

"Yeah. I remember."

"You were right. That *was* the first time you'd kissed the real me. But it took me a while to figure out it was the first time I'd kissed the real you, too."

"The real me." He put the fork back on the plate with a harsh clink and dragged a hand down his face. She could hear the rasp of stubble against his palm, and it sent a

247

shivery bolt of need from her womb to her own palms. She wanted to feel that sweet abrasion against her own skin, against her palms, her throat, her breasts. She squirmed on the bench, trying to ease the strange lightness between her thighs where the skin was so delicate that his whiskers would undoubtedly leave a mark. The lightness became a liquid pull and she had to concentrate on breathing. "Trust me, Georgie, the real me isn't worth your kisses."

She had to swallow before any words would present themselves. "What if I disagree?"

"You'd be a fool." He gripped his knees and shoved to his feet. Pointed at the cinnamon roll. "You finish that."

"I'd rather finish this." She stood, too. Her knees felt like water, and her cheeks burned. Her nipples pushed shamelessly against her thin sweater. She nearly folded her arms over them out of habit but stopped herself. She wanted him. She was about to proposition the man, for heaven's sake. Was she really going to pretend he wasn't doing it for her? Was now really the time to play it cool?

Yes, her mother/brain said. *Now is exactly the time to play it cool. For God's sake, let him come to you.*

Fuck that, her body said. *Feed me.*

"Finish what?" He stood at the sink, his back to her, his big hands gripping the edge.

"This conversation."

"I don't even know what we're talking about."

"You said I'd never really been satisfied," she said. "A few weeks ago. When you kissed me."

"I remember," he said tightly. "Just like I remember that I didn't offer to fix that."

"I know." She swallowed again, her throat dry, her body alive. "But I don't think I ever satisfied you, either. And I *am*

248

offering to fix that. Right now."

CHAPTER 26

PETER GRIPPED THE sink until he couldn't feel his fingers but he kept an eye on them nonetheless. Because if he let those greedy bastards have their way, they'd have been all over Georgie five minutes ago. They'd have helped themselves to her the instant she'd let him feed her, the instant she'd closed her eyes and made that damn *noise* she made every time she tasted something really, really good. Something he'd put in her mouth himself. Something—

Reality rushed in, smothering temptation with a damp slap.

Something he couldn't afford to give her.

The scotch that had first inspired that little moan? He'd stolen it from the taproom.

The cinnamon roll he'd fed her just now? Charity from Addy. He'd tried to buy her a goddamn muffin an hour ago and moths had flown out of his empty wallet. He'd brought her coffee, yeah, but she'd already secured her own, hadn't she? She didn't need a damn thing from him, which was bad enough, but every time she entered his orbit, she ruined clothes he couldn't afford to replace. Every single time they collided, she came away worse off. Which was why there was no way he could, in anything approaching good conscience, let her throw him a gratitude fuck. Even if she insisted.

If there was a God in heaven, she wouldn't insist. He was only human. Flawed, weak, pathetically poor, and *human*.

"Don't do that," he snapped. "I'm not your dog. I don't

need a reward."

"A reward?" Her voice was bewildered behind him and he couldn't bear to turn around. Couldn't bear to witness the confusion and the invitation moving with equal sincerity across that perfect face because, fuck, her honesty was as blinding as her beauty. He couldn't take them both together. "What are you—"

"I cleared Matty and Eli of all public suspicion today, Georgie. I know how you feel about family. I get that that's a big deal to you but I don't need a sexual thank you note, okay?"

"A sexual *thank you note*?"

He gave a tight shrug. "I appreciate the offer but I didn't do it for Matty or Eli, and I definitely didn't do it for you, so you can keep your clothes on. I always knew I'd have to own those fires one day. Today was just my lucky day, I guess." He clamped down on a jag of bitter laughter. Yeah, he'd had all the luck today, hadn't he? Too bad none of it had been good. "Gerte pissed me off and Lainey was trying to make me her plus-one to Addy and Jax's wedding so I—"

"Wait, Lainey asked you out?" Georgie sounded both startled and disgruntled. "I guess I should've seen that one coming. You're my ex-fiancé, and she's never forgiven me for Flynn."

He had no idea who Flynn was, nor did it matter. He stared down at his hands still safely gripping the edge of his dingy sink. "Suffice it to say that drastic measures seemed necessary."

"So what did you say?"

"That I was totally broke and had been for a while. That I'd been trying my hand at insurance fraud via arson over the summer, and Matty and Eli had gotten caught up in the smoke screen. That Bianca had torn me a new one when she found out. That reparations had been made to the tune of whatever was left of my empire. That I've failed catastrophically at being a brother, a fiancé and a small-town tycoon, but I'm trying to be a decent farmer. Failing that, I'm trying to be a decent human. Which is why I'm not going to sleep with you, Georgie." And just saying the words out loud had loss howling through him. Hadn't today sucked enough without fate dangling in front of him the one thing he desperately wanted? The one thing he knew he shouldn't have and didn't deserve? Why did he have to be a good guy today of all days?

"No," Georgie said impatiently, "I meant to Lainey. What did you say to Lainey?"

Shock had him turning around. He found her standing a few feet away in those too-short sweats and ugly rain boots, arms crossed over yesterday's expensive sweater, head tipped like a curious bird, demand blazing in those blue eyes. "To Lainey?"

"Yes, to Lainey. She came home from college with a fiancé who turned out to be a faithless bastard, remember?" That would be Flynn, he surmised, though he didn't remember. He'd been away for years. People forgot that, even if he never did. She wrinkled her nose. "Handsy, too, and a terrible kisser."

Peter narrowed his eyes, an ugly suspicion forming. "Is this hearsay or—"

"Oh, it's personal experience." She grimaced. "Of the against-my-will variety."

Rage smoked to life inside him. "Goddamn it, Georgie—"

"Oh pull yourself together. There's a world of space

between sexual assault and an enthusiastic if misguided pass. Flynn was solidly in the second camp but Lainey wasn't pleased to hear about it. Neither was Gerte. As if they needed another excuse to hate my family." She sighed. "But what was I supposed to do? Let Lainey marry a guy who didn't even wait until he was her husband to cheat on her? Or try to cheat, anyway? We've never been besties but I don't hate the girl."

She didn't say *like she hates me* but Peter heard it just fine. He wondered how often she'd done that, shouldered the blame for a man's bad behavior, then shrugged off the ensuing fury and resentment of the betrayed girlfriend or wife. He considered that stunning face of hers and the equally stunning trust fund, and figured it was probably pretty damn often. Which accounted for all the daylight she'd learned to keep between her public and private selves, never mind that it was eating her alive. Rage smoked stubbornly inside him and he breathed through it. He couldn't convince his fists to relax, though, so he shoved them into his elbows, crossing his arms over the fury trying to crowd his lungs from his chest.

"So?" she prompted. "What did you say when Lainey asked you out?"

"She didn't get that far. We were interrupted."

"What would you have said?"

"What does it matter? I'm not your fiancé anymore, remember? I'm not your anything. If I want to go out with Lainey, I can."

Her eyes narrowed dangerously. "What would you have said, Peter?"

"No." He gave up on concealing the rage. He shoved those angry fists into his pockets and glared at the ceiling.

"I'd have said no, Georgie."

"Why?"

Because she's not you. Because nobody's you, and I don't want anybody who isn't you. Because I want you. Only you. You, you, you.

He brought his eyes down to hers. "Given that I burned Addy's house down and nearly killed both her and Jax in the process, do you really think it's a good idea for me to show up at their wedding, even as Lainey's plus one?"

"Not an answer," she said. "Points for misdirection, though. Bianca's going to love you."

"Bianca hates me."

"She does now," Georgie said serenely. "She'll come around."

"To what?" he asked, increasingly bewildered.

"To you being back in the family."

"We're still doing that?"

"We're not still doing it. It's done. You didn't have to take responsibility for those fires, you know."

"Of course I did."

She nodded slowly. "And that's why Bianca's going to love you."

"Why?"

"Because you're a principled sort of ruthless, and you don't mind bleeding when you need to. You're exactly the kid she deserves."

Hope unspooled inside him, slippery and unwelcome, even as dismay backed him into the sink. "We're not getting engaged again."

"Of course we aren't. Get a hold of yourself, Peter. I don't want to marry you. I only want to sleep with you."

"I already told you that wasn't happening."

"Why not?"

"Because you're not the treat I get for being a good boy."

She laughed. "You've been good, no question, but not that good. I'm worth considerably more than a public confession and a cup of coffee."

"I agree. Unfortunately, a cup of coffee and a public confession is all I can afford." The words fell to the ground between them, weighted with an impossible shame, but he forced himself to continue. "Look around you, Georgie. This farm is barely functional and it's all I own. Everything smells like sheep and dirt and the wood burning stove. Do you really want to take off your clothes in my stinky kitchen and get busy on that cot over there? Because that's my bed until I can afford to turn on the damn furnace. But, oh, wait, the furnace is already on because I have half a dozen Davis relations under my roof. I didn't ask for them but I still have to keep them warm at night, and I have no idea how I'm going to pay that bill come the end of the month."

He kept his eyes mercilessly on hers. She thought he didn't mind bleeding? God. He minded. He bled when he had to but he minded the hell out of it.

"Do you realize that, Georgie? I genuinely have no idea where that money might come from. I went down the hill this morning because there was nothing here for you to eat. My grocery budget covers ramen for one, see, but I've been feeding three lately. Thirteen if we multiply Matty by a factor of ten, which we should because holy God can that kid eat." She stared at him, stricken and pale. She did see. Good. Humiliation clogged his throat but he spoke over it. "But we needed breakfast for five today even without the multiplier so I went down the hill for provisions and ended up at the Wooden Spoon. It was habit more than anything. I used to be a guy who could stand the room a round or three, no problem. But I'm not that guy anymore. I can't even afford a dozen muffins and half a dozen fancy coffees. I remembered that pertinent fact a little late, though, which provided Gerte the distinct pleasure of reshelving the muffins I ordered but couldn't pay for."

He saw her throat work as she cast around for an appropriate response. "Why are you telling me this?"

"Because I have to." He dragged both hands down his face, nearly sick with weariness and with wanting her. Because, yeah, he still wanted her. Was there anything more pathetic than a poor man with expensive taste? He doubted it.

"Why? I know exactly how broke you are. I took great pleasure in following along at home, remember? I'm the *reason* you're so broke." She paused. "Well, no. You're broke because you gambled big and lost."

"And I hurt Bianca's children along the way."

She shrugged lightly. "Nobody drops the hammer like my mom."

"Amen."

"But your net worth has nothing to do with why I want this." She stepped forward, something settling in those clear blue eyes, something freighted and purposeful. Peter wanted to back away but his butt was already up against the sink. And he didn't actually want to back away at all. He wanted to be closer. He wouldn't allow himself that, of course. Wouldn't let himself move to meet her, but he wanted to. Then he didn't have to want anything because she was coming closer all by herself, step by inexorable step. "Neither does what you did for Matty and Eli down at the Wooden Spoon today."

"Why, then?" Desperation twined with desire and knotted itself around his gut. It nailed his feet to the floor and he watched her approach with both resignation and eager anticipation. "Why on earth would you let me touch you? Let me have you?" She was close enough to smell now, and it was all ice and money and…sheep? Of course. She'd been cuddling Bone while Peter had been off kicking lapdogs like some crazed animal abuser.

"Because I'm hungry, Peter." Her body was a handful of crucial inches from his. He felt her words on his own lips, ringing in his own empty spaces. "I'm hungry and you feed me. You're the only one who feeds me."

"Georgie, no."

"But I do have one question, and the answer matters, so think hard and answer honestly." She killed another inch or two, leaned in and rested her palms on the sink on either side of his hips. "Do you want me, Peter? If you don't, just say so. I'll leave and we won't ever talk about this again."

He met her eyes, composed his face and slipped into his old skin like it was a warm bath. He opened his mouth to lie, to say hell no, he didn't want her. Hadn't ever wanted her. All he wanted was for her to go home, take her family with her, and maybe send him a check for next month's gas bill.

He kissed her instead.

He didn't do it with any finesse, either. No, he just sort of…broke. His restraint, his reason, his shame, they all just shattered and blew away like so much dust. He dove at her like a starving man, shoved both hands into that glorious spill of hair and dragged her in. He hauled her up against his body and heard his neural pathways explode. He *heard* them. His higher order thinking came apart with an electric sizzle that he only vaguely noted because he was too busy gobbling up Georgie Davis.

He seized her mouth with his own, and his interior landscape went abruptly dark. It was like the glory of her/ mouth — hot, open and as clumsily eager as his own — had struck him blind. Not that he cared. What was there to see? Georgie was kissing him. God, the scent of her, all winter air and baby sheep and platinum cards. She was both exquisitely familiar and far beyond his touch, except he *was* touching her. And she was letting him.

No, she wasn't simply allowing this. She was *participating*. It floated through his fragmented mind with a sharp wonder. He'd kissed Georgie hundreds of times, maybe thousands, but this was the first time she'd ever kissed him back. He hadn't realized it before, hadn't understood, but if she'd ever kissed him even remotely like this surely he'd have noticed—

She licked into his mouth with wet demand. Hot need shot into his veins, lit up his body like a drug. His cock jumped and he rolled his hips helplessly into hers.

And she made that noise.

"Sweet mother of—" He spun them, shoved her back against his counter and pinned her there with his body, letting her feel every inch of his desire. Showed her with his mouth what every one of those hard, demanding inches had in mind. She met him right there in the middle, too, her tongue as bold and needy as his. His hands flew over her, fast and greedy, skimming over the angles and edges, the brutal geometry imposed on her by pain. He wondered briefly what she'd feel like when he'd fed her back to good health, then decided it didn't matter. It wasn't the size or shape of her that had torn him from his reason, it was the fact of her. It was Georgie herself. It was her need and her courage and her honesty. It was the demand of her mouth and her hands, the unabashed appetite in them both.

Georgie knew how to want, all right. And she wanted him.

Those elegant hands of hers streamed over him like floodwater, a greedy, destructive gush, ripping out trees and houses and streetlights, leaving him reborn in ruins. And he wasn't just happy about it; he was grateful. There wasn't anything in his soul he wouldn't let her destroy, nothing he wanted to keep more than he wanted her to keep touching him. Those hands roved greedily, claiming his scalp, his chest, his arms, his butt. She shoved him back then boosted herself onto the counter and wrapped those endless legs around him. She twisted her hands into his sweater and pinned him with wild blue eyes.

"More," she said, breathless and flushed.

"More," he agreed and dove back in.

CHAPTER 27

GEORGIE WAS GLAD she'd thought to boost herself onto the counter because there was no way she'd have stayed on her feet for Peter's version of more. He took her mouth like plunder and all she could do was hang on. Which was absolutely fine with her. She lifted shaky knees and hooked her ankles together behind him, dragged him closer. God, why couldn't she get close enough? She arched into him, aligned the center of her need with the blunt demand pushing against the front of his jeans. He made some kind of noise and rolled himself into her with a frankly carnal rhythm that flashed her back to the night she'd opened her eyes. The memory of him reaching for satisfaction inside her own body was a dark beauty that filled her mind, fed the sharp-toothed hunger racing through her veins. This time, though, her body was reaching back. Want burned inside her, pooled low and wet between her legs.

She shifted restlessly. More. She needed more. She needed his skin. She plucked at his sweater, desperate to find the skin beneath, and understood only vaguely that he was doing the same. He burrowed a hand up under her sweater, found the edge of her bra and dragged it down. Found the tip of her nipple, already tight and budded. He brushed his fingers experimentally across that shameless point and the need inside her roared onto a plane she'd never experienced before, something akin to pain. Her hands fisted spasmodically. She'd probably scratched him — hell, clawed him — but it was only fair. It was a small pain compared to the hunger keening through her. He brushed his knuckles across that straining point again and her center clenched abruptly. The breath stalled in her lungs and she shoved her breast — meager though it was — greedily into his hand. She didn't just want more; she needed it. She ached for it. She wanted him to take her body like he'd been taking her mouth. She wanted him ungentle, unhinged, impolite. She wanted—

"I know," he murmured against her mouth. "I know. I'm getting there."

"Faster," she muttered and wedged her hands between their bodies. The instant he stepped back, she wrestled herself out of her sweater and tossed it into the sink. Then she was sitting on the counter, knees splayed, chest heaving, her hair a wild cloud of static cling sticking willy-nilly to her cheeks and shoulders, wearing nothing but the bra she'd thrown on under yesterday's sweater.

Which wasn't even really a bra. More of a bralette. Okay, a tank top with delusions of grandeur. It was a dull grey cotton thing whose only purpose in life was to keep her nipples from showing through her clothes, as nipples were pretty much all she could claim in the breast department. It had been pretty once upon a time, with a trio of thin straps rising over each shoulder before criss-crossing between her shoulder blades in back, and a lacy hem that hit right at the bottom of her narrow ribcage. Unfortunately it was also extremely comfortable and she'd worn it nearly to death. It had gone from slim to sloppy months ago, and the lace was a ratty, pilly mess.

And this was a problem. A serious one. Because Georgie wasn't naïve. She understood her value proposition in this world and it didn't involve looking good naked. It involved looking expensive clothed, so expensive that by the time a guy finally got her naked he had no choice but to be grateful. But here she was, trembling with naked need, wearing nothing but her little brother's grimy sweats and an ancient bralette that sagged and bagged far lower than intended over Georgie's essentials. Much lower, in fact, given that it currently exposed several bony inches of her chest and one shameless nipple.

Peter stared, frozen, his brows knit in an ominous frown. Shame leaked into her stomach. She was wearing the matching underwear, too, because they were as comfy as the bralette. They'd been just as cute, too. Once. Now they sported holes big enough to put a thumb through.

"Sorry about—" She shrugged uncomfortably, and one of those worn straps slipped off her shoulder. The elastic was shot. She dragged it back up. "—this." It fell down again and she left it there, defeated.

"This?" He shifted that frown to her saggy strap.

She waved a vague hand at her torso. "I usually dress up when sex is on the agenda."

"I remember." He stepped forward slowly, touched her spread knees with deliberate fingers. A hopeful spark flew from her knees straight to that stupid exposed nipple and she tugged the neckline of her bralette up. He made a disapproving noise — toward her body, she wondered, or the ugly underwear? It slid down again, of course, and the brush of well-worn cotton against her swollen nipple sent a wave of shame-shot hunger crashing over her. Because she was still hungry. He was frowning at her naked body and God help her, she was still so damn hungry. She closed her eyes, paralyzed by the awful humiliation of it.

"Why on earth are you sorry, Georgie?" His voice was a

sonic rumble that whispered over her exquisitely sensitized skin. He cupped her knees in both hands and she gave a violent shiver. He slid his palms to the delicate hollow behind each one and tugged gently. She came helplessly forward, and it put the center of her need — still a howling, ravening thing — a mere whisper from him. It put the truth in her mouth and she gave it to him.

"My naked self is a lot more inspiring in French lingerie."

"Georgie." He dragged a palm slowly up her thigh, until his thumb touched the vulnerable seam where her leg met her pelvis. "You could be wearing a trash bag for all I care."

Her breathing shifted, hitched. "I practically am."

"Great. That's about all I can afford to replace."

His thumb drifted slowly down, tracing that secret line all the way to the curve of her bottom. Her center bloomed, lush and hungry, and she nearly lost the thread. Managed to ask, "Why would you have to replace it?"

"You ruin your clothes every time you come here." And that thumb reversed course, tracing a line back to the point of her hipbone, passing just a fraction closer to her center this time.

"I do not." She sounded breathless, even to herself. And her nipple ached.

"You named my lambs after the sweater you destroyed birthing them." His thumb made a lazy circle around the bony point of her hip and drifted south again, but another fraction of an inch inward. Closer to that pulsing need. Her nipple was so close to his chest. It would be nothing, the work of a moment to arch her back and rub herself shamelessly against the rough wool of his sweater. But she remembered that frown and her courage fled. *Never risk what you can't bear to lose.* "Along with yesterday's skirt and the sweater currently in my sink. But that's not the point."

His thumb reached the inner curve of her bottom again and started slowly back north, another whisper closer to her center. She squirmed restlessly, her need finally trumping her fear. If he wouldn't get his thumb where she needed it then by God she'd get her need to his thumb. But he didn't make another trip south. He leaned forward instead, buried his face in her hair, and pulled in a breath like she was oxygen. Hope spiraled tentatively into the want and the fear, along with a healthy shot of impatience. Fine, her underwear was awful. She could just take it off and they'd move along. *Now.*

"Do you mind getting to the point?" she asked peevishly. "Sometime soonish?"

His voice was a rough caress against the shell of her ear, and want shivered through her. "The point, Georgie, is that this thing you're wearing, while devastating, might as well be a Hefty bag for all it matters to me."

Devastating?

"Don't get me wrong," he said. "I appreciate it. But I'm not in this for the lingerie. If I were, our engagement might've lasted."

Curiosity swirled into that pulsing need, turned it a fascinating shade of compulsion. "What are you in this for, then?"

"I'm hungry, too, Georgie. But I could be blind and you'd still be able to feed me. Because I'm not hungry for your goddamn underwear or how you look in it. I'm hungry for—" He tipped her sideways suddenly and she yelped in surprise. The yelp died in her throat when he dropped his mouth to her aching nipple and took it hungrily between his teeth. At the same moment, he swept his thumb straight down her center, glancing over the tiny knot of her desire. Her core gave a hard clench, lurching her into a wonderland of blazing light and pulsing satisfaction. She jerked, shoved her spasming sex into his palm and moaned helplessly. He worked that knot against her pubic bone with the heel of his hand, drew hard on her nipple and skewered her on the merciless blade of her own satisfaction.

She had no idea how long she stayed there, drowning in it, in him, in the terrifying gift of an orgasm she hadn't given herself. An orgasm so crushingly powerful she didn't even try to manage it, or her face's response. She just tried to survive it. She surfaced to the sound of his voice, a delicious rumble against her skin.

"*That,* Georgie. That's what I'm hungry for. Now give me more."

He dragged at the waistband of her sweats and she rallied. She lifted her bottom and helped him shuck Matty's sweats from her legs. She tugged open the fastening of his jeans and pushed them down his legs with her bare feet. His erection sprang into her hands and she moaned, need blooming at her center again, slippery and hot.

He kicked his jeans and boots aside, dragged her to the edge of the counter and put himself between her knees. But instead of sliding into her, he lifted her from the counter. Her butt filled his palms and she lashed her legs and arms around him, her world tilting and sliding. His sweater was rough against her nipples, and the sweet abrasion had her core fluttering dangerously. She squirmed, tried to hitch herself a little higher, to get herself above the thick heat of him so she could slide down and impale herself on him. Ride him and this impossible hunger into oblivion. But Peter had other ideas.

He turned and shoved one of those heavy kitchen chairs aside with one foot, then laid her out on his big table like a feast. She fell back, the wood cool and delicious against her bare shoulders. Her thighs were spread wide on either side of his hips, the air an exotic kiss against her most private skin. He took his erection in one big hand, stroked himself and met her eyes. Desire blazed there, unhidden and frank.

"Do I need a condom, Georgie?"

Her nipples beaded and ached, her core tightened, and she watched him fist himself. She had to try twice before she could form words. "I'm still on the pill, if that's what you're asking."

"Have you slept with anybody but me lately?"

"No. Only you."

He smiled at her, and a black satisfaction twined into the savage desire filling those dark eyes. The empty ache inside her twisted higher, tighter. "It's only been you for me, too," he told her. "Only you."

"Then no," she managed. "You don't need a condom. You just need to stop talking and—"

Then the blunt head of his cock was right *there*, sliding into her with a hot confidence that had her inner muscles clenching helplessly, gripping him, pulling him. He pushed home, and the mind-bending fullness of it tore a gasp from her. She threw out her arms, seeking something, anything to hold onto. She was dimly aware of a metallic jangle — there went the cinnamon rolls — then her hands found the edge of the table. She locked her ankles together in the small of Peter's back, felt him pulse hot and sure inside her, and she smiled.

"More," she said.

"More," he agreed, and drove her beyond madness.

CHAPTER 28

"Peter."

He had no idea how long it was before Georgie spoke, only that he was vaguely impressed by her ability to form words. His own dazzled brain was still trying to remember what words were.

"Mmmm?" Best he could do.

"Can we move to the cot?"

"The cot?" he mumbled. Progress.

"Yeah." She drifted a hand down his back, cupped one butt cheek then gave it a fond smack. "I think I have frosting in my hair."

He stirred, his body heavy and deliciously slippery against hers. They were...sweaty, he realized. Both of them. It put a glow inside him that had nothing to do with the satisfaction still ringing in his ears and echoing through his body. Because he and Georgie had had sex before, sure. But the kind of ambitious, athletic sex that required *her* to sweat? That was new. And new was good.

He levered himself off her, a stupid grin trying to split his face, and focused with an effort. The cinnamon rolls had indeed splattered to the floor, and were now wearing an upside-down pan like a snail shell. A trail of wet brown sugar streaked across the table, pointing the way to the scene of the crime from under a hank of Georgie's shiny hair. There was a suspiciously sticky patch under his forearm as well. He peeled it off and winced.

She made a moue with well-kissed lips. "You, too?"

"Worth it." He gently disengaged their bodies and that little moue flashed briefly into actual regret. He blinked in surprise. She'd never said as much but he'd always understood this to be Georgie's favorite part of sex — the part where she got her body back. He patted around for his t-shirt and tidied them both up while battling a wave of disorientation. Everything was so weirdly familiar — her body, her scent, her beauty — but nothing was the same at all. This was a brand-new, utterly novel experience and he didn't have his balance.

"Definitely worth it." She closed her eyes and stretched like a well-fed cat, and something primal and endlessly hungry sparked in Peter's blood.

He said, "How attached are you to the cot idea?"

She opened one eye to a narrow slit. "You have a counter-offer?"

The shark in him swam to the surface and he grinned. He always had a counter-offer. He was just a farmer now but some things were in your bones. And counter-offers were in Peter's. "This house has many faults and flaws—"

"This house is incredible," she murmured improbably. "I think it was built by Swedish monks."

"What?"

"Never mind. That's just my stomach talking. This house has many faults and flaws?"

"It does. But — I may have mentioned this before — it has an incredible hot water heater." He propped one hand on the table next to her head and leaned in until his lips were one hot whisper from hers. Her lashes dropped to half-mast and her mouth softened, offered. But he only lifted a lock of her sweat-dampened hair with his other hand. "And I understand you have frosting in your hair."

Her lips curved. "I see where you're going with this." She wrapped a cool hand around the wrist he was leaning on, lifted her head and swiped her tongue up the stickiness on his forearm. That spark in his blood burst into flame and he sucked in a hard breath. "You could use some cleaning up as well."

"I could," he managed. "I absolutely—"

A knock sounded at the front door, tentative but unmistakeable.

"Ignore that," Peter said. "It's nobody."

"It would have to be." She frowned up at him. "Addy sent her guests home, and took Matty and her folks back to Davis Place with her. Who else comes here?"

"Nobody," he assured her, even as the knock sounded again. "The only other person who ever drops by is Willa and I'm pretty sure she and Eli are at the Taproom this morning." He took her mouth in a hot, wet kiss. She met him halfway, then the knock sounded again. She broke away, nudged him back. He sighed and met worried blue eyes.

She said, "What if the babies got out again?"

"You think Tag learned to knock?" But he knew he was losing her. And whoever the hell was at his front door knocked yet again. He sighed and started scooping up clothes. A few seconds later, he was striding barefoot across his chilly dining room, Georgie hard on his heels, to yank open the front door.

His mother stood on the steps, shivering inside a trench coat and shoes that it would take a Georgie to properly appreciate.

"Mom."

"Peter." She smiled but her eyes held the troubled knowledge of his poverty. He watched as she looked beyond him, as that knowledge multiplied itself by the cold unfurnished house, the ugly farmyard she'd walked through, the smell of sheep and want clinging to everything like a toxic fog. This was how her son had turned out.

No smile in the world could conceal her disappointment.

"I'm sorry for stopping by unannounced but I didn't have your number." She gave a helpless shrug. "After what happened at the Wooden Spoon this morning, I thought maybe we could...talk."

Georgie slid a hand into the crook of his elbow. She was warm against his arm but he hardly felt it. Hardly felt *her*. "What happened at the Wooden Spoon this morning?" she asked.

Shay hesitated. If the beautiful woman standing barefoot in his foyer smelling like sex and frosting hadn't yet heard about his humiliating inability to buy her breakfast, Shay wasn't going to tell her. It was, he realized, his mother's version of a gift. One he didn't want or need.

He kept his eyes on Shay, but spoke to Georgie. "I told the world that I was broke, had failed at insurance fraud, and let your mom put me into bankruptcy. And then I couldn't buy you any muffins because I'm too poor."

"Oh, that." Georgie waved a negligent hand and focused on Shay with the regal hauteur of a queen. Or her mother. "We had cinnamon rolls."

Shay's eyes went to Georgie's hair then drifted back to her face. Georgie didn't blink. "I...see."

"Where's your girlfriend?" Georgie asked Shay. "The one from the gallery yesterday."

Peter frowned. Shay and Julia had been to the gallery?

"I'm not sure. I wanted to speak to Peter alone." Shay lifted her shoulders in a pretty shrug. "Julia's the curious sort, though, and friendly. I'm sure she'll find something to occupy her." Her eyes sharpened almost imperceptibly, but Peter had grown up with this woman. Her moods were like quicksilver and he'd learned to read them with brutal accuracy. His shoulders tensed. "Or somebody."

Georgie gave Shay that slow blink that knocked thirty points off her IQ. Shay blinked back, then turned to Peter with an arched brow that said *really?* Peter gave an amiable shrug but he wanted to shake Georgie, wanted to break that vapid shell until she could never wear it again.

"I wonder," Shay said gently to Georgie, "if I might speak to Peter in private."

Georgie gave that another slow blink. "Oh," she said finally. "Sure." She released his arm and patted his cheek. "I should get home anyway. I'm supposed to open the gallery at eleven."

"I'll call you," Peter said lamely.

Georgie gave a vague if dazzling smile and disappeared into the kitchen. She galumphed back out in her rain boots a minute later, gave them both a lazy little finger wave then sailed across his pasture as if it were a catwalk in Milan. He watched her reverse her Rover and disappear down the street. Then he turned back to his mother, now standing in his dining room, taking in the chilly emptiness with wondering eyes.

"So, Mom." He tucked his fingers into his pockets and braced himself. "What's up?"

Five minutes later, Peter was having yet another unexpected experience in his kitchen. His mother was making him breakfast. He dug into the darkest corners of his memory but couldn't come up with a single other image of

Shay standing in front of a stove, competently flicking eggs around a hot pan. As Peter remembered it, her domestic accomplishments (like his own) extended about as far as opening a box of cereal or a can of soup. He scooped the ruined cinnamon rolls off the floor and dumped them in the trash, then took the pan to the sink and began washing it.

Shay looked up from dividing a pile of fluffy scrambled eggs between two plates and chuckled. "Any job worth doing is worth doing right but cleanup is a bitch."

"What does that mean?"

She tipped her head toward the frosting-smeared floor and table. "I don't imagine Georgie Davis is a particularly difficult job but it's good to know that you're doing her right."

"Mom. God."

"Oh, don't be such a prude. It's an accomplishment! Given the circumstances of your broken engagement, it's quite a comeback. You can tell me all about it while we eat." She picked up the plated eggs, eyed the sticky table and paused. "On second thought, why don't we eat here at the counter?"

"Yeah, good thinking."

She handed him a plate and leaned back against the counter, fork in hand, to study him. "So how did you wheedle your way back into the Davis family's good graces? Tell me everything."

"There's nothing to tell," he said easily, but adrenaline snaked into his bloodstream. Maybe Shay had never cooked him breakfast but she'd played this game with him endlessly. An innocent kitchen counter conversation could suddenly be fraught with double and triple meanings, layers of motivations, traps and double-backs. She always wanted something — information, allegiance, admiration — and it was up to Peter to figure out what it was and how to provide it before she got bored. Before she sighed and accused him of being as slow and stupid as his father. Before she abandoned him to get what she needed from somebody else, somebody smarter and more interesting. Somebody worth her time. It was a puzzle strapped to a time bomb and Peter had always loved puzzles.

Or maybe he'd just loved his mother, and had mastered puzzles so he could stay safe and warm in the center of her rapt attention.

Or maybe conversation without bloodshed really was just boring.

"Don't be so modest." Shay forked up a bite of eggs and sighed happily. "Protein. God, how I've missed protein. Julia has her uses but her sweet tooth is killing me. Pie for goddamn breakfast. Who does that?" She shook her head, then pointed a fork at his untouched plate. "Now eat. And spill."

He took a clean fork from the dish drainer and shrugged. "There's nothing to spill, Mom, seriously. You know what this town is like. Girl like Georgie gets an itch, who else is going to scratch it for her? Walt down at the Sugar Rush?"

Shay snorted, and the eggs landed in Peter's stomach like wet cement. He was being a dick. The circumstances demanded it, of course. So did Georgie. She'd specifically asked him to pump Shay for information if the opportunity arose, but his stomach didn't like it. He wondered if this was just a small taste of Georgie's life. No wonder she was so goddamn skinny.

"As if the Davises would stoop to a lowly doughnut boy. At least in public." Shay's mouth tightened bitterly and she scooped up some more eggs. "No, they'd rather swan around this town like royalty. Like they're too good to bang the hot farmer down the road." Her lips curved slyly. "Or take a nice sweaty ride on his mom."

Peter forced down another swallow of eggs and sent his mom a purposefully dubious look. "Georgie's done you, too?"

She gave a startled laugh. "I'm not above it, but no. I was talking about—" She broke off, studied him with bright eyes. "You don't know?"

"What, which Davises you've slept with?"

"Of course." She danced her fork through her fingers. "I assumed you knew."

He shrugged. "There were rumors."

"About?"

"You and Joe."

"Bianca's faithful husband." Her lips curved in a slow, delighted smile. "The rumor mill got hold of that one, did it?"

"It's the only one I ever heard." He arched a brow, and forced himself to finish the eggs. "Why?"

"Well, give credit where it's due." Shay set aside her plate and tapped a finger to her lips. "I didn't think Willa had it in her."

"Willa's a deep pond. She been keeping secrets for you?"

"Just the one."

Peter gave his mother a level stare and she chuckled. "Don't be jealous, sweet pea. You're still my favorite. It was a girl thing, that's all."

It sure as fuck had been. Childbirth was about as girlie as it got.

"Well you couldn't have done better than parking your

275

little secret with Willa, whatever it is. Turns out she's aces in the secret-keeping department."

"Is that so?"

"Oh, yeah." He set his plate aside, too, and leaned in, as if warming up to some good gossip. "You know the baby Davis, the one who looks so much like Diego?"

"Matty," Shay murmured.

"Right. There's been speculation lately that he's not Bianca's menopause baby after all." He slid his mother a conspiratorial smile. "From what I hear, he's more likely to be Diego's bastard." He let a bit of shark surface in his smile. "And Willa's. All these years and I never even suspected. Congratulations, Grandma."

Shay snorted. "Oh, please. Willa may be a deep pond but she's not *that* deep. Matty isn't Willa's baby." The shark swam behind her smile, too. "He's mine."

Peter forced himself to freeze in apparent shock. "*That's* the secret she kept for you?"

"Still keeping it, too, if people think she's the mother." She shook her head in wonder. "I have to admit, I didn't think she would. I wasn't sure what I'd be walking into when I decided to come back to town."

"I can imagine." He leaned back to study her. "What did make you decide to come back, if you weren't planning to drop that little bomb?"

"Who says I'm not?"

"Are you?"

"Not if I don't have to. Not if I get what I want the easy way."

"What's the easy way?"

"Asking for it."

He paused significantly. "Is this the part where you ask

me for it?"

She chuckled. "I don't want a sheep."

"I have a dog you could have. He's an asshole, though."

She grinned. "I'm not much of an animal person."

"Yeah," Peter muttered feelingly. "Me, neither." He'd apologize to Tag later.

"What I want," Shay said, "is a sketch."

Susan Sey

CHAPTER 29

"A SKETCH?" PETER didn't have to fake his frown. What the hell did his mom want with a sketch? "Of Diego's?"

"Who else's?"

"What's it of?"

"Me." She smiled. "Naked." The smile died. "I understand Bianca spent the summer making money off my back. Literally. And I won't have it. I want that sketch."

"What, from the *Diego After Dark* thing? You were—" Understanding rang in his head like a bell, huge and deafening. "Holy fuck, the pencil sketches. Everybody thought they were of Willa. That's how they put two and two together and came up with Matty. She admitted those sketches were of her!"

"Two of them were. The third one was of me."

"I'll be goddamned." He shook his head but it made sense. He tried to remember those sketches but only came up with a vague recollection of skin and hair and sunshine. "And you think Bianca Davis is just going to hand it over?"

"I'd like her to, yes."

"She won't. I'm not rich anymore but I remember it well, and trust me, rich people aren't rich because they give shit away. Especially not valuable shit like an original Diego Davis. Why would Bianca give it to you?"

"I'm sure she doesn't want Matty's true parentage to come to light."

"Diego would've been all of sixteen when he fathered Matty," Peter pointed out. "You think statutory rape will reflect well on you?"

"Truth is a malleable thing," Shay mused, "and so dependent on perspective." And she had a pet reporter, Peter remembered suddenly, who wasn't a fan of the Davis family. "But even if Bianca wants to subject Diego's reputation and Matty's privacy to a long, protracted court battle that will be waged largely in the press, she won't do it."

"Why not?"

"Because I'm a dangerous woman, sweet pea. And if the Davises don't appreciate yet what crossing me has cost them, they will."

Peter gave that a moment of skeptical silence. "And what has crossing you cost them?"

She smiled, a teacher indulging a slow student. "It's strange, isn't it, how many of the Davis men commit suicide? Between Joe's *accidental* death all those years ago, and Diego's passing so young…"

Peter went cold inside but he only allowed himself a skeptical eyebrow. "You really think Diego killed himself? I mean, there was talk but—"

"I can't speak to Diego's death, of course. I wasn't there. But I know exactly how Joe died."

"Carbon monoxide poisoning," Peter said slowly, a prickle of dread cutting through the sweaty adrenaline of trading jabs with a master after so long. "The ventilation on his kiln malfunctioned."

"I know." She blinked big, innocent eyes. "I made sure of it."

"You made sure of it." He injected a note of doubt into his voice but shock was a hard fist in his throat.

"My father was a plumber, remember. It was the work of a moment to loosen a valve here, compromise a gasket there.

279

Not enough to notice, especially not in a junk palace like Joe's old workshop. Just enough that firing the kiln for any length of time would've been...risky." One corner of her mouth tipped up. "*Riskier*, really, as that kiln of his was a homemade jalopy. We'd been waiting for him to blow himself to kingdom come for years. So when he actually did..." She trailed off with a satisfied sigh.

"He didn't blow up," Peter said stupidly, his face numb, his heart stuttering inside his chest. "He just went to sleep and died."

"I know." Her lips flattened with discontent. "It looked very accidental. Too accidental to send Bianca the message I wanted." She brightened. "But I was playing the long game, and it's finally paid off. I have the trump card I need now to get exactly what I want."

"And you want that sketch."

"I do. I have a gallery back in California, you see. Newport Beach. Have you ever been? It's a sweet little ocean town but the art market is wretchedly competitive. I have no problem with competition, of course, but an original Diego Davis would be a delicious coup. Especially if there were rumors about my relationship with the artist. Not that I would ever address those rumors. A true lady understands the value of a little mystery." She sent him a twinkling smile. "And when I'm bored of running a gallery, I'll hold an exclusive auction for major museums and private collectors. It's just a pencil sketch but it should fetch an impressive amount, given how wonderfully stingy Bianca's been about keeping Diego's work impounded here in this frozen backwater." She gave him a brilliant smile. "No offense."

"None taken," he murmured while his brain spun uselessly. What did she want? Why was she telling him this?

What was his role in this disaster? Jesus Christ, his *mother* had killed Georgie's *father*. How the hell were they going to recover from that?

They weren't. The realization was a leaden weight that wrapped itself around that stupid optimism he'd woken up with and dragged it straight to the bottom of the ocean. His mother had killed her father, for God's sake. That wasn't something you recovered from.

"Explain how that's going to work." He dredged up a curious smirk somehow, pasted it to a face that felt like stone. "I don't doubt your persuasive abilities but how is confessing to murder going to make Bianca do anything but press charges?"

"Oh sweet pea." She reached over and cupped his cheek. He barely felt it. "You're so much like your father sometimes." She grinned happily and something deep inside him recoiled like he'd seen a poisonous snake. "Why on earth would I bring this to Bianca when I could bring it to Georgie?"

"You'll tell *Georgie*?" He heard himself ask the question with detached amusement. He really was his mother's creature if he could remember his lines at a moment like this. "Why?"

"Because you're in love with that vapid little princess."

"Oh please," he managed. "I'm not in love—"

"Don't even bother." She waved a languid hand in royal dismissal. "I can smell it on you. It's disgusting."

"Far be it for me to argue with a lady's nose." He shrugged an indulgent *whatever* while his heart ripped in half inside his chest. Because he finally understood. He finally grasped the role his mother intended him to play in this tragedy. "But even if I were in love, Georgie's not.

She's just having kitchen sex with the guy who screwed her family last summer, and you know how the Davises are about family. I couldn't convince her to order Chinese instead of pizza, let alone hand over an original Diego Davis."

"That's not my problem. It's yours. And it's no more than you deserve because honestly, Peter, falling in love? God's sake." She gave a wondering chuckle. "But you made that bed; you can lie in it. You'll be lying in it all alone, though, if you don't convince your beloved to give me that sketch. Because you're right about one thing — the Davises really are pathologically loyal. Once Georgie finds out what really happened to her daddy, even kitchen sex will be off the table." She grinned. "So to speak."

She pushed away from the counter, and the grin fell away. Gone was the girlish sparkle, the fond mother, the impatient teacher, the criminal mastermind. She stood there and gazed impassively at him, her beauty sitting like a cheap mask over the brutal, bloodless truth of her.

"Get me that sketch, Peter."

Georgie shot into a parking spot beside Davis Place and hung up her phone. Her mom wasn't answering but that was Bianca's silver Mercedes sedan she'd just sprayed with gravel, so Georgie felt confident she was in the right place.

It was about all she felt confident of at the moment.

"Mom?" She jogged up the back porch steps and into the kitchen, her rubber boots slapping gracelessly, her crunchy hair bouncing against her back.

"Georgie? Is that you? I saw that you were trying to call but I was talking to—" Bianca sailed through the kitchen door, her phone still in her hand. Her wide, startled eyes flicked over Georgie from head to toe. "God in heaven, are you all right?"

"I'm fine."

"Then why do you look like you slept in a Dumpster?" She came closer, squinted. "Is that *frosting* in your hair?"

Her mother's shocked disapproval snapped Georgie out of the fever dream Peter had woven around her. *Never defend, never excuse*, said the voice in her head. *You control the conversation, not the other way around.*

So Georgie ignored her mother's question and asked one of her own. "Who were you talking to on the phone just now?"

Bianca arched a brow and folded her arms. "Who do you think I was talking to?"

"Julia Gates."

"Interesting guess. And accurate." She stepped over to Addy's industrial-strength coffee maker, a counter-mounted behemoth that required its own plumbing and a manual thicker than a dictionary. She helped herself to one of the pretty china cups hanging on hooks under the cabinet and filled it. "It *was* Julia on the phone. How did you know?"

"I ran into her at the gallery yesterday," Georgie said, her stomach pinched with guilt. She'd had one job yesterday — to give her mom the message Julia had given her. Had she done it? No. She'd done Peter instead. And because Georgie had put her personal wants above the family's needs, her mom had had to engage the enemy with incomplete information. Shame gripped her with icy fingers. "She gave me a message for you."

"Did she?" Bianca leaned back against the counter and sipped her coffee. "Was it goodbye?"

"Goodbye?" Georgie blinked stupidly, and for once it

wasn't an act.

"Goodbye." Bianca smiled over the rim at her daughter, fierce and dangerous. "She and Shay are leaving town this afternoon. They're on their way up now to say goodbye."

CHAPTER 30

THE DOORBELL RANG as Georgie sailed down the stairs, her hair still hot from the blow dryer. Bianca looked up from her seat near the fire and smiled, pleased. She made no move to answer the door.

"You look more yourself," Bianca murmured as Georgie took the chair across from hers, the fireplace crackling comfortably between them.

"I feel more myself," she returned easily, though she wasn't sure that was entirely true. She'd cultivated the appearance of laziness for years but it was like hanging pretty curtains in a junk house. It improved the curb appeal but it didn't fix the mess. Or relieve the constant, grinding pain. But her stomach was fine today, and her muscles were soft with a buttery satisfaction she'd never felt before. She might've been tempted to try her hand at her first genuine nap in years had it not been for the nervy buzz zipping through her veins.

Anticipation, she realized, and pressed a testing hand to her stomach. The fear-tinged kind she assumed soldiers must feel before going into battle, where they knew the next few minutes might be ugly, but once they were over, they were behind you. If you survived, that is. She only hoped her stomach cooperated with the very necessary bit of subterfuge surviving would require.

The doorbell rang again. Bianca ignored it. Georgie did the same.

"How clever of you to keep a change of clothes and a set

of toiletries here at Addy's."

She lifted lazy shoulders. "Winter's coming on, and I have a bride to take care of. I'd hate to pour her into bed one night, then kill myself driving home through a snow storm."

"That would put a damper on the festivities."

"One would hope."

The doorbell rang a third time and Bianca sighed. "Are you ready?"

"Are you?" Georgie had gone over the entire gallery scene with her mother at least four times. If Bianca had wrung any more meaning from it than Georgie had, she'd given no indication.

"I suppose we'll find out." She rose and strolled to the door. Georgie stayed in her chair, but toed off her shoes and tucked her bare feet under her bottom. She heard her mother go through the ritual.

"Julia. How lovely to see you again. And Shay, my goodness. You haven't aged a day!"

"I could say the same to you," Shay returned warmly.

"Come in," Bianca said. "Addy's got a lovely fire going, and we have a few minutes before I'm scheduled to critique the artists in residence." She led the women into Georgie's field of vision, and they were exactly as Georgie remembered them from the gallery. Julia was sharply tailored and colorful, her hair an angled, shiny swing, her glasses frames blue and fashionably studious. Shay was smaller but equally well-groomed. The vast acreage of her hair had been pulled away from her face with a pair of beaten-gold clips but tumbled down her back in a glorious riot of sun-ripened wheat. Georgie recognized her shoes from a recent copy of French Vogue. They were Italian and listed for an amount that would easily put a kid through his first semester or two of community college. A woman should wear shoes like those confidently or not at all, but Shay walked like she was apologizing for something.

"Please, sit." Bianca gestured to a comfortably stuffed leather sofa facing the hearth and took the chair opposite Georgie's. "I understand you ladies are leaving us today."

"We are," Julia said, smiling warmly, first at Bianca, then at Georgie. "It's a shame we weren't able to connect earlier."

"Such a shame. But between wedding preparations and Davis Place's grand opening, every day is just back to back commitments." Bianca lifted graceful shoulders. "I'm sure you understand."

"Of course, of course." Julia waved that away but leaned in. "I don't suppose you'd like to share any of the wedding details with my readers? Color schemes, designers involved? Will there be any mention of Diego?"

"I'm not sure it's in good taste to mention Husband Number One while a lady is marrying Husband Number Two," Georgie offered idly.

"Normally I'd agree," Julia said, glancing only briefly her way before turning back to Bianca. "But Diego wasn't your normal husband, was he?"

"No," Bianca said evenly. "He wasn't."

"And as he continues to be such…" Her eyes drifted around the room, taking in the original Diego Davises gracing the walls, along with the breathtaking lake view that Diego had made famous. "…an important part of Addy's life, one could wonder—" She broke off, tilted her head as if combing her memory. "Did I hear that the wedding will be held right here, actually? Right in front of the Kettle view Diego couldn't stop painting?"

"This place means a great deal to both Addy and Jax,"

Bianca allowed, and Georgie had to admire her mother's conversational jiu jitsu. She'd acknowledged Julia's probe without directly addressing it. For Julia to press further now would require a shift into straight-up reporter mode, at which point Bianca could politely show her the door.

"I'm sure," Julia murmured. She gave a goodnatured shrug. "Well, you can't blame a girl for trying."

Bianca made an agreeable noise that was the furthest thing from agreement Georgie could imagine.

"Speaking of trying." Julia shot a questioning glance at Shay who pulled in a shaky breath and nodded. "There's a reason Shay and I have been trying to get in touch with you."

"Is there?" Bianca tipped her head and radiated grave concern. "Nothing unpleasant, I hope?"

Shay blurted. "I don't want anything from you, if that's what you mean." Her cheeks colored and she dropped her head, stared at the fingers linked in her lap. "I mean, considering the last time I was here, you might think I do but I don't. I just want to—"

Julia put a hand over Shay's knotted fingers, gently cut her off. "Shay's aware that she left something of a mess behind her here in Devil's Kettle. She came back to put some things right."

"I don't want anything from you," Shay hurried to say again. "I just…I need to tell the truth. I've spent years and years lying, and I'm so tired of it. I just want to tell you the truth." She lifted those enormous silver eyes to Bianca, and Georgie felt the punch of her pain across the room. She couldn't imagine how Bianca absorbed it without flinching but she did.

"Why me?" her mother said softly. "Why do you need to tell your truth to me?"

"Because you're his mother."

Georgie's stomach tensed but she only narrowed her eyes to sleepy slits and leaned her chin on her hand. And listened.

"Whose mother?" Bianca asked.

"Matty's. You're his mother now but I was his mother then. It wasn't Willa. It was me."

She buried her face in her hands and sobbed.

Bianca flicked a questioning glance to Julia, who sighed and tightened her mouth while rubbing circles into Shay's shuddering back. Nobody looked at Georgie but she understood her cue nonetheless. She sat up slowly, placed both bare feet on the floor. "I'm sorry but did you just say *you're* Matty's birth mother?"

Shay hauled in a huge breath and shoved her tears away with the heels of her hands. "Yes." She met Georgie's gaze dead on. "I am."

"How on earth…" Bianca began.

"Let her tell you," Julia said. "That's why we're here."

Bianca sat back, her silence an expectation. Georgie mirrored her mother and waited to hear Shay's version of the truth.

"I'm not proud of this," Shay began, "not of any of it. I know Diego was just a boy when Matty was conceived — God, only sixteen — but you have to understand my mental state at the time." Her lips twisted ruefully. "I wish *I'd* understood my mental state at the time but that's not how it works, is it?"

"How what works?" Georgie asked. "Statutory rape?"

"No," Julia said, "battered woman syndrome."

Shay twisted her fingers together in her lap but met Georgie's eyes bravely. "I'd suffered so many years of abuse in my marriage," she said softly. "I don't expect you to remember, Georgie, you were too young, but your mother likely does. The cops were at our house every weekend toward the end, and that kind of long-term fear of your intimate partner does something awful to a woman's self-esteem. It eats away at your boundaries until you can't tell what's right or wrong anymore. You can't tell when you deserve to be hit, and when he just wants to hit somebody. You don't know anymore how to say yes or no and mean it, you only know how to give the answer that's less likely to split your lip." She hesitated. "It left me terribly vulnerable to Diego's…advances."

"You were an adult," Georgie pointed out and Shay dropped shamed eyes to her lap.

"Yes, but her mental state was fragile," Julia countered, "and Diego was as large as a fully grown man. And from what I understand, he could be insistent."

Bianca stiffened. "Are you saying Diego raped her?"

"No, no, no." Shay waved horrified hands as if erasing the words from the air between them. "He was a good kid, a sweet boy. But boys that age are so self-centered." Her smile was tentative. "And as I said, I'd been so damaged, emotionally and physically, that I didn't know how to say no anymore, let alone the kind of no that would dissuade a boy with Diego's confidence. I'm sure he didn't intend…" She trailed off with a broken shrug.

Georgie's stomach seized up. Shay wouldn't call it rape outright but she was flirting around the edges, wasn't she? And with Diego dead, who could gainsay her? Dread crawled up her throat, ugly and dark.

Shay lifted miserable shoulders. "By the time I discovered I was pregnant, Brett and I hadn't been sleeping together for well over a year. He'd know the baby wasn't his, and I was afraid he'd kill me when he found out about it. But Willa was growing up so fast and so pretty, and Brett had never shown any inclination to hit her." She sighed. "It was a horrible gamble, pretending she was the mother. I know that now. An abuser might refuse to even spank a little girl, but once she goes through puberty, she's a woman and it's open season." She shrugged bitterly. "But I didn't know that then, and I didn't think anybody would doubt that Diego had talked Willa into bed, given his reputation."

"His reputation?" Georgie asked idly.

"His nudes are legendary," Julia put in patiently. "And he'd been painting them since, what, fourteen?"

Like she needed to ask. Julia had an encyclopedic knowledge of Diego's work.

"Fourteen," Bianca conceded softly. "Go on."

"There's not that much more to tell." Shay lifted miserable shoulders. "I took Willa to Italy like you told us to so she — well, *I* — could have the baby privately, then you and Georgie came and got him. It was wrong to ask you for money but you have to understand that I didn't have a choice. Once Peter left for college, I knew Willa and I would be at home alone with Brett. And because he'd never lifted a hand to Willa, I was convinced that I was the problem. I thought she'd be safer if I was gone. So I took the money and never looked back. I stayed away for years."

"But you're back now," Georgie observed. "Why?"

"I thought I'd spent those years healing but I hadn't. Time and distance were only a Band-Aid, and Diego's death ripped it right off. There was no way to escape the press coverage, and seeing him, seeing this place, in the news every day dragged up memories and regrets I'd never intended to face. I'd abandoned my children to save myself, sold a badly conceived if much loved baby to the family of the man who fathered him, and disappeared without word or warning." She rolled in trembling lips, bit them and breathed. "I went into a tailspin of suicidal thoughts but eventually found a therapist who saved me. I've spent the years since Diego's death working through to this point, and I've found a certain measure of peace. But the only way to a true and complete healing is facing you, Bianca, and making my amends."

"So that's all you want," Georgie said slowly. "To say you're sorry?"

"I didn't think I could do it," Shay admitted. "I didn't want to be anywhere near Devil's Kettle ever again but then I saw a picture somebody had posted on Twitter."

"Of?"

"Matty. Hashtag DiegoJr." She swallowed audibly and her fingers went to that loose button on her coat again, twisted. "He really is Diego to the life, isn't he?"

"That's what people say." Bianca gave her a polite, close-lipped smile. "It's hard for us to see it. To us Matty is just Matty."

Georgie suppressed a snort but it was a near miss.

"It's an astonishing resemblance," Shay assured her. "Except for his eyes. Those aren't Diego's eyes."

"We've always thought they were Willa's," Georgie put in.

"They are," Shay said. "But they were mine first."

"And now they're Matty's," Bianca said quietly.

"And so lost."

"Pardon?"

Shay moved helpless shoulders. "There was something lost in them. I don't know how else to describe it, but it shamed me. I'd focused on nothing but myself — my pain, my fear, my safety — for years but looking into that boy's lost eyes, even over the internet, made me want to give him what he was looking for, something only I could give him."

Georgie caught her breath. If Shay said *a mother* she was going to throw the woman bodily onto the driveway. If she thought she could come in here after all these years and threaten them with a custody battle, she had no idea who she was dealing with.

"And what's that?" Bianca asked softly. Dangerously. "What is he looking for that I can't give him?"

"The truth. The truth all people deserve about who they are and where they're from. The knowledge that his birth mother loved him as best as she was able, and did her best by him, as screwed up and awful as her best was." She blew out a breath, and those shoulders curved. In defeat? In relief? It was hard to tell. "So that's why I'm here. That's why I came. I don't want anything from anybody, and I have no desire to somehow supplant you as Matty's mother. I could never take your place in his life but—"

But, Georgie knew, just saying the words out loud planted the idea that she *could* like a pernicious weed. Words created a truth of their own.

"But?" Bianca asked blandly.

"You're a mother," Shay said, an edge of desperation creeping into her tone. "You must understand. Once you're a mother, there's a compulsion, a connection. You can't ever really walk away. You have to know your kids are okay. And that picture just tore at me. I didn't know what you'd told him, of course, but speculation about his origins started flying around the internet. And I couldn't bear him thinking his birth mother hadn't wanted him, that I'd sell him or throw him away, that he was worthless. Because I—" Her voice cracked and she lowered her head. Cleared her throat and went on more calmly. "I know what that feeling is. I know the dark places it can take you and I couldn't bear the idea that an innocent child would carry that burden when I had the power to lift it." She squared those tired shoulders and met Bianca's gaze with brave, wet eyes. "I needed to make sure. I needed him to know he's not to blame, not for any of this. If I can do that—" Her voice wobbled again and she paused, drew a steadying breath. "If I can do that, I think I can finally heal. I think we can be okay, all of us."

CHAPTER 31

GEORGIE'S STOMACH HAD behaved reasonably well during the visit, but the instant the door shut behind the two women, Georgie popped to her feet and began pacing. Her bare soles were silent against Addy's pretty hardwood floor but her stomach sighed in relief. Bianca, her back to the door she'd just shut, stared.

"What on earth are you doing?"

"Pacing." Georgie hit the far wall, spun and marched back toward the fireplace.

"Heavens." Bianca's eyes followed her. "Why?"

"My stomach likes it."

"Ah. Well, if it means you can eat again, by all means, continue." She glided across the room and sank into her throne. She watched Georgie's progress to the fireplace, to the far wall, and back to the fireplace. "I've been worried."

"We're in a worrisome situation."

"I'm more concerned about you and Peter."

Georgie's stride nearly faltered. Julia and Shay had spent the last twenty minutes burying landmines and lobbing hand grenades, and Bianca wanted to talk about Peter? "Why?"

"He's poor."

"I know."

"He won't stay that way."

She sent her mother a look on her way by. "And that's a problem?"

"It could be. Money is a powerful god, especially to someone who's been hungry and helpless. Think of what

Peter must have sacrificed to become so wealthy so young, and I'm not talking about all the nights he studied while the other boys partied."

Georgie thought about that shelf of books on sheep husbandry above Peter's cot. "He puts in his hours."

"I'm sure." Bianca flicked unconcerned fingers. "But he didn't just sacrifice his social life on the altar of his ambitions, Georgie. He sacrificed you, too."

"Tried to."

"He would've sentenced you to a lifetime of unrequited love, and himself to a lifetime of intellectual starvation."

"He'd have discovered differently soon enough, on both counts. I wasn't in love with him, and I'm not stupid."

Bianca smiled. "And it would've been delicious to watch him dance at the end of that leash for the rest of your long, interesting lives together. But this isn't about what he would've discovered. It's about what he *believed*. And he believed that avoiding bankruptcy was more important than permanently attaching himself to a vacuous, exquisite shell. He believed that staying rich was more important than your heart, Matty's safety, or his own soul. And *that*, darling girl, concerns me a great deal. Because a man who'd do any one of those things to stay rich will do that and more to get rich again."

"He's not that guy anymore, Mom." Georgie's memory served up a snapshot of Peter walking through a sparkling forest, hunched to protect a dead lamb from the weather. "He's changed."

"I'm sure there's nothing like farming on a shoestring to put a man in touch with his soul," Bianca allowed. "If he has one. But people don't change, Georgie. Not fundamentally. He's the same man today that he was when he mistook you for stupid. When he accepted what he thought was your love in exchange for your money and your family name. When he manipulated a confused boy who should've been family to him into burning down houses. When he burned down this very house we're standing in and nearly killed Jax and Addy." Georgie could feel her mother's eyes on her, sympathetic but unflinching. "Whatever he's said, done, or implied since that makes you think he's changed is nothing but strategy." Bianca tipped her head. "Have you slept with him yet?"

She thought about lying but her stomach twinged, and this was her mother. She'd never been able to lie to Bianca. Plus she'd shown up this morning in rain boots with frosting in her hair. "Yeah. That's changed, too. The sex. It's different."

"Oh, Georgie." Bianca closed her eyes and touched the line between her brows. "The sex hasn't changed. You have." She opened her eyes and pinned Georgie like a butterfly. "You're in love with him."

"I'm not," she said slowly. Her stomach sloshed uneasily, though, as if it didn't know what the truth was. "I don't think so, anyway. How could I be in love with somebody I barely know?"

"You know him. You know him to his bones." Her mother's voice was both hard and weary. "What did he say when you abandoned him with such unseemly haste this morning? I'm going to assume he'd just rocked your world, given the state of your toilette, but you prioritized the family over some fawning pillow talk. How did he handle it?"

"It was fine. Shay had showed up," Georgie said. "She said she wanted to talk to Peter alone, and implied that Julia might be coming up here to wrangle with you. I remembered

297

then that I hadn't told you yet about the gallery scene..." She trailed off, dismay gathering in her throat.

Bianca nodded impassively. "So Shay had a private chat with her son before she and Julia came up here to plant their ugly little seeds, insisting the whole time she doesn't want anything from us."

"She wants something," Georgie whispered, shame and fear knotting her stomach. Would Peter really let Shay use him against her? Against their family? What could Shay promise him that would be worth it? How much money would it take for Peter to betray Georgie a second time? "They always want something."

"And Peter's going to get it for her," Bianca said.

Georgie couldn't argue. She wanted to, but she didn't know how.

"Get him up here, Georgie. We need to have a chat."

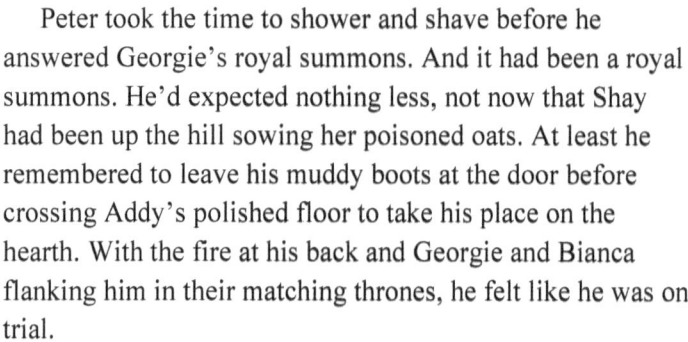

Peter took the time to shower and shave before he answered Georgie's royal summons. And it had been a royal summons. He'd expected nothing less, not now that Shay had been up the hill sowing her poisoned oats. At least he remembered to leave his muddy boots at the door before crossing Addy's polished floor to take his place on the hearth. With the fire at his back and Georgie and Bianca flanking him in their matching thrones, he felt like he was on trial.

Peter couldn't seem to work up the energy to worry about that, though. His entire emotional radar was consumed by Georgie. She sat to his right, curled up in her chair like a cat, her face smooth and serene, her eyes cool and distant, her beauty a brick wall between them. He expected he looked the same to her.

"So, Peter." Bianca folded her hands and placed them in her lap, studied him with dark, pitiless eyes. "Georgie tells us you've had a visit from your mother."

"I have." He could feel Georgie from two yards away. It was like she'd taken a part of his soul with her when she'd left that morning, and it sang to him now, the missing piece of himself, buried irrevocably inside her. He didn't look away from Bianca. He didn't allow himself to. He'd thought he'd known what hell was. He'd had no idea. "She wants a sketch."

Bianca's brows popped up. "That was easy."

"What, you thought you'd have to beat it out of me?"

Her smile implied that she'd had her hopes. "Which sketch?"

"One of Willa's nudes." He leaned forward, elbows on knees, and let his hands dangle. "Evidently one of them's of her."

"Of Shay?" Bianca sat back, considered it. Exchanged a look with Georgie, who nodded.

"The seated one," Georgie murmured. "The line of her spine, the angle of her head. It's…knowing."

"I agree," Bianca said. "I'd thought it was simply a before and after, and chalked the difference up to Willa's having tasted the forbidden fruit." She shook her head in wonder. "It wasn't simply a different perspective. It was a whole different woman."

Peter had no idea what they were talking about.

"Listen, I don't know what went down between you and my mother all those years ago," he said to Bianca, "and I know you have no reason to listen to or to trust a word I say, but if I were you, I'd hand it over. The sketch. Just give it to her."

Bianca smiled. "Why on earth would we do such a thing?"

"Because this place is nice and all, but it's barely open, let alone an established income stream. Because I heard they nailed your money manager recently but I can't imagine they were able to make you anything like whole on what he stole. Because Diego's work and the tourist traffic it generates is still your primary source of income, which makes his reputation as an artist and as a man of paramount importance to your financial well-being. And because Shay's prepared to destroy it unless she gets a piece of it for herself."

"And how will she do that?" Georgie asked, one foot lazily tick-tocking in the air. If Peter didn't know better, he'd swear she was barely awake. "How does she plan to destroy a dead man?"

"She was vague on that point but I surmised it would have something to do with a radical revision of Matty's conception story."

She gave him the slow blink. "She'd paint Diego as a rapist, you mean."

"Yes," Peter said. He couldn't look at her, couldn't bear the distance she'd put between them with that blink. He dropped his eyes to his stocking feet. "She didn't say as much but...yes."

"She's also prepared to wage a custody battle for Matty," Bianca said.

He gripped his fingers together hard enough to crack his knuckles. "She said that?"

"Of course not. But we heard it nonetheless."

Georgie made a low hum of affirmation.

"Is that all she threatened you with?" He didn't want to ask the question but it would only sit in his gut, poisoning him to death, unless he spit it out. "Just the smear campaign and a custody battle?"

"Isn't that enough?" Georgie asked, and his stomach cramped viciously. She had no idea.

"You should give it to her," Peter said again. "Just give her the sketch and she'll go away."

Bianca made a noise that might've been a snort from anybody less elegant. "Please. The Shays of the world don't go away. They're like stray dogs. If you feed them, they'll come back forever. And believe me, I know. I paid her off once, and look how well that worked out." Her mouth flattened. "Fourteen years later, she's sitting in our living room with her hand out."

"And a knife behind her back," Georgie murmured. "People don't change, Peter. They just become more themselves. And Shay's a liar. We can't negotiate with her."

"I agree." Bianca patted her knees with finality. "Thank you for being so forthright with us today, Peter. You've been very helpful."

Peter knew a dismissal when he heard one. He also knew that today's penance wasn't nearly done.

"If you're determined to play hardball with her," he said slowly, "there's something else you should know."

"Oh?" One pale brow crept toward Bianca's hairline.

"I don't know if it's true," he hedged, the weight of Shay's poison sitting like lead in his belly while he worked up the courage to make himself vomit it up. "But if it is, you'll want to take precautions."

Bianca regarded him in expectant silence, brows lifted. Georgie sat with the point of her chin on her palm, her lashes nearly brushing her knuckles with each slow blink.

"Shay came to see me today to make sure I understood

my role in this little transaction," he said finally. "It's my job to convince you that things will get messy if you don't hand over that sketch, pronto. But there's messy and there's *messy*. The first kind of messy involves gossip and lawsuits. Ugly but civilized."

"And the second?"

"The second involves murder."

Georgie's blank blink looked a bit more genuine this time. "She wants you to kill somebody?"

"No." He swallowed. It took him a sweaty second but he managed. "She wants you to know that she already has."

Georgie stared. "Who?"

Peter hesitated and Bianca went eerily still. He focused on her. Only on her.

"Joe," he said. "She told me today that she'd killed your husband Joe." He shifted his eyes to Georgie and finished it. "My mother killed your father, Georgie. And she won't hesitate to kill somebody else you love if you don't give her what she wants."

Georgie froze, as if every bone in her body had turned to glass. "She said that?"

"No," Peter admitted. "But I heard it nonetheless."

Matty stood frozen at the top of the stairs. He had no idea how long had passed since he'd jogged out of the upstairs studio to fetch his mom for a bunch of senior citizens who were somehow impatient for the biting critique Matty avoided like the plague. Better them than him, though, so he'd been cooperatively trotting downstairs to fetch the master.

Then he'd heard *custody battle* and froze.

He'd heard the rest, too.

He gave Peter credit. It couldn't have been easy to walk into this house and face his mother and sister with the kind of news he'd just delivered. Matty himself had never met the man he'd always been told was his father, but in his mind Joe Davis was sort of like Santa Claus, or maybe even God — a benevolent presence that permeated every aspect of the world he lived in. Joe was something you didn't have to see to believe in because the evidence of his goodness was in everything he'd created, from the coffee cups to Jax and Georgie.

Peter's mother had taken Joe from them. On purpose.

It was too huge a horror to fully comprehend, and the courage it must've taken to admit it was staggering. Matty waited until he'd overheard everything he was going to overhear and the front door had closed behind Peter. Then he crept back to the studio and made the trip again, only louder this time. He made sure they heard him coming.

"Mom?" he called. "Georgie? They're ready for you to destroy their hopes and dreams in the upstairs studio!"

"Thanks, Matty," his mother called back. "Be right there."

She always was, Matty thought. She was always right there for him. For them. For the family. There had never been a day that Bianca hadn't been right there, whether he wanted her there or not. Infuriating, demanding, loving and possessive, she'd never failed him. Never failed any of them.

Matty wasn't going to fail her.

CHAPTER 32

"Peter, wait."

He stopped, the farm truck's handle cold against his palm. He'd hoped to get away before Georgie realized how many questions he'd left unanswered. But just like all the rest of today's hopes, it was futile and doomed. That brain of hers was an underrated treasure, demanding answers he didn't want to give her. Answers he'd only just pulled out of his own brain in the reeling, dizzying minutes between Shay leaving his kitchen and Georgie's summons. Answers that made him feel sick and ashamed.

Answers she deserved.

There had been a pair of viciously high heels on the floor in front of Georgie's throne, no friendly rain boots in sight, so he headed back to the front porch. Sure enough she stood there by the railing making bare feet look regal and forbidding.

"What do you need, Georgie?"

"Answers." She folded her arms and gazed down at him. He wanted to drop to his knees before her, a supplicant to her royal highness, and beg for mercy. For forgiveness. He wouldn't. He didn't deserve either.

"I'll try." If his courage held. "Ask."

"Do you believe her?"

"Do I believe Shay killed your father?" He forced himself to meet her eyes without flinching or looking away. "Yes. I do."

Her composure was terrible, her beauty a vast canyon

yawning between them. "Why?"

"Why did she kill him? Or why do I believe she did?"

"Both."

He shrugged uncomfortably. "I can only speculate about her motives—"

"We're not in court, Peter. I'm not going to object to hearsay."

"As long as you understand that this is just an educated guess, and it's over a decade old." She held his gaze and he nodded, defeated. "I was all of seventeen when Shay went to Hill Top House to tell your mom Willa was pregnant. Obviously I wasn't there but I can imagine how it went. Shay shows up, all worry and regret. Your son, my daughter, such a shame but what's done is done and we're going to be grandmas together!"

Her eyes on his were a steady, chilly blue. "My mother will never be anything with your mother."

"I know that." Peter drew in a weary breath and let it out slowly. "Everybody in town knows that. The only person who didn't know that was Shay, but I'll bet your mom made it crystal clear. The idea that Bianca and Shay were even peers, let alone family?" He shook his head. "Not in this universe, or any other."

"You're not wrong. According to my mother, she responded to Shay's pretensions by threatening to file for custody the instant Willa delivered and the baby's paternity was verified. And if Shay made even a token objection, she'd make sure the judge had a copy of every domestic dispute the police had ever responded to at Shay's address."

"Which is both predictable and understandable," Peter allowed. "But ultimately ineffective because scorn doesn't cow Shay at all. It only puts revenge on the agenda. She can't let a humiliation go unpunished, after all, so she ran straight up here to Davis Place. Joe was right where he always was, tinkering in his workshop, which probably delighted Shay."

"Why?"

"Sex is Shay's weapon of choice. It's always easier to get what she wants from a man, and if she can burn down your mother's marriage while getting it, well, bonus."

Georgie's eyes narrowed dangerously. "Are you suggesting my father—"

"You asked me to speculate. Should I stop?" Please say yes. Please stop me. Stop this. Leave something between us, the bare root of something that might grow someday.

"No." She pressed her mouth tight. "Go on."

Peter gave a jerky shrug. "So Shay delivers her sob story. *I'm so afraid, Joe, and don't know where to turn! Your Diego got my Willa pregnant and Brett's going to kill her when he finds out! He's never so much as spanked her before — she's always been his little girl — but once he finds out she's pregnant, she'll be just another cheating whore to him. Just like her mother.*" Peter dragged a hand down his face, sickness crawling up his throat. "I'm sure she told him how Bianca wanted to take the baby and leave her and Willa to Brett's tender mercies and killing fists. I'm sure she worked up some very affecting tears. I'm sure she begged him to talk to Bianca, to change her mind. How was she supposed to protect both herself and Willa with me gone to college in the fall? *I just can't do it all on my own, Joe. I need somebody powerful in my corner, somebody good. Somebody like you, Joe. I'll do whatever you ask, give you whatever you need... You're so strong, Joe. I feel so safe with you. I know I shouldn't but..."*

He swallowed down the sickness, forced himself not to look away from the revulsion in Georgie's face.

"This isn't sounding like hearsay," she said.

"This part isn't. This part I saw."

The expression fell away from her face. There was no surprise, no shock, no horror or betrayal or fury. There was simply nothing. She said, "You saw?"

"I was with Diego that day. We went up to Davis Place so he could get a sketchpad or some pencils or—" He waved an impatient hand. "It doesn't matter what he was getting. The point is, I was standing around in the foyer waiting for him when I heard my mom's voice in the basement studio. So I slid on down the stairs for a better listen. Like most eavesdroppers, though, I didn't hear the beginning of the conversation, so I had no idea that anybody was pregnant. I just heard the part where she offered your dad pretty much anything he wanted if he would just pretty-please give her what she wanted in return. The door was open just enough for me to put an eye to the crack and peek in. Joe's about as uncomfortable as a man can get with a weeping woman. He does that awkward one-armed hug, the kind that doesn't even get you some sideboob. Makes some comforting, avuncular noises. Only Shay's not having avuncular. She's not having paternal. She turns it into something else entirely. She nestles right in, gets nice and close, then looks up at him, all huge wet eyes and available mouth. *I'll do whatever you want, Joe. Anything at all.* She's vulnerable, beautiful, his for the asking."

"And did he ask?" Like she was wondering if her father had been wearing a red shirt or a blue one, not if he'd cheated on her mother. Her courage was staggering, and Peter's heart cracked wide open under the weight of it. And he realized his mother had been right earlier. He *was* in love with Georgie Davis. Deeply, stupidly, irrevocably. Had he really woken up that morning thinking the universe might finally be ready to forgive him? God, he was an idiot. That brief pause in the pain had been the universe switching gears, reaching for a whole new level of torture.

"Did he take what she was offering?" Georgie asked.

"He wasn't even tempted," Peter told her. "Your father performed an impromptu standing long jump that would've qualified for the Olympics. He had a good four yards of daylight between them before I could even blink. He shouted 'Tea!' like a Catholic crossing himself when somebody blasphemes. He was all *Let's have a nice cup of tea and talk this through. I'm sure we can figure something out. Bianca's a good person, not unreasonable, has a temper but blah blah blah.*"

Georgie's composure wavered for a brief moment, as if her true self were underwater and trying to surface. "Tea was Dad's answer to everything."

"Shay doesn't believe in tea," Peter said grimly. "Shay knew she'd just been rejected. Not with anything like your mom's scorn but that made two rejections in one day. Two rejections from one family, and she was furious. Coldly, dangerously furious. I couldn't see your dad's face but I could see hers and there was murder in her eyes. I'd never seen that kind of cold intent before. She'd always been so committed to her role as the victim of domestic abuse. It chilled me to the bone but Joe was already hustling toward the door I was standing behind, hot on the trail of a nice cup of tea. I was back in the foyer like butter wouldn't melt by the time he got to the top of the stairs."

"Did you see her do it?" Georgie asked evenly. "Did you

see her tamper with the kiln?"

"No." He tucked his hands into his pockets and met her gaze without flinching. "Diego found whatever he was looking for and we bailed out. I did my best to forget I'd ever even seen her there." He pushed a hand across his mouth. He didn't want to say the next part but he had to. If he kept it inside, it would poison him. He needed to have it out. "As for whatever I'd seen in her face in that moment? The potential for murder? I let myself forget I'd ever seen that, too. What had I really seen, after all? If the kiln had malfunctioned that night, I might've put more stock in it. I might've said something. But he didn't die that night, did he? Not that night or the next one or the next one. It was months before he ran that kiln long enough to be dangerous, and by that time, I'd put it so far out of my mind, it effectively didn't exist."

"It wasn't a malfunction." Her words snapped like a whip in the chilly air.

"No, it wasn't." Peter couldn't hold her gaze any more. "I know it wasn't."

"But *when* did you know?"

"When did I know what?"

"That it wasn't a malfunction. When did you know your mother killed my father?"

"She told me this morning."

"But when did you *know*?"

He studied her, took in the impassive mask of her beauty, the fierce demand in her eyes. Saw the need for the truth that was clawing her bloody from the inside out. So he screwed up his courage, shoved a hand deep into the blackest recesses of his soul, tore out the truth and handed it over. The hardest, rawest truth he could reach.

"I knew it the minute I saw murder in her face," he said. "Joe was a dead man walking the instant he rejected her, and on some level, I knew it."

It rang between them, that bald admission. Echoed like church bells or tornado sirens, only in complete, brittle silence.

She said, "Get off my family's land."

Peter tucked his fingers into his pockets, kept the mortal wound of his heart tucked into his chest, and nodded. He'd expected nothing less. Deserved nothing less. He hoped like hell the universe didn't have yet another gear of his punishment in reserve, because he wasn't sure he was going to survive this one. He didn't know if he even wanted to.

"I'm sorry, Georgie." They were the hardest, truest words he'd ever spoken but pitifully inadequate once they were out. "For whatever it's worth, I'm so damn sorry."

"Yeah," she said, her eyes fixed on a point somewhere behind him. "So I am."

Georgie didn't miss him. Where would she find the time?

Thanksgiving and Christmas had both come and gone, and between the holidays, her work at the gallery, Addy's wedding preparations, and lending the occasional hand at Davis Place, she was simply too busy to dwell on Peter. If there was an aching void inside her every time she drove past the pastures snow had turned into perfect white quilts, if a pain akin to hunger gnawed at her bones whenever she let her mind go quiet, well, there was always Matty to ferry somewhere. He was a busy kid now that he was no longer sequestered at the farm.

And if driving a teenager all over creation didn't fully occupy her, Julia and Shay were always good for an hour or two's distraction. As much as she hated anticipating their inevitable return, even that was better than dwelling on Peter. On the memory of that awful afternoon when he'd admitted right to her face that he'd known his mother was dangerous. That he'd seen her murderous intentions toward Georgie's father and had done nothing. Said nothing. Created the very silence that had allowed Shay to set the trap that had taken Joe from his family decades before his time, and reduced Georgie's heart to irreparable dust. He'd allowed his mother to take from her the one man on this earth who'd never even paused to admire her face on his way to adore her heart and marvel at her mind.

How could she love the man responsible for the greatest loss of her life?

How could she even have entertained the possibility?

Because Bianca was right. People didn't change. Not really. Peter had shown himself to her again and again and again. He was selfish through and through. He would never value anything above his own skin, and she was well rid of him. Him and his stupid sheep farm and his brutal honesty and his staggering courage and that beautiful, wounded soul he'd damaged over and over but was now determined to protect. *From what? Himself?* Likely.

No. She sucked in a cool, cleansing breath for the fortieth time that evening and blew it out again. Slowly. Temptation crept up on her all the time like that, whispering for her to let go of her anger, or at least to let it die down to embers so the raging heat of it stopped distorting everything on the other side. So she could see clearly and think straight. But the instant the anger ebbed, the pain flooded in, shocking and fresh and breathtaking. And she needed to function. Her stomach complained but the two of them had reached a wary detente recently. She was allowed to present the face she needed to in public, but in private, she paced. She paced and fretted and wept, all night long sometimes. But at least she could eat enough to keep body and soul together. At least she could breathe. At least she could smile for the photos, because Addy and Jax were getting married tomorrow, and it was going to be perfect. As perfect as she could make it.

She'd keep any hint of the imperfect in private, exactly as her mother had taught her. Her wise, prescient mother, who'd seen Peter coming a mile away and tried to warn her.

She pulled in another cool breath, let it out, and dropped the curtain of languid beauty over her private self like a protective blanket.

Willa said, "Jesus Christ, Georgie, you're going to blow out the candles."

"What?" She looked up, startled, her hands frozen over the pine boughs and sugared cranberries she'd been arranging artfully around a tea candle on one of the several round bar-height tables that had taken over Addy's great room for the evening.

Willa marched to the white-draped rectangular table before the fireplace that had temporarily replaced the couch. She set down a generous tray of cheese and crackers and plopped her hands on her hips, eyes narrowed. "You keep sighing like that, you're going to put the candles out. Or, worse, you're going to blow them straight into your stupid pine branches and burn this place down again."

Georgie blinked at the tea candle in front of her that was, indeed, flickering dangerously. "Don't be dramatic." She adjusted a pine needle just so and moved on to the next table. Slid a grouping of sparkly cranberries an inch to the left.

"Dramatic? Me?" Willa snorted inelegantly. "Please.

You're the one having *moods* and making everybody miserable."

"I beg your pardon?"

"You ought to beg Addy's, if you want my opinion."

"Addy's?" Georgie gaped at her, shocked. "I've done nothing but pamper Addy for weeks! I've dealt with the dresses, with the fittings, I've scheduled the pre-event manicures and pedicures, I've engineered her parents' happy reunion, and I personally tended to her hair tonight." She slapped her hands to her hips and glared hotly right back. It felt wonderful. "Her *hair*, Willa. Do you have any idea what a bird's nest she cultivates on top of her head? Do you have any idea what kind of miracle I worked to—"

"Yeah, great." Willa waved that aside with a jerk of her dark head, her own eyes molten silver. "Good for you. You're a goddamn miracle worker. You took care of everything and left the bride — who loves to schedule and arrange and fix stuff herself — nothing to do but worry herself sick about you."

Georgie threw her hands up. "Over what? I'm fine! I'm even eating!"

"Yeah, like food is medicine and you're just waiting for science to come up with nutrition you can breathe." Willa's lip curled. "Okay, I'll grant you, on paper, you're doing a bang up job. Every event goes off like clockwork, and there you are in the middle of it, crossing *T*s and dotting *I*s, dressed like a runway model with that Mona Lisa smile pinned to your perfect face. But you stink of misery the way you stink of French perfume."

Georgie drew back, startled, but her stomach sighed in relief. It liked hearing the truth out loud, even if it was aimed at her like a bullet. She reminded her stomach of the public/private deal and said, "My perfume is glorious. You, on the other hand—" She cast a scathing eye over Willa's perfectly lovely outfit, desperate for an insult to hurl, a fight to start, anything that might distract her from the disconcerting truth Willa had just served up.

"Don't even bother," Willa interrupted flatly. "I'm not going to fight with you. Not today. I'm telling you the bald-ass truth because you need to hear it and Addy's too nice." She set her mouth and squared her shoulders. "And because we're family, damn it."

Georgie shut her mouth and swallowed.

"Your *face* is glorious," Willa said sternly. "But *you're* a disaster, and everybody knows it. Especially our sweet, sensitive, loving bride-to-be. Pretty isn't cutting it this time, Georgie. Addy wants you happy. Everybody who loves you wants you happy." She folded her arms resolutely. "You need to talk to Peter."

CHAPTER 33

GEORGIE STARED. "THE last thing I need is to talk to Peter." But her heart threw itself against her ribs like it was trying to get out. Like it had already started down the hill to that stark, beautiful farm house of his, to the damaged, beautiful man all alone inside it. "He let his mother—"

"Nobody lets Shay do shit," Willa said flatly. "You had one unpleasant conversation with her, and you think you know her? You have no idea who she is, or what she's capable of."

"Like I don't know manipulative mothers? Please. I grew up with Bianca."

"Who loved you — *loves* you — beyond reason, comprehension or logic. So you have no idea. Don't pretend you do."

Georgie jerked a bad-tempered shrug. "Fine. So maybe Peter's not *directly* responsible for my dad's death but that doesn't change the fact that he's still Shay's creature."

"Are you sure about that?"

"Do you doubt it? She was gone for fifteen years, but it took her all of fifteen minutes to make him her messenger boy again." Sickness squirmed greasily in her stomach at the memory of Peter scampering up the hill to deliver his mother's demands. "People don't change, Willa. They just become more themselves."

"I agree," she said improbably.

"You do?"

"Absolutely. Peter wasn't always such an amoral, money-hungry asshole, you know. Back when we were little, he was actually a decent kid. Serious, bookish, earnest. And boy did he love his mom. Unfortunately, his mom was a grade-A whack job and she was determined not to raise a disappointment like her husband. *Real men take care of their women, Peter. Real men make money, real men provide. Look at me in this cheap house, in these cheap clothes, in this cheap town. I'm walking, talking proof that your father's no kind of man. If he were, I'd be wearing diamonds and furs instead of this pretty black eye.*" She pressed her lips into a tight, flat line. "That was her theme song and she sang it to Peter like a goddamn lullaby. It's probably still burned on his brain somewhere. Screw serial killers and child molesters; as far as Shay's concerned, you can't grow up to be anything worse than poor. If you're a dude, that is. If you're living the vag life, substitute *ugly* for *poor*." She snorted. "As if I need to explain that one to Trust Fund Barbie."

Georgie glared. "Fuck you, Willa. We're past Barbie jokes and you know it."

Willa smiled toothily. "I do know it. I just wondered if *you* knew it. Because it wasn't clear based on your recent behavior."

Georgie opened her mouth hotly but Willa held up a hand. "Shut it, Georgie. You have no argument, plus you need to hear this."

Georgie shut it, her pulse thudding uneasily in her ears. Maybe she did need to hear this.

Or are you just that desperate to talk about Peter?

She was starting to hate that voice in her brain. It was so constant, so pitiless, so completely, brutally accurate.

"So in the world according to Shay," Willa went on, "it's

a first-place tie between poor and ugly, depending on your plumbing. Second place loser is gender-neutral, though, and it goes to staying in this inbred hick town when you could be somewhere — anywhere — else. So if you're going to judge Peter for being exactly what his mother made him, take a second to realize that you're playing the same damn game."

"Excuse me?"

"Look at you." Willa folded her arms and gave her the kind of critical up-and-down Georgie was more used to giving than receiving. "You're skinny, unhappy and three shaky steps from a nervous breakdown but you're still being pretty like it's your goddamn job."

"It *is* my job," Georgie snapped, anger sparking to welcome life inside her. "Jax got the competence, Diego got the talent, and I got this." She jerked a thumb toward her face. "Believe me, I'd have chosen otherwise. I'd like to have chosen at all. Lord knows my brothers got to. Either of them could've decided not to use their little gifts from fate, but me? It's my goddamn *face*. It's always just there, for everybody to see and judge and consume."

"You poor thing." Willa blinked huge, unsympathetic eyes. "Imagine! Having to wake up every day pretty enough for the prom."

"Imagine," Georgie returned acidly, "having to go to the prom with somebody so dazzled by your face that he can't even talk to you. Who spends the entire night staring at you like a stroke victim or steering you around the room like you're a hot new sports car. Or trying to get a hand up your skirt. Not because he particularly wants what's under your skirt, mind you, but because he wants to tell all his buddies he not only drove the car, but he popped the hood and changed the oil."

317

Willa winced. "Okay, that would suck but—"

"Imagine," she interrupted, "that that's your entire life. Every minute of every hour of every day."

Willa blanched.

"Yeah, exactly. You can't imagine how jealous I've been over the years of the way you could make yourself invisible."

Her brows popped up. "You noticed that?"

"Of course I noticed that. I notice everything. The dumber people think you are, the less they think you see. They think you comprehend even less. I see all, I know all."

"Damn."

"I was jealous as hell. Why do you think I was such a bitch about calling you out all the time?"

"I thought you were just inherently bitchy," Willa murmured but it was automatic. A reflex. Georgie acknowledged it with a wry smile. They were getting the hang of this sister business.

"Oh, I am. I totally am. But nobody notices because I'm just so darn pretty."

"Or they give you a pass," Willa said slowly, "because your face is the only piece of you that matters."

"Now you're getting it." Georgie gave her a carnival-barker smile. "Welcome to my world."

"I still don't feel sorry for you." Willa frowned at her. "I mean, being the female ideal has to come with an up-side."

"It does," Georgie admitted. "It's just not what you think it is. Why do you think I've been so successful choosing new pieces for the gallery?"

Her brows popped up again. "You do that? I thought Bianca—"

"She used to." Georgie waved that away. "She handed it

over to me once she was sure I knew how to responsibly operate the weapon that is our mutual face."

"You needed an operating manual for your face?" Willa asked doubtfully.

She shrugged. "It's like good art. It provokes a reaction. And just like with art, that reaction isn't about the art, it's about the viewer. Think about the last time you saw something really staggeringly beautiful. Did it satisfy you? Did you come away full and happy?" She leaned closer, flattened her hands on the table between them. "Or did it just remind you of an emptiness inside you, some tiny hungry space that yearns? Did it just make you *want* it?"

"Want what?" Willa asked, those silvery eyes cautious.

"It. Whatever it is you were looking at. You wanted to touch it, didn't you? You wanted to get closer. You wanted to have it, hold it, own it." She tipped her head. "Did you get it?"

"What?"

"The *it*. The thing you wanted so badly. A hot fudge sundae, a great car, an expensive dress."

"Yeah, actually." She cleared her throat and looked away. "I love my bridesmaids dress. That embroidery is incredible, and it fits like it was custom made."

Georgie nodded smugly. "Of course it does. I had the seamstress tear it down to pieces and rebuild it from scratch."

"Making it both off the rack, as requested by the bride, and bespoke, as per Davis family standards." She shook her head admiringly. "Does Addy know that?"

"Hell, no. And you're not going to tell her." She pinned her with demanding eyes. "Tell me, though. Are you satisfied? Will you never want another dress? Is it the only dress you'll ever want or need?"

"Well, no." Her dark brows came together. "Of course not."

"Exactly. Beauty isn't satisfaction. It doesn't actually fill the emptiness inside, it only masks it temporarily. You can close the deal, get the job, win the girl but a week or a month or a year later, you're hungry again. Because that's how beauty works. It isn't about having, it's about wanting. Why do you think people have art collections instead of one perfect painting?"

"Because they keep trying to own the things that make them yearn?"

"Without ever understanding that human beings were designed to yearn." Georgie smiled indulgently. It was a raw deal personally, but had been good to her professionally. "You can't own beauty. You can't even love beauty. You can only ever want it."

Willa's eyes narrowed. "Which explains all your repeat customers."

"It also explains," Georgie pointed out ruthlessly, "why nobody's ever really loved me, and probably never will. Men want me. They *yearn* for me. And every once in a while, they get me, only to discover that I'll never be enough. Yearning becomes disappointment, which becomes contempt. And so on." She rolled a casual hand. "I wasn't ever going to marry for love. I didn't think I'd marry at all, honestly, then your brother came along and offered me the one thing I thought could maybe work. A partnership with a man I liked well enough involving a fair exchange of benefits — my face and family name for his money and ambition — and probably kids at some point. He was my last, best shot, but when he realized I couldn't fill his empty spaces — or his empty wallet — he not only broke up with me, but he blackmailed my brother into burning down our house." She shrugged. "Pretty much business as usual, aside from the sheer scope of it." She gave Willa a wry smile. "Which is why I'm not talking to Peter."

"I used to think you were a straight-up bitch," Willa said slowly. "Entitled, spoiled and mean. But I never thought you were a coward."

Georgie drew back, stung. "I'm not a coward."

"Then why are you hiding like a little bitch?"

"Excuse me?"

"Peter might've been Shay's creature once, but he's not now. You burned that guy right down to the ground. And the guy he's becoming now reminds me a little of the brother I used to have. And I liked that guy. But you?" Willa aimed a finger at her. "You're in love with him."

She closed her eyes but her stomach rejoiced. *Truth, and right out loud! Glory hallelujah!* "I am not," she said weakly. "I can't be."

"Why not? People don't really change, you know. You're right about that. So maybe Shay warped him into thinking he had to be the king of Devil's Kettle to matter, but he stopped being that guy months ago. Now he's just the seriously smart kid I remember who tried too hard and spent too much time alone. You're the one who's still playing Barbie. Why *can't* you be in love with him?"

"Because he's dangerous!" Frustration and fear tangled together and shoved the words out of her before she could stop them. Willa didn't speak. Those dark brows of hers came together over watchful gray eyes and she folded her arms. Not pugnaciously. Patiently. Like Georgie was a wild animal and Willa had dropped into that bottomless stillness she could conjure up that made words almost unnecessary. They poured out of Georgie anyway. "I knew exactly what I was getting with the old Peter but when he threw me over, it still hurt. It hurt a lot, honestly. Worse than it should've, given that I was no more emotionally involved with him than he was with me. Or so I thought. But I must've had feelings for him if his betrayal could hurt me that way. Real feelings. And if that guy could ding my heart, imagine what this new Peter could do to me."

"You're in love with him," Willa repeated stubbornly.

"Maybe I am," she admitted. "Maybe I do love him but it hardly matters because I can't trust him."

"You can." Willa stared at her, disappointment clear in her silver eyes. "You're just too scared to let yourself."

CHAPTER 34

NEW YEAR'S EVE Day dawned brilliant and frigid, the sky a crystal blue dome that looked like it might crack if you hit it with one solid snowball. Of course the snow was far too cold to pack. It would be like throwing a handful of baby powder, only colder. Much, much colder. Peter hunched deeper into his thick jacket and yanked his wool cap down over his numb ears. This, he assumed, was why his hipster farmer had beat feet to Florida, or wherever the hell he'd gone. He'd seen a North Shore winter coming and decided that a masters degree afforded a man warmer options.

Peter had an MBA from Yale that said otherwise.

He trudged back from the far pasture, leaving the gates open behind him as he went. Tag shot past, delivering a solid shoulder check to the back of Peter's leg on the way by. Peter yelped and went down on one knee in the snow. Tag tossed him a broad doggie grin over his shoulder, and since Peter's hand was already in the snow, he scooped up a handful and side-armed it after his disrespectful dog. It fluttered into a million sparkling flakes, exactly as expected. He grinned nonetheless. He couldn't remember the last time he'd thrown a snowball at anybody. Maybe Willa, when they'd been kids. There were some advantages, he decided, to working outdoors. Like pelting the company asshole with a snowball whenever the need arose.

He reached the barn where the company asshole now waited with the dignity of a valued employee. "Yeah," Peter told Tag as he dragged the sliding door aside, "you'd *better* be on your best behavior. It's going to be packing snow one of these days, and you're going to get a taste of your own." Tag didn't so much as twitch an eyebrow. He was on the job now, and Peter was officially beneath his notice.

A humid blast of sheepy air hit Peter as he stepped into the barn, and the chorus went up, twenty-odd sheep delighted to see him. Or delighted at the prospect of a feeder freshly filled with hay. They jostled and circled each other like a bunch of fat, dirty clouds on toothpicks, bawling hungrily.

"All right, ladies, all right. Settle down." He threaded his way to the back of the flock. "There's enough of me to go around." He nodded to the dog now blocking the door, his ears cocked and alert, his eyes eerily intelligent. "Take them to the far pasture, Tag."

Tag turned and trotted away, and the sheep trotted obediently after him. Peter brought up the rear, encouraging the stragglers to keep up. A couple of babies danced in and out of the flock, cavorting and gamboling, delighted with the day and themselves. One of them raced back to him, blew a snotty raspberry against his jeans and leapt into the air, the lamb equivalent, Peter assumed, of hysterical laughter.

"Booger jokes," he said. "Very nice. Go eat, Bone."

Because this, of course, was Georgie's lamb, her mischievous second-born and undeclared favorite. Bone bounced a few steps to the left, putting a couple yards between herself and the flock, then turned back to look at him. *Come on*, she seemed to say, *Georgie's this way! She loves my booger jokes!*

But she didn't love Peter, did she? And while he didn't doubt Georgie would be delighted to see Bone, even with a wedding going on, he doubted he would be as welcome. He stepped around the lamb, gently nudged her back toward the flock. "That way, kiddo. Pretty sure it's black tie only up on the hill today."

Bone heaved a visible sigh — *you're no fun* — and bounced back toward the flock where Rag was waiting for her, all but shaking her head at her sister's undignified antics. Bone gathered herself for a mighty leap, obviously intending to show her sister a thing or two by sailing over her back with stately grace. Instead she clipped Rag with her rear hooves and they both went down in a tumble of skinny legs and outraged bleating. Peter had his phone in his hand, and had thumbed open the camera app before he was even conscious of what he was doing.

He'd been all set to take a video for Georgie, he realized slowly. She loved to see her babies being so naughty and charming. If she were here, she'd have that camera of hers pressed up to her eye, not knowing or caring how weirdly she scrunched up her breathtaking face when she was framing a shot.

The pain of missing her was so familiar, it was like an old friend. He let it settle onto his shoulders, sink to the bottom of his stomach. Georgie was the only person who'd ever seen anything beautiful in this godforsaken place. She was the only one who'd ever looked at Peter's punishment and saw possibility. Who'd ever looked at these messy, stinky animals and seen something worth loving. And she was gone.

Oh, he knew where she was. He always knew where she was. She'd kicked him off her land and out of her life, but she couldn't give him back his stupid heart. It was hers forever, and evidently, it functioned like a homing device. She held a piece of himself, so he always knew where she was.

Today, for example, she was right up the road at Davis Place making Addy and Jax's wedding as perfect as it could be. Not because it was important for the day to be pretty but because family was everything to her. Which was exactly why she might as well be in the next universe, or maybe in the universe beyond that, instead of a mile up the hill. Because family *was* everything to her, and when it mattered, Peter had failed to protect her and hers.

Nothing to be done about that now. He'd made that bed years ago. He had years more to lie in it. He straightened his shoulders, waited until the last sheep was in the far pasture, then shut the electric gate behind them. "Keep an eye on them, Tag."

Tag hopped to the top of the hay feeder and settled in to watch his charges, tail curled around his toes.

Peter headed back to the barn alone to change the oil in the tractor he barely knew how to drive. He had a manual. He'd figure it out. As long as he had a book, he could figure anything out. Too bad Georgie hadn't come with a manual. He might've done better when it mattered.

This live and learn business sucked.

He headed to the barn to stumble his way through Tractor Anatomy 101.

And just like that, Georgie's brother was married to her best friend.

It happened between one blink and the next. One second, Georgie was standing there in a delicious gown the color of a good German chocolate cake, a smattering of hand-beaded snowflakes floating down her bodice to collect in a heavy drift along the hem of her skirt. The next second, her brother was *married*. He was Addy's and Addy was his, and they were both Georgie's family, and he was kissing his bride with a naked gratitude that had tears rushing hot and unexpected into her eyes.

A little sniffling at a wedding was de rigueur but there was nothing polite about the hot clench of tears that gripped Georgie by the throat and shook her like a bad dog. It was only a lifetime of practice that allowed her to keep a small, sleepy smile on her face while she strolled down the aisle after the happy couple. That, and the slice of her brain that spoke with her mother's voice. *The crowd loves a spectacle, Georgie. Don't make yourself one.*

She held it together while the guests filed by, while they kissed Addy's cheek, pumped Jax's hand, and delivered their grinning remarks about honeymoons and future children. Georgie leaned down and air kissed a dozen people, then two dozen. Then four dozen. She had no idea how long it took, was aware only of the rising tide of grief that squeezed her chest and shredded her tender stomach.

Finally everybody was ushered to the upper studio to admire the lake view while the catering staff transformed the great room for dinner and dancing. Georgie shooed one starry-eyed lingerer up the stairs by promising him a dance later. Beside her, Willa said, "I see what you mean about eternal prom night."

"It's a living," Georgie said lightly. "Now go up there and make sure he doesn't come back down until you hear corks popping." She nudged Willa toward the stairs. "I'm going to supervise the kitchen staff."

Willa glowered at her from the bottom riser. "Why do I have to babysit your Romeo? Why can't I supervise the pouring of champagne?"

"I called it first."

"I hate you."

"Back at you, sister."

Willa scowled and marched up the stairs, her snowflake dress swishing and glittering like an actual blizzard. When she was safely out of sight, Georgie peeked into the kitchen and saw a dozen or more bottles of the champagne she'd hand-selected sweating on the counter. Good. She turned away from the kitchen, let herself into an empty bathroom off the great room, and locked the door. She closed the lid of the toilet, lowered herself to sit on top of it, and wept as if her heart were breaking.

She wept for the husband she would never have and hadn't thought she'd even wanted. She wept for the dreams Peter had made her dream, dreams that Shay had poisoned just like she'd poisoned her son and the only chance at love Georgie's heart would accept.

But she also cried with joy. She cried for Jax, for worthy, deserving Jax who'd finally gotten all the happiness he'd earned. And for Addy and her astonishingly generous heart, both of which Georgie's brother would hold precious and keep safe with all the considerable strength of his body and soul for the rest of his life.

And she cried for herself, for whatever had snapped sweetly into place in her soul when Addy had bound herself one layer more deeply into Georgie's family. Her broken heart overflowed with all of it, and she simply wasn't capable of — or interested in — pretending it didn't hurt. Not anymore. When she couldn't breathe for the choke of tears now, she finally respected her heart enough to find a safe place to be brutally, ruthlessly real. The kind of real Peter had taught her she could be, both by example and by demand.

She sucked a breath in all the way to her pinched toes — high heels were murder, albeit a familiar one — and let it out on one last shuddering sob. She rose and leaned into the mirror to inspect the damage. Hell. Her skin was blotchy and raw, her eyes red and puffy inside expertly applied and evidently indestructible makeup. She was just running the cold water and searching for a washcloth to use as a compress when Willa banged on the bathroom door.

"Georgie?"

"Give me a minute," she called back and tossed a washcloth into the sink to soak up the icy water.

"We don't have a minute." Georgie could picture Willa leaning into the door, her brows low over those serious silver eyes. "Julia Gates is here."

"What?" Georgie snapped off the faucet and yanked open the door. Willa practically fell in on top of her. "Where's Shay?" Because if Julia was here, Shay wasn't far behind. She knew it in her bones.

"Still in California, I hope." Willa shoved her farther into the bathroom and snatched the door shut behind them. "Though I doubt it."

"Yeah. Me, too." Georgie wrung out the frigid washcloth, slapped it to her face and started to pace. "God. This is just what today needed."

"Have you been crying?" Willa asked warily.

"Yes." She didn't even flinch at the admission. Her stomach sighed happily and released some of its grip. "Where's Matty?"

Willa's pause filled Georgie with cold dread. "I don't know."

"What do you mean, you don't know?"

"I was going to shove him in a broom closet or something the second I saw Julia."

"Good thinking."

"Yeah. Except I couldn't find him, and I looked everywhere." She met Georgie's stare with troubled silver eyes. "He's gone."

CHAPTER 35

PETER HAD BEEN at it for hours. He'd definitely taken oil out of the tractor — or what he'd hoped was oil — and he'd put oil back in. Whether what he'd removed had actually *been* oil — and whether the tractor would function when he fired it up — was anybody's guess. He'd been trying to test his work most of the day but the tractor refused to run. Was it a botched oil change or something more sinister? Peter had no idea. There was only one way to find out, though.

Several expensive runs to the farm supply store later, he'd replaced the battery, the air filter, the ignition coil, and a few belts and hoses. He'd also installed and calibrated new spark plugs. (Or so the manual assured him.) Night was falling when he climbed wearily into the cracked leather seat, set his jaw against yet another failure and turned the key.

The engine fired up with a roar that startled him so badly he nearly toppled off the damn tractor.

"Yes!" He bounced back into the center of the seat and shot both arms into the air. Triumph filled him, fizzy and bright, raced through his veins and cracked his dirty face into a ridiculous, leering grin. Had the business mogul he'd once been felt this way when he'd closed a sweet deal? When he'd acquired a profitable little property, or a percentage of a start-up with serious potential? Had he felt this way when Georgie had agreed to marry him?

Not even close. This wasn't screwing somebody else so he could have what he wanted. This wasn't beating somebody else so he could win. This was triumph in its purest form, triumph over *himself*. He'd spent an entire day banging his intellect against a machine, and the machine hadn't given in; his brain had. His brain and his hands had shifted to accommodate new information, and he'd acquired a new skill. And he'd used that skill to fix something. Up to this point, he'd done nothing with his life but make money and break shit. But today, he'd *fixed* something. The goddamn tractor *worked*.

The power of that big engine rumbled under his butt, vibrated through his bones, shook his teeth in his head. His eyes stung unexpectedly, and his throat went hot and tight. He knew he couldn't be close to tears. He was a man, for God's sake. Who cried over a tractor? So he threw back his head, opened his mouth and released the ache in his throat in a barbaric yawp that crashed into the tractor's beastly rumble with its claws and fangs out. It was a warrior's song and they shouted it together, Peter and his tractor.

He hopped to the ground, threw open the barn's sliding door and drove out into the twilight, grinning like a maniac. He was going to show his stupid dog what he'd done. He rumbled and jounced over the uneven ground toward the far pasture, singing a tractor song he was making up on the fly entitled *I Fixed This Bitch, How Do You Like Me Now?* It was barely four in the afternoon but he punched on the headlights because it was December on the North Shore and night fell like a hammer up here. He threaded the tractor through the gate to the near pasture, then on into the middle pasture. The far pasture gate was closed, as it should be, but when Peter aimed his headlights at the rusty metal feeder the sheep had been grazing from all day, Tag wasn't sitting on top of it, as he usually was.

Disappointment tangled into his elation and Peter had a moment of wry self-awareness. He was *disappointed* that a dog wasn't there to appreciate his tractor? He really had been spending too much time alone.

Then the alarm took hold. Because Tag wasn't just a dog. He was a better farmer than Peter would ever be. He wouldn't leave the flock, not without a reason.

Oh, God, was another of his ewes giving birth somewhere? But, wait, none of them were pregnant. He was as sure of that as Willa could make him, and when it came to the fertility of his sheep, he trusted his sister completely. But what if another hiker had come by with off-leash dogs? What if the babies had thwarted his electric fence again and wandered off?

He killed the engine and jumped to the ground. He cut the power to the section of the fence that doubled as the gate and swung it open. "Back to the barn, girls," he shouted. "Tag, take them to the barn!"

Tag wasn't anywhere to be seen but the sheep didn't know that. The sheep just knew that this was the part of the day where it got dark, the farmer yelled some words and they went back inside with the dog nipping their heels if they lingered. They all trotted smartly back toward the rectangle of light streaming out of the barn door he'd left open for them. He counted them as they passed, dread growing in his chest as he registered all the ewes and all the lambs. All but one. All but Georgie's baby.

Bone was missing.

Shit.

In his pocket, his phone vibrated with an incoming text. It was probably Georgie demanding he come get his wedding-crashing lamb. He thumbed in his security code, then stared in horror at the message that glowed up at him.

I warned you.

The number was unknown but Peter knew his mother's voice when he heard it.

Then somewhere to the northeast — uphill, across property that wasn't Peter's — Tag barked sharply.

Peter left his fence open and ran.

Georgie shoved Willa toward the stairs. "Get up there and stall," she hissed. "Tell the guests they can see the northern lights if they stare hard enough at the horizon over the lake or something."

Willa stopped on the bottom riser to stare at her. "What kind of moron is going to believe you can see the northern lights in the southern sky at sunset?"

"Make up something better, then! Just keep everybody upstairs until I can figure out what Julia's doing here." Georgie poked Willa up another riser. "I assume Mom has her somewhere?"

"In the library," Willa said and swatted at Georgie's poking fingers. "And why do I have to vamp for the crowd? I want to go look for Matty."

"In that dress? Please. You're a bridesmaid, not the snow queen. You'll freeze to death. Besides, it's entirely possible that I'll find out where Matty is once I talk to Mom. She probably stashed him somewhere herself once she spotted the enemy." She hoped. But fragments of the conversation they'd had with Shay a month or so ago floated through her brain like a chimes from a distant bell, little bits of innuendo and veiled threats, sideways claims to the boy Georgie had fiercely loved since the instant she'd first held him. The boy who was also Shay's biological son.

Willa scowled. "I knew this dress was a mistake."

"You love that dress. You said so."

"I know. That was the mistake." She sighed gustily. "Fine. I'll go upstairs and make nice." She shot an uncompromising finger Georgie's way. "But I want to know what you know the instant you know it."

"Deal." Georgie nudged that finger aside like it was a loaded gun. "Now go."

Willa made an aggrieved noise and stomped up the stairs, all frustration and glittery snowflakes. Georgie turned and jogged to the library, a snug pine-paneled alcove off the great room that smelled of leather and lemon polish. It reminded her of Peter. His properties always smelled of lemon polish, too. Her heart twinged wearily but she was all cried out. The place where she kept her tears was empty, not that she imagined it would stay that way.

"Mom?" She strolled lazily through the arched entry, injected a casually curious note into her tone. "We're about to do the champagne toast. What are you doing—" She stopped, as if surprised. "Oh. Hello, Julia. What are you doing here?"

Julia Gates was perched on the edge of a leather love seat in a sharp tweed skirt suit, her ankles crossed and tucked neatly to one side. "Hello, Georgie." Her mouth was painted a celebratory scarlet, but her eyes sparkled maliciously behind angular frames. "I'm just making a courtesy call."

"On New Year's Eve? During Addy's wedding?" Georgie glanced at Bianca, who sat with one hip hitched onto a curvy-legged writing table by the window.

"I'm not sure courtesy is precisely the word you're looking for, Julia," Bianca murmured with an amused detachment that only barely covered the wariness beneath.

335

The reporter shrugged lightly. "Courtesy isn't precisely what you deserve from me."

"No?"

"After the way you've treated me since Diego's death?" Julia showed her teeth. "You're lucky I'm here at all."

Bianca smiled thinly. "I'm not sure *lucky* is quite the word you're after there, either. But by all means, say what you've come to say. We'll make certain Addison gets the message."

"I'd rather speak to her in person."

"I'm sure you would."

Julia met that with tense silence. Finally she said, "As you like." She folded her hands primly in her lap and met Bianca's eyes. "Shay's agreed to speak on the record about her relationship with Diego and the son that resulted from said relationship."

Georgie gave that a deliberate blink. "What happened to *I don't want anything from you*?"

"She doesn't want anything from you," Julia said, "except that you share with Matty the truth of his birth." Her lips curved. "And she doesn't trust you to do that."

Bianca considered this. "So she enlisted you and your magazine to broadcast the truth to the world."

"I don't see how that's in Matty's best interests," Georgie said. "Unless Shay's planning to use her profits from the piece to buy the kid his own therapist."

Julia ignored that, kept her attention on Georgie's mother. "Can you blame her for wanting to control the public narrative, Bianca? She came to you for help once before, remember, battered and vulnerable. You threatened to not only take her child from her but to publicly paint her as an unfit parent. You all but chased her off your land with torches and pitchforks." She lifted a brow. "It's a habit with you Davises — attacking anybody who dares to suggest that Diego wasn't perfection personified."

"You have no right to decide what Diego was or wasn't," Bianca said coldly. "That right belongs to us, to his mother, to his sister, and to his wife. You were nothing to him but some cheap publicity and an easy lay. You don't know the first thing—"

"Diego was a towering talent and an astonishing personality," Julia snapped, her voice vibrating with an awful love that was more sickness than emotion. A pang of pity took Georgie by surprise. "He was the voice and the vision of his generation, but he was *human*. He wasn't faithful or kind or even particularly principled. But he was fearless and hungry and *real*, and I—" She broke off before she could say the words but Georgie heard them anyway.

I loved him. I love him.

"You what?" Bianca asked disdainfully.

Julia lifted her chin, her skin frighteningly pale aside from the color burning on each cheek. "I don't understand why that can't be enough for you," she said stiffly, but Georgie heard the pain stitching together every word like scar tissue. "He was a genius. Why does he have to be a perfect soul and a faithful husband, too? Why do you have to destroy or silence anybody who suggests otherwise?"

Something glimmered deep inside Georgie's mind, an epiphany sneaking in around the edges. She let the room drop out of focus so she could bend all her attention toward it. Had they had Diego's pet reporter wrong all this time? What if hurting Addy wasn't the goal at all, just an inevitable side effect of Julia's truth? What if Julia was just a woman staggering under the weight of a consuming but unrequited love? And what if grief and rage had turned that love poisonous? Wounds festered and killed people all the time. Was a broken heart really that different? What would it take to lance this woman's wound? To drain the infection and release her from her pain? Could it be as simple as acknowledging the truth of her relationship with Diego, as broken and dirty as it had been?

The truth could be an exquisite relief, as Georgie well knew. Even when it was ugly. Even when it cut. Even when it bled.

"Heaven's sake, Julia," Bianca said impatiently. "Nobody's trying to destroy anybody, nor are we in any way suggesting Diego didn't have his faults. But making them so highly public could damage his legacy beyond redemption. Is that really what you want? To take away from him the one thing he actually earned himself — the right to influence and inspire generations upon generations of artists?"

"Of course not." Julia scowled and dropped her eyes. "I only want—" She stopped and moved miserable shoulders.

"What?" Bianca asked softly. Almost cruelly. "What exactly do you want, Julia?"

"She wants us to make room for her in Diego's story," Georgie said. Both women swung to stare at her but Georgie kept her eyes on the reporter. "Because you weren't just writing his story, were you, Julia? You were part of it. Part of *him*. Isn't that right?"

The relief that flashed through the woman's eyes made Georgie's throat ache.

"Yes." Her skin was tight across blazing cheekbones, her mouth a bright line of defiance. "Because I was, you know. I was part of his life. He didn't love me, not like he loved *her*, but I was important to him. I meant something."

Bianca opened her mouth but Georgie cut her off with a subtle gesture at her side, below Julia's line of vision. "We know you did. But acknowledging that would only hurt Addison, and you know we couldn't endorse that."

"Hurting Addison was never my intention. Not—" She smiled thinly. "—that I would've been overly bothered by it. She was the Angel, after all. She was *his* Angel. She had everything."

"Everything but love and a faithful husband," Georgie pointed out.

"She had him," Julia returned bitterly. "She had his ring and his word and all the devotion of which he was capable."

Such as it was, Georgie thought, but said nothing.

"She was everything to him." Julia twitched a hand, somehow conveying a world of grief and disappointment, and her resignation to it. "But I wasn't nothing. I *wasn't*."

"We know," Georgie said gently. "We saw the paintings. The ones Diego did of you."

Julia closed her eyes. "She deserves to hurt just for burning those paintings. She had no right."

"She had every right," Georgie said calmly. "Diego left them specifically to her, to do with as she liked. She could've used them for tea towels if she'd had the notion."

"She had *no right*." Julia opened her eyes and they glittered with a grief that bordered on madness. "You can't own a painting any more than you can own the talent that created it. Even Diego didn't own his genius. He cared for it and he tended it, but it wasn't his. He was just the steward. He said so all the time."

"An art farmer," Georgie murmured, struck.

"Exactly." Julia barked out a harsh laugh. "He was in the talent husbandry business."

Bianca only stared at them both, bemused.

"What if we agree to acknowledge you and your true role in Diego's life?" Georgie asked, and cut off her mother's inchoate protest with another sharp gesture.

"In exchange for what?" Julia asked, eyes narrowing with equal parts interest and suspicion.

"For not publishing Shay's story." Georgie met those eyes with a level stare. "The truth has a weight and a gravity all its own, Julia. You can't suppress it for long, not without consequences, and I'll bet you know that as well as I do." Julia nodded shortly and Georgie went on. "Which is why Matty already knows everything, and has for some time. But you don't. Not by a long shot."

"What does that mean?" Julia frowned sharply.

"Shay's lying to you. Diego didn't rape her or even pressure her into unwanted sex, and if her pregnancy was an accident, I'm the queen of England. Ask Willa if you don't believe me. She was there. She'll tell you the whole story. Shay's relentlessly ambitious. She wanted to be a Davis and screwing Diego was her opportunity to get there. She's using you," Georgie told her flatly. "You think it's the other way around, that she's your weapon but she's had you aimed at us the whole time. You're just too exhausted and desperate to see it." She waved a weary hand. "I don't blame you. Chronic pain — emotional or physical — takes a vicious toll. You aren't thinking straight."

Julia released an incredulous chuckle. "Are you kidding me? A hard wind would knock that woman back to California. She had a panic attack on the plane ride here."

Georgie suppressed a sick sigh. Bianca actually flinched. Because now they knew for sure what Georgie had previously only feared: Shay had indeed come back to town with Julia. But where was she?

"When she was pregnant with Matty, Shay killed my father." Georgie swung the words like a hammer, cold and merciless. "My mother sneered at her pretensions and my father rejected her advances, so she tampered with the ventilation on Dad's basement kiln in this very house. She left it there like a ticking time bomb, and was innocently gestating Matty in Italy per the agreement when it suffocated my father." Silence stretched between them, heavy with Julia's disbelief and Georgie's grief. "She killed my father and widowed my mother because they didn't give her the proper respect, Julia. Do you really think a woman like that is going to have a panic attack over *flying*?"

The color dropped out of the older woman's cheeks. "You can't know she did anything like murder," she said with uncertain defiance. "If you could prove she'd killed somebody, you'd have—"

"Her own son saw her here the night my father rejected her. She told him what she'd done."

Julia's eyes flew wide. "She *told* him?"

"Yes."

"And you believe him?"

"Yes," she said firmly, because she did. Peter might've been a liar once, but he wasn't anymore. Dishonesty would show on those brutal bones like red wine on a white dress. Now that her heart wasn't awash with pain and fear, she could see that. He'd had every reason to deny all knowledge of what his mother was capable of. But he hadn't lied, had he? He'd looked her dead in the face and he'd told her the truth. His mother was a monster, and he knew it. Had always known it. "He told me what she really wanted from us, too, and it wasn't telling her long-lost son the truth about his birth."

"What was it?" Julia asked, shaken.

"A sketch of Diego's," Georgie said. "One of a trio of pencil sketches from *Diego After Dark*. Nudes."

Her eyes went unfocused. "The ones she asked about at the gallery."

"Yes. Two were of her daughter Willa, but one was of Shay. He drew them both that summer."

"He did more than draw them," Bianca muttered.

"She said she only wanted to prove she was Matty's birth mother," Julia whispered. "She thought if you saw the sketch, you'd see—"

"No," Georgie said. "She knew she couldn't ask us outright for the sketch, not if she wanted to keep up the wounded bird routine for you. So she sent Peter up the hill after the two of you were gone to let us know we could either hand it over, or expect to lose another family member."

"You don't really think she'd—"

"I think you're her final warning," Georgie said coldly. "If the idea of Matty going through this kind of public hell doesn't convince us to show her the proper respect, nothing will." She paused significantly. "And she sent Peter to remind us of how she punishes disrespect."

Julia shook her head slowly, horror dawning in those sharp blue eyes. "I really think you've got her all wrong, Georgie. She's simply not capable of—"

Georgie abruptly lost patience. She turned away from Julia mid-sentence. "Mom? Where's Matty?"

The color drained from Bianca's cheeks, leaving her waxen and chalky. "Isn't he upstairs?"

"No. Willa can't find him. We thought maybe you'd sent

him away."

"No," Bianca whispered, her eyes large and horrified. "I didn't have time."

"Julia?" Georgie turned hard eyes on the reporter.

"No." She lifted helpless shoulders. "I haven't seen him."

"Where's Shay?"

"Waiting for me in the car."

"Are you sure of that?"

Her mouth, so valiantly bright, crumpled. "No," she admitted. "I'm not."

CHAPTER 36

PETER RAN THROUGH the dying light toward the sound of his barking dog. He ran with the determined speed of a man who'd unexpectedly fixed his own tractor and was now possessed by a shaky hope that his luck had changed. That he might land on the side of the angels once again if he just ran fast enough.

He stumbled over the uneven ground and slapped aside the hemlock branches that tore at his jacket until he came across the trail that snaked through the dense woods between his farm and Davis Place. He leaned into the uphill climb, then burst out of the tree line. A few more slippery, rocky yards and he was standing at an intersection in the milky moonlight overlooking the river. It was right where he'd stood with Georgie a lifetime ago, where the trail dead-ended into a choice. Hang a right and you were heading for Davis Place and the Kettle view. Hang a left and you could see the forest fire burn line and go bury a dead lamb.

Tag released another sharp flurry of distant barks and Peter turned right. He'd known he would. His mother had warned him, and Bone wanted his beloved Georgie.

"Damn it," he muttered, and hit the snow-slicked trail at a sprint, praying that crashing a black-tie wedding in tractor-fixing clothes would be his worst sin of the evening. Praying he'd get there before his mother could harm anybody else Georgie loved. Or before some off-leash dog tore the throat out of his happy-go-lucky little lamb.

Tag barked again, and Peter was close enough this time

to catch the warning in it. Tag was reaching the end of his patience, but he wasn't alarmed. Relief sloshed messily inside Peter, and he rounded the final bend. The woods fell away and the trail gave out onto a platform of icy metal grating. It was a tourist overlook, raised above the forbidding slab of basalt that cradled the Kettle itself. He skidded to a halt, caught himself against the blisteringly cold rail. He stood there, panting, listening. The river rushed by on his left, hurtling toward the gaping black maw of the Kettle dead ahead. It flung itself heedlessly over the lip of that hungry hole, and the Kettle gulped it down. Several yards beyond that, the cliff's edge loomed equally ominously, a dark line painted against the purpling sky, with the deadly drop to the lake unseen but heavily implied. Davis Place stood on the cliff's edge to his right, golden light spilling from every window. The back yard was a parking lot tonight, full of cars glittering in the moonlight. He could only see a slice of the front yard beyond the house, but it was enough. A sudden spray of snow flew up beside the house as if kicked up by tiny hooves. It hung glittering in the frozen air like fairy dust. Then Bone was underneath it, bucking and squealing like a kid running through the sprinkler.

Peter dragged a hand down his face and sighed. He ignored the *No Trespassing* signs posted all along the platform and threw a leg carefully over the railing. He shinnied along the outside of the fence until he was positioned over a snowbank big enough to break his fall. He hoped like hell there wasn't a boulder inside it and let himself drop.

He landed with a thud that jarred his bones but didn't break any. He shook off the snow and stepped out on the naked basalt dome, uneasily aware that it was slippery as hell, and he was closer to the hungry mouth of the Kettle than the park service preferred. But he smacked the snow off his filthy jeans and picked his way carefully across the shifting rocks toward Davis Place to retrieve his stupid lamb.

And find his murderous mother.

"Georgie." Willa appeared in the archway between the library and the great room, her expression caught somewhere between impatience and amusement. "You have a visitor."

"I have a what?" Georgie nudged her aside so Bianca could squeeze past with Julia to see if Shay had stayed in the car like a good girl. She doubted it.

Willa caught Bianca's arm. "Hey, wait. Do you know where Matty is?"

"No," Bianca said and shook her off. She took the reporter more firmly by the elbow. "Julia and I are just going to see if Shay would like to come inside and join us for the champagne toast."

"She's here?" Willa asked.

"She's waiting for me in the car," Julia said with desperate certainty.

"We'll see about that," Bianca said and all but perp-walked the reporter out of the library.

Willa watched them go. "I never thought I'd say this but I hope to God my mother's actually in the parking lot. Because if she's not—"

Terror swirled into Georgie's stomach and she threaded her arm through Willa's. Steered her toward the stairs. "We'll know soon enough. Now what's this about a visitor?"

The kitchen door opened and Addy sailed into the great room in a cloud of ivory silk and hand-beaded snowflakes. "One of your lambs is playing in the front yard," she announced. "Everybody's charmed." The catering staff flowed out of the door behind her, armed with trays of full champagne glasses, and started up the stairs. Addy watched them go with the satisfaction of a five-star general. "That ought to keep everybody happy while they're pressed to the glass, falling in love with Rag. Or Bone." She cocked a brow. "Which one's the naughty one?"

"Bone," Georgie said automatically. "You should be with your guests, Addison."

"Oh, I will be. Soon. We all will be. But for now—" She fixed them both with sharp green eyes. "—why don't the two of you tell me what the hell is going on?"

Peter eyed the wide, shallow dip between the dome of basalt under his boots and the edge of Davis Place's lawn. It looked so innocent, like an overgrown ditch blanketed in half a foot of snow but Peter knew exactly what was hiding under there — a three-foot-deep tangle of thorns and brambles the width of a football field. Bone bounced up to the edge of the lawn on the other side of it and peered across at him.

"Bah!" she called delightedly.

"Bah yourself," Peter muttered, but he saw Tag sitting on the rock wall that kept Addy's guests — and Peter's lambs — from tumbling a few hundred feet straight down into the snapping jaws of Lake Superior. Even from a distance, he could see the dog tracking the lamb as it cavorted and tumbled in the yard, occasionally hopping down to nip at her heels when she came too close to the edge. Peter sighed. He knew exactly how pointless it was to chase sheep by yourself. Herding was a two-man job. Or a man and a dog. Or, hell, probably just two dogs would do the trick. Tag was doing the right thing by just putting himself between Bone and the drop, and waiting for reinforcements.

That would be Peter.

He eyed the snowy underbrush again, swore softly and waded in.

Georgie exchanged a glance with Willa, who shrugged and said, "Tell her."

Her stomach voted for the truth, too. It was how her stomach always voted, though. That didn't mean it was the right choice, but in this case it seemed like the only choice.

So Georgie filled Addy in as quickly and thoroughly as possible. Addy took it all in silently, a frown growing between her cinnamon-colored brows. Then the frown turned to anger, which slipped into something foreign and wrong on a face built to smile.

"Addison?" Georgie touched her arm. "Are you all right?"

"No."

Georgie met Willa's eyes, read her own concern in them. "Go get Jax."

"Right." Willa spun for the stairs but Addy shot out a hand, gripped her elbow.

She said, "No."

"No, I shouldn't get Jax?" Willa asked tentatively.

"I mean, no, I won't have it."

Willa sent a helpless look Georgie's way. "Won't have what?"

"I won't have this *woman*," Addy spat viciously, and the depth of her rage sent a shock from Georgie's brain stem to the tips of her fingers, "this conscienceless, murdering *sociopath*, stalking my family and *ruining my wedding*." She released her grip on Willa's arm, turned it into an apologetic pat. "No offense. I know she's your mom."

"None taken," Willa murmured, eyes wide.

"First things first," Addy said briskly. "Let's get Matty back."

"He's probably outside chasing my lamb," Georgie said quickly. She had no idea if she believed any such thing but it was possible. "Let me go look." She sent Willa a look that said *get her back upstairs and give her to Jax.*

"I'm going with you," Addy said.

"Me, too," Willa said, flagrantly ignoring the look.

Georgie glared at them both, side by side, a small but determined army she could either fight with or against. Love for them filled her, even as she tried one last time. "Hell, no. Go upstairs."

"Screw that," Addy said succinctly.

"What she said." Willa nodded toward the dangerously pissed off bride. "If you think you're going out there alone, you're off your nut. You heard Addy. There's a killer on the loose."

"But she's hardly a shoot-you-in-the-face type killer," Georgie said reasonably. "She's more a manufacture-a-plausible-accident type killer." She hoped. "I think I can step into the front yard without incident."

"Great," Addy said implacably. "Then we can all step into the front yard without incident."

Georgie couldn't think of a comeback for that so she threw up her hands. "Fine! You want to drag your wedding dress around in the snow, go for it. But I'm not going to feel sorry for you when the reception photos are a mess."

"I don't want you to feel sorry for me," Addy snapped as they all stomped through the great room toward the front door. "What I want is to go back upstairs and have my damn champagne toast with my damn husband and my entire damn family around me, safe and happy and warm." Tears choked her voice toward the end and she coughed them away. "But if I have to drag my wedding dress — which I know damn well isn't off the rack any more than your bridesmaids dresses are — through the snow or roll around in the yard or dance a naked cha cha on the edge of the Kettle to get it, I will. Because *I am the bride—*" She flung open the door with enough force to bounce it off the side of the house. "*—and I am supposed to get whatever I want today!*"

"Okay, okay!" Willa threw out an arm to stop the door from ricocheting off the siding and knocking the bride back into the house. "Take it easy."

"I will not take it easy! *Matty!*" she roared with a maternal authority that boded well for Georgie's future nieces or nephews being very well-behaved. "You get your skinny butt back inside this *instant* or I swear on all that's holy I will never buy you another doughnut again as long as we both shall live!"

In the yard, Georgie's lamb froze mid-frolic, an ear cocked warily toward the porch. The lawn was a quilt of glittering snow checkered with irregular rectangles of golden light spilling from the house. Peter's dog sat on the center of the rock wall separating the yard from the brutal drop, his eyes patient and stern. For a moment, the world itself waited for Matty's answer. Even the eternal grumble and gnash of the lake far below seemed to pause. But there was nothing.

Finally Bone broke the silence with a joyful bleat, and bounded up the porch steps to say hello. Georgie sighed and bent to meet her naughty lamb. Tag, relieved of duty, hopped off the rock wall and padded over to receive his due. Willa

350

gave it to him, squatting to stroke his ears and murmur lavish compliments. Addy just stood there, fists on hips, scanning the horizon like a radar. Then she said, "Oh dear God."

"What?" Willa shot to her feet. "What is it?"

Georgie followed the trembling finger Addy held out toward the scrubby field between Davis Place and the inky black slab of basalt against the paler black sky. Two silhouettes were moving through the snowy undergrowth, one small and curvy, one long and lanky, but both choosing their footing on the slippery ground with a careful deliberation that made her think of Peter. Recognition was a shock that hollowed out her chest. *Was* that Peter?

No. Her brain caught up with her intuition and she realized the figures only reminded her of Peter. Probably because they were both related to him.

It was Matty and Shay picking their way toward the river. More accurately, it was Shay herding Matty slowly but undeniably to the rim of the Kettle.

CHAPTER 37

PETER HAD BARELY stepped into the frozen brush when Addy's fury had split the night. The front porch of Davis Place had to be half a football field away, but he could see her easily. She glowed like a lighthouse in her wedding dress, flanked by Georgie and Willa. And she was pointing toward the Kettle.

He didn't move. He didn't allow himself the luxury. Instead, he closed his eyes and listened as if his life depended on it. As if Matty's life depended on it. It probably did.

For three long heartbeats, there was nothing but the harsh murmur of the river. Then he heard it, the snap and the snag of legs pushing through the underbrush. It carried clearly on the cold night air, as did the voices.

"You don't have to do this," Matty said, his tone carefully reasonable. "I gave you the sketch."

"Of course I have to do this," Shay returned merrily. "But you've been a very good boy. Much more respectful than that rabid bitch you call mommy. I'll make it quick. You won't suffer."

"But I gave you the sketch. You got what you wanted."

"No," Shay said, resentment creeping in under the cheer. "I didn't."

Dread crawled into Peter's mouth, pooled there like nausea. Matty hadn't spent his childhood at the mercy of Shay's mercurial moods. He hadn't learned to read her the way Peter had. He didn't understand that he was going to get hurt if he kept pushing.

"But the sketch—" Matty started again and Peter opened his eyes in spite of himself. They were maybe a dozen and a half yards farther inland than Peter. Matty had just broken free of the brush and stepped onto the slick stretch of basalt when Shay swung out a casual arm. She clipped the back of his head with whatever she held in her hand. It glinted dully in the moonlight and Peter's heart sank. A gun. She'd just pistol-whipped the kid. Not overly hard, but not just a love tap, either. Jesus.

Matty didn't cry out. His voice just stopped like a sliced thread and he went to his knees. Being hit wasn't like in the movies, Peter knew, especially if you weren't used to it. Pain was an overwhelming, disorienting force that left you silent and stunned.

"What I wanted—" Shay bent to speak to the boy on his hands and knees before her, "—was for Bianca to hand over the sketch, not for you to steal it for me. What I wanted was for your mommy to follow instructions and show some respect. But she just doesn't learn, does she?" She took him by the ear and Matty leapt to his feet with a yelp. Peter winced in sympathy. The ear twist didn't leave a mark but it definitely got your attention. It was a classic for a reason. "But that's all right," Shay went on. "I have time for one more lesson."

Peter knew exactly what kind of lesson Shay wanted to teach Bianca. It wouldn't matter to her one bit that she'd have to murder a child this time. Nor would it matter to her that it was a child of her own body. Nothing mattered to Shay *except* her own body. Except her own wants and needs and desires.

It was something Peter had known on some level for

years but it wasn't until this moment that he *understood* it. That he truly grasped what it meant, and how it functioned in the world. In *his* world.

His mother didn't love him. His mother *couldn't* love him. She couldn't love anybody, or anything. She was broken, and there was nothing Peter could do or buy or earn that would change that. He'd spent years knocking his hard head against the concept, years acquiring vast stores of property, prestige and profits while the rejected little kid inside him hoped in vain that someday it might be enough. Someday his mommy would return, see what he'd made of himself and finally love him.

She would never love him. She didn't know what love was. Not if she thought disrespect and murder were sins of equal weight.

The understanding sank slowly into his bones, both painful and liberating. He wondered how long ago Willa had had this epiphany. Because surely she must have. Maybe that was why she'd been able to be happy while he never had.

Then he realized he was standing there like an idiot having deep thoughts while Shay and Matty, several yards farther inland, moved past him toward the Kettle. When Peter had been between them and the Kettle, his filthy face and tractor-fixing clothes had acted as camouflage against the dark rock rising up behind him. They were abreast of him now, but if they happened to look back as they gained on the Kettle, Peter would be silhouetted against the snowy stretch of brush like a tree trunk.

He eased himself backwards out of the brush as silently as possible and sank down until he was flat against the slippery basalt. Then he began to crawl.

Bianca and Julia emerged from the side yard, Bianca coldly furious, Julia pale and resigned.

"Shay's gone," Bianca announced.

Willa pointed silently toward the silhouettes moving inexorably toward the rim of the Kettle.

Bianca blanched. Julia sank onto the porch steps and put her head in her hands.

"Oh lord, oh lord, oh lord." Addy chanted it, her hands pressed to her waxy cheeks, her eyes fixed helplessly on Matty and Shay. "She's taking him to the Kettle. What do we do? What do we *do?*" Her hands curled into fists and she knocked them against her temples. "Think, think, *think!*"

"I'm going after them," Georgie said. Her blood was beating so hard in her ears she could hardly hear herself speak and her vision was ominously dark at the edges. "Call nine-one-one." She pulled her phone from the clever side pocket she'd had sewn into her bridesmaid dress and held it out to Addison with hands she willed steady with brutal force.

"Wait, you have pockets? And you get to use them? I thought we didn't use pockets!" Willa glared at her. "Also, you're not going after them. Not alone."

"The pocket rule has exceptions. And I'm definitely going after them." The phone buzzed in Georgie's hand and she nearly fumbled it. Then she saw a text from Peter lighting up her screen.

Looking for Bone, found Matty instead. Shay has him. Need distraction. Provide?

Relief nearly unstrung her knees and she swayed. "Oh thank God."

"What?" Addy asked, hope naked in her face.

"Peter's out there." She waved weakly toward the Kettle.

"He was coming after Bone, and must've stumbled across Shay and Matty."

"Shay?" Jax appeared in the open doorway behind her, Eli behind him. Their broad shoulders and deep frowns filled the doorway and blocked the light. "She's here?"

"She's got Matty," Addy cried, and flew into his arms. He closed them around her with a certainty and strength that had Georgie's eyes stinging. "They're out there."

"At the Kettle," Willa told Eli tightly. He didn't wrap her up in his arms like Jax had with Addy, he simply reached out and cupped the nape of her neck. But it made Georgie want to cry, too. She was surrounded by family, and she was alone with her terror. "Peter's with them, though."

"*With them* with them?" Eli frowned. "Or he just happened to be passing by and—"

"Right place, right time, sounds like." Georgie pointed at Bone. "He was out looking for this one."

"Hell." Jax pinched the bridge of his nose. "Tell me you've already called nine-one-one."

She thumb-typed *on my way* and hit send. Then she slapped her phone into his hand. "You do it."

She marched past him to retrieve her rain boots from the hall closet. She came back out to the porch, plopped down on the front step and put them on.

"What are you doing?" Jax asked, Addy still tucked into his side, the phone to his ear.

"Peter said he needs a distraction."

He stared, mouth open, then jumped. "Yes," he said into the phone, "this is Jackson Davis. I'm up at Davis Place. I need to report a hostage situation." He stabbed a finger at Georgie, then at the porch at their feet. *Stay.* She stood, slapped her skirt clean and lifted a middle finger in return.

"Georgie," Bianca snapped. "You're not going anywhere. That woman is dangerous, and your judgment is utterly compromised where Peter's concerned. We have no idea why he wants you out there, but you can be sure it's nothing good, and I'll be damned if I'll lose two children tonight. You're staying right here with me."

She threaded her arm through Georgie's and drew her close. Guilt and fear gripped the back of Georgie's neck with familiar fingers and she hunched automatically. *She's right,* her brain whispered with her mother's voice. *You can't trust him. He's with Shay. He doesn't love you. He doesn't need you. He's using you, and you're a fool to think otherwise.*

She glanced up and found Willa watching her, sympathy and knowledge in those startling eyes. And she knew somehow that this was her last chance. If she caved to that voice in her head right now, she'd be stuck with it forever. She'd have chosen fear and safety over risk and love. She'd have chosen the barren emptiness of the past two months over whatever the future might hold. She had no idea what that future might be, but she was absolutely certain that she couldn't survive another two minutes like the last two months, let alone the rest of her life.

She slid her arm from her mother's and stepped away. "I'm sorry, Mom. I have to go."

"No." Bianca drew herself up regally, her fury magnificent and pure. "I forbid it."

"I love him," she said simply.

"I love *you*."

Tears pinched her throat shut so Georgie hugged her mother, hard and fast. "I trust him."

"You're wrong," Bianca said flatly, but there was something hollow and forlorn under the accusation. "You can't trust—"

"—anybody, I know. You've told me that, over and over." She stepped back, put a careful two feet of space between her mother's demand and her own desperate, knee-jerk desire to obey. "I'm going anyway."

"Georgie, listen to me! You can't just—"

"No," she said firmly. "I'm done listening to you. I've listened to you all my life. I have your voice in my head twenty-four hours a day, reminding me that everybody's watching so I have to be perfect. And I have been. I've been absolutely perfect, Mom. And do you know what that made me?"

"*Safe!*"

She paused, startled. "Oh, Mom." The determination melted away and she reached into that careful space she'd just made. She took her mother's cold, trembling hand. Bianca had lost so much. A husband. A son. The ability to love without wondering how to survive the inevitable heartbreak. "This isn't about my safety. It's about yours."

Bianca drew back, startled, but Georgie held on.

"You want to protect me," she said, "of course you do. You love me. And I love you right back. That's why I've spent so much of my life trying to be perfect enough to please you. And I've done it. I'm exactly what you've always wanted me to be. I'm perfect. Perfectly pretty, perfectly private, perfectly composed, always. But I'm also perfectly alone. God, I'm so alone. In my house, in my head, in my heart. But worse than that, I'm afraid."

"Of what?" Bianca asked. Her face was as coolly composed as ever but her eyes were awash in a pain that wrapped Georgie's heart in barbed wire.

She forced the words out anyway. "Of you."

Bianca closed her eyes and released a single slow breath.

"I'm afraid of disappointing you," Georgie told her gently. "Of letting down the family. Of showing people how I feel in case they use it to hurt me or — God forbid — any of you." She glanced around the porch, saw everybody she loved staring back. "But I can't do it anymore. I can't. Maybe it's stupid, maybe it's risky and maybe it'll break my heart. But I love him. I have to try." She stepped back. "So I'm sorry, but I can't be Georgie Davis anymore."

"Who will you be instead?" Bianca asked softly, bewilderment swimming into the pain in her eyes. "Who else could you possibly be?"

"I don't know. But I'm finally ready to find out. Whatever it costs."

Beside Bianca, Jax pointed again more adamantly at the porch, the phone pressed hard to his ear as he spoke with the first responders. Georgie kissed his cheek and bounded off the steps into the snowy yard. Her lamb bounced joyfully to the edge of the lawn and stood there, waiting for her. Tag lifted a brow, clearly awaiting instructions. Georgie said simply, "Take us to Peter."

"Georgie, no!" Bianca said, but Addy slipped her arm through her mother-in-law's and said, "Go."

Tag trotted up to Bone's heels and barked sharply. The little lamb bleated and shot into the snowy brush toward the Kettle, Tag nipping and nudging and pushing her along.

"Bone!" Georgie shouted, as if the lamb were getting away from her. "Come back here!"

"Georgie, for God's sake!" Jax said, the phone still pressed to his ear, but she gathered her skirt in both hands and ran.

CHAPTER 38

PETER DIDN'T KNOW what he'd expected when he'd asked Georgie to create a distraction, but it wasn't a slo-mo wade through hip-high brush in a bridesmaid's gown. He'd take what he could get, though.

Shay turned at Georgie's shout and shoved Matty to his knees inside one of the baby kettles that pockmarked the basalt shelf on either side of the river. It was a wide, shallow circle, maybe three feet across and two feet deep. She wedged herself in beside him and narrowed her eyes on Georgie, still wading loudly through the underbrush. Peter took the opportunity to scuttle closer. The frozen basalt leached the heat from his fingers as he belly-crawled himself into another shallow depression in the rock between Matty and the maw of the Kettle. He was as cold as he'd ever been, shivering hard enough to rattle the teeth in his head, yet somehow his body was still warm enough to melt the thin slick of ice covering the rocks beneath him. His jeans sponged up the melt water and pressed it to his thighs, which went helpfully numb. He hoped like hell that he'd be able to move when the need arose, or somebody was going to get shot.

A few feet behind him, the river gushed suicidally into the open mouth of the Kettle, sending up a mist that was more ice than water. The roar of it rumbled through Peter's bones and numbed his eardrums. He shouldn't have been able to hear anything over it, but in one of those funny tricks of geography and physics, Shay's voice carried to Peter with perfect clarity.

She hissed, "Don't you say a word, Matisse."

"Why not?" the boy asked dully. "You've been pretty clear that I'm not getting out of this alive."

"You're not. But your sister could. Then again…" Shay paused, as if struck. "Hmm. That's a thought, isn't it?"

Peter's blood stopped in his veins, transformed into pure, frozen terror.

"I wonder," Shay mused, and Peter could hear Georgie getting closer yet, shouting for Bone while Tag barked and Bone bleated with delight over this new game of chase. "What would sting the most, do you suppose? Losing the daughter she created in her own image? Or the only son of her lost boy? Decisions, decisions!"

Matty didn't answer. Peter didn't blame him. He was proud of the kid, in fact. He was bright, and learning fast. You didn't inject yourself into conversations that weren't about you, and you didn't call attention to yourself when crazy people were talking to themselves. Peter stayed on his stomach, kept his eyes pinned to his mother, and waited for his moment.

Then there was the clatter of tiny hooves on loose stone. Bone must've broken free of the brush. The basalt shelf was slightly crowned, and Peter couldn't quite see the edge of the brush from his prone position next to the lip of the Kettle. But he heard Bone bleat cheerfully and start clattering his way. He lifted his head a cautious inch and saw Georgie tear her dress from the last of the brambles and stomp onto the rock face with Tag at her heels.

"Bone!" Georgie snapped, fists on hips. Her bare arms glowed in the moonlight. God, she must be freezing. "Come *back* here! You're going to fall into the Kettle, for mercy's

361

sake!"

Shay said softly, "I could take her, too." She was speaking to herself, weighing the pros and cons. "It could be a murder/suicide. A troubled young boy, a product of rape, driven mad by the shame of his conception and his adoptive mother's lies, decides to kill himself. He's interrupted by his interfering sister, and takes her out as well. Yes, it could work."

Nausea gripped Peter's stomach and twisted it. His numb fingers were fists against the frozen rock, and sharp pebbles cut into his knuckles. Bone trotted guilelessly to the crest of the basalt shelf, spotted Peter and paused to kick up delighted heels. She released an ecstatic whinny, like they were playing hide and seek, and she'd found him. She began trotting his way, then she spotted Matty, too, and found a new register of joy.

Matty hissed, "Bone, no! Go away!"

But Bone had already launched herself into the air with the confidence of the naturally sure-footed. Her little body described a perfect arc in the night sky, and for once she hit her target. Or got close. Peter watched in horror as his lamb landed directly on his mother.

Shay let out a squawk of surprise — no matter how she'd seen this night unfolding, her plans couldn't have included an aerial bombardment by livestock — and pulled the trigger.

Peter's heart stopped but his body didn't. Electric dread pierced him as surely as Shay's bullet must have pierced Bone. It cleared his head and set his muscles in motion. He vaulted up and out of his shallow depression in the rock, sprinted across the open basalt to the baby kettle holding Matty and Shay and a silent lamb. The gunshot was still echoing in the night air when he caught Matty by the collar (or maybe by the hair. It wasn't clear and he didn't have the time or the bandwidth for manners) and dragged him up and out of the pit. He all but threw the kid clear, sent him skidding and tumbling down the slippery rock face toward Georgie who caught him with an inarticulate noise of gratitude and relief.

Shay shot to her feet, outrage and fury twisting her beauty into something awful in the moonlight. "You," she snarled.

"Me," Peter acknowledged. He put both hands in the air, showed their emptiness to her, careful to keep his body between his mother's gun and Georgie and Matty. He hoped to God they quietly crawled back into the brush and got the hell out of here. Shay had already shot his lamb. (She had to have. Bone had been too close to miss, and was too quiet now for there to be any hope.) Georgie would be heartbroken but grieving a lamb was far better than grieving a brother. And Peter didn't want to grieve either Georgie or Matty. And he wouldn't have to, not if they did the smart thing and got the hell away from here.

Somewhere in the distance sirens began to wail. Georgie must've called the cops before diving into the brush. He didn't know if he was relieved or worried about that. A ticking clock was just one more pressure brought to bear on Shay's murderous instability, but there was nothing for it. A smart man used what was at hand rather than wishing for something else.

He tapped one ear. "Hear that, Mom? It's over. You should go."

"I should. I will." She leveled the gun at him with perfectly steady hands, though her face was ablaze with hate and frustration. "But not before I finish this."

Georgie watched Shay level that gun on Peter with cool-eyed intent. Fury and terror coalesced inside her into a hard nugget of blind courage that shoved her to her feet. "No!" she shouted."Don't you dare!"

"Georgie, don't!" Matty hissed and snatched at her billowing skirt. "She's crazy! She already shot your lamb! Don't let her shoot you and Peter, too!"

Bone. Pain swirled through her, was sucked into the black hole of rage forming at her center. It only fed the need rising inside her to go to Peter. To stand with him and declare herself now while she could. While everybody was alive and it still mattered.

"Stay low and get home." She leaned down and kissed his forehead, then tugged her skirt from his hands. Beside Matty, Tag whined and put his butt deliberately on the rock, as if to say *stay*.

"Take him home, Tag," she said gently. "I have to go to Peter."

She turned and picked her way gingerly across the rock in her clumsy boots, careful to keep her body between her brother and the barrel of Shay's gun. She didn't know if either he or the dog would obey her order to leave but she'd given them the best chance she could. She crossed the ice-slicked shelf of stone to where Peter stood, arms out, hands open, making as large a shield of his body as possible. Love for him sloshed up and over the edges of her heart. She loved this man, and she was going to tell him so. Assuming they survived the night.

"Finish what?" Peter asked his mother mildly. "Killing a kid who's not even here anymore?"

Shay's eyes slipped sideways and she swore ripely. Georgie grinned, though she didn't dare even glance away from Shay. Matty must've disappeared. God bless that kid, he knew how to take an order when it counted. If they survived this, she was going to tell him she loved him, too. She stepped to Peter's side and planted herself there, arms crossed.

"Oh my God," Peter muttered, his eyes carefully fixed on his mother even as he spoke to Georgie. "You're supposed to be with Matty. What the hell, Georgie."

"And leave you alone with this crazy woman?" she hissed back. "I don't think so. I'm not going anywhere. Not without you." And she wasn't. Not ever again.

Peter lowered one hand just enough to shove her behind him. "Stay there, goddamn it."

"Fine." She shrugged into his back. God, he was warm. She wanted to wrap her arms around him and never let go but didn't want to distract him. So she stayed put as instructed and watched Shay over his shoulder.

But she saw more than Shay. In the darkness beyond, a shadow-dappled shape moved like a ghost, slipping in and out of the moonlight on silent feet. She notched her chin over Peter's shoulder and breathed, "Look."

He gave no sign of having heard her, only continued to speak to his mother.

"You're too smart for this, Mom." He cocked an ear to the growing wail of the sirens. "Are you really going to let the cops show up and catch you with a loaded weapon?"

And without so much as a black eye or a split lip to generate sympathy? He didn't say that part but Georgie heard it, and she imagined Shay did, too. This wasn't Shay's usual gig. She had to be off-balance.

"Mom, come on. This is ridiculous. You don't want the cops to roll up on a hostage situation and get all hostile." He lowered one hand, tipped it palm-up. "If you're not going to ghost, why don't you at least give me the gun?"

"With my fingerprints all over it?" Shay snorted. "Not likely." She glanced at the Kettle to her left, began sidling carefully toward it. "I'll just dispose of it in the Kettle here before I *ghost*, as you put it."

"That'll work, too," Peter said.

Shay edged carefully to the lip of the Kettle, keeping the gun trained on them as she did. Behind her the river gushed and roared as it flung itself into the bottomless circle it had carved into the rock.

"Stay right where you are," she shouted over the crashing current. She swung the barrel away from them finally, held the gun out over the hungry mouth of the Kettle then jerked her head at Georgie. "Step away from Peter. I'm not getting rid of this gun until I see your empty hands, too."

Georgie stepped sideways, put her hands in the air next to Peter's. Shay smiled and snapped the gun their way again, training the impassive eye of its bore right at Georgie's chest. "But first I'll teach Bianca the lesson I came here to teach her."

Terror drained everything from Georgie's mind, left it a bright, blank sheet billowing on the frigid wind. She kept her hands in the air, kept her eyes on Shay but she spoke to Peter. "She's going to shoot me."

"The fuck she will," he breathed.

"I love you," she told him, just in case.

"Tag," he shouted. *"To me!"*

A number of things happened then in such violently close proximity that Georgie could never completely untangle them into discrete events.

The gun went off. (Did Shay fire it? Or did it just go off?) Shay shouted. (Before the gun went off? After?) Tag shot forward from the shadows behind Shay like a black-and-white bullet, clipping the back of her leg on his way by. Shay's knee buckled and she fell backward, pinwheeled her arms madly. (Was that when she shouted? And then the gun went off?) Her eyes were wide and silver in the moonlight. The gun flew from her hand, leapt up into the night sky and hung there, spinning, spinning. (Surely gravity and time didn't actually suspend themselves? Surely the gun just fell like a normal gun?) Then it dropped into the black gush of the river and was swallowed by the Kettle.

And then Shay followed it down.

She clawed at the air, at the night, at nothing, then dropped into the pitch and rush of the Devil River leaping suicidally into the Kettle.

And then she was gone.

And then Peter was on his knees, his face buried in Tag's coat, rumpling his fur and murmuring praise into his silky ears. And Tag, who'd previously only barely tolerated Peter's presence, butted his head affectionately into Peter's shoulder.

Matty popped up from the underbrush and shot both fists into the sky. "Good *dog*!" he cried. "Good boy, Tag!"

Georgie dropped to her knees and flung her arms around Peter and the dog, crying and laughing and scolding. "Oh thank God. I thought I was dead. I thought *you* were dead. I thought we all were dead and Shay was going to—"

Peter released his dog to wrap Georgie up in his arms. His jacket was wet and cold against her bare shoulders but it was the most glorious thing she'd ever felt. "I thought so, too, honestly. Which is why I'm not going to hold you to that love thing you mentioned, and you're not going to hold this against me."

"Hold what against—"

He kissed her. He lifted her into his mouth and kissed her like he wanted to imprint her on his soul. His mouth was hot on hers, hungry. One hand fisted in her hair, the other plastered her to his body, to the warm, tough, *alive* length of him. He smelled like sheep and motor oil and home, and she'd be damned if he'd give her love a pass. So she kissed him back. She kissed him with all the messy, glorious terror tumbling around inside her. She kissed him with visions of that stark farm house of his dancing behind her eyes, filled with children and dogs and lambs, ringing with laughter and raised voices and muddy boots.

And when sirens screamed into the lot behind Davis Place, when the spotlights flooded the Kettle and cops swarmed over the basalt, Georgie didn't let him go. She grabbed him by the jaw and glared into his dark, honest eyes and said, "You're not giving me a pass on anything. I *love* you, Peter Zinc."

He sighed and seemed to sag. "You know what?"

"What?"

"I think my mom shot me."

CHAPTER 39

His MOTHER HAD, indeed, shot him.

It was only a flesh wound. That last wild shot Shay fired had punched through the sleeve of his jacket and carved a shallow furrow through the meat of his upper arm. It stung like a bitch and bled impressively but was largely harmless. Six inches or so to the left, though, and that bullet would've had Georgie's name on it. And Peter would never forgive that. He certainly didn't expect Georgie to.

He'd cherish that kiss, though. And the fierce declaration of love that came after it. The memories would get him through many a dark, cold winter night, he imagined.

He'd refused the ambulance ride down to Hornby Harbor — insurance was a luxury the self-employed farmer could not afford — but the paramedic threw a few stitches his way in the back of the rig. Eventually, everybody had ended up at Davis Place, some for a wedding reception, some for questioning, some for both. It varied from person to person.

After the cops had taken his statement (separately from Georgie's and Matty's, of course), Peter wanted nothing more than to go home with his heroic dog, take the world's hottest shower, and sleep for eighty-two hours. Georgie had simply stared at him for a long, unreadable moment, then waved her majestic hand. Suddenly Addy's folks were loading Tag into their rental and heading back to babysit the farm for the night, and Peter was tucked into one of Addy's pretty guest rooms with a pink ensuite bathroom and strict instructions to stay put until advised otherwise.

One blistering shower later, Peter was standing by the bed, eyeing the pile of filthy clothes he'd left on the floor. There was no way he was putting any of that back on his body. He was about to steal a bed sheet to fashion a toga when his door opened and Georgie walked in.

He wasn't surprised. He'd been waiting for her.

She closed the door, leaned against it and studied him. He studied her back. She'd obviously showered, too. Her face was scrubbed clean and her hair was a damp, dark gold still striped by the teeth of her comb. Her feet were bare and she wore a pair of slouchy flannel pajama bottoms and a tank top under a soft-looking cardigan. She'd only buttoned the middle two buttons, and he could see a pale slice of her belly where the tank top didn't quite meet the low-slung pjs. He swallowed.

She said, "We should talk."

"We don't need to."

She tipped her head, both hands behind her back, cushioning her spine against the door. "Why not?"

"There's nothing new to say and I'm not really dressed."

"No, I can see that." Her blue eyes roamed his chest, a flicker of hunger in them that made his blood jump. And other unruly body parts. "But I think there are definitely things that need saying."

"Okay, I'll say them, then. You said you loved me tonight but you don't."

"I don't?"

"No, and here's why."

She grinned. "This should be good."

It wasn't good. It was the farthest thing from good. It was a greatest hits album of his most egregious, selfish offenses. He wasn't proud of any of it, but if she needed some context to get her emotional balance back where he was concerned, he'd provide it.

He said, "I told you I loved you when I didn't."

"What, back in the engagement days? I didn't love you, either. Not then."

He ignored that and soldiered on. "I offered to marry you when all I really wanted was your money and your name."

"I accepted that offer because *I* needed *your* money." She came off the door, wandered closer. He had to swallow again to clear the aching desire from his throat.

"I blackmailed Matty into insurance fraud. I had him burn this place to the ground."

"You saved his life tonight," she returned softly, her eyes steady and warm. "Mine, too." She closed the distance between them by another crucial foot. "Keep going."

He jerked a shrug, painfully aware that he was standing there in nothing but a towel. It was fitting, he supposed, that he'd be nearly naked for this recital of his sins. He watched her advance on him, step by sinuous step. Heat stirred in his gut. He wanted her. He always wanted her. And she was grateful to him tonight. Grateful enough to have mistaken gratitude for love. Grateful enough that she might just let him have her. Temptation gnawed at his bones, so he threw out some more awful words, the ones he thought might protect her from him. Might protect him from himself. "My mother killed your father," he blurted. "And I knew it."

"You knew that she could." Another step forward. His stomach quivered. He could feel the air swirling between them. "It wasn't your fault that she did. You were seventeen and your mother was insane. You got out. You got away. You did the right thing."

"She would have killed you tonight." And it put a sick

knot in his stomach just to hear that fact spoken out loud. "You and Matty both."

"And you. Don't forget that your own mother *shot* you." Her eyes dropped to the waterproof bandage on his upper arm and she hissed. "I'd kill her myself for that if I could." Her eyes flickered back up to his. "But you did it for me."

He sucked in a shuddering breath. "And now I'm a killer, too. I killed my own mother."

"She wasn't your mother." Georgie closed the gap between them. Peter's brain sizzled audibly inside his head and he closed his eyes. To endure it? To savor it? He had no idea. He was too consumed by the familiar wonder of her body pressed against his, those long bones and delicate corners, those surprising pockets of softness and give. "She was unnatural and wrong and you didn't kill her. You *survived* her."

"She was my family," he said desperately. He didn't feel that word the way Georgie did but he knew this was the breaking point. Family was everything to Georgie, and in that respect, he was irretrievably broken. His own sister barely tolerated him, and he hadn't spoken to his father in months. And he'd been able to watch his own mother drop into the Kettle tonight and feel nothing but overpowering relief. "I know what family means to you, and I respect that. Hell, I honor that. But whatever Shay was or wasn't, she was my family. That's what I'm from and I can't ever wash that off. I can't ever be what you—"

"No." She took his elbows in her palms, drew him more firmly into her body. She drifted her palms up his biceps, skirted his bandage and wound her fingers together at the nape of his neck. "She wasn't your family. She was never your family. *I'm* your family. *We're* your family, me and

372

Matty. You made us your family when we were out there on that godawful frozen slab of stone tonight and that broken, evil woman tried to hurt us. But you protected us. You *chose* us. She thought she could manipulate you and intimidate you. She thought she knew you but she was wrong. She only knew what she tried to make you. She didn't have the first clue who you are." She lowered her lashes and studied him, her mouth bare inches from his. "But I do. I know who you are, Peter Zinc. And I love you."

He closed his eyes. "How can you say that, Georgie?" It was an agonized whisper. "I have nothing to offer you. I'm *poor*. The kind of poor that has to chose between coffee and muffins, remember?"

"Coffee," she advised him. "Always choose coffee."

"Truth," he admitted, "but *you* shouldn't have to choose." It took every ounce of strength he had but he reached up and found the hands she'd tangled behind his head. He stepped back — goddamn it, he could almost *hear* things breaking in his soul — brought their joined hands down, held them fast in the space he'd made between their bodies. His skin howled for hers but he forced himself to meet her eyes steadily. "You shouldn't have to give up a damn thing. Love should add to you, not subtract. Loving me would diminish you, Georgie. That's how I know it isn't right."

"Can you even hear yourself?" She glared at him. "That's your mother talking. That's Shay's poison working its way through your bloodstream even now."

"What are you talking about?"

"You're not your bank balance, Peter." She gripped his hands fiercely, almost painfully. "What you're worth to me has nothing to do with what you can buy me. I can buy my own damn coffee. But I need something I can't buy, and nobody can give it to me but you."

He stared at her, a little mesmerized. How had he ever
believed this woman was dim? She burned like a flame in
front of him, her eyes alive, her face in constant, fascinating
motion. "What's that?" he managed.

"My goddamn appetite. When I'm with you, I can
actually eat. Everything that's always so tangled up inside
me straightens itself out and I can breathe. I can eat. I can
just be, and it's because of you."

"How?"

"You're so brutally honest, so absolutely real. You don't
cover anything up any more, not how you feel, not how
you've failed. It's all just right out there for the world to
see."

He grimaced. "You're making my point for me,
Georgie."

"I'm making mine, too, so shut up and follow along."

He shut up.

"When I'm with you, it's like I get a contact high off
your courage. Just being around you makes me brave, too.
Brave enough to be exactly what I am. Brave enough to trust
that you see me, the real me inside all—" She jerked her
hand away and waved it impatiently at her face, then circled
it to encompass, he supposed, the massive house, the
staggering fortune, and the family mystique that went with it.
"—this."

She took advantage of the free hand and wrapped it
around his neck again, dragged herself right into his body.
He whimpered. Possibly out loud. "And when you kiss me?
God, when you kiss me." She feathered her lips over his
cheek, over the stubble his girlie shower hadn't been
equipped to remove. Heat crept into his veins, slid along

sinuously, stretched like a cat. "It's *me* you're kissing. It's *me* you're touching, the me no other man has ever seen, or even guessed at, or cared enough to wonder about. You see right past the face to the truth inside me, and believe me, you didn't get there because you're so damn successful. Back when you were rich, you had no idea I existed, not really. But you're honest now. You're true. Fate put your back to the wall tonight, and forced you into an unthinkable choice: The woman who raised you or the woman you love. What's it going to be?"

The woman you love. She knew he loved her. Of course she did. This was Georgie Davis, after all. When was he going to stop underestimating her?

"You," he murmured helplessly. "Always."

"You chose me." Her voice was fierce and satisfied. "I knew you would. Because you're my family and I trusted you. I *trust* you. That's why I love you, and always will."

Something broke inside him. The weary, worn-thin strands holding his self-control to his soul? He'd been clutching so tightly at them, his hands were numb but he opened his fingers now and let them go. Then he filled his hands with her instead, with the warm fact of her body. The scent of expensive shampoo and fresh snow filled his head in an arctic blast, cleared away the clouds and the doubts and the fear, leaving nothing but the bright truth of his heart in her hands.

"I love you, Georgie."

She lifted her mouth to his and he took it. He seized it. He fell into her like a granted wish. He dragged her into his body until that soft and inviting sweater of hers left button prints on his stomach. So he took it off her. She helped him with the towel and then they were together on sheets that smelled like lemon trees and winter mornings. Her hands were wild on his body, fast and hot and demanding. She wanted everything, and he wanted nothing more than to give it to her. Anything he had, anything he was, it was hers.

And when she took him inside herself, when she rocked him into utter mind-splitting bliss, he didn't go there alone. She was there with him, sweaty, hoarse, unbeautiful and satisfied.

Satisfied.

With him.

He wrapped her in his arms, felt his own heartbeat in her chest, and slept.

Epilogue

GEORGIE HAD TAKEN to farming surprisingly well, though why anything surprised Peter about his wife anymore was a mystery. He maneuvered his tractor nimbly in the buttery spring sunlight, stabbed a round bale of hay with the spear attachment and began motoring it to the far pasture. Tag sat on a rise in the middle pasture with his back to the road, keeping watch over the flock while Addy's fresh batch of guest artists swarmed the lambs. The babies had all arrived within the expected window this year, which had been a nice change of pace. Cameras flashed, pencils flew, and Tag ruled like a king.

Peter spotted Georgie leaning carefully over a fence — those things were electric — to zoom in on a mother/baby pair. The mother munched placidly while the baby nursed, and Georgie's shutter clicked and snapped. After losing Bone, they'd both decided that perhaps they weren't cut out for raising meat, and had invested in a ram with more dairy-friendly genes. The babies were adorable black-faced cotton balls on twigs, and Georgie's Instagram feed was blowing up. She'd been featured in *Minnesota Monthly* recently and Peter had been shocked to discover what advertisers would pay to hitch their wagon to a star like hers.

He couldn't say the farm was making anything like the kind of money he'd expected from an investment back in the day, but they weren't doing too badly, all things considered. Addy had insisted on paying a small per-artist fee for each guest she sent to the farm for a morning of *en plain air* work,

Susan Sey

and the field trip to Redemption Dairy was turning out to be a very popular attraction. Between that and Georgie's growing fan base, Peter was starting to wonder if any of that interest could be converted into yet another income stream.

Turned out, it could, and he'd run the numbers to prove it.

All it would take was one frightening/exhilarating bank loan, and they could have a bunkhouse on the property, suitable for weekend warriors and urbanites who'd always secretly wanted to drive a tractor.

The tractor *was* kind of awesome.

He finished with the hay and parked his awesome tractor by the barn. Then he headed out to the pasture to refine his mental pitch and watch his wife work. She was bent over the fence again, and Peter wasn't one to miss an opportunity. He slid a hand over the curve of her bottom. She'd never be curvy by any stretch of the imagination but she'd lost that hollow gauntness since Peter had taken charge of feeding her. Their first meal as a family of two had been chicken noodle soup and fresh bread at the giant farm table, both of which Peter had made himself. And if the farm was now short one violent rooster, well, nobody missed him.

"Watch it, buster," Georgie said mildly, her eye still pressed to the view finder, her face screwed up in that weird *I'm working here* grimace he adored. "My husband's a jealous man."

"That guy? He's a patsy." He slid an arm around her waist and drew her away from the fence. (Carefully. That thing was electric.) "Run away with me. I've got big plans."

"Yeah?" She let the camera dangle from the neck strap and grinned at him. "What kind of plans?"

He tucked his hands into his pockets and rocked back on

his heels. "How would you feel about a bunkhouse?"

She tipped her head and he watched the fascinating machinery of her brain engage.

"You're thinking of taking on guests," she said. "Like, what, a resort/farm deal? Weekend packages on site, involving putting city slickers to work?"

Fascinating and *fast*. He grinned at her. "Damn, you're good. I might be in love with you. Want to get married?"

She wiggled her ring finger at him, and a modest little sapphire — not even a diamond — winked at him. They both loved that ring. "Who are you thinking is going to run this project?" she asked. "Because you're up to here with the farm—" She leveled a hand somewhere above her head. Above his. "—and between the gallery and my internet empire, I'm hands-full, too."

"What about Mike and Jennifer?"

"Addy's parents?" She considered it. "Aren't they still parasailing in Mexico?"

"Yeah. But a couple like that can only parasail for so long. Pretty soon they're going to get hungry for something more substantial. Something that would satisfy Jennifer's need to impose apple-pie order on a farm's worth of chaos."

"We're never short on chaos, it's true," Georgie admitted, not unhappily. "And I'll bet Mike would get a huge kick out of schooling men, women and children alike on the ins and outs of driving a chicken tractor."

"We won't mention proximity to future grandchildren unless we have to," he said virtuously but felt his smile go sharky. He actually hoped they'd have to mention it. He'd made peace with those shark teeth of his. He'd been born with them for a reason. Maybe to defend himself. Maybe to defend those he loved. Maybe just to make a go of an unlikely farm in an unlikely place, filled with an unlikely love.

He was okay with that. And so was Georgie.

ABOUT THE AUTHOR

Once upon a time Susan Sey was a software trainer with nice clothes and free time, but now she has kids. She lives with them and her incredibly patient husband in St. Paul, MN, where she produces smart, sexy contemporary romances on an annual basis. She loves ice cream, her family and happy endings, though not necessarily in that order. She does not enjoy laundry, failure or mowing the lawn, but rises to the occasion as necessary.

You can find her on the web at www.susansey.com, on Facebook or Twitter. Or drop her a line at susan@susansey.com. She dearly loves a good letter.

www.ingramcontent.com/pod-product-compliance
Lightning Source LLC
Chambersburg PA
CBHW032131190626
46814CB00005BA/1641